Joshua — Complete

by
Georg Ebers

Joshua — Complete
by Georg Ebers

Copyright © 2024

All Rights reserved.

No part of this publication may be reproduced, stored in a retrieval system, or transmitted in any form or by any means, electronic, mechanical, photocopying or Otherwise, without the written permission of the publisher.
The author/editor asserts the moral right to be identified as the author/editor of this work.

ISBN: 978-93-62769-18-3

Published by
DOUBLE 9 BOOKS
2/13-B, Ansari Road
Daryaganj, New Delhi – 110002
info@double9books.com
www.double9books.com
Tel. 011-40042856

This book is under public domain

ABOUT THE AUTHOR

Georg Moritz Ebers was a German Egyptologist and author who was born in Berlin on March 1, 1837, and died in Tutzing, Bavaria, on August 7, 1898. He bought the Ebers Papyrus, which is one of the oldest medical records from Egypt and is what made him famous. Georg Ebers was born in Berlin. He was the fifth child in a wealthy family of bankers and someone who made ceramics. After their father killed himself soon after Ebers was born, the children were raised by their mother alone. Smart people like Georg Wilhelm Friedrich Hegel, the Grimm Brothers, and Alexander von Humboldt liked going to the club that his mother ran. Ebers studied law in Gottingen and Oriental languages and history in Berlin. Egyptology was something he studied in depth, so in 1865 he was made Dozent in Egyptian language and antiquities at Jena. In 1868 he was made professor. In 1870, he was hired as a professor at Leipzig to teach these topics. He went to Egypt twice for research reasons. His first important work, Ägypten und die Bücher Moses, came out in 1867 and 1868. In 1874, he edited the famous medical tablet called tablet Ebers, which he had found in Thebes (H. Joachim, 1890).

CONTENTS

PREFACE 7
CHAPTER I 10
CHAPTER II 17
CHAPTER III 22
CHAPTER IV 28
CHAPTER V 34
CHAPTER VI 43
CHAPTER VII 50
CHAPTER VIII 54
CHAPTER IX 58
CHAPTER X 67
CHAPTER XI 75
CHAPTER XII 82
CHAPTER XIII 92
CHAPTER XIV 100
CHAPTER XV 106
CHAPTER XVI 116
CHAPTER XVII 124
CHAPTER XVIII 133
CHAPTER XIX 143
CHAPTER XX 151
CHAPTER XXI 161

CHAPTER XXII	175
CHAPTER XXIII	188
CHAPTER XXIV	199
CHAPTER XXV	213
CHAPTER XXVI	226
CHAPTER XXVII	236
CHAPTER XXVIII	247
CONCLUSION	251

PREFACE

Last winter I resolved to complete this book, and while giving it the form in which it now goes forth into the world, I was constantly reminded of the dear friend to whom I intended to dedicate it. Now I am permitted to offer it only to the manes of Gustav Baur; for a few months ago death snatched him from us.

Every one who was allowed to be on terms of intimacy with this man feels his departure from earth as an unspeakably heavy loss, not only because his sunny, cheerful nature and brilliant intellect brightened the souls of his friends; not only because he poured generously from the overflowing cornucopia of his rich knowledge precious gifts to those with whom he stood in intellectual relations, but above all because of the loving heart which beamed through his clear eyes, and enabled him to share the joys and sorrows of others, and enter into their thoughts and feelings.

To my life's end I shall not forget that during the last few years, himself physically disabled and overburdened by the duties imposed by the office of professor and counsellor of the Consistory, he so often found his way to me, a still greater invalid. The hours he then permitted me to spend in animated conversation with him are among those which, according to old Horace, whom he know so thoroughly and loved so well, must be numbered among the 'good ones'. I have done so, and whenever I gratefully recall them, in my ear rings my friend's question:

"What of the story of the Exodus?"

After I had told him that in the midst of the desert, while following the traces of the departing Hebrews, the idea had occurred to me of treating their wanderings in the form of a romance, he expressed his approval in the eager, enthusiastic manner natural to him. When I finally entered farther into the details of the sketch outlined on the back of a camel, he never ceased to encourage me, though he thoroughly understood my scruples and fully appreciated the difficulties which attended the fulfilment of my task.

So in a certain degree this book is his, and the inability to offer it to the living man and hear his acute judgment is one of the griefs which render it hard to reconcile oneself to the advancing years which in other respects bring many a joy.

Himself one of the most renowned, acute and learned students and interpreters of the Bible, he was perfectly familiar with the critical works the last five years have brought to light in the domain of Old Testament criticism. He had taken a firm stand against the views of the younger school, who seek to banish the Exodus of the Jews from the province of history and represent it as a later production of the myth-making popular mind; a theory we both believed untenable. One of his remarks on this subject has lingered in my memory and ran nearly as follows:

"If the events recorded in the Second Book of Moses—which I believe are true—really never occurred, then nowhere and at no period has a historical event of equally momentous result taken place. For thousands of years the story of the Exodus has lived in the minds of numberless people as something actual, and it still retains its vitality. Therefore it belongs to history no less certainty than the French Revolution and its consequences."

Notwithstanding such encouragement, for a long series of years I lacked courage to finish the story of the Exodus until last winter an unexpected appeal from abroad induced me to resume it. After this I worked uninterruptedly with fresh zeal and I may say renewed pleasure at the perilous yet fascinating task until its completion.

The locality of the romance, the scenery as we say of the drama, I have copied as faithfully as possible from the landscapes I beheld in Goshen and on the Sinai peninsula. It will agree with the conception of many of the readers of "Joshua."

The case will be different with those portions of the story which I have interwoven upon the ground of ancient Egyptian records. They will surprise the laymen; for few have probably asked themselves how the events related in the Bible from the standpoint of the Jews affected the Egyptians, and what political conditions existed in the realm of Pharaoh when the Hebrews left it. I have endeavored to represent these relations with the utmost fidelity to the testimony of the monuments. For the description of the Hebrews, which is mentioned in the Scriptures, the Bible itself offers the best authority. The character of the "Pharaoh of the Exodus" I also copied from the Biblical narrative, and the portraits of the weak King Menephtah, which have been preserved, harmonize admirably with it. What we have learned of later times induced me to weave into the romance the conspiracy of Siptah, the accession to the throne of Seti II., and the person of the Syrian Aarsu who, according to the London Papyrus Harris I., after Siptah had become king, seized the government.

The Naville excavations have fixed the location of Pithom-Succoth beyond question, and have also brought to light the fortified store-house of Pithom (Succoth) mentioned in the Bible; and as the scripture says the Hebrews rested in this place and thence moved farther on, it must be supposed that they overpowered the garrison of the strong building and seized the contents of the spacious granaries, which are in existence at the present day.

In my "Egypt and the Books of Moses" which appeared in 1868, I stated that the Biblical Etham was the same as the Egyptian Chetam, that is, the line of fortresses which protected the isthmus of Suez from the attacks of the nations of the East, and my statement has long since found universal acceptance. Through it, the turning back of the Hebrews before Etham is intelligible.

The mount where the laws were given I believe was the majestic Serbal, not the Sinai of the monks; the reasons for which I explained fully in my work "Through Goshen to Sinai." I have also—in the same volume—attempted to show that the halting-place of the tribes called in the Bible "Dophkah" was the deserted mines of the modern Wadi Maghara.

By the aid of the mental and external experiences of the characters, whose acts have in part been freely guided by the author's imagination, he has endeavored to bring nearer to the sympathizing reader the human side of the mighty destiny of the nation which it was incumbent on him to describe. If he has succeeded in doing so, without belittling the magnificent Biblical narrative, he has accomplished his desire; if he has failed, he must content himself with the remembrance of the pleasure and mental exaltation he experienced during the creation of this work.

Tutzing on the Starnberger See, September 20th, 1889.

GEORG EBERS.

CHAPTER I

"Go down, grandfather: I will watch."

But the old man to whom the entreaty was addressed shook his shaven head.

"Yet you can get no rest here...."

"And the stars? And the tumult below? Who can think of rest in hours like these? Throw my cloak around me! Rest—on such a night of horror!"

"You are shivering. And how your hand and the instrument are shaking."

"Then support my arm."

The youth dutifully obeyed the request; but in a short time he exclaimed: "Vain, all is vain; star after star is shrouded by the murky clouds. Alas, hear the wailing from the city. Ah, it rises from our own house too. I am so anxious, grandfather, feel how my head burns! Come down, perhaps they need help."

"Their fate is in the hands of the gods—my place is here."

"But there—there! Look northward across the lake. No, farther to the west. They are coming from the city of the dead."

"Oh, grandfather! Father—there!" cried the youth, a grandson of the astrologer of Amon-Ra, to whom he was lending his aid. They were standing in the observatory of the temple of this god in Tanis, the Pharaoh's capital in the north of the land of Goshen. He moved away, depriving the old man of the support of his shoulder, as he continued: "There, there! Is the sea sweeping over the land? Have the clouds dropped on the earth to heave to and fro? Oh, grandfather, look yonder! May the Immortals have pity on us! The under-world is yawning, and the giant serpent Apep has come forth from the realm of the dead. It is moving past the temple. I see, I hear it. The great Hebrew's menace is approaching fulfilment. Our race will be effaced from the earth. The serpent! Its head is turned toward the southeast. It will devour the sun when it rises in the morning."

The old man's eyes followed the youth's finger, and he, too, perceived a huge, dark mass, whose outlines blended with the dusky night, come surging through the gloom; he, too, heard, with a thrill of terror, the monster's loud roar.

Both stood straining their eyes and ears to pierce the darkness; but instead of gazing upward the star-reader's eye was bent upon the city, the distant sea, and the level plain. Deep silence, yet no peace reigned above them: the high wind now piled the dark clouds into shapeless masses, anon severed that grey veil and drove the torn fragments far asunder. The moon was invisible to mortal eyes, but the clouds were toying with the bright Southern stars, sometimes hiding them, sometimes affording a free course for their beams. Sky and earth alike showed a constant interchange of pallid light and intense darkness. Sometimes the sheen of the heavenly bodies flashed brightly from sea and bay, the smooth granite surfaces of the obelisks in the precincts of the temple, and the gilded copper roof of the airy royal palace, anon sea and river, the sails in the harbor, the sanctuaries, the streets of the city, and the palm-grown plain which surrounded it vanished in gloom. Eye and ear failed to retain the impression of the objects they sought to discern; for sometimes the silence was so profound that all life, far and near, seemed hushed and dead, then a shrill shriek of anguish pierced the silence of the night, followed at longer or shorter intervals by the loud roar the youthful priest had mistaken for the voice of the serpent of the nether-world, and to which grandfather and grandson listened with increasing suspense.

The dark shape, whose incessant motion could be clearly perceived whenever the starlight broke through the clouds, appeared first near the city of the dead and the strangers' quarter. Both the youth and the old man had been seized with terror, but the latter was the first to regain his self-control, and his keen eye, trained to watch the stars, speedily discovered that it was not a single giant form emerging from the city of the dead upon the plain, but a multitude of moving shapes that seemed to be swaying hither and thither over the meadow lands. The bellowing and bleating, too, did not proceed from one special place, but came now nearer and now farther away. Sometimes it seemed to issue from the bowels of the earth, and at others to float from some airy height.

Fresh horror seized upon the old man. Grasping his grandson's right hand in his, he pointed with his left to the necropolis, exclaiming in tremulous tones: "The dead are too great a multitude. The under-world is overflowing, as the river does when its bed is not wide enough for the waters from the south. How they swarm and surge and roll onward! How they scatter and sway to and fro. They are the souls of the thousands whom grim death has snatched away, laden with the curse of the Hebrew, unburied, unshielded from corruption, to descend the rounds of the ladder leading to the eternal world."

"Yes, yes, those are their wandering ghosts," shrieked the youth in absolute faith, snatching his hand from the grey-beard's grasp and striking his burning brow, exclaiming, almost incapable of speech in his horror: "Ay, those are the souls of the damned. The wind has swept them into the sea, whose waters cast them forth again upon the land, but the sacred earth spurns them and flings them into the air. The pure ether of Shu hurls them back to the ground and now—oh look, listen—they are seeking the way to the wilderness."

"To the fire!" cried the old astrologer. "Purify them, ye flames; cleanse them, water."

The youth joined his grandfather's form of exorcism, and while still chanting together, the trap-door leading to this observatory on the top of the highest gate of the temple was opened, and a priest of inferior rank called: "Cease thy toil. Who cares to question the stars when the light of life is departing from all the denizens of earth!"

The old man listened silently till the priest, in faltering accents, added that the astrologer's wife had sent him, then he stammered:

"Hora? Has my son, too, been stricken?"

The messenger bent his head, and the two listeners wept bitterly, for the astrologer had lost his first-born son and the youth a beloved father.

But as the lad, shivering with the chill of fever, sank ill and powerless on the old man's breast, the latter hastily released himself from his embrace and hurried to the trap-door. Though the priest had announced himself to be the herald of death, a father's heart needs more than the mere words of another ere resigning all hope of the life of his child.

Down the stone stairs, through the lofty halls and wide courts of the temple he hurried, closely followed by the youth, though his trembling limbs could scarcely support his fevered body. The blow that had fallen upon his own little circle had made the old man forget the awful vision which perchance menaced the whole universe with destruction; but his grandson could not banish the sight and, when he had passed the fore-court and was approaching the outermost pylons his imagination, under the tension of anxiety and grief, made the shadows of the obelisks appear to be dancing, while the two stone statues of King Rameses, on the corner pillars of the lofty gate, beat time with the crook they held in their hands.

Then the fever struck the youth to the ground. His face was distorted by the convulsions which tossed his limbs to and fro, and the old man, failing on his knees, strove to protect the beautiful head, covered with clustering curls, from striking the stone flags, moaning under his breath "Now fate has overtaken him too."

Then calming himself, he shouted again and again for help, but in vain. At last, as he lowered his tones to seek comfort in prayer, he heard the sound of voices in the avenue of sphinxes beyond the pylons, and fresh hope animated his heart.

Who was coming at so late an hour?

Loud wails of grief blended with the songs of the priests, the clinking and tinkling of the metal sistrums, shaken by the holy women in the service of the god, and the measured tread of men praying as they marched in the procession which was approaching the temple.

Faithful to the habits of a long life, the astrologer raised his eyes and, after a glance at the double row of granite pillars, the colossal statues and obelisks in the fore-court, fixed them on the starlit skies. Even amid his grief a bitter smile hovered around his sunken lips; to-night the gods themselves were deprived of the honors which were their due.

For on this, the first night after the new moon in the month of Pharmuthi, the sanctuary in bygone years was always adorned with flowers. As soon as the darkness of this moonless night passed away, the high festival of the spring equinox and the harvest celebration would begin.

A grand procession in honor of the great goddess Neith, of Rennut, who bestows the blessings of the fields, and of Horus at whose sign the seeds begin to germinate, passed, in accordance with the rules prescribed by the Book of the Divine Birth of the Sun, through the city to the river and harbor; but to-day the silence of death reigned throughout the sanctuary, whose courts at this hour were usually thronged with men, women, and children, bringing offerings to lay on the very spot where death's finger had now touched his grandson's heart.

A flood of light streamed into the vast space, hitherto but dimly illumined by a few lamps. Could the throng be so frenzied as to imagine that the joyous festival might be celebrated, spite of the unspeakable horrors of the night.

Yet, the evening before, the council of priests had resolved that, on account of the rage of the merciless pestilence, the temple should not be adorned nor the procession be marshalled. In the afternoon many whose houses had been visited by the plague had remained absent, and now while he, the astrologer, had been watching the course of the stars, the pest had made its way into this sanctuary, else why had it been forsaken by the watchers and the other astrologers who had entered with him at sunset, and whose duty it was to watch through the night?

He again turned with tender solicitude to the sufferer, but instantly started to his feet, for the gates were flung wide open and the light of torches and lanterns streamed into the court. A swift glance at the sky told him that it was a little after midnight, yet his fears seemed to have been true—the priests were crowding into the temples to prepare for the harvest festival to-morrow.

But he was wrong. When had they ever entered the sanctuary for this purpose in orderly procession, solemnly chanting hymns? Nor was the train composed only of servants of the deity. The population had joined them, for the shrill lamentations of women and wild cries of despair, such as he had never heard before in all his long life within these sacred walls, blended in the solemn litany.

Or were his senses playing him false? Was the groaning throng of restless spirits which his grandson had pointed out to him from the observatory, pouring into the sanctuary of the gods?

New horror seized upon him; with arms flung upward to bid the specters avaunt he muttered the exorcism against the wiles of evil spirits. But he soon let his hands fall again; for among the throng he noted some of his friends who yesterday, at least, had still walked among living men. First, the tall form of the second prophet of the god, then the women consecrated to the service of Amon-Ra, the singers and the holy fathers and, when he perceived behind the singers, astrologers, and pastophori his own brother-in-law, whose house had yesterday been spared by the plague, he summoned fresh courage and spoke to him. But his voice was smothered by the shouts of the advancing multitude.

The courtyard was now lighted, but each individual was so engrossed by his own sorrows that no one noticed the old astrologer. Tearing the cloak from his shivering limbs to make a pillow for the lad's tossing head, he heard, while tending him with fatherly affection, fierce imprecations on the Hebrews who had brought this woe on Pharaoh and his people, mingling with the chants and shouts of the approaching crowd and, recurring again and again, the name of Prince Rameses, the heir to the throne, while the tone in which it was uttered, the formulas of lamentation associated with it, announced the tidings that the eyes of the monarch's first-born son were closed in death.

The astrologer gazed at his grandson's wan features with increasing anxiety, and even while the wailing for the prince rose louder and louder a slight touch of gratification stirred his soul at the thought of the impartial justice Death metes out alike to the sovereign on his throne and the beggar by the roadside. He now realized what had brought the noisy multitude to the temple!

With as much swiftness as his aged limbs would permit, he hastened forward to meet the mourners; but ere he reached them he saw the gate-keeper and his wife come out of their house, carrying between them on a mat the dead body of a boy. The husband held one end, his fragile little wife the other, and the gigantic warder was forced to stoop low to keep the rigid form in a horizontal position and not let it slip toward the woman. Three children, preceded by a little girl carrying a lantern, closed the mournful procession.

Perhaps no one would have noticed the group, had not the gate-keeper's little wife shrieked so wildly and piteously that no one could help hearing her lamentations. The second prophet of Amon, and then his companions, turned toward them. The procession halted, and as some of the priests approached the corpse the gate-keeper shouted loudly: "Away, away from the plague! It has stricken our first-born son."

The wife meantime had snatched the lantern from her little girl's hand and casting its light full on the dead boy's rigid face, she screamed:

"The god hath suffered it to happen. Ay, he permitted the horror to enter beneath his own roof. Not his will, but the curse of the stranger rules us and our lives. Look, this was our first-born son, and the plague has also stricken two of the temple-servants. One already lies dead in our room, and there lies Kamus, grandson of the astrologer Rameri. We heard the old man call, and saw what was happening; but who can prop another's house when his own is falling? Take heed while there is time; for the gods have opened their own sanctuaries to the horror. If the whole world crumbles into ruin, I shall neither marvel nor grieve. My lord priests, I am only a poor lowly woman, but am I not right when I ask: Do our gods sleep, or has some one paralyzed them, or what are they doing that they leave us and our children in the power of the base Hebrew brood?"

"Overthrow them! Down with the foreigners! Death to the sorcerer Mesu, — [Mesu is the Egyptian name of Moses] — hurl him into the sea." Such were the imprecations that followed the woman's curse, as an echo follows a shout, and the aged astrologer's brother-in-law Hornecht, captain of the archers, whose hot blood seethed in his veins at the sight of the dying form of his beloved nephew, waved his short sword, crying frantically: "Let all men who have hearts follow me. Upon them! A life for a life! Ten Hebrews for each Egyptian whom the sorcerer has slain!"

As a flock rushes into a fire when the ram leads the way, the warrior's summons fired the throng. Women forced themselves in front of the men, pressing after him into the gateway, and when the servants of the temple lingered to await the verdict of the prophet of Amon, the latter drew his stately figure to its full height, and said calmly: "Let all who wear priestly garments remain and pray with me. The populace is heaven's instrument to mete out vengeance. We will remain here to pray for their success."

CHAPTER II

Bai, the second prophet of Amon, who acted as the representative of the aged and feeble chief-prophet and high-priest Rui, went into the holy of holies, the throng of inferior servants of the divinity pursued their various duties, and the frenzied mob rushed through the streets of the city towards the distant Hebrew quarter.

As the flood, pouring into the valley, sweeps everything before it, the people, rushing to seek vengeance, forced every one they met to join them. No Egyptian from whom death had snatched a loved one failed to follow the swelling torrent, which increased till hundreds became thousands. Men, women, and children, freedmen and slaves, winged by the ardent longing to bring death and destruction on the hated Hebrews, darted to the remote quarter where they dwelt.

How the workman had grasped a hatchet, the housewife an axe, they themselves scarcely knew. They were dashing forward to deal death and ruin and had had no occasion to search for weapons—they had been close at hand.

The first to feel the weight of their vengeance must be Nun, an aged Hebrew, rich in herds, loved and esteemed by many an Egyptian whom he had benefitted—but when hate and revenge speak, gratitude shrinks timidly into the background.

His property, like the houses and hovels of his people, was in the strangers' quarter, west of Tanis, and lay nearest to the streets inhabited by the Egyptians themselves.

Usually at this hour herds of cattle and flocks of sheep were being watered or driven to pasture and the great yard before his house was filled with cattle, servants of both sexes, carts, and agricultural implements. The owner usually overlooked the departure of the flocks and herds, and the mob had marked him and his family for the first victims of their fury.

The swiftest of the avengers had now reached his extensive farm-buildings, among them Hornecht, captain of the archers, brother-in-law of the old astrologer. House and barns were brightly illumined by the first light of the young day. A stalwart smith kicked violently on the stout door; but the unbolted sides yielded so easily that he was forced to cling to the doorpost to save himself from falling. Others, Hornecht among them, pressed past him into the yard. What did this mean?

Had some new spell been displayed to attest the power of the Hebrew leader Mesu, who had brought such terrible plagues on the land,—and of his God.

The yard was absolutely empty. The stalls contained a few dead cattle and sheep, killed because they had been crippled in some way, while a lame lamb limped off at sight of the mob. The carts and wagons, too, had vanished. The lowing, bleating throng which the priests had imagined to be the souls of the damned was the Hebrew host, departing by night from their old home with all their flocks under the guidance of Moses.

The captain of the archers dropped his sword, and a spectator might have believed that the sight was a pleasant surprise to him; but his neighbor, a clerk from the king's treasure-house, gazed around the empty space with the disappointed air of a man who has been defrauded.

The flood of schemes and passions, which had surged so high during the night, ebbed under the clear light of day. Even the soldier's quickly awakened wrath had long since subsided into composure. The populace might have wreaked their utmost fury on the other Hebrews, but not upon Nun, whose son, Hosea, had been his comrade in arms, one of the most distinguished leaders in the army, and an intimate family friend: Had he thought of him and foreseen that his father's dwelling would be first attacked, he would never have headed the mob in their pursuit of vengeance; nay, he bitterly repented having forgotten the deliberate judgment which befitted his years.

While many of the throng began to plunder and destroy Nun's deserted home, men and women came to report that not a soul was to be found in any of the neighboring dwellings. Others told of cats cowering on the deserted hearthstones, of slaughtered cattle and shattered furniture; but at last the furious avengers dragged out a Hebrew with his family and a half-witted grey-haired woman found hidden among some straw. The crone, amid imbecile laughter, said her people had made themselves hoarse calling her, but Meliela was too wise to walk on and on as they meant to do; besides her feet were too tender, and she had not even a pair of shoes.

The man, a frightfully ugly Jew, whom few of his own race would have pitied, protested, sometimes with a humility akin to fawning, sometimes with the insolence which was a trait of his character, that he had nothing to do with the god of lies in whose name the seducer Moses had led away his people to ruin; he himself, his wife, and his child had always been on friendly terms with the Egyptians. Indeed, many knew him, he was a moneylender and when the rest of his nation had set forth on their pilgrimage, he had concealed himself, hoping to pursue his dishonest calling and sustain no loss.

Some of his debtors, however, were among the infuriated populace, though even without their presence he was a doomed man; for he was the first person on whom the excited mob could show that they were resolved upon revenge. Rushing upon him with savage yells, the lifeless bodies of the luckless wretch and his family were soon strewn over the ground. Nobody knew who had done this first bloody deed; too many had dashed forward at once.

Not a few others who had remained in the houses and huts also fell victims to the people's thirst for vengeance, though many had time to escape, and while streams of blood were flowing, axes were wielded, and walls and doors were battered down with beams and posts to efface the abodes of the detested race from the earth.

The burning embers brought by some frantic women were extinguished and trampled out; the more prudent warned them of the peril that would menace their own homes and the whole city of Tanis, if the strangers' quarter should be fired.

So the Hebrews' dwellings escaped the flames; but as the sun mounted higher dense clouds of white dust shrouded the abodes they had forsaken, and where, only yesterday, thousands of people had possessed happy homes and numerous herds had quenched their thirst in fresh waters, the glowing soil was covered with rubbish and stone, shattered beams, and broken woodwork. Dogs and cats left behind by their owners wandered among the ruins and were joined by women and children who lived in the beggars' hovels on the edge of the necropolis close by, and now, holding their hands over their mouths, searched amid the stifling dust and rubbish for any household utensil or food which might have been left by the fugitives and overlooked by the mob.

During the afternoon Fai, the second prophet of Amon, was carried past the ruined quarter. He did not come to gloat over the spectacle of destruction, it was his nearest way from the necropolis to his home. Yet a satisfied smile hovered around his stern mouth as he noticed how thoroughly the people had performed their work. His own purpose, it is true, had not been fulfilled, the leader of the fugitives had escaped their vengeance, but hate, though never sated, can yet be gratified. Even the smallest pangs of an enemy are a satisfaction, and the priest had just come from the grieving Pharaoh. He had not succeeded in releasing him entirely from the bonds of the Hebrew magician, but he had loosened them.

The resolute, ambitious man, by no means wont to hold converse with himself, had repeated over and over again, while sitting alone in the sanctuary reflecting on what had occurred and what yet remained to be done, these little words, and the words were: "Bless me too!"

Pharaoh had uttered them, and the entreaty had been addressed neither to old Rui, the chief priest, nor to himself, the only persons who could possess the privilege of blessing the monarch, nay—but to the most atrocious wretch that breathed, to the foreigner the Hebrew, Mesu, whom he hated more than any other man on earth.

"Bless me too!" The pious entreaty, which wells so trustingly from the human heart in the hour of anguish, had pierced his soul like a dagger. It had seemed as if such a petition, uttered by the royal lips to such a man, had broken the crozier in the hand of the whole body of Egyptian priests, stripped the panther-skin from their shoulders, and branded with shame the whole people whom he loved.

He knew full well that Moses was one of the wisest sages who had ever graduated from the Egyptian schools, knew that Pharaoh was completely under the thrall of this man who had grown up in the royal household and been a friend of his father Rameses the Great. He had seen the monarch pardon deeds committed by Moses which would have cost the life of any other mortal, though he were the highest noble in the land—and what must the Hebrew be to Pharaoh, the sun-god incarnate on the throne of the world, when standing by the death-bed of his own son, he could yield to the impulse to uplift his hands to him and cry "Bless me too!"

He had told himself all these things, maturely considered them, yet he would not yield to the might of the strangers. The destruction of this man and all his race was in his eyes the holiest, most urgent duty—to accomplish which he would not shrink even from assailing the throne. Nay, in his eyes Pharaoh Menephtah's shameful entreaty: "Bless me too!" had deprived him of all the rights of sovereignty.

Moses had murdered Pharaoh's first-born son, but he and the aged chief-priest of Amon held the weal or woe of the dead prince's soul in their hands,—a weapon sharp and strong, for he knew the monarch's weak and vacillating heart. If the high-priest of Amon—the only man whose authority surpassed his own—did not thwart him by some of the unaccountable whims of age, it would be the merest trifle to force Pharaoh to yield; but any concession made to-day would be withdrawn to-morrow, should the Hebrew succeed in coming between the irresolute monarch and his Egyptian advisers. This very day the unworthy son of the great Rameses had covered his face and trembled like a timid fawn at the bare mention of the sorcerer's name, and to-morrow he might curse him and pronounce a death sentence upon him. Perhaps he might be induced to do this, and on the following one he would recall him and again sue for his blessing.

Down with such monarchs! Let the feeble reed on the throne be hurled into the dust! Already he had chosen a successor from among the princes of the blood, and when the time was ripe—when Rui, the high-priest of Amon, had passed the limits of life decreed by the gods to mortals and closed his eyes in death, he, Bai, would occupy his place, a new life for Egypt, and Moses and his race would commence would perish.

While the prophet was absorbed in these reflections a pair of ravens fluttered around his head and, croaking loudly, alighted on the dusty ruins of one of the shattered houses. He involuntarily glanced around him and noted that they had perched on the corpse of a murdered Hebrew, lying half concealed amid the rubbish. A smile which the priests of lower rank who surrounded his litter knew not how to interpret, flitted over his shrewd, defiant countenance.

CHAPTER III

Hornecht, commander of the archers, was among the prophet's companions. Indeed they were on terms of intimacy, for the soldier was a leader amid the nobles who had conspired to dethrone Pharaoh.

As they approached Nun's ruined dwelling, the prophet pointed to the wreck and said: "The former owner of this abode is the only Hebrew I would gladly spare. He was a man of genuine worth, and his son, Hosea...."

"Will be one of us," the captain interrupted. "There are few better men in Pharaoh's army, and," he added, lowering his voice, "I rely on him when the decisive hour comes."

"We will discuss that before fewer witnesses," replied Bai. "But I am greatly indebted to him. During the Libyan war—you are aware of the fact—I fell into the hands of the enemy, and Hosea, at the head of his little troop, rescued me from the savage hordes." Sinking his tones, he went on in his most instructive manner, as though apologizing for the mischief wrought: "Such is the course of earthly affairs! Where a whole body of men merit punishment, the innocent must suffer with the guilty. Under such circumstances the gods themselves cannot separate the individual from the multitude; nay, even the innocent animals share the penalty. Look at the flocks of doves fluttering around the ruins; they are seeking their cotes in vain. And the cat with her kittens yonder. Go and take them, Beki; it is our duty to save the sacred animals from starving to death."

And this man, who had just been planning the destruction of so many of his fellow-mortals, was so warmly interested in kindly caring for the senseless beasts, that he stopped his litter and watched his servants catch the cats.

This was less quickly accomplished than he had hoped; for one had taken refuge in the nearest cellar, whose opening was too narrow for the men to follow. The youngest, a slender Nubian, undertook the task; but he had scarcely approached the hole when he started back, calling: "There is a human being there who seems to be alive. Yes, he is raising his hand. It is a boy or a youth, and assuredly no slave; his head is covered with long waving locks, and—a sunbeam is shining into the cellar—I can see a broad gold circlet on his arm."

"Perhaps it is one of Nun's kindred, who has been forgotten," said Hornecht, and Bai eagerly added:

"It is an interposition from the gods! Their sacred animals have pointed out the way by which I can render a service to the man to whom I am so much indebted. Try to get in, Beki, and bring the youth out."

Meanwhile the Nubian had removed the stone whose fall had choked the opening, and soon after he lifted toward his companions a motionless young form which they brought into the open air and bore to a well whose cool water speedily restored consciousness.

As he regained his senses, he rubbed his eyes, gazed around him bewildered, as if uncertain where he was, then his head drooped as though overwhelmed with grief and horror, revealing that the locks at the back were matted together with black clots of dried blood.

The prophet had the deep wound, inflicted on the lad by a falling stone, washed at the well and, after it had been bandaged, summoned him to his own litter, which was protected from the sun.

The young Hebrew, bringing a message, had arrived at the house of his grandfather Nun, before sunrise, after a long night walk from Pithom, called by the Hebrews Succoth, but finding it deserted had lain down in one of the rooms to rest a while. Roused by the shouts of the infuriated mob, he had heard the curses on his race which rang through the whole quarter and fled to the cellar. The roof, which had injured him in its fall, proved his deliverance; for the clouds of dust which had concealed everything as it came down hid him from the sight of the rioters.

The prophet looked at him intently and, though the youth was unwashed, wan, and disfigured by the bloody bandage round his head, he saw that the lad he had recalled to life was a handsome, well-grown boy just nearing manhood.

His sympathy was roused, and his stern glance softened as he asked kindly whence he came and what had brought him to Tanis; for the rescued youth's features gave no clue to his race. He might readily have declared himself an Egyptian, but he frankly admitted that he was a grandson of Nun. He had just attained his eighteenth year, his name was Ephraim, like that of his forefather, the son of Joseph, and he had come to visit his grandfather. The words expressed steadfast self-respect and pride in his illustrious ancestry.

He delayed a short time ere answering the question whether he brought a message; but soon collected his thoughts and, looking the prophet fearlessly in the face, replied:

"Whoever you may be, I have been taught to speak the truth, so I will tell you that I have another relative in Tanis, Hosea, the son of Nun, a chief in Pharaoh's army, for whom I have a message."

"And I will tell you," the priest replied, "that it was for the sake of this very Hosea I tarried here and ordered my servants to bring you out of the ruined house. I owe him a debt of gratitude, and though most of your nation have committed deeds worthy of the harshest punishment, for the sake of his worth you shall remain among us free and unharmed."

The boy raised his eyes to the priest with a proud, fiery glance, but ere he could find words, Bai went on with encouraging kindness.

"I believe I can read in your face, my lad, that you have come to seek admittance to Pharaoh's army under your uncle Hosea. Your figure is well-suited to the trade of war, and you surely are not wanting in courage."

A smile of flattered vanity rested on Ephraim's lips, and toying with the broad gold bracelet on his arm, perhaps unconsciously, he replied with eagerness:

"Ay, my lord, I have often proved my courage in the hunting field; but at home we have plenty of sheep and cattle, which even now I call my own, and it seems to me a more enviable lot to wander freely and rule the shepherds than to obey the commands of others."

"Aha!" said the priest. "Perhaps Hosea may instil different and better views. To rule—a lofty ambition for youth. The misfortune is that we who have attained it are but servants whose burdens grow heavier with the increasing number of those who obey us. You understand me, Hornecht, and you, my lad, will comprehend my meaning later, when you become the palm-tree the promise of your youth foretells. But we are losing time. Who sent you to Hosea?"

The youth cast down his eyes irresolutely, but when the prophet broke the silence with the query: "And what has become of the frankness you were taught?" he responded promptly and resolutely:

"I came for the sake of a woman whom you know not."

"A woman?" the prophet repeated, casting an enquiring glance at Hornecht. "When a bold warrior and a fair woman seek each other, the Hathors—[The Egyptian goddesses of love, who are frequently represented with cords in their hands,]—are apt to appear and use the binding cords; but it does not befit a servant of the divinity to witness such goings on, so I forbear farther questioning. Take charge of the lad, captain, and aid him to deliver his message to Hosea. The only doubt is whether he is in the city."

"No," the soldier answered, "but he is expected with thousands of his men at the armory to-day."

"Then may the Hathors, who are partial to love messengers, bring these two together to-morrow at latest," said the priest.

But the lad indignantly retorted: "I am the bearer of no love message."

The prophet, pleased with the bold rejoinder, answered pleasantly: "I had forgotten that I was accosting a young shepherd-prince." Then he added in graver tones: "When you have found Hosea, greet him from me and tell him that Bai, the second prophet of Amon sought to discharge a part of the debt of gratitude he owed for his release from the hands of the Libyans by extending his protection to you, his nephew. Perhaps, my brave boy, you do not know that you have escaped as if by a miracle a double peril; the savage populace would no more have spared your life than would the stifling dust of the falling houses. Remember this, and tell Hosea also from me, Bai, that I am sure when he beholds the woe wrought by the magic arts of one of your race on the house of Pharaoh, to which he vowed fealty, and with it on this city and the whole country, he will tear himself with abhorrence from his kindred. They have fled like cowards, after dealing the sorest blows, robbing of their dearest possessions those among whom they dwelt in peace, whose protection they enjoyed, and who for long years have given them work and ample food. All this they have done and, if I know him aright, he will turn his back upon men who have committed such crimes. Tell him also that this has been voluntarily done by the Hebrew officers and men under the command of the Syrian Aarsu. This very morning—Hosea will have heard the news from other sources—they offered sacrifices not only to Baal and Seth, their own gods, whom so many of you were ready to serve ere the accursed sorcerer, Mesu, seduced you, but also to Father Amon and the sacred nine of our eternal deities. If he will do the same, we will rise hand in hand to the highest place, of that he may be sure—and well he merits it. The obligation still due him I shall gratefully discharge in other ways, which must for the present remain secret. But you may tell your uncle now from me that I shall find means to protect Nun, his noble father, when the vengeance of the gods and of Pharaoh falls upon the rest of your race. Already—tell him this also—the sword is whetted, and a pitiless judgment is impending. Bid him ask himself what fugitive shepherds can do against the power of the army among whose ablest leaders he is numbered. Is your father still alive, my son?"

"No, he was borne to his last resting-place long ago," replied the youth in a faltering voice.

Was the fever of his wound attacking him? Or did the shame of belonging to a race capable of acts so base overwhelm the young heart? Or did the lad cling to his kindred, and was it wrath and resentment at hearing them so bitterly reviled which made his color vary from red to pale and roused such a tumult in his soul that he was scarcely capable of speech? No matter! This lad was certainly no suitable bearer of the message the prophet desired to send to his uncle, and Bai beckoned to Hornecht to come with him under the shadow of a broad-limbed sycamore-tree.

The point was to secure Hosea's services in the army at any cost, so he laid his hand on his friend's shoulder, saying:

"You know that it was my wife who won you and others over to our cause. She serves us better and more eagerly than many a man, and while I appreciate your daughter's beauty, she never tires of lauding the winning charm of her innocence."

"And Kasana is to take part in the plot?" cried the soldier angrily.

"Not as an active worker, like my wife,—certainly not."

"She would be ill-suited to such a task," replied the other in a calmer tone, "she is scarcely more than a child."

"Yet through her aid we might bring to our cause a man whose good-will seems to me priceless."

"You mean Hosea?" asked the captain, his brow darkening again, but the prophet added:

"And if I do? Is he still a real Hebrew? Can you deem it unworthy the daughter of a distinguished warrior to bestow her band on a man who, if our plans prosper, will be commander-in-chief of all the troops in the land?"

"No, my lord!" cried Hornecht. "But one of my motives for rebelling against Pharaoh and upholding Siptah is that the king's mother was a foreigner, while our own blood courses through Siptah's veins. The mother decides the race to which a man belongs, and Hosea's mother was a Hebrew woman. He is my friend, I value his talents; Kasana likes him...."

"Yet you desire a more distinguished son-in-law?" interrupted his companion. "How is our arduous enterprise to prosper, if those who are to peril their lives for its success consider the first sacrifice too great? You say that your daughter favors Hosea?"

"Yes, she did care for him," the soldier answered; "yes, he was her heart's desire. But I compelled her to obey me, and now that she is a widow, am I to give her to the man whom—the gods alone know with how much difficulty—I forced her to resign? When was such an act heard of in Egypt?"

"Ever since the men and women who dwell by the Nile have submitted, for the sake of a great cause, to demands opposed to their wishes," replied the priest.

"Consider all this, and remember that Hosea's ancestress—he boasted of it in your own presence—was an Egyptian, the daughter of a man of my own class."

"How many generations have passed to the tomb since?"

"No matter! It brings us into closer relations with him. That must suffice. Farewell until this evening. Meanwhile, will you extend your hospitality to Hosea's nephew and commend him to your fair daughter's nursing; he seems in sore need of care."

CHAPTER IV

The house of Hornecht, like nearly every other dwelling in the city, was the scene of the deepest mourning. The men had shaved their hair, and the women had put dust on their foreheads. The archer's wife had died long before, but his daughter and her women received him with waving veils and loud lamentations; for the astrologer, his brother-in-law, had lost both his first-born son and his grandson, and the plague had snatched its victims from the homes of many a friend.

But the senseless youth soon demanded all the care the women could bestow, and after bathing him and binding a healing ointment on the dangerous wound in his head, strong wine and food were placed before him, after which, refreshed and strengthened, he obeyed the summons of the daughter of his host.

The dust-covered, worn-out fellow was transformed into a handsome youth. His perfumed hair fell in long curling locks from beneath the fresh white bandage, and gold-bordered Egyptian robes from the wardrobe of Kasana's dead husband covered his pliant bronzed limbs. He seemed pleased with the finery of his garments, which exhaled a subtle odor of spikenard new to his senses; for the eyes in his handsome face sparkled brilliantly.

It was many a day since the captain's daughter, herself a woman of unusual beauty and charm, had seen a handsomer youth. Within the year she had married a man she did not love Kasana had returned a widow to her father's house, which lacked a mistress, and the great wealth bequeathed to her, at her husband's death, made it possible for her to bring into the soldier's unpretending home the luxury and ease which to her had now become a second nature.

Her father, a stern man prone to sudden fits of passion, now yielded absolutely to her will. Formerly he had pitilessly enforced his own, compelling the girl of fifteen to wed a man many years her senior. This had been done because he perceived that Kasana had given her young heart to Hosea, the soldier, and he deemed it beneath his dignity to receive the Hebrew, who at that time held no prominent position in the army, as his son-in-law. An Egyptian girl had no choice save to accept the husband chosen by her father and Kasana submitted, though she shed so many bitter tears that the archer rejoiced when, in obedience to his will, she had wedded an unloved husband.

But even as a widow Kasana's heart clung to the Hebrew. When the army was in the field her anxiety was ceaseless; day and night were spent in restlessness and watching. When news came from the troops she asked only about Hosea, and her father with deep annoyance attributed to her love for the Hebrew her rejection of suitor after suitor. As a widow she had a right to the bestowal of her own hand, and the tender, gentle-natured woman astonished Hornecht by the resolute decision displayed, not alone to him and lovers of her own rank, but to Prince Siptah, whose cause the captain had espoused as his own.

To-day Kasana expressed her delight at the Hebrew's return with such entire frankness and absence of reserve that the quick-tempered man rushed out of the house lest he might be tempted into some thoughtless act or word. His young guest was left to the care of his daughter and her nurse.

How deeply the lad's sensitive nature was impressed by the airy rooms, the open verandas supported by many pillars, the brilliant hues of the painting, the artistic household utensils, the soft cushions, and the sweet perfume everywhere! All these things were novel and strange to the son of a herdsman who had always lived within the grey walls of a spacious, but absolutely plain abode, and spent months together in canvas tents among shepherds and flocks, nay was more accustomed to be in the open air than under any shelter! He felt as though some wizard had borne him into a higher and more beautiful world, where he was entirely at home in his magnificent garb, with his perfumed curls and limbs fresh from the bath. True, the whole earth was fair, even out in the pastures among the flocks or round the fire in front of the tent in the cool of the evening, when the shepherds sang, the hunters told tales of daring exploits, and the stars sparkled brightly overhead.

But all these pleasures were preceded by weary, hateful labor; here it was a delight merely to see and to breathe and, when the curtains parted and the young widow, giving him a friendly greeting, made him sit down opposite to her, sometimes questioning him and sometimes listening with earnest sympathy to his replies, he almost imagined his senses had failed him as they had done under the ruins of the fallen house, and he was enjoying the sweetest of dreams. The feeling that threatened to stifle him and frequently interrupted the flow of words was the rapture bestowed upon him by great Aschera, the companion of Baal, of whom the Phoenician traders who supplied the shepherds with many good things had told him such marvels, and whom the stern Miriam forbade him ever to name at home.

His family had instilled into his young heart hatred of the Egyptians as the oppressors of his race, but could they be so wicked, could he detest a people among whom were creatures like this lovely, gentle woman, who gazed into his eyes so softly, so tenderly, whose voice fell on his ear like harmonious music, and whose glance made his blood course so swiftly that he could scarce endure it and pressed his hand upon his heart to quiet its wild pulsation.

Kasana sat opposite to him on a seat covered with a panther-skin, drawing the fine wool from the distaff. He had pleased her and she had received him kindly because he was related to the man whom she had loved from childhood. She imagined that she could trace a resemblance between him and Hosea, though the youth lacked the grave earnestness of the man to whom she had yielded her young heart, she knew not why nor when, though he had never sought her love.

A lotus blossom rested among her dark waving curls, and its stem fell in a graceful curve on her bent neck, round which clustered a mass of soft locks. When she lifted her eyes to his, he felt as though two springs had opened to pour floods of bliss into his young breast, and he had already clasped in greeting the dainty hand which held the yarn.

She now questioned him about Hosea and the woman who had sent the message, whether she was young and fair and whether any tie of love bound her to his uncle.

Ephraim laughed merrily. She who had sent him was so grave and earnest that the bare thought of her being capable of any tender emotion wakened his mirth. As to her beauty, he had never asked himself the question.

The young widow interpreted the laugh as the reply she most desired and, much relieved, laid aside the spindle and invited Ephraim to go into the garden.

How fragrant and full of bloom it was, how well-kept were the beds, the paths, the arbors, and the pond.

His unpretending home adjoined a dreary yard, wholly unadorned and filled with pens for sheep and cattle. Yet he knew that at some future day he would be owner of great possessions, for he was the sole child and heir of a wealthy father and his mother was the daughter of the rich Nun. The men servants had told him this more than once, and it angered him to see that his own home was scarcely better than Hornecht's slave-quarters, to which Kasana had called his attention.

During their stroll through the garden Ephraim was asked to help her cull the flowers and, when the basket he carried was filled, she invited him to sit with her in a bower and aid her to twine the wreaths. These were intended for the dear departed. Her uncle and a beloved cousin—who bore some resemblance to Ephraim—had been snatched away the night before by the plague which his people had brought upon Tanis.

From the street which adjoined the garden-wall they heard the wails of women lamenting the dead or bearing a corpse to the tomb. Once, when the cries of woe rose more loudly and clearly than ever, Kasana gently reproached him for all that the people of Tanis had suffered through the Hebrews, and asked if he could deny that the Egyptians had good reason to hate a race which had brought such anguish upon them.

It was hard for Ephraim to find a fitting answer; he had been told that the God of his race had punished the Egyptians to rescue his own people from shame and bondage, and he could neither condemn nor scorn the men of his own blood. So he kept silence that he might neither speak falsely nor blaspheme; but Kasana allowed him no peace, and he at last replied that aught which caused her sorrow was grief to him, but his people had no power over life and health, and when a Hebrew was ill, he often sent for an Egyptian physician. What had occurred was doubtless the will of the great God of his fathers, whose power far surpassed the might of any other deity. He himself was a Hebrew, yet she would surely believe his assurance that he was guiltless of the plague and would gladly recall her uncle and cousin to life, had he the power to do so. For her sake he would undertake the most difficult enterprise.

She smiled kindly and replied:

"My poor boy! If I see any guilt in you, it is only that you are one of a race which knows no ruth, no patience. Our beloved, hapless dead! They must even lose the lamentations of their kindred; for the house where they rest is plague-stricken and no one is permitted to enter."

She silently wiped her eyes and went on arranging her garlands, but tear after tear coursed down her cheeks.

Ephraim knew not what to say, and mutely handed her the leaves and blossoms. Whenever his hand touched hers a thrill ran through his veins.

His head and the wound began to ache, and he sometimes felt a slight chill. He knew that the fever was increasing, as it had done once before when he nearly lost his life in the red disease; but he was ashamed to own it and battled bravely against his pain.

When the sun was nearing the horizon Hornecht entered the garden. He had already seen Hosea, and though heartily glad to greet his old friend once more, it had vexed him that the soldier's first enquiry was for his daughter. He did not withhold this from the young widow, but his flashing eyes betrayed the displeasure with which he delivered the Hebrew's message. Then, turning to Ephraim, he told him that Hosea and his men would encamp outside of the city, pitching their tents, on account of the pestilence, between Tanis and the sea. They would soon march by. His uncle sent Ephraim word that he must seek him in his tent.

When he noticed that the youth was aiding his daughter to weave the garlands, he smiled, and said:

"Only this morning this young fellow declared his intention of remaining free and a ruler all his life. Now he has taken service with you, Kasana. You need not blush, young friend. If either your mistress or your uncle can persuade you to join us and embrace the noblest trade—that of the soldier—so much the better for you. Look at me! I've wielded the bow more than forty years and still rejoice in my profession. I must obey, it is true, but it is also my privilege to command, and the thousands who obey me are not sheep and cattle, but brave men. Consider the matter again. He would make a splendid leader of the archers. What say you, Kasana?"

"Certainly," replied the young widow. And she was about to say more, but the regular tramp of approaching troops was heard on the other side of the garden-wall. A slight flush crimsoned Kasana's cheeks, her eyes sparkled with a light that startled Ephraim and, regardless of her father or her guest, she darted past the pond, across paths and flower-beds, to a grassy bank beside the wall, whence she gazed eagerly toward the road and the armed host which soon marched by.

Hosea, in full armor, headed his men. As he passed Hornecht's garden he turned his grave head, and seeing Kasana lowered his battle-axe in friendly salutation.

Ephraim had followed the captain of the archers, who pointed out the youth's uncle, saying: "Shining armor would become you also, and when drums are beating, pipes squeaking shrilly, and banners waving, a man marches as lightly as if he had wings. To-day the martial music is hushed by the terrible woe brought upon us by that Hebrew villain. True, Hosea is one of his race yet, though I cannot forget that fact, I must admit that he is a genuine soldier, a model for the rising generation. Tell him what I think of him on this score. Now bid farewell to Kasana quickly and follow the men; the little side-door in the wall is open." He turned towards the house as he spoke, and Ephraim held out his hand to bid the young widow farewell.

She clasped it, but hurriedly withdrew her own, exclaiming anxiously: "How burning hot your hand is! You have a fever!"

"No, no," faltered the youth, but even while speaking he fell upon his knees and the veil of unconsciousness descended upon the sufferer's soul, which had been the prey of so many conflicting emotions.

Kasana was alarmed, but speedily regained her composure and began to cool his brow and head by bathing them with water from the neighboring pond. Yes, in his boyhood the man she loved must have resembled this youth. Her heart throbbed more quickly and, while supporting his head in her hands, she gently kissed him.

She supposed him to be unconscious, but the refreshing water had already dispelled the brief swoon, and he felt the caress with a thrill of rapture. But he kept his eyes closed, and would gladly have lain for a lifetime with his head pillowed on her breast in the hope that her lips might once more meet his. But instead of kissing him a second time she called loudly for aid. He raised himself, gave one wild, ardent look into her face and, ere she could stay him, rushed like a strong man to the garden gate, flung it open, and followed the troops. He soon overtook the rear ranks, passed on in advance of the others, and at last reached their leader's side and, calling his uncle by name, gave his own. Hosea, in his joy and astonishment, held out his arms, but ere Ephraim could fall upon his breast, he again lost consciousness, and stalwart soldiers bore the senseless lad into the tent the quartermaster had already pitched on a dune by the sea.

CHAPTER V

It was midnight. A fire was blazing in front of Hosea's tent, and he sat alone before it, gazing mournfully now into the flames and anon over the distant country. Inside the canvas walls Ephraim was lying on his uncle's camp-bed.

The surgeon who attended the soldiers had bandaged the youth's wounds, given him an invigorating cordial, and commanded him to keep still; for the violence with which the fever had attacked the lad alarmed him.

But in spite of the leech's prescription Ephraim continued restless. Sometimes Kasana's image rose before his eyes, increasing the fever of his over-heated blood, sometimes he recalled the counsel to become a warrior like his uncle. The advice seemed wise—at least he tried to persuade himself that it was—because it promised honor and fame, but in reality he wished to follow it because it would bring her for whom his soul yearned nearer to him.

Then his pride rose as he remembered the insults which she and her father had heaped on those to whom by every tie of blood and affection, he belonged. His hand clenched as he thought of the ruined home of his grandfather, whom he had ever regarded one of the noblest of men. Nor was his message forgotten. Miriam had repeated it again and again, and his clear memory retained every syllable, for he had unweariedly iterated it to himself during his solitary walk to Tanis. He was striving to do the same thing now but, ere he could finish, his mind always reverted to thoughts of Kasana. The leech had told Hosea to forbid the sufferer to talk and, when the youth attempted to deliver his message, the uncle ordered him to keep silence. Then the soldier arranged his pillow with a mother's tenderness, gave him his medicine, and kissed him on the forehead. At last he took his seat by the fire before the tent and only rose to give Ephraim a drink when he saw by the stars that an hour had passed.

The flames illumined Hosea's bronzed features, revealing the countenance of a man who had confronted many a peril and vanquished all by steadfast perseverance and wise consideration. His black eyes had an imperious look, and his full, firmly-compressed lips suggested a quick temper and, still more, the iron will of a resolute man. His broad-shouldered form leaned against some lances thrust crosswise into the earth, and when he passed his strong hand through his thick black locks or smoothed his dark beard, and his eyes sparkled with ire, it was evident that his soul was stirred by conflicting emotions and that he stood on the threshold of a great resolve. The lion was resting, but when he starts up, let his foes beware!

His soldiers had often compared their fearless, resolute leader, with his luxuriant hair, to the king of beasts, and as he now shook his fist, while the muscles of his bronzed arm swelled as though they would burst the gold armlet that encircled them, and his eyes flashed fire, his awe-inspiring mien did not invite approach.

Westward, the direction toward which his eyes were turned, lay the necropolis and the ruined strangers' quarter. But a few hours ago he had led his troops through the ruins around which the ravens were circling and past his father's devastated home.

Silently, as duty required, he marched on. Not until he halted to seek quarters for the soldiers did he hear from Hornecht, the captain of the archers, what had happened during the night. He listened silently, without the quiver of an eye-lash, or a word of questioning, until his men had pitched their tents. He had but just gone to rest when a Hebrew maiden, spite of the menaces of the guard, made her way in to implore him, in the name of Eliab, one of the oldest slaves of his family, to go with her to the old man, her grandfather. The latter, whose weakness prevented journeying, had been left behind, and directly after the departure of the Hebrews he and his wife had been carried on an ass to the little but near the harbor, which generous Nun, his master, had bestowed on the faithful slave.

The grand-daughter had been left to care for the feeble pair, and now the old servant's heart yearned for one more sight of his lord's first-born son whom, when a child, he had carried in his arms. He had charged the girl to tell Hosea that Nun had promised his people that his son would abandon the Egyptians and cleave to his own race. The tribe of Ephraim, nay the whole Hebrew nation had hailed these tidings with the utmost joy. Eliab would give him fuller details; she herself had been well nigh dazed with weeping and anxiety. He would earn the richest blessings if he would only follow her.

The soldier realized at once that he must fulfil this desire, but he was obliged to defer his visit to the old slave until the nest morning. The messenger, however, even in her haste, had told him many incidents she had seen herself or heard from others.

At last she left him. He rekindled the fire and, so long as the flames burned brightly, his gaze was bent with a gloomy, thoughtful expression upon the west. Not till they had devoured the fuel and merely flickered with a faint bluish light around the charred embers did he fix his eyes on the whirling sparks. And the longer he did so, the deeper, the more unconquerable became the conflict in his soul, whose every energy, but yesterday, had been bent upon a single glorious goal.

The war against the Libyan rebels had detained him eighteen months from his home, and he had seen ten crescent moons grow full since any news had reached him of his kindred. A few weeks before he had been ordered to return, and when to-day he approached nearer and nearer to the obelisks towering above Tanis, the city of Rameses, his heart had pulsed with as much joy and hopefulness as if the man of thirty were once more a boy.

Within a few short hours he should again see his beloved, noble father, who had needed great deliberation and much persuasion from Hosea's mother—long since dead—ere he would permit his son to follow the bent of his inclinations and enter upon a military life in Pharaoh's army. He had anticipated that very day surprising him with the news that he had been promoted above men many years his seniors and of Egyptian lineage. Instead of the slights Nun had dreaded, Hosea's gallant bearing, courage and, as he modestly added, good-fortune had gained him promotion, yet he had remained a Hebrew. When he felt the necessity of offering to some god sacrifices and prayer, he had bowed before Seth, to whose temple Nun had led him when a child, and whom in those days all the people in Goshen in whose veins flowed Semitic blood had worshipped. But he also owed allegiance to another god, not the God of his fathers, but the deity revered by all the Egyptians who had been initiated. He remained unknown to the masses, who could not have understood him; yet he was adored not only by the adepts but by the majority of those who had obtained high positions in civil or military life-whether they were servants of the divinity or not—and Hosea, the initiated and the stranger, knew him also. Everybody understood when allusion was made to "the God," the "Sum of All," the "Creator of Himself," and the "Great One." Hymns extolled him, inscriptions on the monuments, which all could read, spoke of him, the one God, who manifested himself to the world, pervaded the universe, and existed throughout creation not alone as the vital spark animates the human organism, but as himself the sum of creation, the world with its perpetual growth, decay, and renewal, obeying the laws he had himself ordained. His spirit, existing in every form of nature, dwelt also in man, and wherever a mortal gazed he could discern the rule of the "One." Nothing could be imagined without him, therefore he was one like the God of Israel. Nothing could be created nor happen on earth apart from him, therefore, like Jehovah, he was omnipotent. Hosea had long regarded both as alike in spirit, varying only in name. Whoever adored one was a servant of the other, so the warrior could have entered his father's presence with a clear conscience, and told him that although in the service of the king he had remained loyal to the God of his nation.

Another thought had made his heart pulse faster and more joyously as he saw in the distance the pylons and obelisks of Tanis; for on countless marches through the silent wilderness and in many a lonely camp he had beheld in imagination a virgin of his own race, whom he had known as a singular child, stirred by marvellous thoughts, and whom, just before leading his troops to the Libyan war, he had again met, now a dignified maiden of stern and unapproachable beauty. She had journeyed from Succoth to Tanis to attend his mother's funeral, and her image had been deeply imprinted on his heart, as his—he ventured to hope—on hers. She had since become a prophetess, who heard the voice of her God. While the other maidens of his people were kept in strict seclusion, she was free to come and go at will, even among men, and spite of her hate of the Egyptians and of Hosea's rank among them, she did not deny that it was grief to part and that she would never cease thinking of him. His future wife must be as strong, as earnest, as himself. Miriam was both, and quite eclipsed a younger and brighter vision which he had once conjured before his memory with joy.

He loved children, and a lovelier girl than Kasana he had never met, either in Egypt or in alien lands. The interest with which the fair daughter of his companion-in-arms watched his deeds and his destiny, the modest yet ardent devotion afterwards displayed by the much sought-after young widow, who coldly repelled all other suitors, had been a delight to him in times of peace. Prior to her marriage he had thought of her as the future mistress of his home, but her wedding another, and Hornecht's oft-repeated declaration that he would never give his child to a foreigner, had hurt his pride and cooled his passion. Then he met Miriam and was fired with an ardent desire to make her his wife. Still, on the homeward march the thought of seeing Kasana again had been a pleasant one. It was fortunate he no longer wished to wed Hornecht's daughter; it could have led to naught save trouble. Both Hebrews and Egyptians held it to be an abomination to eat at the same board, or use the same seats or knives. Though he himself was treated by his comrades as one of themselves, and had often heard Kasana's father speak kindly of his kindred, yet "strangers" were hateful in the eyes of the captain of the archers, and of all free Egyptians.

He had found in Miriam the noblest of women. He hoped that Kasana might make another happy. To him she would ever be the charming child from whom we expect nothing save the delight of her presence.

He had come to ask from her, as a tried friend ever ready for leal service, a joyous glance. From Miriam he would ask herself, with all her majesty and beauty, for he had borne the solitude of the camp long enough, and now that on his return no mother's arms opened to welcome him, he felt for the first time the desolation of a single life. He longed to enjoy the time of peace when, after dangers and privations of every kind, he could lay aside his weapons. It was his duty to lead a wife home to his father's hearth and to provide against the extinction of the noble race of which he was the sole representative. Ephraim was the son of his sister.

Filled with the happiest thoughts, he had advanced toward Tannis and, on reaching the goal of all his hopes and wishes, found it lying before him like a ripening grain-field devastated by hail and swarms of locusts.

As if in derision, fate led him first to the Hebrew quarter. A heap of dusty ruins marked the site of the house where he had spent his childhood, and for which his heart had longed; and where his loved ones had watched his departure, beggars were now greedily searching for plunder among the debris.

The first man to greet him in Tanis was Kasana's father. Instead of a friendly glance from her eyes, he had received from him tidings that pierced his inmost heart. He had expected to bring home a wife, and the house where she was to reign as mistress was razed to the ground. The father, for whose blessing he longed, and who was to have been gladdened by his advancement, had journeyed far away and must henceforward be the foe of the sovereign to whom he owed his prosperity.

He had been proud of rising, despite his origin, to place and power. Now he would be able, as leader of a great host, to show the prowess of which he was capable. His inventive brain had never lacked schemes which, if executed by his superiors, would have had good results; now he could fulfil them according to his own will, and instead of the tool become the guiding power.

These reflections had awakened a keen sense of exultation in his breast and winged his steps on his homeward march and, now that he had reached the goal, so long desired, must he turn back to join the shepherds and builders to whom—it now seemed a sore misfortune—he belonged by the accident of birth and ancestry, though, denial was futile, he felt as utterly alien to the Hebrews as he was to the Libyans whom he had confronted on the battle-field. In almost every pursuit he valued, he had nothing in common with his people. He had believed he might truthfully answer yes to his father's enquiry whether he had returned a Hebrew, yet he now felt it would be only a reluctant and half-hearted assent.

He clung with his whole soul to the standards beneath which he had gone to battle and might now himself lead to victory. Was it possible to wrench his heart from them, renounce what his own deeds had won? Yet Eliab's granddaughter had told him that the Hebrews expected him to leave the army and join them. A message from his father must soon reach him — and among the Hebrews a son never opposed a parent's command.

There was still another to whom implicit obedience was due, Pharaoh, to whom he had solemnly vowed loyal service, sworn to follow his summons without hesitation or demur, through fire and water, by day and night.

How often he had branded the soldier who deserted to the foe or rebelled against the orders of his commander as a base scoundrel and villain, and by his orders many a renegade from his standard had died a shameful death on the gallows under his own eyes. Was he now to commit the deed for which he had despised and killed others? His prompt decision was known throughout the army, how quickly in the most difficult situations he could resolve upon the right course and carry it into action; but during this dark and lonely hour of the night he seemed to himself a mere swaying reed, and felt as helpless as a forsaken orphan.

Wrath against himself preyed upon him, and when he thrust a spear into the flames, scattering the embers and sending a shower of bright sparks upward, it was rage at his own wavering will that guided his hand.

Had recent events imposed upon him the virile duty of vengeance, doubt and hesitation would have vanished and his father's summons would have spurred him on to action; but who had been the heaviest sufferers here? Surely it was the Egyptians whom Moses' curse had robbed of thousands of beloved lives, while the Hebrews had escaped their revenge by flight. His wrath had been kindled by the destruction of the Hebrews' houses, but he saw no sufficient cause for a bloody revenge, when he remembered the unspeakable anguish inflicted upon Pharaoh and his subjects by the men of his own race.

Nay; he had nothing to avenge; he seemed to himself like a man who beholds his father and mother in mortal peril, owns that he cannot save both, yet knows that while staking his life to rescue one he must leave the other to perish. If he obeyed the summons of his people, he would lose his honor, which he had kept as untarnished as his brazen helm, and with it the highest goal of his life; if he remained loyal to Pharaoh and his oath, he must betray his own race, have all his future days darkened by his father's curse, and resign the brightest dream he cherished; for Miriam was a true child of her people and he would be blest indeed if her lofty soul could be as ardent in love as it was bitter in hate.

Stately and beautiful, but with gloomy eyes and hand upraised in warning, her image rose before his mental vision as he sat gazing over the smouldering fire out into the darkness. And now the pride of his manhood rebelled, and it seemed base cowardice to cast aside, from dread of a woman's wrath and censure, all that a warrior held most dear.

"Nay, nay," he murmured, and the scale containing duty, love, and filial obedience suddenly kicked the beam. He was what he was—the leader of ten thousand men in Pharaoh's army. He had vowed fealty to him—and to none other. Let his people fly from the Egyptian yoke, if they desired. He, Hosea, scorned flight. Bondage had sorely oppressed them, but the highest in the land had received him as an equal and held him worthy of the loftiest honor. To repay them with treachery and desertion was foreign to his nature and, drawing a long breath, he sprang to his feet with the conviction that he had chosen aright. A fair woman and the weak yearning of a loving heart should not make him a recreant to grave duties and the loftiest purposes of his life.

"I will stay!" cried a loud voice in his breast. "Father is wise and kind, and when he learns the reasons for my choice he will approve them and bless, instead of cursing me. I will write to him, and the boy Miriam sent me shall be the messenger."

A call from the tent startled him and when, springing up, he glanced at the stars, he found that he had forgotten his duty to the suffering lad and hurried to his couch.

Ephraim was sitting up in his bed, watching for him, and exclaimed: "I have been waiting a long, long time to see you. So many thoughts crowd my brain and, above all, Miriam's message. I can get no rest until I have delivered it—so listen now."

Hosea nodded assent and, after drinking the healing potion handed to him, Ephraim began:

"Miriam the daughter of Amram and Jochebed greets the son of Nun the Ephraimite. Thy name is Hosea, 'the Help,' and the Lord our God hath chosen thee to be the helper of His people. But henceforward, by His command, thou shalt be called Joshua,—[Jehoshua, he who helps Jehova]—the help of Jehovah; for through Miriam's lips the God of her fathers, who is the God of thy fathers likewise, bids thee be the sword and buckler of thy people. In Him dwells all power, and he promises to steel thine arm that He may smite the foe."

Ephraim had begun in a low voice, but gradually his tones grew more resonant and the last words rang loudly and solemnly through the stillness of the night.

Thus had Miriam uttered them, laying her hands on the lad's head and gazing earnestly into his face with eyes deep and dark as night, and while repeating them he had felt as though some secret power were constraining him to shout them aloud to Hosea, just as he had heard them from the lips of the prophetess. Then, with a sigh of relief, he turned his face toward the canvas wall of the tent, saying quietly:

"Now I will go to sleep."

But Hosea laid his hand on his shoulder, exclaiming imperiously: "Say it again."

The youth obeyed, but this time he repeated the words in a low, careless tone, then saying beseechingly:

"Let me rest now," put his hand under his cheek and closed his eyes.

Hosea let him have his way, carefully applied a fresh bandage to his burning head, extinguished the light, and flung more fuel on the smouldering fire outside; but the alert, resolute man performed every act as if in a dream. At last he sat down, and propping his elbows on his knees and his head in his hands, stared alternately, now into vacancy, and anon into the flames.

Who was this God who summoned him through Miriam's lips to be, under His guidance, the sword and shield of His people?

He was to be known by a new name, and in the minds of the Egyptians the name was everything "Honor to the name of Pharaoh," not "Honor to Tharaoh" was spoken and written. And if henceforward he was to be called Joshua, the behest involved casting aside his former self, and becoming a new man.

The will of the God of his fathers announced to him by Miriam meant no less a thing than the command to transform himself from the Egyptian his life had made him, into the Hebrew he had been when a lad. He must learn to act and feel like an Israelite! Miriam's summons called him back to his people. The God of his race, through her, commanded him to fulfil his father's expectations. Instead of the Egyptian troops whom he must forsake, he was in future to lead the men of his own blood forth to battle! This was the meaning of her bidding, and when the noble virgin and prophetess who addressed him, asserted that God Himself spoke through her lips, it was no idle boast, she was really obeying the will of the Most High. And now the image of the woman whom he had ventured to love, rose in unapproachable majesty before him. Many things which he had heard in his childhood concerning the God of Abraham, and His promises returned to his mind, and the scale which hitherto had been the heavier, rose higher and higher. The resolve just matured, now seemed uncertain, and he again confronted the terrible conflict he had believed was overpast.

How loud, how potent was the call he heard! Ringing in his ears, it disturbed the clearness and serenity of his mind, and instead of calmly reflecting on the matter, memories of his boyhood, which he had imagined were buried long ago, raised their voices, and incoherent flashes of thought darted through his brain.

Sometimes he felt impelled to turn in prayer to the God who summoned him, but whenever he attempted to calm himself and uplift his heart and eyes to Him, he remembered the oath he must break, the soldiers he must abandon to lead, instead of well-disciplined, brave, obedient bands of brothers-in-arms, a wretched rabble of cowardly slaves, and rude, obstinate shepherds, accustomed to the heavy yoke of bondage.

The third hour after midnight had come, the guards had been relieved, and Hosea thought he might now permit himself a few hours repose. He would think all these things over again by daylight with his usual clear judgment, which he strove in vain to obtain now. But when he entered the tent and heard Ephraim's regular breathing, he fancied that the boy's solemn message was again echoing in his ears. Startled, he was in the act of repeating it himself, when loud voices in violent altercation among the sentinels disturbed the stillness of the night.

The interruption was welcome, and he hurried to the outposts.

CHAPTER VI

Hogla, the old slave's granddaughter, had come to beseech Hosea to go with her at once to her grandfather, who had suddenly broken down, and who feeling the approach of death could not perish without having once more seen and blessed him.

The warrior told her to wait and, after assuring himself that Ephraim was sleeping quietly, ordered a trusty man to watch beside his bed and went away with Hogla.

The girl walked before him, carrying a small lantern, and as its light fell on her face and figure, he saw how unlovely she was, for the hard toil of slavery had bowed the poor thing's back before its time. Her voice had the harsh accents frequently heard in the tones of women whose strength has been pitilessly tasked; but her words were kind and tender, and Hosea forgot her appearance when she told him that her lover had gone with the departing tribes, yet she had remained with her grandparents because she could not bring herself to leave the old couple alone. Because she had no beauty no man had sought her for his wife till Assir came, who did not care for her looks because he toiled industriously, like herself, and expected her to add to his savings. He would gladly have stayed with her, but his father had commanded him to go forth, so there was no choice for them save to obey and part forever.

The words were simple and the accents harsh, yet they pierced the heart of the man who was preparing to follow his own path in opposition to his father's will.

As they approached the harbor and Hosea saw the embankments, and the vast fortified storehouses built by his own people, he remembered the ragged laborers whom he had so often beheld crouching before the Egyptian overseers or fighting savagely among themselves. He had heard, too, that they shrunk from no lies, no fraud to escape their toil, and how difficult was the task of compelling them to obey and fulfil their duty.

The most repulsive forms among these luckless hordes rose distinctly before his vision, and the thought that it might henceforward be his destiny to command such a wretched rabble seemed to him ignominy which the lowest of his brave officers, the leader of but fifty men, would seek to avoid. True, Pharaoh's armies contained many a Hebrew mercenary who had won renown for bravery and endurance; but these men were the sons of owners of herds or people who had once been shepherds. The toiling slaves, whose clay huts could be upset by a kick, formed the majority of those to whom he was required to return.

Resolute in his purpose to remain loyal to the oath which bound him to the Egyptian standard, yet moved to the very depths of his heart, he entered the slave's little hut, and his anger rose when he saw old Eliab sitting up, mixing some wine and water with his own hands. So he had been summoned from his nephew's sick-bed, and robbed of his night's rest, on a false pretence, in order that a slave, in his eyes scarcely entitled to rank as a man, might have his way. Here he himself experienced a specimen of the selfish craft of which the Egyptians accused his people, and which certainly did not attract him, Hosea, to them. But the anger of the just, keen sighted-man quickly subsided at the sight of the girl's unfeigned joy in her grandfather's speedy recovery. Besides he soon learned from the old man's aged wife that, shortly after Hogla's departure, she remembered the wine they had, and as soon as he swallowed the first draught her husband, whom she had believed had one foot in the grave, grew better and better. Now he was mixing some more of God's gift to strengthen himself occasionally by a sip.

Here Eliab interrupted her to say that they owed this and many more valuable things to the goodness of Nun, Hosea's father, who had given them, besides their little hut, wine, meal for bread, a milch cow, and also an ass, so that he could often ride out into the fresh air. He had likewise left them their granddaughter and some pieces of silver, so that they could look forward without fear to the end of their days, especially as they had behind the house a bit of ground, where Hogla meant to raise radishes, onions, and leeks for their own table. But the best gift of all was the written document making them and the girl free forever. Ay, Nun was a true master and father to his people, and the blessing of Jehovah had followed his gifts; for soon after the departure of the Hebrews, he and his wife had been brought hither unmolested by the aid of Assir, Hogla's lover.

"We old people shall die here," Eliab's wife added. But Assir promised Hogla that he would come back for her when she had discharged her filial duties to the end.

Then, turning to her granddaughter, she said encouragingly: "And we cannot live much longer now."

Hogla raised her blue gown to wipe the tears from her eyes, exclaiming

"May it be a long, long time yet. I am young and can wait."

Hosea heard the words, and again it seemed as though the poor, forsaken, unlovely girl was giving him a lesson.

He had listened patiently to the freed slaves' talk, but his time was limited and he now asked whether Eliab had summoned him for any special purpose.

"Ay," he replied; "I was obliged to send, not only to still the yearning of my old heart, but because my lord Nun commanded me to do so."

"Thou hast attained a grand and noble manhood, and hast now become the hope of Israel. Thy father promised the slaves and freedmen of his household that after his death, thou wouldst be heir, lord and master. His words were full of thy praise, and great rejoicing hailed his statement that thou wouldst follow the departing Hebrews. And my lord deigned to command me to tell thee, if thou should'st return ere his messenger arrived, that Nun, thy father, expected his son. Whithersoever thy nation may wander, thou art to follow. Toward sunrise, or at latest by the noon-tide hour, the tribes will tarry to rest at Succoth. He will conceal in the hollow sycamore that stands in front of Amminadab's house a letter which will inform thee whither they will next turn their steps. His blessing and that of our God will attend thy every step."

As Eliab uttered the last words, Hosea bowed his head as if inviting invisible hands to be laid upon it. Then he thanked the old man and asked, in subdued tones, whether all the Hebrews had willingly obeyed the summons to leave house and lands.

His aged wife clasped her hands, exclaiming: "Oh no, my lord, certainly not. What wailing and weeping filled the air before their departure! Many refused to go, others fled, or sought some hiding-place. But all resistance was futile. In the house of our neighbor Deuel—you know him—his young wife had just given birth to their first son. How was she to fare on the journey? She wept bitterly and her husband uttered fierce curses, but it was all in vain. She was put in a cart with her babe, and as the arrangements went on, both submitted like all the rest—even Phineas who crept into a pigeon-house with his wife and five children, and crooked grave-haunting Kusaja. Do you remember her? Adonai! She had seen father, mother, husband, and three noble sons, all that the Lord had given her to love, borne to the tomb. They lay side by side in our burying ground, and every morning and evening she went there and, sitting on a log of wood which she had rolled close to the gravestones, moved her lips constantly, not in prayer—no, I have listened often when she did not know I was near—no; she talked to the dead, as though they could hear her in the sepulchre, and understand her words like those who walk alive beneath the sun. She is near seventy, and for thrice seven years she has gone by the name of grave-haunting Kusaja. It was in sooth a foolish thing to do; yet perhaps that was why she found it all the harder to give it up, and go she would not, but hid herself among the bushes. When Ahieser, the overseer, dragged her out, her wailing made one's heart sore, yet when the time for departure came, the longing to go seized upon her also, and she found it as hard to resist as the others."

"What had happened to the poor creatures, what possessed them?" asked Hosea, interrupting the old wife's speech; for in imagination he again beheld the people he must lead, if he valued his father's blessing as the most priceless boon the world could offer, and beheld them in all their wretchedness.

The startled dame, fearing that she had offended her master's first-born son, the great and powerful chieftain, stammered:

"What possessed them, my lord? Ah, well—I am but a poor lowly slave-woman; yet, my lord, had you but seen it.... "

"Well, even then?" interrupted the warrior in harsh, impatient tones, for this was the first time he had ever found himself compelled to act against his desires and belief.

Eliab tried to come to the assistance of the terrified woman, saying timidly,

"Ah, my lord, no tongue can relate, no human mind can picture it. It came from the Almighty and, if I could describe how great was its influence on the souls of the people...."

"Try," Hosea broke in, "but my time is brief. So they were compelled to depart, and set forth reluctantly on their wanderings. Even the Egyptians have long known that they obeyed the bidding of Moses and Aaron as the sheep follow the shepherd. Have those who brought the terrible pestilence on so many guiltless human beings also wrought the miracle of blinding the minds of you and of your wife?"

The old man stretched out his hands to the soldier, and answered in a troubled voice and a tone of the most humble entreaty:

"Oh, my lord, you are my master's first-born son, the greatest and loftiest of your race, if it is your pleasure you can trample me into the dust like a beetle, yet I must lift up my voice and say: 'You have heard false tales!' You were away in foreign lands when mighty things were done in our midst, and far from Zoan,—[The Hebrew name for Tanis]—as I hear, when the exodus took place. Any son of our people who witnessed it would rather his tongue should wither than mock at the marvels the Lord permitted him to behold. Ah, if you had patience to suffer me to tell the tale...."

"Speak on!" cried Hosea, astonished at the old man's solemn fervor. Eliab thanked him with an ardent glance, exclaiming:

"Oh, would that Aaron, or Eleasar, or my lord your father were here in my stead, or would that Jehovah would bestow on me the might of their eloquence! But be it as it is! True, I imagine I can again see and hear everything as though it were happening once more before my eyes, but how am I to describe it? How can such things be given in words? Yet, with God's assistance, I will try."

Here he paused and Hosea, noticing that the old man's hands and lips were trembling, gave him the cup of wine, and Eliab gratefully quaffed it to the dregs. Then, half-closing his eyes, he began his story and his wrinkled features grew sharper as he went on:

"My wife has already told you what occurred after the people learned the command that had been issued. We, too, were among those who lost courage and murmured. But last night, all who belonged to the household of Nun—and also the shepherds, the slaves, and the poor—were summoned to a feast, and there was abundance of roast lamb, fresh, unleavened bread, and wine, more than usual at the harvest festival, which began that night, and which you, my lord, have often attended in your boyhood. We sat rejoicing, and our lord, your father, comforted us, and told us of the God of our fathers and the wonders He had wrought for them. It was now His will that we should go forth from this land where we had suffered contempt and bondage. This was no sacrifice like that of Abraham when, at the command of the Most High, he had whetted his knife to shed the blood of his son Isaac, though it would be hard for many of us to quit a home that had grown dear to us and forego many a familiar custom. But it will be a great happiness for us all. For, he said, we were not to journey forth to an unknown country, but to a beautiful region which God Himself had set apart for us. He had promised us, instead of this place of bondage, a new and delightful home where we should dwell free men, amid fruitful fields and rich pastures, which would supply food to every man and his family and make all hearts rejoice. Just as laborers must work hard to earn high wages, we must endure a brief period of want and suffering to gain for ourselves and for our children the beautiful new home which the Lord had promised. God's own land it must be, for it was a gift of the Most High.

"Having spoken thus, he blessed us all and promised that thou, too, wouldst shake the dust from off thy feet, and join us to fight for our cause with a strong arm as a trained soldier and a dutiful son.

"Shouts of joy rang forth and, when we assembled in the market-place and found that all the bondmen had escaped from the overseers, many gained fresh courage. Then Aaron stepped into our midst, stood upon the auctioneer's bench, and told us with his own lips all that we had heard from my master Nun at the festival. The words he uttered sounded sometimes like pealing thunder, and anon like the sweet melody of lutes, and every one felt that the Lord our God Himself was speaking through him; for even the most rebellious were so deeply moved that they no longer complained and murmured. And when he finally announced to the throng that no erring mortal, but the Lord our God Himself would be our leader, and described the wonders of the land whose gates He would open unto us, and where we might live, trammelled by no bondage, as free and happy men, owing no obedience to any ruler save the God of our fathers and those whom we ourselves chose for our leaders, every man present felt as though he were drunk with sweet wine, and, instead of faring forth across a barren wilderness to an unknown goal, was on the way to a great festal banquet, prepared by the Most High Himself. Even those who had not heard Aaron's words were inspired with wondrous faith; men and women behaved even more joyously and noisily than usual at the harvest festival, for every heart was overflowing with genuine gratitude.

"The old people caught the universal spirit! Your grandfather Elishama, bowed by the weight of his hundred years, who, as you know, has long sat bent and silent in his corner, straightened his drooping form, and with sparkling eyes poured forth a flood of eloquent words. The spirit of the Lord had descended upon him and upon us all. I myself felt as though the vigor of youth had returned to mind and body, and when I passed the throngs who were preparing to set forth, I saw the young mother Elisheba in her litter. Her face was as radiant as on her marriage morn, and she was pressing her nursling to her breast, and rejoicing over his happy fate in growing up in freedom in the Promised Land. Her spouse, Deuel, who had poured forth such bitter imprecations, now waved his staff, kissed his wife and child with tears of joy, and shouted with delight like a vintager at the harvest season, when jars and wine skins are too few to hold the blessing. Old grave-haunting Kusaja, who had been dragged away from the sepulchre of her kindred, was sitting in a cart with other infirm folk, waving her veil and joining in the hymn of praise Elkanah and Abiasaph, the sons of Korah, had begun. So they went forth; we who were left behind fell into each other's arms, uncertain whether the tears we shed streamed from our eyes for grief or for sheer joy at seeing the throng of our loved ones so full of hope and gladness.

"So it came to pass.

"As soon as the pitch torches borne at the head of the procession, which seemed to me to shine more brightly than the lamps lighted by the Egyptians on the gates of the temple of the great goddess Neith, had vanished in the darkness, we set out, that we might not delay Assir too long, and while passing through the streets, which resounded with the wailing of the citizens, we softly sang the hymn of the sons of Korah, and great joy and peace filled our hearts, for we knew that the Lord our God would defend and guide His people."

The old man paused, but his wife and Hogla, who had listened with sparkling eyes, leaned one on the other and, without any prompting, began the hymn of praise of the sons of Korah, the old woman's faint voice mingling with touching fervor with the tones of the girl, whose harsh notes thrilled with the loftiest enthusiasm.

Hosea felt that it would be criminal to interrupt the outpouring of these earnest hearts, but Eliab soon stopped them and gazed with evident anxiety into the stern face of his lord's first-born son.

Had Hosea understood him?

Did this warrior, who served under Pharaoh's banner, realize how entirely the Lord God Himself had ruled the souls of his people at their departure.

Had the life among the Egyptians so estranged him from his people and his God, rendered him so degenerate, that he would bid defiance to the wishes and commands of his own father?

Was the man on whom the Hebrews' highest hopes were fixed a renegade, forever lost to his people?

He received no verbal answer to these mute questions, but when Hosea grasped his callous right hand in both his own and pressed it as he would have clasped a friend's, when he bade him farewell with tearful eyes, murmuring: "You shall hear from me!" he felt that he knew enough and, overwhelmed with passionate delight, he pressed kiss after kiss upon the warrior's arms and clothing.

CHAPTER VII

Hosea returned to the camp with drooping head. The conflict in his soul was at an end. He now knew what duty required. He must obey his father's summons.

And the God of his race!

The old man's tale had given new life to the memories of his childhood, and he now knew that He was not the same God as the Seth of the Asiatics in Lower Egypt, nor the "One" and the "Sum of All" of the adepts.

The prayers he had uttered ere he fell asleep, the history of the creation of the world, which he could never hear sufficiently often, because it showed so clearly the gradual development of everything on earth and in heaven until man came to possess and enjoy all, the story of Abraham and Isaac, of Jacob, Esau, and his own ancestor, Joseph—how gladly he had listened to these tales as they fell from the lips of the gentle woman who had given him life, and from those of his nurse, and his grandfather Elishama. Yet he imagined that they had faded from his memory long ago.

But in old Eliab's hovel he could have repeated the stories word for word, and he now knew that there was indeed one invisible, omnipotent God, who had preferred his race above all others, and had promised to make them a mighty people.

The truths concealed by the Egyptians under the greatest mystery were the common property of his race. Every beggar, every slave might raise his hands in supplication to the one invisible God who had revealed Himself unto Abraham.

Shrewd Egyptians, who had divined His existence and shrouded His image with monstrous shapes, born of their own thoughts and imaginations, had drawn a thick veil over Him, hidden Him from the masses. Among the Hebrews alone did He really live and display His power in all its mighty, heart-stirring grandeur.

He was not nature, with whom the initiated in the temples confounded Him. No, the God of his fathers was far above all created things and the whole visible universe, far above man, His last, most perfect work, whom

He had formed in His own image; and every living creature was subject to His will. The Mightiest of Kings, He ruled the universe with stern justice, and though He withdrew Himself from the sight and understanding of man, His image, He was nevertheless a living, thinking, moving Being, though His span of existence was eternity, His mind omniscience, His sphere of sovereignty infinitude.

And this God had made Himself the leader of His people! There was no warrior who could venture to cope with His might. If the spirit of prophecy had not deceived Miriam, and the Lord had indeed commanded Hosea to wield His sword, how dared he resist, what higher position could earth offer? And his people? The rabble of whom he had thought so scornfully, what a transformation seemed to have been wrought in them by the power of the Most High, since he had listened to old Eliab's tale! Now he longed to be their leader, and midway to the camp he paused on a sand-hill, whence he could see the limitless expanse of the sea shimmering under the sheen of the twinkling stars of heaven, and for the first time in many a long, long year, he raised his arms and eyes to the God whom he had found once more.

He began with a little prayer his mother had taught him; then he cried out to the Almighty as to a powerful counselor, imploring him with fervent zeal to point out the way in which he should walk without being disobedient to Him or to his father, or breaking the oath he had sworn to Pharaoh and becoming a dishonored man in the eyes of those to whom he owed so great a debt of gratitude.

"Thy chosen people praise Thee as the God of Truth, Who dost punish those who forswear their oaths," he prayed. "How canst Thou command me to be faithless and break the vow that I have made. Whatever I am, whatever I may accomplish, belongs to Thee, Oh Mighty Lord, and I am ready to devote my blood, my life to my people. But rather than render me a dishonored and perjured man, take me away from earth and commit the work which Thou hast chosen Thy servant to perform, to the hands of one who is bound by no solemn oath."

So he prayed, and it seemed as if he clasped in his embrace a long-lost friend. Then he walked on in silence through the vanishing dusk, and when the first grey light of morning dawned, the flood of feeling ebbed, and the clear-headed warrior regained his calmness of thought.

He had vowed to do nothing against the will of his father or his God, but he was no less firmly resolved to be neither perjurer nor renegade. His duty was clear and plain. He must leave Pharaoh's service, first telling his superiors that, as a dutiful son, he must obey his father's commands, and share his fate and that of his people.

Yet he did not conceal from himself that his request might be refused, that he might be detained by force, nay, perchance, if he insisted on carrying out his purpose with unshaken will, he might be menaced with death, or if the worst should come, even delivered over to the executioner. But if this should be his doom, if his purpose cost him his life, he would still have done what was right, and his comrades, whose esteem he valued, could still think of him as a brave brother-in-arms. Nor would his father and Miriam be angry with him, nay, they would mourn the faithful son, the upright man, who chose death rather than dishonor.

Calm and resolute, he gave the pass-word with haughty bearing to the sentinel and entered his tent. Ephraim was still lying on his couch, smiling as if under the thrall of pleasant dreams. Hosea threw himself on a mat beside him to seek strength for the hard duties of the coming day. Soon his eyes closed, too, and, after an hour's sound sleep, he woke without being roused and called for his holiday attire, his helmet, and the gilt coat-of-mail he wore at great festivals or in the presence of Egypt's king.

Meantime Ephraim, too, awoke, looked with mingled curiosity and delight at his uncle, who stood before him in all the splendor of his manhood and glittering panoply of war, and exclaimed:

"It must be a proud feeling to wear such garments and lead thousands to battle."

Hosea shrugged his shoulders and replied:

"Obey thy God, give no man, from the loftiest to the lowliest, a right to regard you save with respect, and you can hold your head as high as the proudest warrior who ever wore purple robe and golden armor."

"But you have done great deeds among the Egyptians," Ephraim continued. "They hold you in high regard; even captain Homecht and his daughter, Kasana."

"Do they?" asked the soldier smiling, and then bid his nephew keep quiet; for his brow, though less fevered than the night before, was still burning.

"Don't go into the open air until the leech has seen you," Hosea added, "and wait here till my return."

"Shall you be absent long?" asked the lad.

Hosea paused for a moment, lost in thought then, with a kindly glance at him answered, gravely "Whoever serves a master knows not how long he may be detained." Then, changing his tone, he continued less earnestly. "To-day—this morning—perchance I may finish my business speedily and return in a few hours. If not, if I do not come back to you this evening or early to-morrow morning, then...." he laid his hand on the lad's shoulder as he spoke "then go home at your utmost speed. When you reach Succoth, if the people have gone before your coming, you will find in the hollow sycamore before Amminadab's house a letter which will tell you whither they have turned their steps. When you overtake them, give my greetings to my father, to my grandfather Elishama, and to Miriam. Tell them that Hosea will be mindful of the commands of his God and of his father. In future he will call himself Joshua—Joshua, do you hear? Tell this to Miriam first. Finally, tell them that if I remain behind and am not suffered to follow them, as I would like to, that the Most High has made a different disposal of His servant and has broken the sword which He had chosen, ere He used it. Do you understand me, boy?"

Ephraim nodded, and answered:

"You mean that death alone can stay you from obeying the summons of God, and your father's command."

"Ay, that was my meaning," replied the chief. "If they ask why I did not slip away from Pharaoh and escape his power, say that Hosea desired to enter on his new office as a true man, unstained by perjury or, if it is the will of God, to die one. Now repeat the message."

Ephraim obeyed; his uncle's remarks must have sunk deep into his soul; for he neither forgot nor altered a single word. But scarcely had he performed the task of repetition when, with impetuous earnestness, he grasped Hosea's hand and besought him to tell him whether he had any cause to fear for his life.

The warrior clasped him affectionately in his arms and answered that he hoped he had entrusted this message to him only to have it forgotten. "Perhaps," he added, "they will strive to keep me by force, but by God's help I shall soon be with you again, and we will ride to Succoth together."

With these words he hurried out, unheeding the questions his nephew called after him; for he had heard the rattle of wheels outside. Two chariots, drawn by mettled steeds, rapidly approached the tent and stopped directly before the entrance.

CHAPTER VIII

The men who stepped from the chariots were old acquaintances of Hosea. They were the head chamberlain and one of the king's chief scribes, come to summon him to the Sublime Porte.

[Palace of the king. The name of Pharaoh means "the Sublime Porte."]

No hesitation nor escape was possible, and Hosea, feeling more surprise than anxiety, entered the second chariot with the chief scribe. Both officials wore mourning robes, and instead of the white ostrich plume, the insignia of office, black ones waved over the temples of both. The horses and runners of the two-wheeled chariots were also decked with all the emblems of the deepest woe. And yet the monarch's messengers seemed cheerful rather than depressed; for the eagle they were to bear to Pharaoh was ready to obey his behest, and they had feared that they would find his eyrie abandoned.

Swift as the wind the long-limbed bays of royal breed bore the light vehicles over the uneven sandy road and the smooth highway toward the palace.

Ephraim, with the curiosity of youth, had gone out of the tent to view a scene so novel to his eyes. The soldiers were pleased by the Pharaoh's sending his own carriage for their commander, and the lad's vanity was flattered to see his uncle drive away in such state. But he was not permitted the pleasure of watching him long; dense clouds of dust soon hid the vehicles.

The scorching desert wind which, during the Spring months, so often blows through the valley of the Nile, had risen, and though the bright blue sky which had been visible by night and day was still cloudless, it was veiled by a whitish mist.

The sun, a motionless ball, glared down on the heads of men like a blind man's eye. The burning heat it diffused seemed to have consumed its rays, which to-day were invisible. The eye protected by the mist could gaze at it undazzled, yet its scorching power was undiminished. The light breeze, which usually fanned the brow in the morning, touched it now like the hot breath of a ravening beast of prey. Loaded with the fine scorching sand borne from the desert, it transformed the pleasure of breathing into a painful torture. The air of an Egyptian March morning, which was wont to be so balmy, now oppressed both man and beast, choking their lungs and seeming to weigh upon them like a burden destroying all joy in life.

The higher the pale rayless globe mounted into the sky, the greyer became the fog, the more densely and swiftly blew the sand-clouds from the desert.

Ephraim was still standing in front of the tent, gazing at the spot where Pharaoh's chariots had disappeared. His knees trembled, but he attributed it to the wind sent by Seth-Typhon, at whose blowing even the strongest felt an invisible burden clinging to their feet.

Hosea had gone, but he might come back in a few hours, then he, Ephraim, would be obliged to go with him to Succoth, and the bright dreams and hopes which yesterday had bestowed and whose magical charms were heightened by his fevered brain, would be lost to him forever.

During the night he had firmly resolved to enter Pharaoh's army, that he might remain near Tanis and Kasana; but though he had only half comprehended Hosea's message, he could plainly discern that he intended to turn his back upon Egypt and his high position and meant to take Ephraim with him, should he make his escape. So he must renounce his longing to see Kasana once more. But this thought was unbearable and an inward voice whispered that, having neither father nor mother, he was free to act according to his own will. His guardian, his dead father's brother, in whose household he had grown up, had died not long before, and no new guardian had been named because the lad was now past childhood. He was destined at some future day to be one of the chiefs of his proud tribe and until yesterday he had desired no better fate.

He had obeyed the impulse of his heart when, with the pride of a shepherd prince, he had refused the priest's suggestion that he should become one of Pharaoh's soldiers, but he now told himself that he had been childish and foolish to reject a thing of which he was ignorant, nay, which had ever been intentionally represented to him in a false and hateful light in order to bind him more firmly to his own people.

The Egyptians had always been described as detestable enemies and oppressors, yet how enchanting everything seemed in the house of the first Egyptian warrior he had entered.

And Kasana!

What must she think of him, if he left Tanis without a word of greeting, of farewell. Must it not grieve and wound him to remain in her memory a clumsy peasant shepherd? Nay, it would be positively dishonest not to return the costly raiment she had lent him. Gratitude was reckoned among the Hebrews also as the first duty of noble hearts. He would be worthy of hate his whole life long, if he did not seek her once more!

But there was need of haste. When Hosea returned, he must find him ready for departure.

He at once began to bind his sandals on his feet, but he did it slowly, and could not understand why the task seemed so hard to-day.

He passed through the camp unmolested. The pylons and obelisks before the temples, which appeared to quiver in the heated air, marked the direction he was to pursue, and he soon reached the broad road which led to the market-place—a panting merchant whose ass was bearing skins of wine to the troops, told him the way.

Dense clouds of dust lay on the road and whirled around him, the sun beat fiercely down on his bare head, his wound began to ache again, the fine sand which filled the air entered his eyes and mouth and stung his face and bare limbs like burning needles. He was tortured by thirst and was often compelled to stop, his feet grew so heavy. At last he reached a well dug for travelers by a pious Egyptian, and though it was adorned with the image of a god and Miriam had taught him that this was an abomination from which he should turn aside, he drank again and again, thinking he had never tasted aught so refreshing.

The fear of losing consciousness, as he had done the day before, passed away and, though his feet were still heavy, he walked rapidly toward the alluring goal. But soon his strength again deserted him, the sweat poured from his brow, his wound began to throb and beat, and he felt as though his skull was compressed by an iron circle. His keen eyes, too, failed, for the objects he tried to see blended with the dust of the road, the horizon reeled up and down before his eyes, and he felt as though the hard pavement had turned to a yielding bog under his feet.

Yet he took little heed of all these things, for never before had such bright visions filled his mind. His thoughts grew marvellously vivid, and image after image rose before the wide eyes of his soul, not at his own behest, but as if summoned by a secret will outside of his consciousness. Now he fancied that he was lying at Kasana's feet, resting his head on her lap while he gazed upward into her lovely face—anon he saw Hosea standing before him in his glittering armor, as he had beheld him a short time ago, only his garb was still more gorgeous and, instead of the dim light in the tent, a ruddy glow like that of fire surrounded him. Then the finest oxen and rams in his herds passed before him and sentences from the messages he had learned darted through his mind; nay he sometimes imagined that they were being shouted to him aloud. But ere he could grasp their import, some new dazzling vision or loud rushing noise seemed to fill his mental eye and ear.

He pressed onward, staggering like a drunken man, with drops of sweat standing on his brow and with parched mouth. Sometimes he unconsciously raised his hand to wipe the dust from his burning eyes, but he cared little that he saw very indistinctly what was passing around him, for there could be nothing more beautiful than what he beheld with his inward vision.

True, he was often aware that he was suffering intensely, and he longed to throw himself exhausted on the ground, but a strange sense of happiness sustained him. At last he was seized with the delusion that his head was swelling and growing till it attained the size of the head of the colossus he had seen the day before in front of a temple gate, then it rose to the height of the palm-trees by the road-side, and finally it reached the mist shrouding the firmament, then far above it. Then it suddenly seemed as though this head of his was as large as the whole world, and he pressed his hands on his temples to clasp his brow; for his neck and shoulders were too weak to support the weight of so enormous a head and, mastered by this strange delusion, he shrieked aloud, his shaking knees gave way, and he fell unconscious in the dust.

CHAPTER IX

At the same hour a chamberlain was ushering Hosea into the audience chamber.

Usually subjects summoned to the presence of the king were kept waiting for hours, but the Hebrew's patience was not tried long. During this period of the deepest mourning the spacious rooms of the palace, commonly tenanted by a gay and noisy multitude, were hushed to the stillness of death; for not only the slaves and warders, but many men and women in close attendance on the royal couple had fled from the pestilence, quitting the palace without leave.

Here and there a solitary priest, official, or courtier leaned against a pillar or crouched on the floor, hiding his face in his hands, while awaiting some order. Sentries paced to and fro with lowered weapons, lost in melancholy thoughts. Now and then a few young priests in mourning robes glided through the infected rooms, silently swinging silver censers which diffused a pungent scent of resin and juniper.

A nightmare seemed to weigh upon the palace and its occupants; for in addition to grief for their beloved prince, which saddened many a heart, the dread of death and the desert wind paralyzed alike the energy of mind and body.

Here in the immediate vicinity of the throne where, in former days, all eyes had sparkled with hope, ambition, gratitude, fear, loyalty, or hate, Hosea now encountered only drooping heads and downcast looks.

Bai, the second prophet of Amon, alone seemed untouched alike by sorrow, anxiety, or the enervating atmosphere of the day; he greeted the warrior in the ante-room as vigorously and cheerily as ever, and assured him—though in the lowest whisper—that no one thought of holding him responsible for the misdeeds of his people. But when Hosea volunteered the acknowledgment that, at the moment of his summons to the king, he had been in the act of going to the commander-in-chief to beg a release from military service, the priest interrupted him to remind him of the debt of gratitude he, Bai, owed to him as the preserver of his life. Then he added that he would make every effort in his power to keep him in the army and show that the Egyptians—even against Pharaoh's will, or which he would speak farther with him privately—knew how to honor genuine merit without distinction of person or birth.

The Hebrew had little time to repeat his resolve; the head chamberlain interrupted them to lead Hosea into the presence of the "good god."

The sovereign awaited Hosea in the smaller audience-room adjoining the royal apartments.

It was a stately chamber, and to-day looked more spacious than when, as of yore, it was filled with obsequious throngs. Only a few courtiers and priests, with some of the queen's ladies-in-waiting, all clad in deep mourning, stood in groups near the throne. Opposite to Pharaoh, squatting in a circle on the floor, were the king's councillors and interpreters, each adorned with an ostrich plume.

All wore tokens of mourning, and the monotonous, piteous plaint of the wailing women, which ever and anon rose into a loud, shrill, tremulous shriek, echoed through the silent rooms within to this hall, announcing that death had claimed a victim even in the royal dwelling.

The king and queen sat on a gold and ivory couch, heavily draped with black. Instead of their usual splendid attire, both wore dark robes, and the royal consort and mother, who mourned her first-born son, leaned motionless, with drooping head, against her kingly husband's shoulder.

Pharaoh, too, gazed fixedly into space, as though lost in a dream. The sceptre had slipped from his hand and lay in his lap.

The queen had been torn away from the corpse of her son, which was now delivered to the embalmers, and it was not until she reached the entrance of the audience-chamber that she had succeeded in checking her tears. She had no thought of resistance; the inexorable ceremonial of court etiquette required the queen to be present at any audience of importance. To-day she would gladly have shunned the task, but Pharaoh had commanded her presence, and she knew and approved the course to be pursued; for she was full of dread of the power of the Hebrew Mesu, called by his own people Moses, and of his God, who had brought such terrible woe on the Egyptians. She had other children to lose, and she had known Mesu from her childhood, and was well aware how highly the great Rameses, her husband's father and predecessor, had prized the wisdom of this stranger who had been reared with his own sons.

Ah, if it were only possible to conciliate this man. But Mesu had departed with the Israelites, and she knew his iron will and had learned that the terrible prophet was armed, not alone against Pharaoh's threats, but also against her own fervent entreaties.

She was now expecting Hosea. He, the son of Nun, the foremost man of all the Hebrews in Tanis, would succeed, if any one could, in carrying out the plan which she and her royal husband deemed best for all parties,—a plan supported also by Rui, the hoary high-priest and first prophet of Amon, the head of the whole Egyptian priesthood, who held the offices of chief judge, chief treasurer, and viceroy of the kingdom, and had followed the court from Thebes to Tanis.

Ere going to the audience hall, she had been twining wreaths for her loved dead and the lotus flowers, larkspurs, mallow and willow-leaves, from which she was to weave them, had been brought there by her desire. They were lying on a small table and in her lap; but she felt paralyzed, and the hand she stretched toward them refused to obey her will.

Rui, the first prophet of Amon, an aged man long past his ninetieth birthday, squatted on a mat at Pharaoh's left hand. A pair of bright eyes, shaded by bushy white brows, glittered in his brown face—seamed and wrinkled like the bark of a gnarled oaklike gay flowers amid withered leaves, forming a strange contrast to his lean, bowed, and shrivelled form.

The old man had long since resigned the management of business affairs to the second prophet, Bai, but he held firmly to his honors, his seat at Pharaoh's side, and his place in the council, where, though he said little, his opinion was more frequently followed than that of the eloquent, ardent second prophet, who was many years his junior.

The old man had not quitted Pharaoh's side since the plague entered the palace, yet to-day he felt more vigorous than usual; the hot desert wind, which weakened others, refreshed him. He was constantly shivering, despite the panther-skin which hung over his back and shoulders, and the heat of the day warmed his chilly old blood.

Moses, the Hebrew, had been his pupil, and never had he instructed a nobler nature, a youth more richly endowed with all the gifts of intellect. He had initiated the Israelite into all the highest mysteries, anticipating the greatest results for Egypt and the priesthood, and when the Hebrew one day slew an overseer who had mercilessly beaten one of his race, and then fled into the desert, Rui had secretly mourned the evil deed as if his own son had committed it and must suffer the consequences. His intercession had secured Mesu's pardon; but when the latter returned to Egypt and the change had occurred which other priests termed his "apostasy," the old man had grieved even more keenly than over his flight. Had he, Rui, been younger, he would have hated the man who had thus robbed him of his fairest hopes; but the aged priest, who read men's hearts like an open book and could judge the souls of his fellow-mortals with the calm impartiality of an unclouded mind, confessed that he had been to blame in failing to foresee his pupil's change of thought.

Education and precept had made Mesu an Egyptian priest according to his own heart and that of the divinity; but after having once raised his hand in the defence of his own people against those to whom he had been bound only by human craft and human will, he was lost to the Egyptians and became once more a true son of his race. And where this man of the strong will and lofty soul led the way, others could not fail to follow.

Rui knew likewise full well what the renegade meant to give to his race; he had confessed it himself to the priest-faith in the one God. Mesu had rejected the accusation of perjury, declaring that he would never betray the mysteries to the Hebrews, his sole desire was to lead them back to the God whom they had worshipped ere Joseph and his family came to Egypt. True, the "One" of the initiated resembled the God of the Hebrews in many things, but this very fact had soothed the old sage; for experience had taught him that the masses are not content with a single invisible God, an idea which many, even among the more advanced of his own pupils found difficult to comprehend. The men and women of the lower classes needed visible symbols of every important thing whose influence they perceived in and around them, and the Egyptian religion supplied these images. What could an invisible creative power guiding the course of the universe be to a love-sick girl? She sought the friendly Hathor, whose gentle hands held the cords that bound heart to heart, the beautiful mighty representative of her sex—to her she could trustingly pour forth all the sorrows that burdened her bosom. What was the petty grief of a mother who sought to snatch her darling child from death, to the mighty and incomprehensible Deity who governed the entire universe? But the good Isis, who herself had wept her eyes red in bitter anguish, could understand her woe. And how often in Egypt it was the wife who determined her husband's relations to the gods!

Rui had frequently seen Hebrew men and women praying fervently in Egyptian temples. Even if Mesu should induce them to acknowledge his God, the experienced sage clearly foresaw that they would speedily turn from the invisible Spirit, who must ever remain aloof and incomprehensible, and return by hundreds to the gods they understood.

Now Egypt was threatened with the loss of the laborers and builders she so greatly needed, but Rui believed that they might be won back.

"When fair words will answer our purpose, put aside sword and bow," he had replied to Bai, who demanded that the fugitives should be pursued and slain. "We have already too many corpses in our country; what we want is workers. Let us hold fast what we seem on the verge of losing."

These mild words were in full harmony with the mood of Pharaoh, who had had sufficient sorrow, and would have thought it wiser to venture unarmed into a lion's cage than to again defy the wrath of the terrible Hebrew.

So he had closed his ears to the exhortations of the second prophet, whose steadfast, energetic will usually exercised all the greater influence upon him on account of his own irresolution, and upheld old Rui's suggestion that the warrior, Hosea, should be sent after his people to deal with them in Pharaoh's name—a plan that soothed his mind and renewed his hopes.

The second prophet, Bai, had finally assented to the plan; for it afforded a new chance of undermining the throne he intended to overthrow. If the Hebrews were once more settled in the land, Prince Siptah, who regarded no punishment too severe for the race he hated, might perhaps seize the sceptre of the cowardly king Menephtah.

But the fugitives must first be stopped, and Hosea was the right man to do this. But in Bai's eyes no one would be more able to gain the confidence of an unsuspicious soldier than Pharaoh and his royal consort. The venerable high-priest Rui, though wholly unaware of the conspiracy, shared this opinion, and thus the sovereigns had been persuaded to interrupt the mourning for the dead and speak in person to the Hebrew.

Hosea had prostrated himself before the throne and, when he rose, the king's weary face was bent toward him, sadly, it is true, yet graciously.

According to custom, the hair and beard of the father who had lost his first-born son had been shaven. Formerly they had encircled his face in a frame of glossy black, but twenty years of anxious government had made them grey, and his figure, too, had lost its erect carriage and seemed bent and feeble, though he had scarcely passed his fifth decade. His regular features were still beautiful in their symmetry, and there was a touch of pathos in their mournful gentleness, so evidently incapable of any firm resolve, especially when a smile lent his mouth a bewitching charm.

The languid indolence of his movements scarcely impaired the natural dignity of his presence, yet his musical voice was wont to have a feeble, beseeching tone. He was no born ruler; thirteen older brothers had died ere the throne of Pharaoh had become his heritage, and up to early manhood he had led a careless, joyous existence—as the handsomest youth in the whole land, the darling of women, the light-hearted favorite of fortune. Then he succeeded his father the great Rameses, but he had scarcely grasped the sceptre ere the Libyans, with numerous allies, rebelled against Egypt. The trained troops and their leaders, who had fought in his predecessor's wars, gained him victory, but during the twenty years which had now passed since Rameses' death, the soldiers had rarely had any rest. Insurrections constantly occurred, sometimes in the East, anon in the West and, instead of living in Thebes, where he had spent many years of happiness, and following the bent of his inclination by enjoying in the splendid palace the blessing of peace and the society of the famous scholars and poets who then made that city their home, he was compelled sometimes to lead his armies in the field, sometimes to live in Tanis, the capital of Lower Egypt, to settle the disturbances of the border land.

This was the desire of the venerable Rui, and the king willingly followed his guidance. During the latter years of Rameses' reign, the temple at Thebes, and with it the chief priest, had risen to power and wealth greater than that possessed by royalty itself, and Menephtah's indolent nature was better suited to be a tool than a guiding hand, so long as he received all the external honors due to Pharaoh. These he guarded with a determination which he never roused himself to display in matters of graver import.

The condescending graciousness of Pharaoh's reception awakened feelings of mingled pleasure and distrust in Hosea's mind, but he summoned courage to frankly express his desire to be relieved from his office and the oath he had sworn to his sovereign.

Pharaoh listened quietly. Not until Hosea confessed that he was induced to take this step by his father's command did he beckon to the high-priest, who began in low, almost inaudible tones:

"The son who resigns great things to remain obedient to his father will be the most loyal of the 'good god's' servants. Go, obey the summons of Nun. The son of the sun, the Lord of Upper and Lower Egypt, sets you free; but through me, the slave of his master, he imposes one condition."

"What is that?" asked Hosea.

Pharaoh signed to Rui a second time and, as the monarch sank back upon his throne, the old man, fixing his keen eyes on Hosea, replied:

"The demand which the lord of both worlds makes upon you by my lips is easy to fulfil. You must return to be once more his servant and one of us, as soon as your people and their leader, who have brought such terrible woe upon this land, shall have clasped the divine hand which the son of the sun extends to them in reconciliation, and shall have returned to the beneficent shadow of his throne. He intends to attach them to his person and his realm by rich tokens of his favor, as soon as they return from the desert to which they have gone forth to sacrifice to their God. Understand me fully! All the burdens which have oppressed the people of your race shall be removed. The 'great god' will secure to them, by a new law, privileges and great freedom, and whatever we promise shall be written down and witnessed on our part and yours as a new and valid covenant binding on our children and our children's children. When such a compact has been made with an honest purpose on our part to keep it for all time, and your tribes have consented to accept it, will you promise that you will then be one of us again?"

"Accept the office of mediator, Hosea," the queen here interrupted in a low tone, with her sorrowful eyes fixed imploringly on Hosea's face. "I dread the fury of Mesu, and everything in our power shall be done to regain his old friendship. Mention my name and recall the time when he taught little Isisnefert the names of the plants she brought to him and explained to her and her sister their beneficial or their harmful qualities, during his visits to the queen, his second mother, in the women's apartments. The wounds he has dealt our hearts shall be pardoned and forgotten. Be our envoy. Hosea, do not deny us."

"Such words from royal lips are a strict mandate," replied the Hebrew. "And yet they make the heart rejoice. I will accept the office of mediator."

The hoary high-priest nodded approvingly, exclaiming:

"I hope a long period of blessing may arise from this brief hour. But note this. Where potions can aid, surgery must be shunned. Where a bridge spans the stream, beware of swimming through the whirlpool."

"Yes, by all means shun the whirlpool," Pharaoh repeated, and the queen uttered the same words, then once more bent her eyes on the flowers in her lap.

A council now began.

Three private scribes took seats on the floor close by Rui, in order to catch his low tones, and the scribes and councillors in the circle before the throne seized their writing-materials and, holding the papyrus in their left hands, wrote with reed or brush; for nothing which was debated and determined in Pharaoh's presence was suffered to be left unrecorded.

During the continuance of this debate no voice in the audience chamber was raised above a whisper; the courtiers and guards stood motionless at their posts, and the royal pair gazed mutely into vacancy as though lost in reverie.

Neither Pharaoh nor his queen could possibly have heard the muttered conversation between the men; yet the Egyptians, at the close of every sentence, glanced upward at the king as if to ensure his approbation. Hosea, to whom the custom was perfectly familiar, did the same and, like the rest, lowered his tones. Whenever the voices of Bai or of the chief of the scribes waxed somewhat louder, Pharaoh raised his head and repeated the words of Rui: "Where a bridge spans the stream, beware of swimming through the whirlpool;" for this saying precisely expressed his own desires and those of the queen. No strife! Let us live at peace with the Hebrews, and escape from the anger of their awful leader and his God, without losing the thousands of industrious workers in the departed tribes.

So the discussion went on, and when the murmuring of the debaters and the scratching of the scribes' reeds had continued at least an hour the queen remained in the same position; but Pharaoh began to move and lift up his voice, fearing that the second prophet, who had detested the man whose benedictions he had implored and whose enmity seemed so terrible, was imposing on the mediator requirements impossible to fulfil.

Yet he said nothing save to repeat the warning about the bridge, but his questioning look caused the chief of the scribes to soothe him with the assurance that everything was progressing as well as possible. Hosea had only requested that, in future, the overseers of the workmen should not be of Libyan birth, but Hebrews themselves, chosen by the elders of their tribes with the approval of the Egyptian government.

Pharaoh cast a glance of imploring anxiety at Bai, the second prophet, and the other councillors; but the former shrugged his shoulders deprecatingly and, pretending to yield his own opinion to the divine wisdom of Pharaoh, acceded to Hosea's request.

The divinity on the throne of the world accepted, with a grateful bend of the head, this concession from a man whose wishes had so often opposed his own, and after the "repeater" or herald had read aloud all the separate conditions of the agreement, Hosea was forced to make a solemn vow to return in any case to Tanis, and report to the Sublime Porte how his people had received the king's proposals.

But the wary chief, versed in the wiles and tricks with which the government was but too well supplied, uttered the vow with great reluctance, and only after he had received a written assurance that, whatever might be the result of the negotiations, his liberty should not be restricted in any respect, after he had proved that he had used his utmost efforts to induce the leader of the Hebrews to accept the compact.

At last Pharaoh extended his hand for the warrior to kiss, and when the latter had also pressed his lips to the edge of the queen's garments, Rui signed to the head-chamberlain, who made obeisance to Pharaoh, and the sovereign knew that the hour had come when he might retire. He did so gladly and with a lighter heart; for he believed that he had done his best to secure his own welfare and that of his people.

A sunny expression flitted across his handsome, worn features, and when the queen also rose and saw his smile of satisfaction it was reflected on her face. Pharaoh uttered a sigh of relief as he crossed the threshold of the audience chamber and, accosting his wife, said:

"If Hosea wins his cause, we shall cross the bridge safely."

"And need not swim through the whirlpool," the queen answered in the same tone.

"And if the chief succeeds in soothing Mesu, and induces the Hebrews to stay in the land," Pharaoh added:

"Then you will enrol this Hosea—he looks noble and upright—among the kindred of the king," Isisnefert interrupted.

But upon this Pharaoh drew up his languid, drooping figure, exclaiming eagerly:

"How can I? A Hebrew! Were we to admit him among the 'friends' or 'fan-bearers' it would be the highest favor we could bestow! It is no easy matter in such a case to choose between too great or too small a recompense."

The farther the royal pair advanced toward the interior of the palace, the louder rose the wailing voices of the mourning women. Tears once more filled the eyes of the queen; but Pharaoh continued to ponder over what office at court he could bestow on Hosea, should his mission prove successful.

CHAPTER X

Hosea was forced to hurry in order to overtake the tribes in time; for the farther they proceeded, the harder it would be to induce Moses and the leaders of the people to return and accept the treaty.

The events which had befallen him that morning seemed so strange that he regarded them as a dispensation of the God whom he had found again; he recollected, too, that the name "Joshua," "he who helps Jehovah," had been received through Miriam's message. He would gladly bear it; for though it was no easy matter to resign the name for which he had won renown, still many of his comrades had done likewise. His new one was attesting its truth grandly; never had God's help been more manifest to him than this morning. He had entered Pharaoh's palace expecting to be imprisoned or delivered over to the executioner, as soon as he insisted upon following his people, and how speedily the bonds that held him in the Egyptian army had been sundered. And he had been appointed to discharge a task which seemed in his eyes so grand, so lofty, that he was on the point of believing that the God of his fathers had summoned him to perform it.

He loved Egypt. It was a fair country. Where could his people find a more delightful home? It was only the circumstances under which they had lived there which had been intolerable. Happier times were now in store. The tribes were given the choice between returning to Goshen, or settling on the lake land west of the Nile, with whose fertility and ample supply of water he was well acquainted. No one would have a right to reduce them to bondage, and whoever gave his labor to the service of the state was to have for overseer no stern and cruel foreigner, but a man of his own blood.

True, he knew that the Hebrews must remain under subjection to Pharaoh. But had not Joseph, Ephraim, and his sons, Hosea's ancestors, been called his subjects and lived content to be numbered among the Egyptians.

If the covenant was made, the elders of the tribes were to direct the private concerns of the people. Spite of Bai's opposition, Moses had been named regent of the new territory, while he, Hosea, himself was to command the soldiers who would defend the frontiers, and marshal fresh troops from the Israelite mercenaries, who had already borne themselves valiantly in many a fray. Ere he had quitted the palace, Bai had made various mysterious allusions, which though vague in purport, betrayed that the priest was cherishing important plans and, as soon as the guidance of the government passed from old Rui's hands into his, a high position, perhaps the command of the whole army, now led by a Syrian named Aarsu, would be conferred on him, Hosea.

But this prospect caused him more anxiety than pleasure, though great was his satisfaction at having gained the concession that every third year the eastern frontiers of the country should be thrown open to his people, that they might go to the desert and there offer sacrifices to their God. Moses had seemed to lay the utmost stress upon this privilege, and according to the existing law, no one was permitted to cross the narrow fortified frontier on the east without the permission of the government. Perhaps granting this desire of the mighty leader might win him to accept a compact so desirable for his nation.

During these negotiations Hosea had again realized his estrangement from his people, he was not even aware—for what purpose the sacrifice in the desert was offered. He also frankly acknowledged to Pharaoh's councillors that he knew neither the grievances nor the requirements of the tribes, a course he pursued to secure to the Hebrews the right of changing or revising in any respect the offers he was to convey.

What better proposals could they or their leader desire?

The future was full of fresh hopes of happiness for his people and himself. If the compact was made, the time had arrived for him to establish a home of his own, and Miriam's image again appeared in all its loftiness and beauty. The thought of gaining this splendid maiden was fairly intoxicating, and he wondered whether he was worthy of her, and if it would not be presumptuous to aspire to the hand of the divinely-inspired, majestic virgin and prophetess.

He was experienced in the affairs of life and knew full well how little reliance could be placed upon the promises of the vacillating man, who found the sceptre too heavy for his feeble hand. But he had exercised caution and, if the elders of the people could but be won over, the agreement would be inscribed on metal tables, sentence by sentence, and hung in the temple at Thebes, with the signatures of Pharaoh and the envoys of the Hebrews, like every other binding agreement between Egypt and a foreign nation. Such documents—he had learned this from the treaty of peace concluded with the Cheta—assured and lengthened the brief "eternity" of national covenants. He had certainly neglected no precaution to secure his people from treachery and perjury. Never had he felt more vigorous, more confident, more joyous than when he again entered Pharaoh's chariot to take leave of his subordinates. Bai's mysterious hints and suggestions troubled him very little; he was accustomed to leave future anxieties to be cared for in the future. But at the camp he encountered a grief which belonged to the present; surprised, angry, and troubled, he learned that Ephraim had secretly left the tent, telling no one whither he was going. A hurried investigation drew out the information that the youth had been seen on the road to Tanis, and Hosea hastily bade his trusty shield-bearer search the city for the youth and, if he found him, to order him to follow his uncle to Succoth.

After the chief had said farewell to his men, he set off, attended only by his old groom. He was pleased to have the adone—[Corresponding to the rank of adjutant.]—and subaltern officers who had been with him, the stern warriors, with whom he had shared everything in war and peace, in want and privation, show so plainly the pain of parting. Tears streamed down the bronzed cheeks of many a man who had grown grey in warfare, as he clasped his hand for the last time. Many a bearded lip was pressed to the hem of his robe, to his feet, and to the sleek skin of the noble Libyan steed which, pressing forward with arching neck only to be curbed by its rider's strength, bore him through the ranks. For the first time since his mother's death his own eyes grew dim, as shouts of farewell rang warmly and loudly from the manly breasts of his soldiers.

Never before had he so deeply realized how firmly he was bound to these men, and how he loved his noble profession.

Yet the duty he was now fulfilling was also great and glorious, and the God who had absolved him from his oath and smoothed the way for him to obey his father's commands as a true and upright man, would perhaps bring him back to his comrades in arms, whose cordial farewell he still fancied he heard long after he was out of reach of their voices.

The greatness of the work assigned to him, the enthusiasm of a man who devotes himself with devout earnestness to the performance of a difficult task, the rapturous joy of the lover, who with well-founded hopes of the fulfilment of the purest and fairest desires of his heart, hastens to meet the woman of his choice, first dawned upon him when he had left the city behind and was dashing at a rapid trot toward the south-east across the flat, well-watered plain with its wealth of palm-groves.

While forcing his steed to a slower pace as he passed through the streets of the capital, and the region near the harbor, his mind was so engrossed by his recent experiences and his anxiety concerning the runaway youth, that he paid little attention to the throng of vessels lying at anchor, the motley crowd of ship owners, traders, sailors, and laborers, representatives of all the nations of Africa and Asia, who sought a livelihood here, and the officials, soldiers, and petitioners, who had followed Pharaoh from Thebes to the city of Rameses.

He had even failed to see two men of high rank, though one, Hornecht, the captain of the archers, had waved his hand to him.

They had retired into the deep gateway formed by the pylons at the entrance of the temple of Seth, to escape the clouds of dust which the desert wind was still blowing along the road.

While Hornecht was vainly trying to arrest the horseman's attention, his companion, Bai, the second prophet of Amon, whispered: "Let him go! He will learn where his nephew is soon enough."

"As you desire," replied the soldier. Then he eagerly continued the story he had just begun. "When they brought the lad in, he looked like a piece of clay in the potter's workshop."

"No wonder," replied the priest; "he had lain long enough in the road in the dust of Typhon. But what was your steward seeking among the soldiers?"

"We had heard from my adon, whom I sent to the camp last evening, that the poor youth was attacked by a severe fever, so Kasana put up some wine and her nurse's balsam, and dispatched the old creature with them to the camp."

"To the youth or to Hosea?" asked the prophet with a mischievous smile.

"To the sufferer," replied Hornecht positively, a frown darkening his brow. But, restraining himself, he added as if apologizing: "Her heart is as soft as wax, and the Hebrew youth—you saw him yesterday...."

"Is a splendid lad, just fitted to win a woman's heart!" replied the priest laughing. "Besides, whoever shows kindness to the nephew does not harm the uncle."

"That was not in her mind," replied Hornecht bluntly. "But the invisible God of the Hebrews is not less watchful of his children than the Immortals whom you serve; for he led Hotepu to the youth just as he was at the point of death. The dreamer would undoubtedly have ridden past him; for the dust had already...."

"Transformed him into a bit of potter's clay. But then?"

"Then the old man suddenly saw a glint of gold in the dusty heap."

"And the stiffest neck will stoop for that."

"Quite true. My Hotepu did so, and the broad gold circlet the lad wore flashed in the sunlight and preserved his life a second time."

"The luckiest thing is that we have the lad in our possession."

"Yes, I was rejoiced to have him open his eyes once more. Then his recovery grew more and more rapid; the doctor says he is like a kitten, and all these mishaps will not cost him his life. But he is in a violent fever, and in his delirium says all sorts of senseless things, which even my daughter's nurse, a native of Ascalon, cannot clearly comprehend. Only she thought she caught Kasana's name."

"So it is once more a woman who is the source of the trouble."

"Stop these jests, holy father," replied Hornecht, biting his lips. "A modest widow, and that boy with the down still on his lips."

"At his age," replied the unabashed priest, "fullblown roses have a stronger attraction for young beetles than do buds; and in this instance," he added more gravely, "it is a most fortunate accident. We have Hosea's nephew in the snare, and it will be your part not to let him escape."

"Do you mean that we are to deprive him of his liberty?" cried the warrior.

"Even so."

"Yet you value his uncle?"

"Certainly. But the state has a higher claim."

"This boy...."

"Is a desirable hostage. Hosea's sword was an extremely useful tool to us; but if the hand that guides it is directed by the man whose power ever greater things we know...."

"You mean the Hebrew, Mesu?"

"Then Hosea will deal us wounds as deep as those he erst inflicted on our foes."

"Yet I have heard you say more than once that he was incapable of perjury."

"And so I say still, he has given wonderful proof of it to-day. Merely for the sake of being released from his oath, he thrust his head into the crocodile's jaws. But though the son of Nun is a lion, he will find his master in Mesu. That man is the mortal foe of the Egyptians, the bare thought of him stirs my gall."

"The cries of the wailing women behind this door admonish us loudly enough to hate him."

"Yet the weakling on the throne has forgotten vengeance, and is now sending Hosea on an errand of reconciliation."

"With your sanction, I think?"

"Ay," replied the priest with a mocking smile. "We send him to build a bridge! Oh, this bridge! A grey-beard's withered brain recommends it to be thrown across the stream, and the idea just suits this pitiful son of a great father, who would certainly never have shunned swimming through the wildest whirlpool, especially when revenge was to be sought. Let Hosea essay the bridge! If it leads him back across the stream to us, I will offer him a right warm and cordial welcome; but as soon as this one man stands on our shores, may its supports sink under the leaders of his people; we, the only brave souls in Egypt, must see to that."

"So be it. Yet I fear we shall lose the chief, too, if justice overtakes his people."

"It might almost seem so."

"You have greater wisdom than I."

"Yet here you believe me in error."

"How could I venture to...."

"As a member of the military council you are entitled to your own opinion, and I consider myself bound to show you the end of the path along which you have hitherto followed us with blindfold eyes. So listen, and judge accordingly when your turn comes to speak in the council. The chief-priest Rui is old...."

"And you now fill half his offices."

"Would that he might soon be relieved of the last half of his burden. Not on my own account. I love strife, but for the welfare of our native land. It is a deep-seated feeling of our natures to regard the utterances and mandates of age as wisdom, so there are few among the councillors who do not follow the old man's opinions; yet his policy limps on crutches, like himself. All good projects are swamped under his weak, fainthearted guidance."

"That is the very reason my vote is at your disposal," cried the warrior. "That is why I am ready to use all my might to hurl this sleeper from the throne and get rid of his foolish advisers."

The prophet laid his finger on his lips to warn his companion to be more cautious, drew nearer to him, pointed to his litter, and said in a low, hurried tone:

"I am expected at the Sublime Porte, so listen. If Hosea's mission is successful his people will return—the guilty with the innocent—and the latter will suffer. Among the former we can include the whole of Hosea's tribe, who call themselves the sons of Ephraim, from old Nun down to the youth in your dwelling."

"We may spare them; but Mesu, too, is a Hebrew, and what we do to him...."

"Will not occur in the public street, and it is child's play to sow enmity between two men who desire to rule in the same sphere. I will make sure that Hosea shall shut his eyes to the other's death; but Pharaoh, whether his name is Meneptah or"—he lowered his voice—"Siptah, must then raise him to so great a height—and he merits it—that his giddy eyes will never discern aught we desire to conceal. There is one dish that never palls on any man who has once tasted it."

"And what is that?"

"Power, Hornecht—mighty power! As ruler of a whole province, commander of all the mercenaries in Aarsu's stead, he will take care not to break with us. I know him. If I can succeed in making him believe Mesu has wronged him—and the imperious man will afford some pretext for it—and can bring him to the conviction that the law directs the punishment we mete out to the sorcerer and the worst of his adherents, he will not only assent but approve it."

"And if he fails in his mission?"

"He will return at any rate; for he would not be false to his oath. But if Mesu, from whom we may expect anything, should detain him by force, the boy will be of service to us; for Hosea loves him, his people value his life, and he belongs to one of their noblest tribes. In any case Pharaoh must threaten the lad; we will guard him, and that will unite his uncle to us by fresh ties and lead him to join those who are angry with the king."

"Excellent!"

"The surest way to attain our object will be by forging still another chain. In short—now I beg you to be quiet, your temper is far too hot for your grey hairs—in short, our Hebrew brother-in-arms, the saviour of my life, the ablest man in the army, who is certain to win the highest place, must be your son-in-law. Kasana's heart is his—my wife has told me so." Hornecht frowned again, and struggled painfully to control his anger. He perceived that he must overcome his objection to giving his daughter to the man whose birth he scorned, much as he liked and esteemed his character. He could not refrain from uttering an oath under his breath, but his answer to the prophet was more calm and sensible than the latter had anticipated. If Kasana was so possessed by demons that this stranger infatuated her, let her have her will. But Hosea had not yet sued for her.

"By the red god Seth, and his seventy companions," he added wrathfully, "neither you, nor any one shall induce me to offer my daughter, who has twenty suitors, to a man who terms himself our friend, yet finds no leisure to greet us in our own house! To keep fast hold of the lad is another thing, I will see to that."

CHAPTER XI

The midnight heavens, decked with countless stars, spanned with their cloudless azure vault the flat plains of the eastern Delta and the city of Succoth, called by the Egyptians, from their sanctuary, the place of the god Tum, or Pithom.

The March night was drawing toward its end, pallid mists floated over the canal, the work of Hebrew bondmen which, as far as the eye could reach, intersected the plain, watering the fields and pastures along its course.

Eastward and southward the sky was shrouded by dense veils of mist that rose from the large lakes and from the narrow estuaries that ran far up into the isthmus. The hot and dusty desert wind, which the day before had swept over the parched grass and the tents and houses of Succoth, had subsided at nightfall; and the cool atmosphere which in March, even in Egypt, precedes the approach of dawn, made itself felt.

Whoever had formerly entered, between midnight and morning, the humble frontier hamlet with its shepherd tents, wretched hovels of Nile mud, and by no means handsome farms and dwellings, would scarcely have recognized it now. Even the one noticeable building in the place—besides the stately temple of the sungod Tum—the large fortified store-house, presented at this hour an unfamiliar aspect. Its long white-washed walls, it is true, glimmered through the gloom as distinctly as ever, but instead of towering—as usual at this time—mute and lifeless above the slumbering town—the most active bustle was going on within and around it. It was intended also as a defense against the predatory hordes of the Shasu,

[Bedouins, who dwelt as nomads in the desert adjacent to Egypt, now regarded as part of Asia.]

who had made a circuit around the fortified works on the isthmus, and its indestructible walls contained an Egyptian garrison, who could easily defend it against a force greatly superior in numbers.

To-day it looked as if the sons of the desert had assailed it; but the men and women who were bustling about below and on the broad parapet of the gigantic building were Hebrews, not Shasu. With loud outcries and gesticulations of delight they were seizing the thousands of measures of wheat, barley, rye, and durra, the stores of pulse, dates, and onions they found in the well-filled granaries, and even before sunset had begun to empty the store-rooms and put their contents into sacks, pails, and skins, trays, jugs, and aprons, which were let down by ropes or carried to the ground on ladders.

The better classes took no share in this work, but among the busy throng, spite of the lateness of the hour, were children of all ages, carrying away in pots, jugs, and dishes—borrowed from their mothers' cooking utensils—as much as they could.

Above, beside the unroofed openings of the storerooms, into which the stars were shining, and also at the foot of the ladders, women held torches or lanterns to light the others at their toil.

Pans of blazing pitch were set in front of the strong locked doors of the real fortress, and in their light armed shepherds were pacing to and fro. When heavy stones or kicks belabored the brazen-bound door from within, and threats were uttered in the Egyptian tongue, the Hebrews outside did not fail to retort in words of mockery and scorn.

On the day of the harvest festival, during the first evening watch, runners arrived at Succoth and announced to the Israelites, whose numbers were twenty-fold greater than those of the Egyptians, that they had quitted Tanis in the morning and the tribes intended to leave at night; their kindred in Succoth must be ready to go forth with them. There was great rejoicing among the Hebrews, who like those of their blood in the city of Rameses, had assembled in every house at a festive repast on the night of the new moon after the vernal equinox when the harvest festival usually began. The heads of the tribes had informed them that the day of liberation had arrived, and the Lord would lead them into the Promised Land.

Here, too, as in Tanis, many had been faint-hearted and rebellious, and others had endeavored to separate their lot from the rest and remain behind; but here, too, they were carried away by the majority. Eleasar, the son of Aaron, and the distinguished heads of the tribe of Judah, Hur and Naashon, had addressed the multitude, as Aaron and Nun had done in the city of Rameses. But Miriam, the virgin, the sister of Moses, had gone from house to house, everywhere awakening the fire of enthusiasm in men's hearts, and telling the women that the morrow's sun would usher in for them and their children a new day of happiness, prosperity, and freedom.

Few had been deaf to the appeals of the prophetess; there was an air of majesty, which compelled obedience, in the bearing of this maiden, whose large black eyes, surmounted by heavy dark eye-brows, which met in the middle, pierced the hearts of those on whom her gaze was bent and seemed to threaten the rebellious with their gloomy radiance.

The members of every household went to rest after the festival with hearts uplifted and full of hope. But what a change had passed over them during the second day, the night that followed it, and the next morning! It seemed as though the desert wind had buried all their courage and confidence in the dust it swept before it. The dread of going forth to face an unknown future had stolen into every heart, and many a man who had waved his staff full of trust and joyful enterprise was now held, as if with clamps and fetters, to his well-tilled garden, the home of his ancestors, and the harvest in the fields, which had just been half gathered.

The Egyptian garrison in the fortified store-house had not failed to notice that the Hebrews were under some special excitement, but they supposed it due to the harvest festival. The commander of the garrison had learned that Moses desired to lead his people into the wilderness to offer sacrifices to their God, and had asked for a reinforcement. But he knew nothing more; for until the morning when the desert wind blew, no Hebrew had disclosed the plans of his kindred. But the more sorely the heat of the day oppressed them, the greater became the dread of the faint-hearted of the pilgrimage through the hot, dusty, waterless desert. The terrible day had given them a foretaste of what was impending and when, toward noon, the dust grew thicker, the air more and more oppressive, a Hebrew trader, from whom the Egyptian soldiers purchased goods, stole into the store-house to ask the commander to prevent his people from rushing to their doom.

Even among the leaders the voices of malcontents had grown loud. Asarja and Michael, with their sons, who grudged the power of Moses and Aaron, had even gone from one to another to try to persuade them, ere departing, to summon the elders again and charge then to enter into fresh negotiations with the Egyptians. While these malcontents were successfully gathering adherents, and the traitor had sought the commander of the Egyptian garrison, two more messengers arrived with tidings that the fugitives would arrive in Succoth between midnight and morning.

Breathless, speechless, dripping with perspiration, and with bleeding lips, the elder messenger sank on the threshold of Amminadab's house, now the home of Miriam also. Both the exhausted men were refreshed with wine and food, ere the least wearied was fully capable of speech. Then, in a hoarse voice, but from a heart overflowing with gratitude and ardent enthusiasm, he reported the scenes which had occurred at the exodus, and how the God of their fathers had filled every heart with His spirit, and instilled new faith into the souls of the cowards.

Miriam had listened to this story with sparkling eyes; at its close she flung her veil over her head and bade the servants of the household, who had assembled around the messengers, to summon the whole Hebrew people under the sycamore, whose broad summit, the growth of a thousand years, protected a wide space of earth from the scorching sunbeams.

The desert wind was still blowing, but the glad news seemed to have destroyed the baneful power it exerted on man, and when many hundreds of people had flocked together under the sycamore, Miriam had given her hand to Eleasar, the son of her brother Aaron, sprung upon the bench which rested against the huge hollow trunk of the tree, raised her hands and eyes toward heaven in an ecstasy, and began in a loud voice to address a prayer to the Lord, as if she beheld him with her earthly vision.

Then she permitted the messenger to speak, and when the latter again described the events which had occurred in the city of Rameses, and then announced that the fugitives from Tanis would arrive in a few hours, loud shouts of joy burst from the throng. Eleasar, the son of Aaron, proclaimed with glowing enthusiasm what the Lord had done for his people and had promised to them, their children, and children's children.

Each word from the lips of the inspired speaker fell upon the hearts of the Hebrews like the fresh dew of morning on the parched grass. The trusting hearers pressed around him and Miriam with shouts of joy, and the drooping courage of the timorous appeared to put forth new wings. Asarja, Michael, and their followers no longer murmured, nay, most of them had been infected by the general enthusiasm, and when a Hebrew mercenary stole out from the garrison of the store-house and disclosed what had been betrayed to his commander, Eleasar, Naashon, Hur, and others took counsel together, gathered all the shepherds around them, and with glowing words urged them to show in this hour that they were men indeed and did not fear, with their God's mighty aid, to fight for their people and their liberty.

There was no lack of axes, clubs, sickles, brazen spears, heavy staves, slings, the shepherds' weapons of defence against the wild beasts of the desert, or bows and arrows, and as soon as a goodly number of strong men had joined him, Hur fell upon the Egyptian overseers who were watching the labor of several hundred Hebrew slaves. Shouting: "They are coming! Down with the oppressors! The Lord our God is our leader!" they rushed upon the Lybian warders, put them to rout, and released their fellows who were digging the earth, and laying bricks. As soon as the illustrious

Naashon had pressed one of the oldest of these hapless men like a brother to his heart, the other liberated bondsmen had flung themselves into the shepherds' arms and thus, still shouting: "They are coming!" and "The Lord, the God of our fathers, is our leader!" they pressed forward in an increasing multitude. When at last the little band of shepherds had grown to a body of several thousand men, Hur led them against the Egyptian soldiers, whom they largely outnumbered.

The Egyptian bowmen had already discharged a shower of arrows, and stones hurled from the slings of the powerful shepherds had dealt fatal wounds in the front ranks of the foe, when the blast of a trumpet rang out, summoning the garrison of the fortress behind the sloping walls and solid door. The Hebrews seemed to the commander too superior a force to fight, but duty required him to hold the fort until the arrival of the reinforcements he had requested.

Hur, however, had not been satisfied with his first victory. Success had kindled the courage of his followers, as a sharp gust of wind fans a smouldering fire, and wherever an Egyptian showed himself on the battlements of the store-house, the round stone from a shepherd's sling struck heavily upon him. At Naashon's bidding ladders had been brought and, in the twinkling of an eye, hundreds climbed up the building from every direction and, after a short, bloodless struggle, the granaries fell into the Hebrews' hands, though the Egyptians had succeeded in still retaining the fort. During the passage of these events the desert wind had subsided. Some of the liberated bondsmen, furious with rage, had heaped straw, wood, and faggots against the gate of the courtyard into which the Egyptians had been forced. It would have been a light task for the assailants to destroy every one of their foes by fire; but Hur, Naashon, and other prudent leaders had not suffered this to be done, lest the provisions still in the store-rooms should be burned.

It had been no easy matter, in truth, to deter the younger of the ill-treated bondsmen from this act of vengeance; but each one was a member of some family, and when Hur's admonitions were supported by those of the fathers and mothers, they not only allowed themselves to be pacified, but aided the elders to distribute the contents of the magazines among the heads of families and pack them on the beasts of burden and into the carts which were to accompany the fugitives.

The work went forward amid the broad glare of torches, and became a new festival; for neither Hur, Naashon, nor Eleasar could prevent the men and women from opening the wine-jars and skins. They succeeded, however, in preserving the lion's share of the precious booty for a time of need, and thus averted much drunkenness, though the spirit of the grape-juice and the pleasure in obtaining so rich a prize doubtless enhanced the grateful excitement of the throng. When Eleasar finally went among them for the second time to tell them of the Promised Land, men and women listened with uplifted hearts, and joined in the hymn Miriam began to sing.

Devout enthusiasm now took possession of every heart in Succoth, as it had done in Tanis during the hour that preceded the exodus, and when seventy Hebrew men and women, who had concealed themselves in the temple of Turn, heard the jubilant hymn, they came forth into the open air, joined the others, and packed their possessions with as much glad hopefulness and warm trust in the God of their fathers, as if they had never shrunk from the departure.

As the stars sank lower in the heavens, the joyous excitement increased. Men and women thronged the road to Tanis to meet their approaching kindred. Many a father led his boy by the hand, and many a mother carried her child in her arms; the multitude drawing near contained numerous beloved relatives to be greeted, and the coming dawn could not fail to bring solemn hours of which one would wish no beloved heart to be deprived, and which would linger in the souls of the little ones till they themselves had children and grandchildren.

No bed in tent, hovel, or house was occupied; for everywhere the final packing was going on. The throng of workers at the granaries had lessened; most of them were now supplied with as much food as they could carry.

Men and women equipped for travelling lay around fires hurriedly lighted in front of many tents and houses, and in the larger farms shepherds were driving the cattle and slaughtering the oxen and sheep which were unable to go with the people. The blows of axes and hammers and the creaking of saws were heard in front of many a house; for litters to transport the sick and feeble must be made. Carts and wains were still to be loaded, and the heads of families had a hard task with the women; for a woman's heart often clings more closely to things apparently worthless than to those of the greatest value. When the weaver Rebecca was more eager to find room in the cart for the rude cradle in which her darling had died, than for the beautiful ebony chest inlaid with ivory an Egyptian had pawned to her husband, who could blame her?

Light shone from all the window openings and tent doors, while from the roofs of the largest houses the blaze of torches or lanterns greeted the approaching Hebrews.

At the banquet served on the night of the harvest festival, no table had lacked a roast lamb; during this hour of waiting the housewife offered her family what she could.

The narrow streets of the humble little town were full of active life, and never had the setting stars shone upon features so cheerful, eyes sparkling so brightly with enthusiasm, and faces so transfigured by hope and devout piety.

CHAPTER XII

When morning dawned, all who had not gone down to meet the fugitives who were to make their first long halt here, had assembled on the roof of one of the largest houses in Succoth.

One after another fleet-footed man or boy, hurrying in advance of the rest, had reached Succoth. Amminadab's house was the goal sought by the majority. It consisted of two buildings, one occupied by Naashon, the owner's son, and his family, the other, a larger dwelling, which sheltered, besides the grey-haired owner and his wife, his son-in-law Aaron with his wife, children, and grand-children, and Miriam. The aged leader of his tribe, who had assigned the duties of his position to his son Naashon, extended his hand to every messenger and listened to his story with sparkling eyes, often dimmed by tears. He had induced his old wife to sit in the armchair in which she was to be carried after the people, that she might become accustomed to it, and for the same reason he now occupied his own.

When the old dame heard the messengers boast that the fair future promised to the people was now close at hand, her eyes often sought her husband, and she exclaimed: "Yes, Moses!" for she held her son-in-law's brother in high esteem, and rejoiced to see his prophecy fulfilled. The old people were proud of Aaron, too; but all their love was lavished upon Eleasar, their grandson, whom they beheld growing up into a second Moses. Miriam had been for some time a new and welcome member of the household. True, the warm-hearted old couple's liking for the grave maiden had not increased to parental tenderness, and their daughter Elisheba, Aaron's active wife, had no greater inclination to share the cares of the large family with the prophetess than her son Naashon's spouse, who, moreover, dwelt with her immediate family under her own roof. Yet the old people owed Miriam a debt of gratitude for the care she bestowed upon their granddaughter Milcah, the daughter of Aaron and Elisheba, whom a great misfortune had transformed from a merry-hearted child into a melancholy woman, whose heart seemed dead to every joy.

A few days after her marriage to a beloved husband the latter, carried away by passion, had raised his hand against an Egyptian tax-gatherer, who, while Pharaoh was passing through Succoth toward the east, had attempted to drive off a herd of his finest cattle for "the kitchen of the lord of both worlds." For this act of self-defence the hapless man had been conveyed to the mines as a prisoner of state, and every one knew that the convicts there perished, soul and body, from torturing labor far beyond their strength. Through the influence of old Nun, Hosea's father, the wife and relatives of the condemned man had been saved from sharing his punishment, as the law prescribed. But Milcah languished under the blow, and the only person who could rouse the pale, silent woman from brooding over her grief was Miriam. The desolate heart clung to the prophetess, and she accompanied her when she practised in the huts of the poor the medical skill she had learned and took them medicines and alms.

The last messengers Amninadab and his wife received on the roof described the hardships of the journey and the misery they had witnessed in dark hues; but if one, more tender-hearted than the rest, broke into lamentations over the sufferings endured by the women and children during the prevalence of the desert wind, and recalling the worst horrors impressed upon his memory, uttered mournful predictions for the future, the old man spoke cheering words, telling him of the omnipotence of God, and how custom would inure one to hardship. His wrinkled features expressed firm confidence, while one could read in Miriam's beautiful, yet stern countenance, little of the courageous hope, which youth is wont to possess in a far higher degree than age.

During the arrival and departure of the messengers she did not quit the old couple's side, leaving to her sister-in-law Elisheba and her servants the duty of offering refreshments to the wearied men. She herself listened intently, with panting breath, but what she heard seemed to awaken her anxiety; for she knew that no one came to the house which sheltered Aaron save those who were adherents of her brothers, the leaders of the people. If such men's blitheness was already waning, what must the outlook be to the lukewarm and refractory!

She rarely added a question of her own to those asked by the old man and, when she did so, the messengers who heard her voice for the first time looked at her in surprise; though musical, the tones were unusually deep.

After several messengers, in reply to her inquiries, declared that Hosea, the son of Nun, had not come with the others, her head drooped and she asked nothing more, till pallid Milcah, who followed her everywhere, raised her dark eyes beseechingly and murmured the name of Reuben, her captive husband. The prophetess kissed the poor desolate wife's forehead, glanced at her as if she had neglected her in some way, and then questioned the messengers with urgent eagerness concerning their news of Reuben, who had been dragged to the mines. One only had learned from a released prisoner that Milcah's husband was living in the copper mines of the province of Bech, in the neighborhood of Mt. Sinai, and Miriam seized upon these tidings to assure Milcah, with great vivacity and warmth, that if the tribes moved eastward they would surely pass the mines and release the Hebrews imprisoned there.

These were welcome words, and Milcah, who nestled to her comforter's breast, would gladly have heard more; but great restlessness had seized upon the people gazing into the distance from the roof of Amminadab's house; a dense cloud of dust was approaching from the north, and soon after a strange murmur arose, then a loud uproar, and finally shouts and cries from thousands of voices, lowing, neighing, and bleating, such as none of the listeners had ever heard,—and then on surged the many-limbed and many-voiced multitude, the endless stream of human beings and herds, which the astrologer's grandson on the observatory of the temple at Tanis had mistaken for the serpent of the nether-world.

Now, too, in the light of early dawn, it might easily have been imagined a host of bodiless spirits driven forth from the realms of the dead; for a whitish-grey column of dust extending to the blue vault of heaven moved before it, and the vast whole, with its many parts and voices, veiled by the clouds of sand, had the appearance of a single form. Often, however, a metal spear-head or a brazen kettle, smitten by a sunbeam, flashed brightly, and individual voices, shouting loudly, fell upon the ear.

The foremost billows of the flood had now reached Amminadab's house, before which pasture lands extended as far as the eye could reach.

Words of command rang on the air, the procession halted, dispersing as a mountain lake overflows in spring, sending rivulets and streams hither and thither; but the various small runlets speedily united, taking possession of broad patches of the dewy pastures, and wherever such portions of the torrent of human beings and animals rested, the shroud of dust which had concealed them disappeared.

The road remained hidden by the cloud a long time, but on the meadows the morning sunlight shone upon men, women, and children, cattle and donkeys, sheep and goats, and soon tent after tent was pitched on the green sward in front of the dwellings of Amminadab and Naashon, herds were surrounded by pens, stakes and posts were driven into the hard ground, awnings were stretched, cows were fastened to ropes, cattle and sheep were led to water, fires were lighted, and long lines of women, balancing jars on their heads, with their slender, beautifully curved arms, went to the well behind the old sycamore or to the side of the neighboring canal.

This morning, as on every other working-day, a pied ox with a large hump was turning the wheel that raised the water. It watered the land, though the owner of the cattle intended to leave it on the morrow; but the slave who drove it had no thought beyond the present and, as no one forbade him, moistened as he was wont the grass for the foe into whose hands it was to fall.

Hours elapsed ere the advancing multitude reached the camp, and Miriam who stood describing to Amminadab, whose eyes were no longer keen enough to discern distant objects, what was passing below, witnessed many an incident from which she would fain have averted her gaze.

She dared not frankly tell the old man what she beheld, it would have clouded his joyous hope.

Relying, with all the might of an inspired soul upon the God of her fathers and his omnipotence, she had but yesterday fully shared Amminadab's confidence; but the Lord had bestowed upon her spirit the fatal gift of seeing things and hearing words incomprehensible to all other human beings. Usually she distinguished them in dreams, but they often came to her also in solitary hours, when she was deeply absorbed by thoughts of the past or the future.

The words Ephraim had announced to Hosea in her name, as a message from the Most High, had been uttered by unseen lips while she was thinking under the sycamore of the exodus and the man whom she had loved from her childhood—and when that day, between midnight and morning, she again sat beneath the venerable tree and was overpowered by weariness, she had believed she heard the same voice. The words had vanished from her memory when she awoke, but she knew that their purport had been sorrowful and of ill omen.

Spite of the vagueness of the monition, it disturbed her, and the outcries rising from the pastures certainly were not evoked by joy that the people had joined her brothers and the first goal of their wanderings had been successfully gained, as the old man at her side supposed; no, they were the furious shouts of wrathful, undisciplined men, wrangling and fighting with fierce hostility on the meadow for a good place to pitch their tents or the best spot at the wells or on the brink of the canals to water their cattle.

Wrath, disappointment, despair echoed in the shouts, and when her gaze sought the point whence they rose loudest, she saw the corpse of a woman borne on a piece of tent-cloth by railing bondmen and a pale, death-stricken infant held on the arm of a half naked, frantic man, its father, who shook his disengaged hand in menace toward the spot where she saw her brothers.

The next moment she beheld a grey-haired old man, bowed by heavy toil, raise his fist against Moses. He would have struck him, had he not been dragged away by others.

She could not bear to stay longer on the roof. Pale and panting for breath, she hurried to the camp. Milcah followed, and wherever they encountered people who lived in Succoth, they received respectful greetings.

The new comers from Zoan,—as the Hebrews called Tanis,—Pha-kos, and Bubastis, whom they met on the way, did not know Miriam, yet the tall figure and stately dignity of the prophetess led them also to make way respectfully or pause to answer her questions.

The things she learned were evil and heart-rending; for joyously as the procession had marched forward on the first day, it dragged along sadly and hopelessly on the second. The desert wind had robbed many of the strong of their power of resistance and energy; others, like the bondman's wife and nursling, had been attacked by fever on the pilgrimage through the dust and the oppressive heat of the day, and they pointed out to her the procession which was approaching the burial-place of the Hebrews of Succoth. Those who were being conveyed to the bourn whence there is no return were not only women and children, or those who had been brought from their homes ill, that they might not be left behind, but also men who were in robust health the day before and had broken down under burdens too heavy for their strength, or who had recklessly exposed themselves, while working, to the beams of the noon-day sun.

In one tent, where a young mother was shaking with the chill of a severe attack of fever, Miriam asked the pallid Milcah to bring her medicine chest, and the desolate wife went on her errand with joyous alacrity. On the way she stopped many and timidly asked about her captive husband, but could obtain no news of him. Miriam, however, heard from Nun, Hosea's father, that Eliab, the freedman whom he had left behind, had informed him that his son would be ready to join his people. She also learned that the wounded Ephraim had found shelter in his uncle's tent.

Was the lad's illness serious, or what other cause detained Hosea in Tanis? These questions filled Miriam's heart with fresh anxiety, yet with rare energy she nevertheless lavished help and comfort wherever she went.

Old Nun's cordial greeting had cheered her, and a more vigorous, kind, and lovable old man could not be imagined.

The mere sight of his venerable head, with its thick snow-white hair and beard, his regular features, and eyes sparkling with the fire of youth, was a pleasure to her, and as, in his vivacious, winning manner, he expressed his joy at meeting her again, as he drew her to his heart and kissed her brow, after she had told him that, in the name of the Most High, she had called Hosea "Joshua" and summoned him back to his people that he might command their forces, she felt as if she had found in him some compensation for her dead father's loss, and devoted herself with fresh vigor to the arduous duties which everywhere demanded her attention.

And it was no trivial matter for the high-souled maiden to devote herself, with sweet self-sacrifice, to those whose roughness and uncouth manners wounded her. The women, it is true, gladly accepted her aid, but the men, who had grown up under the rod of the overseer, knew neither reserve nor consideration. Their natures were as rude as their persons and when, as soon as they learned her name, they began to assail her with harsh reproaches, asserting that her brother had lured them from an endurable situation to plunge them into the most horrible position, when she heard imprecations and blasphemy, and saw the furious wrath of the black eyes that flashed in the brown faces framed by masses of tangled hair and beards, her heart failed her.

But she succeeded in mastering dread and aversion, and though her heart throbbed violently, and she expected to meet the worst, she reminded those who were repulsive to her and from whom her woman's weakness urged her to flee, of the God of their fathers and His promises.

She now thought she knew what the sorrowful warning voice under the sycamore had portended, and beside the couch of the young dying mother she raised her hands and heart to Heaven and took an oath unto the Most High that she would exert every power of her being to battle against the faint-hearted lack of faith and rude obstinacy, which threatened to plunge the people into sore perils. Jehovah had promised them the fairest future and they must not be robbed of it by the short-sightedness and defiance of a few deluded individuals; but God himself could scarcely be wroth with those who, content if their bodily wants were satisfied, had unresistingly borne insults and blows like cattle. The multitude even now did not realize that they must pass through the darkness of misery to be worthy of the bright day that awaited them.

The medicines administered by Miriam seemed to relieve the sufferer, and filled with fresh confidence, she left the tent to seek her brothers.

There had been little change in the state of affairs in the camp, and she again beheld scenes from which she recoiled and which made her regret that the sensitive Milcah was her companion.

Some rascally bondmen who had seized cattle and utensils belonging to others had been bound to a palmtree, and the ravens that followed the procession; and had found ample sustenance on the way, now croaked greedily around the quickly established place of execution.

No one knew who had been judge or executioner of the sentence; but those who took part in the swift retribution considered it well justified, and rejoiced in the deed.

With rapid steps and averted head Miriam drew the trembling Milcah on and gave her to the care of her uncle Naashon to lead home. The latter had just parted from the man who with him ruled the sons of Judah as a prince of the tribe—Hur, who at the head of the shepherds had won the first victory against the Egyptians, and who now led to the maiden with joyful pride a man and a boy, his son and grandson. Both had been in the service of the Egyptians, practising the trade of goldsmith and worker in metals for Pharaoh at Memphis. The former's skill had won him the name of Uri, which in Egyptian means 'great', and this artificer's son Bezaleel, Hur's grandson, though scarcely beyond boyhood, was reputed to surpass his father in the gifts of genius.

Hur gazed with justifiable pride at son and grandson; for though both had attained much consideration among the Egyptians they had followed their father's messenger without demur, leaving behind them many who were dear to their hearts, and the property gained in Memphis, to join their wandering nation and share its uncertain destiny.

Miriam greeted the new arrivals with the utmost warmth, and the men who, representing three generations, stood before her, presented a picture on which the eyes of any well-disposed person could not fail to rest with pleasure.

The grandfather was approaching his sixtieth year, and though many threads of silver mingled with his ebon-black hair, he held himself as erect as a youth, while his thin, sharply-cut features expressed the unyielding determination, which explained his son's and grandson's prompt obedience to his will.

Uri, too, was a stately man, and Bezaleel a youth who showed that he had industriously utilized his nineteen years and already attained an independent position. His artist eye sparkled with special brilliancy, and after he and his father had taken leave of Miriam to greet Caleb, their grandfather and great-grandfather, she heartily congratulated the man who was one of her brother's most loyal friends, upon such scions of his noble race.

Hur seized her hand and, with a warmth of emotion gushing from a grateful heart that was by no means usual to the stern, imperious nature of this chief of an unruly shepherd tribe, exclaimed:

"Ay, they have remained good, true, and obedient. God has guarded them and prepared this day of happiness for me. Now it depends on you to make it the fairest of all festivals. You must have long perceived that my eyes have followed you and that you have been dear to my heart. To work for our people and their welfare is my highest aim as a man, yours as a woman, and that is a strong bond. But I desired to have a still firmer one unite us, and since your parents are dead, and I cannot go with the bridal dower to Amram, to buy you from him, I now bring my suit to you in person, high-souled maiden. But ere you say yes or no, you should learn that my son and grandson are ready to pay you the same honor as head of our household that they render me, and your brothers willingly permitted me to approach you as a suitor."

Miriam had listened to this offer in silent surprise. She had a high esteem and warm regard for the man who so fervently desired her love. Spite of his age, he stood before her in the full flush of manhood and stately dignity, and the beseeching expression of eyes whose glance was wont to be so imperious and steadfast stirred the inmost depths of her soul.

She, however, was waiting with ardent longing for another, so her sole answer was a troubled shake of the head.

But this man of mature years, a prince of his tribe, who was accustomed to carry his plans persistently into execution, undeterred by her mute refusal, continued even more warmly than before.

"Do not destroy in one short moment the yearning repressed with so much difficulty for years! Do you object to my age?"

Miriam shook her head a second time, but Hur went on:

"That was the source of my anxiety, though I can still vie with many a younger man in vigor. But, if you can overlook your lover's grey hairs, perhaps you may be induced to weigh the words he now utters. Of the faith and devotion of my soul I will say nothing. No man of my years woos a woman, unless his heart's strong impulse urges him on. But there is something else which, meseems, is of equal import. I said that I would lead you to my house. Yonder it stands, a building firm and spacious enough; but from to-morrow a tent will be our home, the camp our dwelling-place, and there will be wild work enough within its bounds. No one is secure, not even of life, least of all a woman, however strong she may be, who has made common cause with those against whom thousands murmur. Your parents are dead, your brothers might protect you, but should the people lay hands on them, the same stones on which you cross the stream would drag you down into the depths with them."

"And were I your wife, you also," replied Miriam, her thick eye-brows contracting in a heavy frown.

"I will take the risk," Hur answered. "The destinies of all are in God's hands, my faith is as firm as yours, and behind me stands the tribe of Judah, who follow me and Naashon as the sheep follow the shepherds. Old Nun and the Ephraimites are with us, and should matters come to the worst, it would mean perishing according to God's will, or in faithful union, power, and prosperity, awaiting old age in the Promised Land."

Miriam fearlessly gazed full into his stern eyes, laid her hand on his arm, and answered: "Those words are worthy of the man whom I have honored from childhood, and who has reared such sons; but I cannot be your wife."

"You cannot?"

"No, my lord, I cannot."

"A hard sentence, but it must suffice," replied the other, his head drooping in sorrow; but Miriam exclaimed:

"Nay, Hur, you have a right to ask the cause of my refusal, and because I honor you, I owe you the truth. Another man of our race reigns in my heart. He met me for the first time when I was still a child. Like your son and grandson, he has lived among the Egyptians, but the summons of our God and of his father reached him as did the message to your sons, and like Uri and Bezaleel, he showed himself obedient. If he still desires to wed me, I shall become his wife, if it is the will of the God whom I serve, and who shows me the favor of suffering me to hear his voice. But I shall think of you with gratitude forever."

Her large eyes had been glittering through tears as she uttered the words, and there was a tremor in the grey-haired lover's voice as he asked in hesitating, embarrassed tones:

"And if the man for whom you are waiting—I do not ask his name— shuts his ears to the call that has reached him, if he declines to share the uncertain destiny of his people?"

"That will never happen!" Miriam interrupted, a chill creeping through her veins, but Hur exclaimed:

"There is no 'never,' no 'surely,' save with God. If, spite of your firm faith, the result should be different from your expectations, will you resign to the Lord the wish which began to stir in your heart, when you were still a foolish child?"

"He who has guided me until now will show me the right way."

"Well then," replied Hur, "put your trust in Him, and if the man of your choice is worthy of you, and becomes your lord, my soul will rejoice without envy when the Most High blesses your union. But if God wills otherwise, and you need a strong arm for your support, I am here. The tent and the heart of Hur will ever be open to you."

With these words he turned away; but Miriam gazed thoughtfully after him as long as the old chief's stately figure was visible.

At last, still pondering, she moved toward her host's house, but at the road leading to Tanis, she paused and gazed northward. The dust had subsided, and she could see a long distance, but the one person whom it was to lead back to her and to his people did not appear. Sighing sadly, she moved onward with drooping head, and started violently when her brother Moses' deep voice called to her from the old sycamore.

CHAPTER XIII

Aaron and Eleasar, with fiery eloquence, had reminded the murmuring, disheartened people of the power and promises of their God. Whoever had stretched his limbs undisturbed to comfortable rest, whoever had been strengthened by food and drink regained the confidence that had been lost. The liberated bondmen were told of the hard labor and dishonoring blows which they had escaped and admonished that they must recognize as God's dispensation, among other things, that Pharaoh had not pursued them; but the rich booty still found in the plundered storehouse had no small share in the revival of their drooping courage, and the bondmen and lepers—for many of the latter had accompanied them and rested outside the camp—in short, all for whose support Pharaoh had provided, saw themselves safe for a long time from care and privation. Yet there was no lack of malcontents, and here and there, though no one knew who instigated the question, loud discussion arose whether it would not be more advisable to return to Pharaoh and rely on his favor. Whoever raised it, did the work secretly, and was often compelled to submit to sharp, threatening retorts.

Miriam had talked with her brothers and shared the heavy anxieties that oppressed them. Why had the desert wind so speedily destroyed the courage of the people during their brief pilgrimage? How impatient, how weak in faith, how rebellious they had showed themselves at the first obstacle they had encountered, how uncontrollable they had been in following their fierce impulses. When summoned to prayer just before sunrise during their journey, some had turned toward the day-star rising in the east, others had taken out a small idol they had brought with them, and others still had uplifted their eyes to the Nile acacia, which in some provinces of Egypt was regarded as a sacred tree. What did they know of the God who had commanded them to cast so much behind them and take upon themselves such heavy burdens? Even now many were despairing, though they had confronted no serious dangers; for Moses had intended to lead the Hebrews in Succoth over the road to Philistia direct to the Promised Land in Palestine, but the conduct of the people forced him to resign this plan and form another.

To reach the great highway connecting Asia and Africa it was necessary to cross the isthmus, which rather divided than united the two continents; for it was most thoroughly guarded from intruders and, partly by natural, partly by artificial obstacles, barred the path of every fugitive; a series of deep lakes rolled their waves upon its soil, and where these did not stay the march of the travelers strong fortifications, garrisoned by trained Egyptian troops, rose before them.

This chain of forts was called Chetam—or in the Hebrew tongue—Etham, and wayfarers leaving Succoth would reach the nearest and strongest of these forts in a few hours.

When the tribes, full of enthusiasm for their God, and ready for the most arduous enterprises, shook off their chains and, exulting in their new liberty, rushed forward to the Promised Land Moses, and with him the majority of the elders, had believed that, like a mountain torrent, bursting dams and sluices, they would destroy and overthrow everything that ventured to oppose their progress. With these enthusiastic masses, to whom bold advance would secure the highest good, and timid hesitation could bring nothing save death and ruin, they had expected to rush over the Etham line as if it were a pile of faggots. But now since a short chain of difficulties and suffering had stifled the fire of their souls, now that wherever the eye turned, there were two calm and five dissatisfied or anxious individuals to one upheld by joyous anticipation, to storm the Etham line would have cost rivers of blood and moreover jeopardized all that had been already gained.

The overpowering of the little garrison in the storehouse of Pithom had occurred under specially favorable circumstances, which could hardly be expected to happen again, so the original plan must be changed, and an attempt made to take a circuit around the fortifications. Instead of moving toward the northeast, the tribes must turn southward.

But, ere carrying this plan into execution, Moses, accompanied by a few trusty men, desired to examine the new route and ascertain whether it would be passable for the great wandering people.

These matters were discussed under the great sycamore in front of Amminadab's house, and Miriam was present, a mute witness.

Women,—even those like herself,—were forced to keep silence when men were holding counsel; yet it was hard for her to remain speechless when it was decided to abstain from attacking the forts, even should the trained warrior, Hosea, whom God Himself had chosen to be his sword, return to his people.

"What avails the best leader, if there is no army to obey him?" Naashon, Amminadab's son, had exclaimed, and the others shared his opinion.

When the council finally broke up, Moses took leave of his sister with fraternal affection. She knew that he was in the act of plunging into fresh dangers and—in the modest manner in which she was always wont to accost the brother who so far surpassed all others in every gift of mind and body,—expressed her anxiety. He looked into her eyes with friendly reproach and raised his right hand toward heaven; but she understood his meaning, and kissing his hand with grateful warmth, replied:

"You stand under the protection of the Most High, and I fear no longer."

Pressing his lips upon her brow, he bade her give him a tablet, wrote a few words on it, flung it into the hollow trunk of the sycamore, and said:

"For Hosea, no, for Joshua, the son of Nun, if he comes while I am absent. The Lord has great deeds for him to accomplish, when he learns to expect loftier things from the Most High than from the mighty ones of earth."

With these words he left her; but Aaron who, as the oldest, was the head of her tribe, lingered and told her that a man of worth sought her hand. Miriam, with blanching face, replied:

"I know it...."

He looked at her in surprise and with earnest monition, added:

"As you choose; yet it will be wise to consider this. Your heart belongs to your God and to your people, and the man whom you wed must be ready, like yourself, to serve both; for two must be one in marriage, and if the highest aim of one is not also that of the other, they will remain two till the end. The voice of the senses, which drew them together, will soon be mute and nothing will be left to them save discord."

Having said this, he went away, and she, too, was preparing to leave the others; for on the eve of departure she might be needed in the house whose hospitality she enjoyed. But a new incident detained her, as though bound with fetters, under the sycamore.

What cared she for the packing of perishable wares and providing for bodily needs, when affairs which occupied her whole soul were under discussion! Elisheba, Naashon's wife, any housekeeper and faithful slave could attend to the former wants. Higher things were to be determined here—the weal or woe of her people.

Several men of distinction in the tribes had joined the elders under the sycamore; but Hur had already departed with Moses.

Uri, the son of the former, now appeared beneath the ancient tree. The worker in metals, who had just come from Egypt, had talked in Memphis with persons who were near to the king and learned that Pharaoh was ready to remove great burdens from the Hebrews and grant them new favors, if Moses would render the God whom he served propitious to him and induce the people to return after they had offered sacrifices in the wilderness. Therefore it would be advisable to send envoys to Tanis and enter into negotiations with the Sublime Porte.

These proposals, which Uri had not yet ventured to moot to his father, he, with good intentions, brought before the assembled elders; he hoped that their acceptance might spare the people great suffering. But scarcely had he concluded his clear and convincing speech, when old Nun, Hosea's father, who had with difficulty held his feelings in check, broke in.

The old man's face, usually so cheerful, glowed with wrath, and its fiery hue formed a strange contrast to the thick white locks which framed it. A few hours before he had heard Moses repel similar propositions with harsh decision and crushing reasons; now he had heard them again brought forward and noted many a gesture of assent among the listeners, and saw the whole great enterprise imperilled, the enterprise for whose success he had himself risked and sacrificed more than any other man.

This was too much for the active old man who, with flashing eyes and hand upraised in menace, burst forth "What do you mean? Are we to pick up the ends of the rope the Lord our God has severed? Do you counsel us to fasten it anew, with a looser knot, which will hold as long as the whim of a vacillating weakling who has broken his promises to us and to Moses a score of times? Do you wish to lead us back to the cage whence the Almighty released us by a miracle? Are we to treat the Lord our God like a bad debtor and prefer the spurious gold ring we are offered to the royal treasures He promises? Oh, messenger from the Egyptians—I would...."

Here the hot-blooded grey-beard raised his clenched fist in menace but, ere he had uttered the threat that hovered on his lips, he let his arm fall; for Gabriel, the oldest member of the tribe of Zebulun, shouted:

"Remember your own son, who is to-day among the foes of his people."

The words struck home; yet they only dimmed the fiery old man's glad self-reliance a moment and, amid the voices uttering disapproval of the malicious Gabriel and the few who upheld the Zebulunite, he cried:

"And because I am perhaps in danger of losing, not only the ten thousand acres of land I flung behind me, but a noble son, it is my right to speak here."

His broad chest heaved with his labored breathing and his eyes, shadowed by thick white brows, rested with a milder expression on the son of Hur, whose face had paled at his vehement words, as he continued:

"Uri is a good and dutiful son to his father and has also been obliged to make great sacrifices in leaving the place where his work was so much praised and his own house in Memphis. The blessing of the Most High will not fail him. But for the very reason that he has hitherto obeyed the command, he must not now seek to destroy what we have commenced under the guidance of the Most High. To you, Gabriel, I answer that my son probably will not tarry among our foes, but obedient to my summons, will join us, like Uri, the first-born of Hur. What still detains him is doubtless some important matter of which Hosea will have as little cause to be ashamed as I, his father. I know and trust him, and whoever expects aught else will sooner or later, by my son's course of action, be proved a liar."

Here he paused to push his white hair back from his burning brow and, as no one contradicted him, he turned to the worker in metals, and added with cordial friendliness:

"What angered me, Uri, was certainly not your purpose. That is a good one; but you have measured the greatness and majesty of the God of our fathers by the standard of the false gods of the Egyptians, who die and rise again and, as Aaron has just said, represent only minor attributes of Him who is in all and transcends everything. To serve God, until Moses taught me a better counsel, I deemed meant to sacrifice an ox, a lamb, or a goose upon the altar like the Egyptians; but your eyes, as befell me through Moses, will not be opened to Him who rules the world and has made us His people, until, like me, you, and all of us, and probably my son also, shall each have kindled in his own breast the sacrificial fire which never goes out and consumes everything that does not relate to Him in love and loyalty, faith and reverence. Through Moses, His servant, God has promised us the greatest blessings—deliverance from bondage, the privilege of ruling on our own land as free men in a beautiful country, our own possession and the heritage of our children. We are going forth to receive His gift, and whoever seeks to stop us on our way, whoever urges us to turn and creep back into the net whose brazen meshes we have burst, advises his people to run once more like sheep into the fire from which they have escaped. I am not angry with you; your face shows that you perceive how foolishly you have erred; but all ye who are here must know that I heard only a few hours ago from Moses' own lips these words: 'Whoever counsels return and the making of covenants with the Egyptians, I will denounce as a scorner of Jehovah our God, and the destroyer and worst foe of his people!'"

Uri went to the old man, gave him his hand, and deeply convinced of the justice of his reproaches, exclaimed: "No treaty, no covenant with the Egyptians! I am grateful to you, Nun, for opening my eyes. To me, also, the hour will doubtless come in which you, or some one who stands nearer to Him than I, will teach me to know your God, who is also mine."

As he ceased speaking, he went away with Nun, who put his arm around his shoulders; but Miriam had listened breathlessly to Uri's last words, and as he expressed a desire to know the God of his people, her eyes had sparkled with the light of enthusiasm. She felt that her soul was filled with the greatness of the Most High and that she had the gift of speech to make another familiar with the knowledge she herself possessed. But this time also custom required her to keep silence. Her heart ached, and as she again moved among the multitude and convinced herself that Hosea had not yet come, she went home, as twilight was beginning to gather, and joined the others on the roof.

No one there appeared to have missed her, not even poor melancholy Milcah, and she felt unutterably lonely in this house.

If Hosea would only come, if she might have a strong breast on which to lean, if this sense of being a stranger in her own home, this useless life beneath the roof she was obliged to call hers, though she never felt thoroughly at home under it, would but cease. Moses and Aaron, too, had gone away, taking Hur's grandson with them; but no one had deemed her, who lived and breathed solely for her people and their welfare, worthy to learn whither their journey led or what was its purpose.

Why had the God to whom she devoted her whole life and being made her a woman, yet given her the mind and soul of a man?

She waited, as if to test whether any of the circle of kindly-natured people to which she belonged really loved her, for some one of the elders or the children to accost her; but Eleasar's little ones were pressing around their grandparents, and she had never understood how to make herself agreeable to children. Elisheba was directing the slaves who were putting the finishing touches to the packing; Milcah sat with her cat in her lap, gazing into vacancy. No one heeded or spoke to her.

Bitter pain overpowered Miriam, and after she had shared the evening meal with the others, and forced herself not to disturb by her own sorrowful mood, the joyous excitement of the children, who looked forward to the pilgrimage as a great pleasure, she longed to go out of doors.

Closely veiled, she passed alone through the camp and what she beheld there was certainly ill-suited to dispel the mood that oppressed her. There was plenty of noise, and though sometimes devout hymns, full of joy and hope, echoed on the air, she heard far more frequently savage quarrelling and rebellious words. When her ear caught threats or reproaches levelled against her noble brother, she quickened her pace, but she could not escape her anxiety concerning what would happen at the departure after sunrise on the morrow, should the malcontents obtain supremacy.

She knew that the people would be forced to press forward; but her dread of Pharaoh's military power had never permitted her to be at peace—to her it was as it were embodied in Hosea's heroic figure. If the Lord Himself did not fight in the ranks of the wretched bondmen and shepherds who were quarrelling and disputing around her, how were they to withstand the well-trained and equipped hosts of the Egyptians, with their horses and chariots?

She had heard that guards had been posted in all parts of the camp, with orders to sound the horn or strike the cymbal at the approach of the foe, until the men had flocked to the spot whence the warning first echoed.

She had long listened for such an alarm, yet how much more intently for the hoof-beats of a single steed, the firm step and deep voice of the warrior for whom she yearned. On his account she constantly returned to the northern part of the camp which adjoined the road coming from Tanis and where now, at Moses' bidding, the tents of most of the men capable of bearing arms were pitched. Here she had hoped to find true confidence; but as she listened to the talk of the armed soldiers who surrounded the camp-fires in dense circles, she heard that Uri's proposal had reached them also. Most of them were husbands and fathers, had left behind a house, a bit of land, a business, or an office, and though many spoke of the command of the Most High and the beautiful new home God had promised, not a few were disposed to return. How gladly she would have gone among these blinded mortals and exhorted them to obey with fresh faith and confidence the command of the Lord and of her brother. But here, too, she was forced to keep silence. She was permitted to listen only, and she was most strongly attracted to the very places where she might expect to hear rebellious words and proposals.

There was a mysterious charm in this cruel excitement and she felt as if she were deprived of something desirable when many a fire was extinguished, the soldiers went to sleep, and conversation ceased.

She now turned for the last time toward the road leading from Tanis; but nothing was stirring there save the sentries pacing to and fro.

She had not yet doubted Hosea's coming; for the summons she had sent to him in the name of the Lord had undoubtedly reached him; but now that the stars showed her it was past midnight, the thought came vividly before her mind of the many years he had spent among the Egyptians, and that he might perhaps deem it unworthy of a man to obey the call of a woman, even if she uplifted her voice in the name of the Most High. She had experienced humiliations enough that day, why should not this be decreed also?

CHAPTER XIV

Deeply disturbed and tortured by such thoughts, Miriam walked toward Amminadab's house to seek repose; but just as she was in the act of crossing the threshold, she paused and again listened for sounds coming from the north.

Hosea must arrive from that direction.

But she heard nothing save the footsteps of a sentinel and the voice of Hur, who was patrolling the camp with a body of armed men.

He, too, had been unable to stay in the house.

The night was mild and starry, the time seemed just suited for dreams under the sycamore. Her bench beneath the venerable tree was empty, and with drooping head she approached the beloved resting-place, which she must leave forever on the morrow.

But ere she had reached the spot so close at hand, she paused with her figure drawn up to its full height and her hand pressed upon her throbbing bosom. This time she was not mistaken, the beat of hoofs echoed on the air, and it came from the north.

Were Pharaoh's chariots approaching to attack the camp? Should she shout to wake the warriors? Or could it be he whom she so longingly expected? Yes, yes, yes! It was the tramp of a single steed, and must be a new arrival; for there were loud voices in the tents, the dogs barked, and shouts, questions, and answers came nearer and nearer with the rider.

It was Hosea, she felt sure. His riding alone through the night, released from the bonds that united him to Pharaoh and his comrades in arms, was a sign of his obedience! Love had steeled his will and quickened the pace of his steed, and the gratitude of answering affection, the reward she could bestow, should be withheld no longer. In her arms he should blissfully perceive that he had resigned great possessions to obtain something still fairer and sweeter! She felt as though the darkness around had suddenly brightened into broad day, as her ear told her that the approaching horseman was riding straight toward the house of her host Amminadab.

She now knew that he was obeying her summons, that he had come to find her. Hosea was seeking her ere he went to his own father, who had found shelter in the big empty house of his grandson, Ephraim.

He would gladly have dashed toward her at the swiftest pace of his steed, but it would not do to ride rapidly through the camp. Ah, how long the time seemed ere she at last saw the horseman, ere he swung himself to the ground, and his companion flung the reins of the horse to a man who followed him.

It was he, it was Hosea!

But his companion—she had recognized him distinctly and shrank a little—his companion was Hur, the man who a few hours before had sought her for his wife.

There stood her two suitors side by side in the starlight, illumined by the glare of the pitch torches blazing beside the carts and household utensils which had been packed for the morrow's journey.

The tall figure of the elder Hebrew towered over the sinewy form of the warrior, and the shepherd prince bore himself no whit less erect than the Egyptian hero. Both voices sounded earnest and manly, yet her lover's seemed to Miriam stronger and deeper. They had now advanced so near that she could understand their conversation.

Hur was telling the newcomer that Moses had gone on a reconnoitring expedition, and Hosea was expressing his regret, because he had important matters to discuss with him.

Then he must set out with the tribes the next morning, Hur replied, for Moses intended to join them on the way.

Then he pointed to Amminadab's house, from which no ray of light gleamed through the darkness, and asked Hosea to spend the remainder of the night beneath his roof, as he probably would not wish to disturb his aged father at so late an hour.

Miriam saw her friend hesitate and gaze intently up to the women's apartments and the roof of her host's house. Knowing what he sought, she could no longer resist the impulse of her heart, but stepped forth from the shadow of the sycamore and gave Hosea a cordial and tender welcome.

He, too, disdained to conceal the joy of his heart, and Hur stood beside the reunited lovers, as they clasped each other's hands, and exchanged greetings, at first mutely, then with warm words.

"I knew you would come!" cried the maiden, and Hosea answered with joyful emotion.

"You might easily suppose so, oh Prophetess; for your own voice was among those that summoned me here."

Then in a calmer tone, he added: "I hoped to find your brother also; I am the bearer of a message of grave import to him, to us, and to the people. I see that you, too, are ready to depart and should grieve to behold the comfort of your aged hosts destroyed by hasty acts that may yet be needless."

"What do you mean?" asked Hur, advancing a step nearer to the other. "I mean," replied Hosea, "that if Moses persists in leading the tribes eastward, much blood will flow uselessly to-morrow; for I learned at Tanis that the garrison of Etham has been ordered to let no man pass, still less the countless throng, whose magnitude surprised me as I rode through the camp. I know Apu, who commands the fortifications and the legions whom he leads. There would be a terrible, fruitless massacre of our half-armed, untrained people, there would be—in short, I have urgent business to discuss with Moses, urgent and immediate, to avert the heaviest misfortune ere it is too late."

"What you fear has not escaped our notice," replied Hur, "and it is in order to guard against this peril that Moses has set forth on a dangerous quest."

"Whither?" asked Hosea.

"That is the secret of the leaders of the tribes."

"Of which my father is one."

"Certainly; and I have already offered to take you to him. If he assumes the responsibility of informing you...."

"Should he deem it a breach of duty, he will keep silence. Who is to command the wandering hosts tomorrow?"

"I."

"You?" asked Hosea in astonishment, and Hur answered calmly:

"You marvel at the audacity of the shepherd who ventures to lead an army; but the Lord of all armies, to whom we trust our cause, is our leader; I rely solely on His guidance."

"And so do I," replied Hosea. "No one save the God through whom Miriam summoned me to this spot, entrusted me—of that I am confident—with the important message which brings me here. I must find Moses ere it is too late."

"You have already heard that he will be beyond the reach of any one, myself included, until to-morrow, perhaps the day after. Will you speak to Aaron?"

"Is he in the camp?"

"No; but we expect his return before the departure of the people, that is in a few hours."

"Has he the power to decide important matters in Moses' absence?"

"No, he merely announces to the people in eloquent language what his illustrious brother commands."

The warrior bent his eyes with a disappointed expression on the ground, and after a brief pause for reflection eagerly added, fixing his gaze on Miriam:

"It is Moses to whom the Lord our God announces his will; but to you, his august maiden sister, the Most High also reveals himself, to you..."

"Oh, Hosea!" interrupted the prophetess, extending her hands toward him with a gesture of mingled entreaty and warning; but the chief, instead of heeding her monition, went on:

"The Lord our God hath commanded you to summon me, His servant, back to the people; He hath commanded you to give me the name for which I am to exchange the one my father and mother bestowed upon me, and which I have borne in honor for thirty years. Obedient to your summons, I have cast aside all that could make me great among men; but on my way through Egypt,—bearing in my heart the image of my God and of you,—braving death, the message I now have to deliver was entrusted to me, and I believe that it came from the Most High Himself. It is my duty to convey it to the leaders of the people; but as I am unable to find Moses, I can confide it to no better one than you who, though only a woman, stand,—next to your brother—nearest to the Most High, so I implore you to listen to me. The tidings I bring are not yet ripe for the ears of a third person."

Hur drew his figure to a still greater height and, interrupting Hosea, asked Miriam whether she desired to hear the son of Nun without witnesses; she answered with a quiet "yes."

Then Hur turned haughtily and coldly to the warrior:

"I think that Miriam knows the Lord's will, as well as her brother's, and is aware of what beseems the women of Israel. If I am not mistaken, it was under this tree that your own father, the worthy Nun, gave to my son Uri the sole answer which Moses must also make to every bearer of a message akin to yours."

"Do you know it?" asked Hosea in a tone of curt reproof.

"No," replied the other, "but I suspect its purport, and look here."

While speaking he stooped with youthful agility and, raising two large stones with his powerful arms, propped them against each other, rolled several smaller ones to their sides, and then, with panting breath, exclaimed:

"Let this heap be a witness between me and thee, like the stones named Mizpah which Jacob and Laban erected. And as the latter called upon the Lord to watch between him and the other, so do I likewise. I point to this heap that you may remember it, when we are parted one from the other. I lay my hand upon these stones and bear witness that I, Hur, son of Caleb and Ephrath, put my trust in no other than the Lord, the God of our fathers, and am ready to obey His command, which calls us forth from the kingdom of Pharaoh into a land which He promised to us. But of thee, Hosea, son of Nun, I ask and the Lord our God hears thee: Dost thou, too, expect no other help save from the God of Abraham, who has made thy race His chosen people? And wilt thou also testify whether thou wilt ever regard the Egyptians who oppressed us, and from whose bondage the Lord our God delivered us, as the mortal foes of thy God and of thy race?"

The warrior's bearded features quivered, and he longed to overthrow the heap and answer the troublesome questioner with wrathful words, but Miriam had laid her hand on the top of the pile of stones, and clasping his right hand, exclaimed:

"He is questioning you in the presence of our God and Lord, who is your witness."

Hosea succeeded in controlling his wrath, and pressing the maiden's hand more closely, he answered earnestly:

"He questions, but I may not answer; 'yea' or 'nay' will be of little service here; but I, too, call God to witness, and before this heap you, Miriam, but you alone, shall hear what I propose and for what purpose I have come. Look, Hur! Like you I lay my hand upon this heap and bear witness that I, Hosea, son of Nun, put my sole trust in the Lord and God of our fathers. He stands as a witness between me and thee, and shall decide whether my way is His, or that of an erring mortal. I will obey His will, which He has made known to Moses and to this noble maiden. This I swear by an oath whose witness is the Lord our God."

Hur had listened intently and, impressed by the earnestness of the words, now exclaimed:

"The Lord our God has heard your vow and against your oath I, in the presence of this heap, take another: If the hour comes when, mindful of this heap of stones, you give the testimony you have refused me, there shall henceforward be no ill-will between us, and if it is in accordance with the will of the Most High, I will cheerfully resign to you the office of commander, which you, trained in many wars, would be better suited to fill than I, who hitherto have ruled only my flocks and shepherds. But you, Miriam, I charge to remember that this heap of stones will also be a witness of the colloquy you are to hold with this man in the presence of God. I remind you of the reproving words you heard beneath this tree from the lips of his father, and call God to witness that I would have darkened the life of my son Uri, who is the joy of my heart, with a father's curse if he had gone among the people to induce them to favor the message he brought; for it would have turned those of little faith from their God. Remember this, maiden, and let me say again:

"If you seek me you will find me, and the door I opened will remain open to you, whatever may happen!"

With these words Hur turned his back upon Miriam and the warrior.

Neither knew what had befallen them, but he who during the long ride beset by many a peril had yearned with ardent anticipations for the hour which was to once more unite him to the object of his love, gazed on the ground full of bewilderment and profound anxiety, while Miriam who, at his approach, had been ready to bestow upon him the highest, sweetest gifts with which a loving woman rewards fidelity and love, had sunk to the earth before the ominous pile of stones close beside the tree and pressed her forehead against its gnarled, hollow trunk.

CHAPTER XV

For a long time nothing was heard beneath the sycamore save Miriam's low moans and the impatient footsteps of the warrior who, while struggling for composure, did not venture to disturb her.

He could not yet understand what had suddenly towered like a mountain between him and the object of his love.

He had learned from Hur's words that his father and Moses rejected all mediation, yet the promises he was bearing to the people seemed to him a merciful gift from the Most High. None of his race yet knew it and, if Moses was the man whom he believed him to be, the Lord must open his eyes and show him that he had chosen him, Hosea, to lead the people through his mediation to a fairer future; nor did he doubt that He could easily win his father over to his side. He would even have declared a second time, with the firmest faith, that it was the Most High who had pointed out his path, and after reflecting upon all this he approached Miriam, who had at last risen, with fresh confidence. His loving heart prompted him to clasp her in his arms, but she thrust him back and her voice, usually so pure and clear, sounded harsh and muffled as she asked why he had lingered so long and what he intended to confide to her.

While cowering under the sycamore, she had not only struggled and prayed for composure, but also gazed into her own soul. She loved Hosea, but she suspected that he came with proposals similar to those of Uri, and the wrathful words of hoary Nun rang in her ears more loudly than ever. The fear that the man she loved was walking in mistaken paths, and the startling act of Hur had made the towering waves of her passion subside and her mind, now capable of calmer reflection, desired first of all to know what had so long detained him whom she had summoned in the name of her God, and why he came alone, without Ephraim.

The clear sky was full of stars, and these heavenly bodies, which seem to have been appointed to look down upon the bliss of united human lovers, now witnessed the anxious questions of a tortured girl and the impatient answers of a fiery, bitterly disappointed man.

He began with the assurance of his love and that he had come to make her his wife; but, though she permitted him to hold her hand in his clasp, she entreated him to cease pleading his suit and first tell her what she desired to know.

On his way he had received various reports concerning Ephraim through a brother-in-arms from Tanis, so he could tell her that the lad had been disobedient and, probably from foolish curiosity, had gone, ill and wounded, to the city, where he had found shelter and care in the house of a friend. But this troubled Miriam, who seemed to regard it as a reproach to know that the orphaned, inexperienced lad, who had grown up under her own eyes and whom she herself had sent forth among strangers, was beneath an Egyptian roof.

But Hosea declared that he would undertake the task of bringing him back to his people and as, nevertheless she continued to show her anxiety, asked whether he had forfeited her confidence and love. Instead of giving him a consoling answer, she began to put more questions, desiring to know what had delayed his coming, and so, with a sorely troubled and wounded heart, he was forced to make his report and, in truth, begin at the end of his story.

While she listened, leaning against the trunk of the sycamore, he paced to and fro, urged by longing and impatience, sometimes pausing directly in front of her. Naught in this hour seemed to him worthy of being clothed in words, save the hope and passion which filled his heart. Had he been sure that hers was estranged he would have dashed away again, after having revealed his whole soul to his father, and risked the ride into unknown regions to seek Moses. To win Miriam and save himself from perjury were his only desires, and momentous as had been his experiences and expectations, during the last few days, he answered her questions hastily, as if they concerned the most trivial things.

He began his narrative in hurried words, and the more frequently she interrupted him, the more impatiently he bore it, the deeper grew the lines in his forehead.

Hosea, accompanied by his attendant, had ridden southward several hours full of gladsome courage and rich in budding hopes, when just before dusk he saw a vast multitude moving in advance of him. At first he supposed he had encountered the rear-guard of the migrating Hebrews, and had urged his horse to greater speed. But, ere he overtook the wayfarers, some peasants and carters who had abandoned their wains and beasts of burden rushed past him with loud outcries and shouts of warning which told him that the people moving in front were lepers. And the fugitives' warning had been but too well founded; for the first, who turned with the heart-rending cry: "Unclean! Unclean!" bore the signs of those attacked by the fell disease, and from their distorted faces covered with white dust and scurf, lustreless eyes, destitute of brows, gazed at him.

Hosea soon recognized individuals, here Egyptian priests with shaven heads, yonder Hebrew men and women. With the stern composure of a soldier, he questioned both and learned that they were marching from the stone quarries opposite Memphis to their place of isolation on the eastern shore of the Nile. Several of the Hebrews among them had heard from their relatives that their people had left Egypt and gone to seek a land which the Lord had promised them. Many had therefore resolved to put their trust also in the mighty God of their fathers and follow the wanderers; the Egyptian priests, bound to the Hebrews by the tie of a common misfortune, had accompanied them, and fixed upon Succoth as the goal of their journey, knowing that Moses intended to lead his people there first. But every one who could have directed them on their way had fled before them, so they had kept too far northward and wandered near the fortress of Thabne. Hosea had met them a mile from this spot and advised them to turn back, that they might not bring their misfortune upon their fugitive brethren.

During this conversation, a body of Egyptian soldiers had marched from the fortress toward the lepers to drive them from the road; but their commander, who knew Hosea, used no violence, and both men persuaded the leaders of the lepers to accept the proposal to be guided to the peninsula of Sinai, where in the midst of the mountains, not far from the mines, a colony of lepers had settled. They had agreed to this plan because Hosea promised them that, if the tribes went eastward, they would meet them and receive everyone who was healed; but if the Hebrews remained in Egypt, nevertheless the pure air of the desert would bring health to many a sufferer, and every one who recovered would be free to return home.

These negotiations had consumed much time, and the first delay was followed by many others; for as Hosea had been in such close contact with the lepers, he was obliged to ride to Thabne, there with the commander of the garrison, who had stood by his side, to be sprinkled with bird's blood, put on new garments, and submit to certain ceremonies which he himself considered necessary and which could be performed only in the bright sunlight. His servant had been kept in the fortress because the kind-hearted man had shaken hands with a relative whom he met among the hapless wretches.

The cause of the delay had been both sorrowful and repulsive, and not until after Hosea had left Thabne in the afternoon and proceeded on his way to Succoth, did hope and joy again revive at the thought of seeing Miriam once more and bringing to his people a message that promised so much good.

His heart had never throbbed faster or with more joyous anticipation than on the nocturnal ride which led him to his father and the woman he loved, and on reaching his goal, instead of the utmost happiness, he now found only bitter disappointment.

He had reluctantly described in brief, disconnected sentences his meeting with the lepers, though he believed he had done his best for the welfare of these unfortunates. All of his warrior comrades had uttered a word of praise; but when he paused she whose approval he valued above aught else, pointed to a portion of the camp and said sadly: "They are of our blood, and our God is theirs. The lepers in Zoan, Pha-kos and Phibeseth followed the others at a certain distance, and their tents are pitched outside the camp. Those in Succoth—there are not many—will also be permitted to go forth with us; for when the Lord promised the people the Land for which they long, He meant lofty and lowly, poor and humble, and surely also the hapless ones who must now remain in the hands of the foe. Would you not have done better to separate the Hebrews from the Egyptians, and guide those of our own blood to us?"

The warrior's manly pride rebelled and his answer sounded grave and stern: "In war we must resolve to sacrifice hundreds in order to save thousands. The shepherds separate the scabby sheep to protect the flock."

"True," replied Miriam eagerly; "for the shepherd is a feeble man, who knows no remedy against contagion; but the Lord, who calls all His people, will suffer no harm to arise from rigid obedience."

"That is a woman's mode of thought," replied Hosea; "but what pity dictates to her must not weigh too heavily in the balance in the councils of men. You willingly obey the voice of the heart, which is most proper, but you should not forget what befits you and your sex."

A deep flush crimsoned Miriam's cheeks; for she felt the sting contained in this speech with two-fold pain because it was Hosea who dealt the thrust. How many pangs she had been compelled to endure that day on account of her sex, and now he, too, made her feel that she was not his peer because she was a woman. In the presence of the stones Hur had gathered, and on which her hand now rested, he had appealed to her verdict, as though she were one of the leaders of the people, and now he abruptly thrust her, who felt herself inferior to no man in intellect and talent, back into a woman's narrow sphere.

But he, too, felt his dignity wounded, and her bearing showed him that this hour would decide whether he or she would have the mastery in their future union. He stood proudly before her, his mien stern in its majesty—never before had he seemed so manly, so worthy of admiration. Yet the desire to battle for her insulted womanly dignity gained supremacy over every other feeling, and it was she who at last broke the brief, painful silence that had followed his last words, and with a composure won only by the exertion of all her strength of will, she began:

"We have both forgotten what detains us here so late at night. You wished to confide to me what brings you to your people and to hear, not what Miriam, the weak woman, but the confidante of the Lord decides."

"I hoped also to hear the voice of the maiden on whose love I rely," he answered gloomily.

"You shall hear it," she replied quickly, taking her hand from the stones. "Yet it may be that I cannot agree with the opinion of the man whose strength and wisdom are so far superior to mine, yet you have just shown that you cannot tolerate the opposition of a woman, not even mine."

"Miriam," he interrupted reproachfully, but she continued still more eagerly: "I have felt it, and because it would be the greatest grief of my life to lose your heart, you must learn to understand me, ere you call upon me to express my opinion."

"First hear my message."

"No, no!" she answered quickly. "The reply would die upon my lips. Let me first tell you of the woman who has a loving heart, and yet knows something else that stands higher than love. Do you smile? You have a right to do so, you have so long been a stranger to the secret I mean to confide...."

"Speak then!" he interrupted, in a tone which betrayed how difficult it was for him to control his impatience.

"I thank you," she answered warmly. Then leaning against the trunk of the ancient tree, while he sank down on the bench, gazing alternately at the ground and into her face, she began:

"Childhood already lies behind me, and youth will soon follow. When I was a little girl, there was not much to distinguish me from others. I played like them and, though my mother had taught me to pray to the God of our fathers, I was well pleased to listen to the other children's tales of the goddess Isis. Nay, I stole into her temple, bought spices, plundered our little garden for her, anointed her altar, and brought flowers for offerings. I was taller and stronger than many of my companions, and was also the daughter of Amram, so they followed me and readily did what I suggested. When I was eight years old, we moved hither from Zoan. Ere I again found a girl-playfellow, you came to Gamaliel, your sister's husband, to be cured of the wound dealt by a Libyan's lance. Do you remember that time when you, a youth, made the little girl a companion? I brought you what you needed and prattled to you of the things I knew, but you told me of bloody battles and victories, of flashing armor, and the steeds and chariots of the warrior, You showed me the ring your daring had won, and when the wound in your breast was cured, we roved over the pastures. Isis, whom you also loved, had a temple here, and how often I secretly slipped into the forecourt to pray for you and offer her my holiday-cakes. I had heard so much from you of Pharaoh and his splendor, of the Egyptians, and their wisdom, their art, and luxurious life, that my little heart longed to live among them in the capital; besides, it had reached my ears that my brother Moses had received great favors in Pharaoh's palace and risen to distinction in the priesthood. I no longer cared for our own people; they seemed to me inferior to the Egyptians in all respects.

"Then came the parting from you and, as my little heart was devout and expected all good gifts from the divine power, no matter what name it bore, I prayed for Pharaoh and his army, in whose ranks you were fighting.

"My mother sometimes spoke of the God of our fathers as a mighty protector, to whom the people in former days owed much gratitude, and told me many beautiful tales of Him; but she herself often offered sacrifices in the temple of Seth, or carried clover blossoms to the sacred bull of the sun-god. She, too, was kindly disposed toward the Egyptians, among whom her pride and joy, our Moses, had attained such high honors.

"So in happy intercourse with the others I reached my fifteenth year. In the evening, when the shepherds returned home, I sat with the young people around the fire, and was pleased when the sons of the shepherd princes preferred me to my companions and sought my love; but I refused them all, even the Egyptian captain who commanded the garrison of the storehouse; for I remembered you, the companion of my youth. My best possession would not have seemed too dear a price to pay for some magic spell that would have brought you to us when, at the festal games, I danced and sang to the tambourine while the loudest shouts of applause greeted me. Whenever many were listening I thought of you—then I poured forth like the lark the feelings that filled my heart, then my song was inspired by you and not by the fame of the Most High, to whom it was consecrated."

Here passion, with renewed power, seized the man, to whom the woman he loved was confessing so many blissful memories. Suddenly starting up, he extended his arms toward her; but she sternly repulsed him, that she might control the yearning which threatened to overpower her also.

Yet her deep voice had gained a new, strange tone as, at first rapidly and softly, then in louder and firmer accents, she continued:

"So I attained my eighteenth year and was no longer satisfied to dwell in Succoth. An indescribable longing, and not for you only, had taken possession of my soul. What had formerly afforded me pleasure now seemed shallow, and the monotony of life here in the remote frontier city amid shepherds and flocks, appeared dull and pitiful.

"Eleasar, Aaron's son, had taught me to read and brought me books, full of tales which could never have happened, yet which stirred the heart. Many also contained hymns and fervent songs such as one lover sings to another. These made a deep impression on my soul and, whenever I was alone in the evening, or at noon-day when the shepherds and flocks were far away in the fields, I repeated these songs or composed new ones, most of which were hymns in praise of the deity. Sometimes they extolled Amon with the ram's head, sometimes cow-headed Isis, and often, too, the great and omnipotent God who revealed Himself to Abraham, and of whom my mother spoke more and more frequently as she advanced in years. To compose such hymns in quiet hours, wait for visions revealing God's grandeur and splendor, or beautiful angels and horrible demons, became my favorite occupation. The merry child had grown a dreamy maiden, who let household affairs go as they would. And there was no one who could have warned me, for my mother had followed my father to the grave; and I now lived alone with my old aunt Rachel, unhappy myself, and a source of joy to no one. Aaron, the oldest of our family, had removed to the dwelling of his father-in-law Amminadab: the house of Amram, his heritage, had become too small and plain for him and he left it to me. My companions avoided me; for my mirthfulness had departed and I patronized them with wretched arrogance because I could compose songs and beheld more in my visions than all the other maidens.

"Nineteen years passed and, on the evening of my birthday, which no one remembered save Milcah, Eleasar's daughter, the Most High for the first time sent me a messenger. He came in the guise of an angel, and bade me set the house in order; for a guest, the person dearest to me on earth, was on the way.

"It was early and under this very tree; but I went home and, with old Rachel's help, set the house in order, and provided food, wine, and all else we offer to an honored guest. Noon came, the afternoon passed away, evening deepened into night, and morning returned, yet I still waited for the guest. But when the sum of that day was nearing the western horizon, the dogs began to bark loudly, and when I went to the door a powerful man, with tangled grey hair and beard, clad in the tattered white robes of a priest, hurried toward me. The dogs shrank back whining; but I recognized my brother.

"Our meeting after so long a separation at first brought me more fear than pleasure; for Moses was flying from the officers of the law because he had slain the overseer. You know the story.

"Wrath still glowed in his flashing eyes. He seemed to me like the god Seth in his fury, and each one of his slow words was graven upon my soul as by a hammer and chisel. Thrice seven days and nights he remained under my roof, and as I was alone with him and deaf Rachel, and he was compelled to remain concealed, no one came between us, and he taught me to know Him who is the God of our fathers.

"Trembling and despairing, I listened to his powerful words, which seemed to fall like rocks upon my breast, when he admonished me of God's requirements, or described the grandeur and wrath of Him whom no mind can comprehend, and no name can describe. Ah, when he spoke of Him and of the Egyptian gods, it seemed as if the God of my people stood before me like a giant, whose head touched the sky, and the other gods were creeping in the dust at his feet like whining curs.

"He taught me also that we alone were the people whom the Lord had chosen, we and no other. Then for the first time I was filled with pride at being a descendant of Abraham, and every Hebrew seemed a brother, every daughter of Israel a sister. Now, too, I perceived how cruelly my people had been enslaved and tortured. I had been blind to their suffering, but Moses opened my eyes and sowed in my heart hate, intense hate of their oppressors, and from this hate sprang love for the victims. I vowed to follow my brother and await the summons of my God. And lo, he did not tarry and Jehovah's voice spoke to me as with tongues.

"Old Rachel died. At Moses' bidding I gave up my solitary life and accepted the invitation of Aaron and Amminadab.

"So I became a guest in their household, yet led a separate life among them all. They did not interfere with me, and the sycamore here on their land became my special property. Beneath its shadow God commanded me to summon you and bestow on you the name 'Help of Jehovah'—and you, no longer Hosea, but Joshua, will obey the mandate of God and His prophetess."

Here the warrior interrupted the maiden's words, to which he had listened earnestly, yet with increasing disappointment:

"Ay, I have obeyed you and the Most High. But what it cost me you disdain to ask. Your story has reached the present time, yet you have made no mention of the days following my mother's death, during which you were our guest in Tanis. Have you forgotten what first your eyes and then your lips confessed? Have the day of your departure and the evening on the sea, when you bade me hope for and remember you, quite vanished from your memory? Did the hatred Moses implanted in your heart kill love as well as every other feeling?"

"Love?" asked Miriam, raising her large eyes mournfully to his. "Oh no. How could I forget that time, the happiest of my life! Yet from the day Moses returned from the wilderness by God's command to release the people from bondage—three months after my separation from you—I have taken no note of years and months, days and nights."

"Then you have forgotten those also?" Hosea asked harshly.

"Not so," Miriam answered, gazing beseechingly into his face. "The love that grew up in the child and did not wither in the maiden's heart, cannot be killed; but whoever consecrates one's life to the Lord...."

Here she suddenly paused, raised her hands and eyes rapturously, as if borne out of herself, and cried imploringly: "Thou art near me, Omnipotent One, and seest my heart! Thou knowest why Miriam took no note of days and years, and asked nothing save to be Thy instrument until her people, who are, also, this man's people, received what Thou didst promise."

During this appeal, which rose from the inmost depths of the maiden's heart, the light wind which precedes the coming of dawn had risen, and the foliage in the thick crown of the sycamore above Miriam's head rustled; but Hosea fairly devoured with his eyes the tall majestic figure, half illumined, half veiled by the faint glimmering light. What he heard and saw seemed like a miracle. The lofty future she anticipated for her people, and which must be realized ere she would permit herself to yield to the desire of her own heart, he believed that he was hearing to them as a messenger of the Lord. As if rapt by the noble enthusiasm of her soul, he rushed toward her, seized her hand, and cried in glad emotion: "Then the hour has come which will again permit you to distinguish months from days and listen to the wishes of your own soul. For to I, Joshua, no longer Hosea, but Joshua, come as the envoy of the Lord, and my message promises to the people whom I will learn to love as you do, new prosperity, and thus fulfils the promise of a new and better home, bestowed by the Most High."

Miriam's eyes sparkled brightly and, overwhelmed with grateful joy, she exclaimed:

"Thou hast come to lead us into the land which Jehovah promised to His people? Oh Lord, how measureless is thy goodness! He, he comes as Thy messenger."

"He comes, he is here!" Joshua enthusiastically replied, and she did not resist when he clasped her to his breast and, thrilling with joy, she returned his kiss.

CHAPTER XVI

Fear of her own weakness soon made Miriam release herself from her lover's embrace, but she listened with eager happiness, seeking some new sign from the Most High in Joshua's brief account of everything he had felt and experienced since her summons.

He first described the terrible conflict he endured, then how he regained entire faith and, obedient to the God of his people and his father's summons, went to the palace expecting imprisonment or death, to obtain release from his oath.

He told her how graciously the sorrowing royal pair had received him, and how he had at last taken upon himself the office of urging the leaders of his nation to guide them into the wilderness for a short time only, and then take them home to Egypt, where a new and beautiful region on the western bank of the river should be allotted to them. There no foreign overseer should henceforward oppress the workmen, but the affairs of the Hebrews should be directed by their own elders, and a man chosen by themselves appointed their head.

Lastly he said that he, Joshua, would be placed in command of the Hebrew forces and, as regent, mediate and settle disputes between them and the Egyptians whenever it seemed necessary.

United to her, a happy husband, he would care in the new land for even the lowliest of his race. On the ride hither he had felt as men do after a bloody battle, when the blast of trumpets proclaim victory. He had indeed a right to regard himself as the envoy of the Most High.

Here, however, he interrupted himself; for Miriam, who at first had listened with open ears and sparkling eyes, now showed a more and more anxious and troubled mien. When he at last spoke of making the people happy as her husband, she withdrew her hand, gazed timidly at his manly features, glowing with joyful excitement, and then as if striving to maintain her calmness, fixed her eyes upon the ground.

Without suspecting what was passing in her mind, Hosea drew nearer. He supposed that her tongue was paralyzed by maidenly shame at the first token of favor she had bestowed upon a man. But when at his last words, designating himself as the true messenger of God, she shook her head disapprovingly, he burst forth again, almost incapable of self-control in his sore disappointment:

"So you believe that the Lord has protected me by a miracle from the wrath of the mightiest sovereign, and permitted me to obtain from his powerful hand favors for my people, such as the stronger never grant to the weaker, simply to trifle with the joyous confidence of a man whom he Himself summoned to serve Him."

Miriam, struggling to force back her tears, answered in a hollow tone: "The stronger to the weaker! If that is your opinion, you compel me to ask, in the words of your own father: 'Who is the more powerful, the Lord our God or the weakling on the throne, whose first-born son withered like grass at a sign from the Most High. Oh, Hosea! Hosea!'"

"Joshua!" he interrupted fiercely. "Do you grudge me even the name your God bestowed? I relied upon His help when I entered the palace of the mighty king. I sought under God's guidance rescue and salvation for the people, and I found them. But you, you...."

"Your father and Moses, nay, all the believing heads of the tribes, see no salvation for us among the Egyptians," she answered, panting for breath. "What they promise the Hebrews will be their ruin. The grass sowed by us withers where their feet touch it! And you, whose honest heart they deceive, are the whistler whom the bird-catcher uses to decoy his feathered victims into the snare. They put the hammer into your hand to rivet more firmly than before the chains which, with God's aid, we have sundered. Before my mind's eye I perceive...."

"Too much!" replied the warrior, grinding his teeth with rage. "Hate dims your clear intellect. If the bird-catcher really—what was your comparison—if the bird-catcher really made me his whistler, deceived and misled me, he might learn from you, ay, from you! Encouraged by you, I relied upon your love and faith. From you I hoped all things—and where is this love? As you spared me nothing that could cause me pain, I will, pitiless to myself, confess the whole truth to you. It was not alone because the God of my fathers called me, but because His summons reached me through you and my father that I came. You yearn for a land in the far uncertain distance, which the Lord has promised you; but I opened to the people the door of a new and sure home. Not for their sakes—what hitherto have they been to me?—but first of all to live there in happiness with you whom I loved, and my old father. Yet you, whose cold heart knows naught of love, with my kiss still on your lips, disdain what I offer, from hatred of the hand to which I owe it. Your life, your conflicts have made you masculine. What other women would trample the highest blessings under foot?"

Miriam could bear no more and, sobbing aloud, covered her convulsed face with her hands.

At the grey light of dawn the sleepers in the camp began to stir, and men and maid servants came out of the dwellings of Amminadab and Naashon. All whom the morning had roused were moving toward the wells and watering places, but she did not see them.

How her heart had expanded and rejoiced when her lover exclaimed that he had come to lead them to the land which the Lord had promised to his people. Gladly had she rested on his breast to enjoy one brief moment of the greatest bliss; but how quickly had bitter disappointment expelled joy! While the morning breeze had stirred the crown of the sycamore and Joshua had told her what Pharaoh would grant to the Hebrews, the rustling among the branches had seemed to her like the voice of God's wrath and she fancied she again heard the angry words of hoary-headed Nun. The latter's reproaches had dismayed Uri like the flash of lightning, the roll of thunder, yet how did Joshua's proposition differ from Uri's?

The people—she had heard it also from the lips of Moses—were lost if, faithless to their God, they yielded to the temptations of Pharaoh. To wed a man who came to destroy all for which she, her brothers, and his own father lived and labored, was base treachery. Yet she loved Joshua and, instead of harshly repulsing him, she would have again nestled ah, how gladly, to the heart which she knew loved her so ardently.

But the leaves in the top of the tree continued to rustle and it seemed as if they reminded her of Aaron's warning, so she forced herself to remain firm.

The whispering above came from God, who had chosen her for His prophetess, and when Joshua, in passionate excitement, owned that the longing for her was his principal motive for toiling for the people, who were as unknown to him as they were dear to her, her heart suddenly seemed to stop beating and, in her mortal agony, she could not help sobbing aloud.

Unheeding Joshua, or the stir in the camp, she again flung herself down with uplifted arms under the sycamore, gazing upward with dilated, tearful eyes, as if expecting a new revelation. But the morning breeze continued to rustle in the summit of the tree, and suddenly everything seemed as bright as sunshine, not only within but around her, as always happened when she, the prophetess, was to behold a vision. And in this light she saw a figure whose face startled her, not Joshua, but another to whom her heart did not incline. Yet there he stood before the eyes of her soul in all his stately height, surrounded by radiance, and with a solemn gesture he laid his hand on the stones he had piled up.

With quickened breath, she gazed upward to the face, yet she would gladly have closed her eyes and lost her hearing, that she might neither see it nor catch the voices from the tree. But suddenly the figure vanished, the voices died away, and she appeared to behold in a bright, fiery glow, the first man her virgin lips had kissed, as with uplifted sword, leading the shepherds of her people, he dashed toward an invisible foe.

Swiftly as the going and coming of a flash of lightning, the vision appeared and vanished, yet ere it had wholly disappeared she knew its meaning.

The man whom she called "Joshua" and who seemed fitted in every respect to be the shield and leader of his people, must not be turned aside by love from the lofty duty to which the Most High had summoned him. None of the people must learn the message he brought, lest it should tempt them to turn aside from the dangerous path they had entered.

Her course was as plain as the vision which had just vanished. And, as if the Most High desired to show her that she had rightly understood its meaning, Hur's voice was heard near the sycamore—ere she had risen to prepare her lover for the sorrow to which she must condemn herself and him—commanding the multitude flocking from all directions to prepare for the departure.

The way to save him from himself lay before her; but Joshua had not yet ventured to disturb her devotions.

He had been wounded and angered to the inmost depths of his soul by her denial. But as he gazed down at her and saw her tall figure shaken by a sudden chill, and her eyes and hands raised heavenward as though, spellbound, he had felt that something grand and sacred dwelt within her breast which it would be sacrilege to disturb; nay, he had been unable to resist the feeling that it would be presumptuous to seek to wed a woman united to the Lord by so close a tie. It must be bliss indeed to call this exalted creature his own, yet it would be hard to see her place another, even though it were the Almighty Himself, so far above her lover and husband.

Men and cattle had already passed close by the sycamore and just as he was in the act of calling Miriam and pointing to the approaching throng, she rose, turned toward him, and forced from her troubled breast the words:

"I have communed with the Lord, Joshua, and now know His will. Do you remember the words by which God called you?"

He bent his head in assent; but she went on:

"Well then, you must also know what the Most High confided to your father, to Moses, and to me. He desires to lead us out of the land of Egypt, to a distant country where neither Pharaoh nor his viceroy shall rule over us, and He alone shall be our king. That is His will, and if He requires you to serve Him, you must follow us and, in case of war, command the men of our people."

Joshua struck his broad breast, exclaiming in violent agitation: "An oath binds me to return to Tanis to inform Pharaoh how the leaders of the people received the message with which I was sent forth. Though my heart should break, I cannot perjure myself."

"And mine shall break," gasped Miriam, "ere I will be disloyal to the Lord our God. We have both chosen, so let what once united us be sundered before these stones."

He rushed frantically toward her to seize her hand; but with an imperious gesture she waved him back, turned away, and went toward the multitude which, with sheep and cattle, were pressing around the wells.

Old and young respectfully made way for her as, with haughty bearing, she approached Hur, who was giving orders to the shepherds; but he came forward to meet her and, after hearing the promise she whispered, he laid his hand upon her head and said with solemn earnestness:

"Then may the Lord bless our alliance."

Hand in hand with the grey-haired man to whom she had given herself, Miriam approached Joshua. Nothing betrayed the deep emotion of her soul, save the rapid rise and fall of her bosom, for though her cheeks were pale, her eyes were tearless and her bearing was as erect as ever.

She left to Hur to explain to the lover whom she had forever resigned what she had granted him, and when Joshua heard it, he started back as though a gulf yawned at his feet.

His lips were bloodless as he stared at the unequally matched pair. A jeering laugh seemed the only fitting answer to such a surprise, but Miriam's grave face helped him to repress it and conceal the tumult of his soul by trivial words.

But he felt that he could not long succeed in maintaining a successful display of indifference, so he took leave of Miriam. He must greet his father, he said hastily, and induce him to summon the elders.

Ere he finished several shepherds hurried up, disputing wrathfully and appealed to Hur to decide what place in the procession belonged to each tribe. He followed them, and as soon as Miriam found herself alone with Joshua, she said softly, yet earnestly, with beseeching eyes:

"A hasty deed was needful to sever the tie that bound us, but a loftier hope unites us. As I sacrificed what was dearest to my heart to remain faithful to my God and people, do you, too, renounce everything to which your soul clings. Obey the Most High, who called you Joshua! This hour transformed the sweetest joy to bitter grief; may it be the salvation of our people! Remain a son of the race which gave you your father and mother! Be what the Lord called you to become, a leader of your race! If you insist on fulfilling your oath to Pharaoh, and tell the elders the promises with which you came, you will win them over, I know. Few will resist you, but of those few the first will surely be your own father. I can hear him raise his voice loudly and angrily against his own dear son; but if you close your ears even to his warning, the people will follow your summons instead of God's, and you will rule the Hebrews as a mighty man. But when the time comes that the Egyptian casts his promises to the winds, when you see your people in still worse bondage than before and behold them turn from the God of their fathers to again worship animal-headed idols, your father's curse will overtake you, the wrath of the Most High will strike the blinded man, and despair will be the lot of him who led to ruin the weak masses for whose shield the Most High chose him. So I, a feeble woman, yet the servant of the Most High and the maiden who was dearer to you than life, cry in tones of warning: Fear your father's curse and the punishment of the Lord! Beware of tempting the people."

Here she was interrupted by a female slave, who summoned her to her house—and she added in low, hurried accents: "Only this one thing more. If you do not desire to be weaker than the woman whose opposition roused your wrath, sacrifice your own wishes for the welfare of yonder thousands, who are of the same blood! With your hand on these stones you must swear...."

But here her voice failed. Her hands groped vainly for some support, and with a loud cry she sank on her knees beside Hur's token.

Joshua's strong arms saved her from falling prostrate, and several women who hurried up at his shout soon recalled the fainting maiden to life.

Her eyes wandered restlessly from one to another, and not until her glance rested on Joshua's anxious face did she become conscious where she was and what she had done. Then she hurriedly drank the water a shepherd's wife handed to her, wiped the tears from her eyes, sighed painfully, and with a faint smile whispered to Joshua: "I am but a weak woman after all."

Then she walked toward the house, but after the first few steps turned, beckoned to the warrior, and said softly:

"You see how they are forming into ranks. They will soon begin to move. Is your resolution still unshaken? There is still time to call the elders."

He shook his head, and as he met her tearful, grateful glance, answered gently:

"I shall remember these stones and this hour, wife of Hur. Greet my father for me and tell him that I love him. Repeat to him also the name by which his son, according to the command of the Most High, will henceforth be called, that its promise of Jehovah's aid may give him confidence when he hears whither I am going to keep the oath I have sworn."

With these words he waved his hand to Miriam and turned toward the camp, where his horse had been fed and watered; but she called after him: "Only one last word: Moses left a message for you in the hollow trunk of the tree."

Joshua turned back to the sycamore and read what the man of God had written for him. "Be strong and steadfast" were the brief contents, and raising his head he joyfully exclaimed: "Those words are balm to my soul. We meet here for the last time, wife of Hur, and, if I go to my death, be sure that I shall know how to die strong and steadfast; but show my old father what kindness you can."

He swung himself upon his horse and while trotting toward Tanis, faithful to his oath, his soul was free from fear, though he did not conceal from himself that he was going to meet great perils. His fairest hopes were destroyed, yet deep grief struggled with glad exaltation. A new and lofty emotion, which pervaded his whole being, had waked within him and was but slightly dimmed, though he had experienced a sorrow bitter enough to darken the light of any other man's existence. Naught could surpass the noble objects to which he intended to devote his blood and life—his God and his people. He perceived with amazement this new feeling which had power to thrust far into the background every other emotion of his breast— even love.

True, his head often drooped sorrowfully when he thought of his old father; but he had done right in repressing the eager yearning to clasp him to his heart. The old man would scarcely have understood his motives, and it was better for both to part without seeing each other rather than in open strife.

Often it seemed as though his experiences had been but a dream, and while he felt bewildered by the excitements of the last few hours, his strong frame was little wearied by the fatigues he had undergone.

At a well-known hostelry on the road, where he met many soldiers and among them several military commanders with whom he was well acquainted, he at last allowed his horse and himself a little rest and food; and as he rode on refreshed active life asserted its claims; for as far as the gate of the city of Rameses he passed bands of soldiers, and learned that they were ordered to join the cohorts he had himself brought from Libya.

At last he rode into the capital and as he passed the temple of Amon he heard loud lamentations, though he had learned on the way that the plague had ceased. What many a sign told him was confirmed at last by some passing guards—the first prophet and high-priest of Amon, the grey-haired Rui, had died in the ninety-eighth year of his life. Bai, the second prophet, who had so warmly protested his friendship and gratitude to Hosea, had now become Rui's successor and was high-priest and judge, keeper of the seals and treasurer, in short, the most powerful man in the realm.

∴

CHAPTER XVII

"Help of Jehovah!" murmured a state-prisoner, laden with heavy chains, five days later, smiling bitterly as, with forty companions in misfortune, he was led through the gate of victory in Tanis toward the east.

The mines in the Sinai peninsula, where more convict labor was needed, were the goal of these unfortunate men.

The prisoner's smile lingered a short time, then drawing up his muscular frame, his bearded lips murmured: "Strong and steadfast!" and as if he desired to transmit the support he had himself found he whispered to the youth marching at his side: "Courage, Ephraim, courage! Don't gaze down at the dust, but upward, whatever may come."

"Silence in the ranks!" shouted one of the armed Libyan guards, who accompanied the convicts, to the older prisoner, raising his whip with a significant gesture. The man thus threatened was Joshua, and his companion in suffering Ephraim, who had been sentenced to share his fate.

What this was every child in Egypt knew, for "May I be sent to the mines!" was one of the most terrible oaths of the common people, and no prisoner's lot was half so hard as that of the convicted state-criminals.

A series of the most terrible humiliations and tortures awaited them. The vigor of the robust was broken by unmitigated toil; the exhausted were forced to execute tasks so far beyond their strength that they soon found the eternal rest for which their tortured souls longed. To be sent to the mines meant to be doomed to a slow, torturing death; yet life is so dear to men that it was considered a milder punishment to be dragged to forced labor in the mines than to be delivered up to the executioner.

Joshua's encouraging words had little effect upon Ephraim; but when, a few minutes later, a chariot shaded by an umbrella, passed the prisoners, a chariot in which a slender woman of aristocratic bearing stood beside a matron behind the driver, he turned with a hasty movement and gazed after the equipage with sparkling eyes till it vanished in the dust of the road.

The younger woman had been closely veiled, but Ephraim thought he recognized her for whose sake he had gone to his ruin, and whose lightest sign he would still have obeyed.

And he was right; the lady in the chariot was Kasana, the daughter of Hornecht, captain of the archers, and the matron was her nurse.

At a little temple by the road-side, where, in the midst of a grove of Nile acacias, a well was maintained for travellers, she bade the matron wait for her and, springing lightly from the chariot which had left the prisoners some distance behind, she began to pace up and down with drooping head in the shadow of the trees, until the whirling clouds of dust announced the approach of the convicts.

Taking from her robe the gold rings she had ready for this purpose, she went to the man who was riding at its head on an ass and who led the mournful procession. While she was talking with him and pointing to Joshua, the guard cast a sly glance at the rings which had been slipped into his hand, and seeing a welcome yellow glitter when his modesty had expected only silver, his features instantly assumed an expression of obliging good-will.

True, his face darkened at Kasana's request, but another promise from the young widow brightened it again, and he now turned eagerly to his subordinates, exclaiming: "To the well with the moles, men! Let them drink. They must be fresh and healthy under the ground!"

Then riding up to the prisoners, he shouted to Joshua:

"You once commanded many soldiers, and look more stiff-necked now than beseems you and me. Watch the others, guards, I have a word or two to say to this man alone."

He clapped his hands as if he were driving hens out of a garden, and while the prisoners took pails and with the guards, enjoyed the refreshing drink, their leader drew Joshua and Ephraim away from the road—they could not be separated on account of the chain which bound their ancles together.

The little temple soon hid them from the eyes of the others, and the warder sat down on a step some distance off, first showing the two Hebrews, with a gesture whose meaning was easily understood, the heavy spear he carried in his hand and the hounds which lay at his feet.

He kept his eyes open, too, during the conversation that followed. They could say whatever they chose; he knew the duties of his office and though, for the sake of good money he could wink at a farewell, for twenty years, though there had been many attempts to escape, not one of his moles—a name he was fond of giving to the future miners—had succeeded in eluding his watchfulness.

Yonder fair lady doubtless loved the stately man who, he had been told, was formerly a chief in the army. But he had already numbered among his "moles," personages even more distinguished, and if the veiled woman managed to slip files or gold into the prisoner's hands, he would not object, for that very evening the persons of both would be thoroughly searched, even the youth's black locks, which would not have remained unshorn, had not everything been in confusion prior to the departure of the convicts, which took place just before the march of Pharaoh's army.

The watcher could not hear the whispered words exchanged between the degraded chief and the lady, but her humble manner and bearing led him to suppose that it was she who had brought the proud warrior to his ruin. Ah, these women! And the fettered youth! The looks he fixed upon the slender figure were ardent enough to scorch her veil. But patience! Mighty Father Amon! His moles were going to a school where people learned modesty!

Now the lady had removed her veil. She was a beautiful woman! It must be hard to part from such a sweetheart. And now she was weeping.

The rude warder's heart grew as soft as his office permitted; but he would fain have raised his scourge against the older prisoner; for was it not a shame to have such a sweetheart and stand there like a stone?

At first the wretch did not even hold out his hand to the woman who evidently loved him, while he, the watcher, would gladly have witnessed both a kiss and an embrace.

Or was this beauty the prisoner's wife who had betrayed him? No, no! How kindly he was now gazing at her. That was the manner of a father speaking to his child; but his mole was probably too young to have such a daughter. A mystery! But he felt no anxiety concerning its solution; during the march he had the power to make the most reserved convict an open book.

Yet not only the rude gaoler, but anyone would have marvelled what had brought this beautiful, aristocratic woman, in the grey light of dawn, out on the highway to meet the hapless man loaded with chains.

In sooth, nothing would have induced Kasana to take this step save the torturing dread of being scorned and execrated as a base traitress by the man whom she loved. A terrible destiny awaited him, and her vivid imagination had shown her Joshua in the mines, languishing, disheartened, drooping, dying, always with a curse upon her on his lips.

On the evening of, the day Ephraim bad been brought to the house, shivering with the chill caused by burning fever, and half stifled with the dust of the road, her father lead told her that in the youthful Hebrew they possessed a hostage to compel Hosea to return to Tanis and submit to the wishes of the prophet Bai, with whom she knew her father was leagued in a secret conspiracy. He also confided to her that not only great distinction and high offices, but a marriage with herself had been arranged to bind Hosea to the Egyptians and to a cause from which the chief of the archers expected the greatest blessings for himself, his house, and his whole country.

These tidings had filled her heart with joyous hope of a long desired happiness, and she confessed it to the prisoner with drooping head amid floods of tears, by the little wayside temple; for he was now forever lost to her, and though he did not return the love she had lavished on him from his childhood, he must not hate and condemn her without having heard her story.

Joshua listened willingly and assured her that nothing would lighten his heart more than to have her clear herself from the charge of having consigned him and the youth at his side to their most terrible fate.

Kasana sobbed aloud and was forced to struggle hard for composure ere she succeeded in telling her tale with some degree of calmness.

Shortly after Hosea's departure the chief-priest died and, on the same day Bai, the second prophet, became his successor. Many changes now took place, and the most powerful man in the kingdom filled Pharaoh with hatred of the Hebrews and their leader, Mesu, whom he and the queen had hitherto protected and feared. He had even persuaded the monarch to pursue the fugitives, and an army had been instantly summoned to compel their return. Kasana had feared that Hosea could not be induced to fight against the men of his own blood, and that he must feel incensed at being sent to make treaties which the Egyptians began to violate even before they knew whether their offers had been accepted.

When he returned—as he knew only too well—Pharaoh had had him watched like a prisoner and would not suffer him to leave his presence until he had sworn to again lead his troops and be a faithful servant to the king. Bai, the new chief priest, however, had not forgotten that Hosea had saved his life and showed himself well disposed and grateful to him; she knew also that he hoped to involve him in a secret enterprise, with which her father, too, was associated. It was Bai who had prevailed upon Pharaoh, if Hosea would renew his oath of fealty, to absolve him from fighting against his own race, put him in command of the foreign mercenaries and raise him to the rank of a "friend of the king." All these events, of course, were familiar to him; for the new chief priest had himself set before him the tempting dishes which, with such strong, manly defiance, he had thrust aside.

Her father had also sided with him, and for the first time ceased to reproach him with his origin.

But, on the third day after Hosea's return, Hornecht had gone to talk with him and since then everything had changed for the worse. He must be best aware what had caused the man of whom she, his daughter, must think no evil, to be changed from a friend to a mortal foe.

She had looked enquiringly at him as she spoke, and he did not refuse to answer—Hornecht had told him that he would be a welcome son-in-law.

"And you?" asked Kasana, gazing anxiously into his face.

"I," replied the prisoner, "was forced to say that though you had been dear and precious to me from your childhood, many causes forbade me to unite a woman's fate to mine."

Kasana's eyes flashed, and she exclaimed:

"Because you love another, a woman of your own people, the one who sent Ephraim to you!"

But Joshua shook his head and answered pleasantly:

"You are wrong, Kasana! She of whom you speak is the wife of another."

"Then," cried the young widow with fresh animation, gazing at him with loving entreaty, "why were you compelled to rebuff my father so harshly?"

"That was far from my intention, dear child," he replied warmly, laying his hand on her head. "I thought of you with all the tenderness of which my nature is capable. If I could not fulfil his wish, it was because grave necessity forbids me to yearn for the peaceful happiness by my own hearth-stone for which others strive. Had they given me my liberty, my life would have been one of restlessness and conflict."

"Yet how many bear sword and shield," replied Kasana, "and still, on their return, rejoice in the love of their wives and the dear ones sheltered beneath their roof."

"True, true," he answered gravely; "but special duties, unknown to the Egyptians, summon me. I am a son of my people."

"And you intend to serve them?" asked Kasana. "Oh, I understand you. Yet.... why then did you return to Tanis? Why did you put yourself into Pharaoh's power?"

"Because a sacred oath compelled me, poor child," he answered kindly.

"An oath," she cried, "which places death and imprisonment between you and those whom you love and still desire to serve. Oh, would that you had never returned to this abode of injustice, treachery, and ingratitude! To how many hearts this vow will bring grief and tears! But what do you men care for the suffering you inflict on others? You have spoiled all the pleasure of life for my hapless self, and among your own people dwells a noble father whose only son you are. How often I have seen the dear old man, the stately figure with sparkling eyes and snow-white hair. So would you look when you, too, had reached a ripe old age, as I said to myself, when I met him at the harbor, or in the fore-court of the palace, directing the shepherds who were driving the cattle and fleecy sheep to the tax-receiver's table. And now his son's obstinacy must embitter every day of his old age."

"Now," replied Joshua, "he has a son who is going, laden with chains, to endure a life of misery, but who can hold his head higher than those who betrayed him. They, and Pharaoh at their head, have forgotten that he has shed his heart's blood for them on many a battlefield, and kept faith with the king at every peril. Menephtah, his vice-roy and chief, whose life I saved, and many who formerly called me friend, have abandoned and hurled me and this guiltless boy into wretchedness, but those who have done this, woman, who have committed this crime, may they all...."

"Do not curse them!" interrupted Kasana with glowing cheeks.

But Joshua, unheeding her entreaty, exclaimed "Should I be a man, if I forgot vengeance?"

The young widow clung anxiously to his arm, gasping in beseeching accents:

"How could you forgive him? Only you must not curse him; for my father became your foe through love for me. You know his hot blood, which so easily carries him to extremes, despite his years. He concealed from me what he regarded as an insult; for he saw many woo me, and I am his greatest treasure. Pharaoh can pardon rebels more easily than my father can forgive the man who disdained his jewel. He behaved like one possessed when he returned. Every word he uttered was an invective. He could not endure to stay at home and raged just as furiously elsewhere. But no doubt he would have calmed himself at last, as he so often did before, had not some one who desired to pour oil on the flames met him in the fore-court of the palace. I learned all this from Bai's wife; for she, too, repents what she did to injure you; her husband used every effort to save you. She, who is as brave as any man, was ready to aid him and open the door of your prison; for she has not forgotten that you saved her husband's life in Libya. Ephraim's chains were to fall with yours, and everything was ready to aid your flight."

"I know it," Hosea interrupted gloomily, "and I will thank the God of my fathers if those were wrong from whom I heard that you are to blame, Kasana, for having our dungeon door locked more firmly."

"Should I be here, if that were so!" cried the beautiful, grieving woman with impassioned eagerness. "True, resentment did stir within me as it does in every woman whose lover scorns her; but the misfortune that befell you speedily transformed resentment into compassion, and fanned the old flames anew. So surely as I hope for a mild judgment before the tribunal of the dead, I am innocent and have not ceased to hope for your liberation. Not until yesterday evening, when all was too late, did I learn that Bai's proposal had been futile. The chief priest can do much, but he will not oppose the man who made himself my father's ally."

"You mean Prince Siptah, Pharaoh's nephew!" cried Joshua in excited tones. "They intimated to me the scheme they were weaving in his interest; they wished to put me in the place of the Syrian Aarsu, the commander of the mercenaries, if I would consent to let them have their way with my people and desert those of my own blood. But I would rather die twenty deaths than sully myself with such treachery. Aarsu is better suited to carry out their dark plans, but he will finally betray them all. So far as I am concerned, the prince has good reason to hate me."

Kasana laid her hand upon his lips, pointed anxiously to Ephraim and the guide, and said gently:

"Spare my father! The prince—what roused his enmity...."

"The profligate seeks to lure you into his snare and has learned that you favor me," the warrior broke in. She bent her head with a gesture of assent, and added blushing:

"That is why Aarsu, whom he has won over to his cause, watches you so strictly."

"And the Syrian will keep his eyes sufficiently wide open," cried Joshua. "Now let us talk no more of this. I believe you and thank you warmly for following us hapless mortals. How fondly I used to think, while serving in the field, of the pretty child, whom I saw blooming into maidenhood."

"And you will think of her still with neither wrath nor rancor?"

"Gladly, most gladly."

The young widow, with passionate emotion, seized the prisoner's hand to raise it to her lips, but he withdrew it; and, gazing at him with tears in her eyes, she said mournfully:

"You deny me the favor a benefactor does not refuse even to a beggar." Then, suddenly drawing herself up to her full height, she exclaimed so loudly that the warder started and glanced at the sun: "But I tell you the time will come when you will sue for the favor of kissing this hand in gratitude. For when the messenger arrives bringing to you and to this youth the liberty for which you have longed, it will be Kasana to whom you owe it."

Rapt by the fervor of the wish that animated her, her beautiful face glowed with a crimson flush. Joshua seized her right hand, exclaiming:

"Ah, if you could attain what your loyal soul desires! How could I dissuade you from mitigating the great misfortune which overtook this youth in your house? Yet, as an honest man, I must tell you that I shall never return to the service of the Egyptians; for, come what may, I shall in future cleave, body and soul, to those you persecute and despise, and to whom belonged the mother who bore me."

Kasana's graceful head drooped; but directly after she raised it again, saying:

"No other man is so noble, so truthful, that I have known from my childhood. If I can find no one among my own nation whom I can honor, I will remember you, whose every thought is true and lofty, whose nature is faultless. Put if poor Kasana succeeds in liberating you, do not scorn her, if you find her worse than when you left her, for however she may humiliate herself, whatever shame may come upon her...."

"What do you intend?" Hosea anxiously interrupted; but she had no time to answer; for the captain of the guard had risen and, clapping his hands, shouted: "Forward, you moles!" and "Step briskly."

The warrior's stout heart was overwhelmed with tender sadness and, obeying a hasty impulse, he kissed the beautiful unhappy woman on the brow and hair, whispering:

"Leave me in my misery, if our freedom will cost your humiliation. We shall probably never meet again; for, whatever may happen, my life will henceforth be nothing but battle and sacrifice. Darkness will shroud us in deeper and deeper gloom, but however black the night may be, one star will still shine for this boy and for me—the remembrance of you, my faithful, beloved child."

He pointed to Ephraim as he spoke and the youth, as if out of his senses, pressed his lips on the hand and arm of the sobbing woman.

"Forward!" shouted the leader again, and with a grateful smile helped the generous lady into the chariot, marvelling at the happy, radiant gaze with which her tearful eyes followed the convicts.

The horses started, fresh shouts arose, blows from the whips fell on bare shoulders, now and then a cry of pain rang on the morning air, and the train of prisoners again moved eastward. The chain on the ancles of the companions in suffering stirred the dust, which shrouded the little band like the grief, hate, and fear darkening the soul of each.

∴

CHAPTER XVIII

A long hour's walk beyond the little temple where the prisoners had rested the road, leading to Succoth and the western arm of the Red Sea, branched off from the one that ran in a southeasterly direction past the fortifications on the isthmus to the mines.

Shortly after the departure of the prisoners, the army which had been gathered to pursue the Hebrews left the city of Rameses, and as the convicts had rested some time at the well, the troops almost overtook them. They had not proceeded far when several runners came hurrying up to clear the road for the advancing army. They ordered the prisoners to move aside and defer their march until the swifter baggage train, bearing Pharaoh's tents and travelling equipments, whose chariot wheels could already be heard, had passed them.

The prisoners' guards were glad to stop, they were in no hurry. The day was hot, and if they reached their destination later, it would be the fault of the army.

The interruption was welcome to Joshua, too; for his young companion had been gazing into vacancy as if bewildered, and either made no answer to his questions or gave such incoherent ones that the older man grew anxious; he knew how many of those sentenced to forced labor went mad or fell into melancholy. Now a portion of the army would pass them, and the spectacle was new to Ephraim and promised to put an end to his dull brooding.

A sand-hill overgrown with tamarisk bushes rose beside the road, and thither the leader guided the party of convicts. He was a stern man, but not a cruel one, so he permitted his "moles" to lie down on the sand, for the troops would doubtless be a long time in passing. As soon as the convicts had thrown themselves on the ground the rattle of wheels, the neighing of fiery steeds, shouts of command, and sometimes the disagreeable braying of an ass were heard.

When the first chariots appeared Ephraim asked if Pharaoh was coming; but Joshua, smiling, informed him that when the king accompanied the troops to the field, the camp equipage followed directly behind the vanguard, for Pharaoh and his dignitaries wished to find the tents pitched and the tables laid, when the day's march was over and the soldiers and officers expected a night's repose.

Joshua had not finished speaking when a number of empty carts and unladen asses appeared. They were to carry the contributions of bread and meal, animals and poultry, wine and beer, levied on every village the sovereign passed on the march, and which had been delivered to the tax-gatherers the day before.

Soon after a division of chariot warriors followed. Every pair of horses drew a small, two-wheeled chariot, cased in bronze, and in each stood a warrior and the driver of the team. Huge quivers were fastened to the front of the chariots, and the soldiers leaned on their lances or on gigantic bows. Shirts covered with brazen scales, or padded coats of mail with gay overmantle, a helmet, and the front of the chariot protected the warrior from the missiles of the foe. This troop, which Joshua said was the van, went by at a slow trot and was followed by a great number of carts and wagons, drawn by horses, mules, or oxen, as well as whole troops of heavily-laden asses.

The uncle now pointed out to his nephew the long masts, poles, and heavy rolls of costly stuffs intended for the royal tent, and borne by numerous beasts of burden, as well as the asses and carts with the kitchen utensils and field forges. Among the baggage heaped on the asses, which were followed by nimble drivers, rode the physicians, tailors, salve-makers, cooks, weavers of garlands, attendants, and slaves belonging to the camp. Their departure had been so recent that they were still fresh and inclined to jest, and whoever caught sight of the convicts, flung them, in the Egyptian fashion, a caustic quip which many sought to palliate by the gift of alms. Others, who said nothing, also sent by the ass-drivers fruit and trifling gifts; for those who were free to-day might share the fate of these hapless men to-morrow. The captain permitted it, and when a passing slave, whom Joshua had sold for thieving, shouted the name of Hosea, pointing to him with a malicious gesture, the rough but kind-hearted officer offered his insulted prisoner a sip of wine from his own flask.

Ephraim, who had walked from Succoth to Tanis with a staff in his hand, and a small bundle containing bread, dried lamb, radishes, and dates, expressed his amazement at the countless people and things a single man needed for his comfort, and then relapsed into his former melancholy until his uncle roused him with farther explanations.

As soon as the baggage train had passed, the commander of the band of prisoners wished to set off, but the "openers of the way," who preceded the archers, forbade him, because it was not seemly for convicts to mingle with soldiers. So they remained on their hillock and continued to watch the troops.

The archers were followed by heavily-armed troops, bearing shields covered with strong hide so large that they extended from the feet to above the middle of the tallest men, and Hosea now told the youth that in the evening they set them side by side, thus surrounding the royal tent like a fence. Besides this weapon of defence they carried a lance, a short dagger-like sword, or a battle-sickle, and as these thousands were succeeded by a body of men armed with slings Ephraim for the first time spoke without being questioned and said that the slings the shepherds had taught him to make were far better than those of the soldiers and, encouraged by his uncle, he described in language so eager that the prisoners lying by his side listened, how he had succeeded in slaying not only jackals, wolves, and panthers, but even vultures, with stones hurled from a sling. Meanwhile he interrupted himself to ask the meaning of the standards and the names of the separate divisions.

Many thousands had already passed, when another troop of warriors in chariots appeared, and the chief warder of the prisoners exclaimed:

"The good god! The lord of two worlds! May life, happiness, and health be his!" With these words he fell upon his knees in the attitude of worship, while the convicts prostrated themselves to kiss the earth and be ready to obey the captain's bidding and join at the right moment in the cry: "Life, happiness, and health!"

But they had a long time to wait ere the expected sovereign appeared; for, after the warriors in the chariots had passed, the body-guard followed, foot-soldiers of foreign birth with singular ornaments on their helmets and huge swords, and then numerous images of the gods, a large band of priests and wearers of plumes. They were followed by more body-guards, and then Pharaoh appeared with his attendants. At their head rode the chief priest Bai in a gilded battle-chariot drawn by magnificent bay stallions. He who had formerly led troops in the field, had assumed the command of this pursuing expedition ordered by the gods and, though clad in priestly robes, he also wore the helmet and battle-axe of a general. At last, directly behind his equipage, came Pharaoh himself; but he did not go to battle like his warlike predecessors in a war-chariot, but preferred to be carried on a throne. A magnificent canopy protected him above, and large, thick, round ostrich feather fans, carried by his fan-bearers, sheltered him on both sides from the scorching rays of the sun.

After Menephtah had left the city and the gate of victory behind him, and the exulting acclamations of the multitude had ceased to amuse him, he had gone to sleep and the shading fans would have concealed his face and figure from the prisoners, had not their shouts been loud enough to rouse him and induce him to turn his head toward them. The gracious wave of his right hand showed that he had expected to see different people from convicts and, ere the shouts of the hapless men had died away, his eyes again closed.

Ephraim's silent brooding had now yielded to the deepest interest, and as the empty golden war-chariot of the king, before which pranced the most superb steeds he had ever seen, rolled by, he burst into loud exclamations of admiration.

These noble animals, on whose intelligent heads large bunches of feathers nodded, and whose rich harness glittered with gold and gems, were indeed a splendid sight. The large gold quivers set with emeralds, fastened on the sides of the chariot, were filled with arrows.

The feeble man to whose weak hand the guidance of a great nation was entrusted, the weakling who shrunk from every exertion, regained his lost energy whenever hunting was in prospect; he considered this campaign a chase on the grandest scale and as it seemed royal pastime to discharge his arrows at the human beings he had so lately feared, instead of at game, he had obeyed the chief priest's summons and joined the expedition. It had been undertaken by the mandate of the great god Amon, so he had little to dread from Mesu's terrible power.

When he captured him he would make him atone for having caused Pharaoh and his queen to tremble before him and shed so many tears on his account.

While Joshua was still telling the youth from which Phoenician city the golden chariots came, he suddenly felt Ephraim's right hand clutch his wrist, and heard him exclaim: "She! She! Look yonder! It is she!" The youth had flushed crimson, and he was not mistaken; the beautiful Kasana was passing amid Pharaoh's train in the same chariot in which she had pursued the convicts, and with her came a considerable number of ladies who had joined what the commander of the foot-soldiers, a brave old warrior, who had served under the great Rameses, termed "a pleasure party."

On campaigns through the desert and into Syria, Libya, or Ethiopia the sovereign was accompanied only by a chosen band of concubines in curtained chariots, guarded by eunuchs; but this time, though the queen had remained at home, the wife of the chief priest Bai and other aristocratic ladies had set the example of joining the troops, and it was doubtless tempting enough to many to enjoy the excitements of war without peril.

Kasana had surprised her friend by her appearance an hour before; only yesterday the young widow could not be persuaded to accompany the troops. Obeying an inspiration, without consulting her father, so unprepared that she lacked the necessary traveling equipments, she had joined the expedition, and it seemed as if a man whom she had hitherto avoided, though he was no less a personage than Siptah, the king's nephew, had become a magnet to her.

When she passed the prisoners, the prince was standing in the chariot beside the young beauty in her nurse's place, explaining in jesting tones the significance of the flowers in a bouquet, which Kasana declared could not possibly have been intended for her, because an hour and a quarter before she had not thought of going with the army.

But Siptah protested that the Hathors had revealed at sunrise the happiness in store for him, and that the choice of each single blossom proved his assertion.

Several young courtiers who were walking in front of their chariots, surrounded them and joined in the laughter and merry conversation, in which the vivacious wife of the chief priest shared, having left her large travelling-chariot to be carried in a litter.

None of these things escaped Joshua's notice and, as he saw Kasana, who a short time before had thought of the prince with aversion, now saucily tap his hand with her fan, his brow darkened and he asked himself whether the young widow was not carelessly trifling with his misery.

But the prisoners' chief warder had now noticed the locks on Siptah's temples, which marked him as a prince of the royal household and his loud "Hail! Hall!" in which the other guards and the captives joined, was heard by Kasana and her companions. They looked toward the tamarisk-bushes, whence the cry proceeded, and Joshua saw the young widow turn pale and then point with a hasty gesture to the convicts. She must undoubtedly have given Siptah some command, for the latter at first shrugged his shoulders disapprovingly then, after a somewhat lengthy discussion, half grave, half jesting, he sprang from the chariot and beckoned to the chief gaoler.

"Have these men," he called from the road so loudly that Kasana could not fail to hear, "seen the face of the good god, the lord of both worlds?" And when he received a reluctant answer, he went on arrogantly:

"No matter! At least they beheld mine and that of the fairest of women, and if they hope for favor on that account they are right. You know who I am. Let the chains that bind them together be removed." Then, beckoning to the man, he whispered:

"But keep your eyes open all the wider; I have no liking for the fellow beside the bush, the ex-chief Hosea. After returning home, report to me and bring news of this man. The quieter he has become, the deeper my hand will sink in my purse. Do you understand?"

The warder bowed, thinking: "I'll take care, my prince, and also see that no one attempts to take the life of any of my moles. The greater the rank of these gentlemen, the more bloody and strange are their requests! How many have come to me with similar ones. He releases the poor wretches' feet, and wants me to burden my soul with a shameful murder. Siptah has tried the wrong man! Here, Heter, bring the bag of tools and open the moles' chains."

While the files were grating on the sand-hill by the road and the prisoners were being released from the fetters on their ancles,—though for the sake of security each man's arms were bound together,—Pharaoh's host marched by.

Kasana had commanded Prince Siptah to release from their iron burden the unfortunates who were being dragged to a life of misery, openly confessing that she could not bear to see a chief who had so often been a guest of her house so cruelly humiliated. Bai's wife had supported her wish, and the prince was obliged to yield.

Joshua knew to whom he and Ephraim owed this favor, and received it with grateful joy.

Walking had been made easier for him, but his mind was more and more sorely oppressed with anxious cares.

The army passing yonder would have been enough to destroy down to the last man a force ten times greater than the number of his people. His people, and with them his father and Miriam,—who had caused him such keen suffering, yet to whom he was indebted for having found the way which, even in prison, he had recognized as the only right one—seemed to him marked out for a bloody doom; for, however powerful might be the God whose greatness the prophetess had praised in such glowing words, and to whom he himself had learned to look up with devout admiration,—untrained and unarmed bands of shepherds must surely and hopelessly succumb to the assault of this army. This certainty, strengthened by each advancing division, pierced his very soul. Never before had he felt such burning anguish, which was terribly sharpened when he beheld the familiar faces of his own troops, which he had so lately commanded, pass before him under the leadership of another. This time they were taking the field to hew down men of his own blood. This was pain indeed, and Ephraim's conduct gave him cause for fresh anxiety; since Kasana's appearance and interference in behalf of him and his companions in suffering, the youth had again lapsed into silence and gazed with wandering eyes at the army or into vacancy.

Now he, too, was freed from the chain, and Joshua asked in a whisper if he did not long to return to his people to help them resist so powerful a force, but Ephraim merely answered:

"When confronted with those hosts, they can do nothing but yield. What did we lack before the exodus? You were a Hebrew, and yet became a mighty chief among the Egyptians ere you obeyed Miriam's summons. In your place, I would have pursued a different course."

"What would you have done?" asked Joshua sternly.

"What?" replied the youth, the fire of his young soul blazing. "What? Only this, I would have remained where there is honor and fame and everything beautiful. You might have been the greatest of the great, the happiest of the happy—this I have learned, but you made a different choice."

"Because duty commanded it," Joshua answered gravely, "because I will no longer serve any one save the people among whom I was born."

"The people?" exclaimed Ephraim, contemptuously. "I know them, and you met them at Succoth. The poor are miserable wretches who cringe under the lash; the rich value their cattle above all else and, if they are the heads of the tribes, quarrel with one another. No one knows aught of what pleases the eye and the heart. They call me one of the richest of the race and yet I shudder when I think of the house I inherited, one of the best and largest. One who has seen more beautiful ones ceases to long for such an abode."

The vein on Joshua's brow swelled, and he wrathfully rebuked the youth for denying his own blood, and being a traitor to his people.

The guard commanded silence, for Joshua had raised his reproving voice louder, and this order seemed welcome to the defiant youth. When, during their march, his uncle looked sternly into his face or asked whether he had thought of his words, he turned angrily away, and remained mute and sullen until the first star had risen, the night camp had been made under the open sky, and the scanty prison rations had been served.

Joshua dug with his hands a resting place in the sand, and with care and skill helped the youth to prepare a similar one.

Ephraim silently accepted this help; but as they lay side by side, and the uncle began to speak to his nephew of the God of his people on whose aid they must rely, if they were not to fall victims to despair in the mines, the youth interrupted him, exclaiming in low tones, but with fierce resolution:

"They will not take me to the mines alive! I would rather die, while making my escape, than pine away in such wretchedness."

Joshua whispered words of warning, and again reminded him of his duties to his people. But Ephraim begged to be let alone; yet soon after he touched his uncle and asked softly:

"What are they planning with Prince Siptah?"

"I don't know; nothing good, that is certain."

"And where is Aarsu, the Syrian, your foe, who commands the Asiatic mercenaries, and who was to watch us with such fierce zeal? I did not see him with the others."

"He remained in Tanis with his troops."

"To guard the palace?"

"Undoubtedly."

"Then he commands many soldiers, and Pharaoh has confidence in him?"

"The utmost, though he ill deserves it."

"And he is a Syrian, and therefore of our blood."

"And more closely allied to us than to the Egyptians, at least so far as language and appearance are concerned."

"I should have taken him for a man of our race, yet he is, as you were, one of the leaders in the army."

"Other Syrians and Libyans command large troops of mercenaries, and the herald Ben Mazana, one of the highest dignitaries of the court—the Egyptians call him Rameses in the sanctuary of Ra—has a Hebrew father."

"And neither he nor the others are scorned on account of their birth?"

"This is not quite so. But why do you ask these questions?"

"I could not sleep."

"And so such thoughts came to you. But you have some definite idea in your mind and, if my inference is correct, it would cause me pain. You wished to enter Pharaoh's service!"

Both were silent a long time, then Ephraim spoke again and, though he addressed Joshua, it seemed as if he were talking to himself:

"They will destroy our people; bondage and shame await those who survive. My house is now left to ruin, not a head of my splendid herds of cattle remains, and the gold and silver I inherited, of which there was said to be a goodly store, they are carrying with them, for your father has charge of my wealth, and it will soon fall as booty into the hands of the Egyptians. Shall I, if I obtain my liberty, return to my people and make bricks? Shall I bow my back and suffer blows and abuse?"

Joshua eagerly whispered:

"You must appeal to the God of your fathers, that he may protect and defend His people. Yet, if the Most High has willed the destruction of our race, be a man and learn to hate with all the might of your young soul those who trample your people under their feet. Fly to the Syrians, offer them your strong young arm, and take no rest till you have avenged yourself on those who have shed the blood of your people and load you, though innocent, with chains."

Again silence reigned for some time, nothing was heard from Ephraim's rude couch save a dull, low moan from his oppressed breast; but at last he answered softly:

"The chains no longer weigh upon us, and how could I hate her who released us from them?"

"Remain grateful to Kasana," was the whispered reply, "but hate her nation."

Hosea heard the youth toss restlessly, and again sigh heavily and moan.

It was past midnight, the waxing moon rode high in the heavens, and the sleepless man did not cease to listen for sounds from the youth; but the latter remained silent, though slumber had evidently fled from him also; for a noise as if he were grinding his teeth came from his place of rest. Or had mice wandered to this barren place, where hard brown blades of grass grew between the crusts of salt and the bare spots, and were gnawing the prisoners' hard bread?

Such gnawing and grinding disturb the sleep of one who longs for slumber; but Joshua desired to keep awake to continue to open the eyes of the blinded youth, yet he waited in vain for any sign of life from his nephew.

At last he was about to lay his hand on the lad's shoulder, but paused as by the moonlight he saw Ephraim raise one arm though, before he lay down, both hands were tied more firmly than before.

Joshua now knew that it was the youth's sharp teeth gnawing the rope which had caused the noise that had just surprised him, and he immediately stood up and looked first upward and then around him.

Holding his breath, the older man watched every movement, and his heart began to throb anxiously. Ephraim meant to fly, and the first step toward escape had already succeeded! Would that the others might prosper too! But he feared that the liberated youth might enter the wrong path. He was the only son of his beloved sister, a fatherless and motherless lad, so he had never enjoyed the uninterrupted succession of precepts and lessons which only a mother can give and a defiant young spirit will accept from her alone. The hands of strangers had bound the sapling to a stake and it had shot straight upward, but a mother's love would have ennobled it with carefully chosen grafts. He had grown up beside another hearth than his parents', yet the latter is the only true home for youth. What marvel if he felt himself a stranger among his people.

Amid such thoughts a great sense of compassion stole over Joshua and, with it, the consciousness that he was deeply accountable for this youth who, for his sake, while on the way to bring him a message, had fallen into such sore misfortune. But much as he longed to warn him once more against treason and perjury, he refrained, fearing to imperil his success. Any noise might attract the attention of the guards, and he took as keen an interest in the attempt at liberation, as if Ephraim had made it at his suggestion.

So instead of annoying the youth with fruitless warnings, he kept watch for him; life had taught him that good advice is more frequently unheeded than followed, and only personal experiences possess resistless power of instruction.

The chief's practiced eye soon showed him the way by which Ephraim, if fortune favored him, could escape.

He called softly, and directly after his nephew whispered:

"I'll loose your ropes, if you will hold up your hands to me. Mine are free!"

Joshua's tense features brightened.

The defiant lad was a noble fellow, after all, and risked his own chance in behalf of one who, if he escaped with him, threatened to bar the way in which, in youthful blindness, he hoped to find happiness.

CHAPTER XIX

Joshua gazed intently around him. The sky was still bright, but if the north wind continued to blow, the clouds which seemed to be rising from the sea must soon cover it.

The air had grown sultry, but the guards kept awake and regularly relieved one another. It was difficult to elude their attention; yet close by Ephraim's couch, which his uncle, for greater comfort, had helped him make on the side of a gently sloping hill, a narrow ravine ran down to the valley. White veins of gypsum and glittering mica sparkled in the moonlight along its bare edges. If the agile youth could reach this cleft unseen, and crawl through as far as the pool of saltwater, overgrown with tall grass and tangled desert shrubs, at which it ended, he might, aided by the clouds, succeed.

After arriving at this conviction Joshua considered, as deliberately as if the matter concerned directing one of his soldiers on his way, whether he himself, in case he regained the use of his hands, could succeed in following Ephraim without endangering his project. And he was forced to answer this question in the negative; for the guard who sometimes sat, sometimes paced to and fro on a higher part of the crest of the hill a few paces away, could but too easily perceive, by the moonlight, the youth's efforts to loose the firmly-knotted bonds. The cloud approaching the moon might perhaps darken it, ere the work was completed. Thus Ephraim might, on his account, incur the peril of losing the one fortunate moment which promised escape. Would it not be the basest of crimes, merely for the sake of the uncertain chance of flight, to bar the path to liberty of the youth whose natural protector he was? So he whispered to Ephraim:

"I cannot go with you. Creep through the chasm at your right to the salt-pool. I will watch the guards. As soon as the cloud passes over the moon and I clear my throat, start off. If you escape, join our people. Greet my old father, assure him of my love and fidelity, and tell him where I am being taken. Listen to his advice and Miriam's; theirs is the best counsel. The cloud is approaching the moon,—not another word now!"

As Ephraim still continued to urge him in a whisper to hold up his pinioned arms, he ordered him to keep silence and, as soon as the moon was obscured and the guard, who was pacing to and fro above their heads began a conversation with the man who came to relieve him, Joshua cleared his throat and, holding his breath, listened with a throbbing heart for some sound in the direction of the chasm.

He first heard a faint scraping and, by the light of the fire which the guards kept on the hill-top as a protection against wild beasts, he saw Ephraim's empty couch.

He uttered a sigh of relief; for the youth must have entered the ravine. But though he strained his ears to follow the crawling or sliding of the fugitive he heard nothing save the footsteps and voices of the warders.

Yet he caught only the sound, not the meaning of their words, so intently did he fix his powers of hearing upon the course taken by the fugitive. How nimbly and cautiously the agile fellow must move! He was still in the chasm, yet meanwhile the moon struggled victoriously with the clouds and suddenly her silver disk pierced the heavy black curtain that concealed her from the gaze of men, and her light was reflected like a slender, glittering pillar from the motionless pool of salt-water, enabling the watching Joshua to see what was passing below; but he perceived nothing that resembled a human form.

Had the fugitive encountered any obstacle in the chasm? Did some precipice or abyss hold him in its gloomy depths? Had—and at the thought he fancied that his heart had stopped beating—Had some gulf swallowed the lad when he was groping his way through the night?

How he longed for some noise, even the faintest, from the ravine! The silence was terrible. But now! Oh, would that it had continued! Now the sound of falling stones and the crash of earth sliding after echoed loudly through the still night air. Again the moonlight burst through the cloud-curtain, and Joshua perceived near the pool a living creature which resembled an animal more than a human being, for it seemed to be crawling on four feet. Now the water sent up a shower of glittering spray. The figure below had leaped into the pool. Then the clouds again swallowed the lamp of night, and darkness covered everything.

With a sigh of relief Joshua told himself that he had seen the flying Ephraim and that, come what might, the escaping youth had gained a considerable start of his pursuers.

But the latter neither remained inert nor allowed themselves to be deceived; for though, to mislead them, he had shouted loudly: "A jackal!" they uttered a long, shrill whistle, which roused their sleeping comrades. A few seconds later the chief warder stood before him with a burning torch, threw its light on his face, and sighed with relief when he saw him. Not in vain had he bound him with double ropes; for he would have been called to a severe reckoning at home had this particular man escaped.

But while he was feeling the ropes on the prisoner's arms, the glare of the burning torch, which lighted him, fell on the fugitive's rude, deserted couch. There, as if in mockery, lay the gnawed rope. Taking it up, he flung it at Joshua's feet, blew his whistle again and again, and shouted: "Escaped! The Hebrew! Young Curly-head!"

Paying no farther heed to Joshua, he began the pursuit. Hoarse with fury, he issued order after order, each one sensible and eagerly obeyed.

While some of the guards dragged the prisoners together, counted them, and tied them with ropes, their commander, with the others and his dogs, set off on the track of the fugitive.

Joshua saw him make the intelligent animals smell Ephraim's gnawed bonds and resting-place, and beheld them instantly rush to the ravine. Gasping for breath, he also noted that they remained in it quite a long time, and at last—the moon meanwhile scattered the clouds more and more—darted out of the ravine, and dashed to the water. He felt that it was fortunate Ephraim had waded through instead of passing round it; for at its edge the dogs lost the scent, and minute after minute elapsed while the commander of the guards walked along the shore with the eager animals, which fairly thrust their noses into the fugitive's steps, in order to again get on the right trail. Their loud, joyous barking at last announced that they had found it. Yet, even if they persisted in following the runaway, the captive warrior no longer feared the worst, for Ephraim had gained a long advance of his pursuers. Still, his heart beat loudly enough and time seemed to stand still until the chief-warder returned exhausted and unsuccessful.

The older man, it is true, could never have overtaken the swift-footed youth, but the youngest and most active guards had been sent after the fugitive. This statement the captain of the guards himself made with an angry jeer.

The kindly-natured man seemed completely transformed,—for he felt what had occurred as a disgrace which could scarcely be overcome, nay, a positive misfortune.

The prisoner who had tried to deceive him by the shout of 'jackal!' was doubtless the fugitive's accomplice. Prince Siptah, too, who had interfered with the duties of his office, he loudly cursed. But nothing of the sort should happen again; and he would make the whole band feel what had fallen to his lot through Ephraim. Therefore he ordered the prisoners to be again loaded with chains, the ex-chief fastened to a coughing old man, and all made to stand in rank and file before the fire till morning dawned.

Joshua gave no answer to the questions his new companion-in-chains addressed to him; he was waiting with an anxious heart for the return of the pursuers. At times he strove to collect his thoughts to pray, and commended to the God who had promised His aid, his own destiny and that of the fugitive boy. True, he was often rudely interrupted by the captain of the guards, who vented his rage upon him.

Yet the man who had once commanded thousands of soldiers quietly submitted to everything, forcing himself to accept it like the unavoidable discomfort of hail or rain; nay, it cost him an effort to conceal his joyful emotion when, toward sunrise, the young warders sent in pursuit returned with tangled hair, panting for breath, and bringing nothing save one of the dogs with a broken skull.

The only thing left for the captain of the guards to do was to report what had occurred at the first fortress on the Etham border, which the prisoners were obliged in any case to pass, and toward this they were now driven.

Since Ephraim's flight a new and more cruel spirit had taken possession of the warders. While yesterday they had permitted the unfortunate men to move forward at an easy pace, they now forced them to the utmost possible speed. Besides, the atmosphere was sultry, and the scorching sun struggled with the thunderclouds gathering in heavy masses at the north.

Joshua's frame, inured to fatigues of every kind, resisted the tortures of this hurried march; but his weaker companion, who had grown grey in a scribe's duties, often gave way and at last lay prostrate beside him.

The captain was obliged to have the hapless man placed on an ass and chain another prisoner to Joshua. He was his former yoke-mate's brother, an inspector of the king's stables, a stalwart Egyptian, condemned to the mines solely on account of the unfortunate circumstance of being the nearest blood relative of a state criminal.

It was easier to walk with this vigorous companion, and Joshua listened with deep sympathy and tried to comfort him when, in a low voice, he made him the confidant of his yearning, and lamented the heaviness of heart with which he had left wife and child in want and suffering. Two sons had died of the pestilence, and it sorely oppressed his soul that he had been unable to provide for their burial—now his darlings would be lost to him in the other world also and forever.

At the second halt the troubled father became franker still. An ardent thirst for vengeance filled his soul, and he attributed the same feeling to his stern-eyed companion, whom he saw had plunged into misfortune from a high station in life. The ex-inspector of the stables had a sister-in-law, who was one of Pharaoh's concubines, and through her and his wife, her sister, he had learned that a conspiracy was brewing against the king in the House of the Separated.—[Harem]. He even knew whom the women desired to place in Menephtah's place.

As Joshua looked at him, half questioning, half doubting, his companion whispered. "Siptah, the king's nephew, and his noble mother, are at the head of the plot. When I am once more free, I will remember you, for my sister-in-law certainly will not forget me." Then he asked what was taking his companion to the mines, and Joshua frankly told his name. But when the Egyptian learned that he was fettered to a Hebrew, he tore wildly at his chain and cursed his fate. His rage, however, soon subsided in the presence of the strange composure with which his companion in misfortune bore the rudest insults, and Joshua was glad to have the other beset him less frequently with complaints and questions.

He now walked on for hours undisturbed, free to yield to his longing to collect his thoughts, analyze the new and lofty emotions which had ruled his soul during the past few days, and accommodate himself to his novel and terrible position.

This quiet reflection and self-examination relieved him and, during the following night, he was invigorated by a deep, refreshing sleep.

When he awoke the setting stars were still in the sky and reminded him of the sycamore in Succoth, and the momentous morning when his lost love had won him for his God and his people. The glittering firmament arched over his head, and he had never so distinctly felt the presence of the Most High. He believed in His limitless power and, for the first time, felt a dawning hope that the Mighty Lord who had created heaven and earth would find ways and means to save His chosen people from the thousands of the Egyptian hosts.

After fervently imploring God to extend His protecting hand over the feeble bands who, obedient to His command, had left so much behind them and marched so confidently through an unknown and distant land, and commended to His special charge the aged father whom he himself could not defend, a wonderful sense of peace filled his soul.

The shouts of the guards, the rattling of the chain, his wretched companions in misfortune, nay, all that surrounded him, could not fail to recall the fate awaiting him. He was to grow grey in slavish toil within a close, hot pit, whose atmosphere choked the lungs, deprived of the bliss of breathing the fresh air and beholding the sunlight; loaded with chains, beaten and insulted, starving and thirsting, spending days and nights in a monotony destructive alike to soul and body,—yet not for one moment did he lose the confident belief that this horrible lot might befall any one rather than himself, and something must interpose to save him.

On the march farther eastward, which began with the first grey dawn of morning, he called this resolute confidence folly, yet strove to retain it and succeeded.

The road led through the desert, and at the end of a few hours' rapid march they reached the first fort, called the Fortress of Seti. Long before, they had seen it through the clear desert air, apparently within a bowshot.

Unrelieved by the green foliage of bush or palmtree, it rose from the bare, stony, sandy soil, with its wooden palisades, its rampart, its escarped walls, and its lookout, with broad, flat roof, swarming with armed warriors. The latter had heard from Pithom that the Hebrews were preparing to break through the chain of fortresses on the isthmus and had at first mistaken the approaching band of prisoners for the vanguard of the wandering Israelites.

From the summits of the strong projections, which jutted like galleries from every direction along the entire height of the escarped walls to prevent the planting of scaling-ladders, soldiers looked through the embrasures at the advancing convicts; yet the archers had replaced their arrows in the quivers, for the watchmen in the towers perceived how few were the numbers of the approaching troop, and a messenger had already delivered to the commander of the garrison an order from his superior authorizing him to permit the passage of the prisoners.

The gate of the palisade was now opened, and the captain of the guards allowed the prisoners to lie down on the glowing pavement within.

No one could escape hence, even if the guards withdrew; for the high fence was almost insurmountable, and from the battlements on the top of the jutting walls darts could easily reach a fugitive.

The ex-chief did not fail to note that everything was ready, as if in the midst of war, for defence against a foe. Every man was at his post, and beside the huge brazen disk on the tower stood sentinels, each holding in his hand a heavy club to deal a blow at the approach of the expected enemy; for though as far as the eye could reach, neither tree nor house was visible, the sound of the metal plate would be heard at the next fortress in the Etham line, and warn or summon its garrison.

To be stationed in the solitude of this wilderness was not a punishment, but a misfortune; and the commander of the army therefore provided that the same troops should never remain long in the desert.

Joshua himself, in former days, had been in command of the most southerly of these fortresses, called the Migdol of the South; for each one of the fortifications bore the name of Migdol, which in the Semitic tongue means the tower of a fortress.

His people were evidently expected here; and it was not to be supposed that Moses had led the tribes back to Egypt. So they must have remained in Succoth or have turned southward. But in that direction rolled the waters of the Bitter Lakes and the Red Sea, and how could the Hebrew hosts pass through the deep waters?

Hosea's heart throbbed anxiously at this thought, and all his fears were to find speedy confirmation; for he heard the commander of the fortress tell the captain of the prisoners' guards, that the Hebrews had approached the line of fortifications several days before, but soon after, without assaulting the garrison, had turned southward. Since then they seemed to have been wandering in the desert between Pithom and the Red Sea.

All this had been instantly reported at Tanis, but the king was forced to delay the departure of the army for several days until the week of general mourning for the heir to the throne had expired. The fugitives might have turned this to account, but news had come by a carrier dove that the blinded multitude had encamped at Pihahiroth, not far from the Red Sea. So it would be easy for the army to drive them into the water like a herd of cattle; there was no escape for them in any other direction.

The captain listened to these tidings with satisfaction; then he whispered a few words to the commander of the fortress and pointed with his finger to Joshua, who had long recognized him as a brother-in-arms who had commanded a hundred men in his own cohorts and to whom he had done many a kindness. He was reluctant to reveal his identity in this wretched plight to his former subordinate, who was also his debtor; but the commander flushed as he saw him, shrugged his shoulders as though he desired to express to Joshua regret for his fate and the impossibility of doing anything for him, and then exclaimed so loudly that he could not fail to hear:

"The regulations forbid any conversation with prisoners of state, but I knew this man in better days, and will send you some wine which I beg you to share with him."

As he walked with the other to the gate, and the latter remarked that Hosea deserved such favor less than the meanest of the band, because he had connived at the escape of the fugitive of whom he had just spoken, the commander ran his hand through his hair, and answered:

"I would gladly have shown him some kindness, though he is much indebted to me; but if that is the case, we will omit the wine; you have rested long enough at any rate."

The captain angrily gave the order for departure, and drove the hapless band deeper into the desert toward the mines.

This time Joshua walked with drooping head. Every fibre of his being rebelled against the misfortune of being dragged through the wilderness at this decisive hour, far from his people and the father whom he knew to be in such imminent danger. Under his guidance the wanderers might perchance have found some means of escape. His fist clenched when he thought of the fettered limbs which forbade him to utilize the plans his brain devised for the welfare of his people; yet he would not lose courage, and whenever he said to himself that the Hebrews were lost and must succumb in this struggle, he heard the new name God Himself had bestowed upon him ring in his ears and at the same moment the flames of hate and vengeance on all Egyptians, which had been fanned anew by the fortress commander's base conduct, blazed up still more brightly. His whole nature was in the most violent tumult and as the captain noted his flushed cheeks and the gloomy light in his eyes he thought that this strong man, too, had been seized by the fever to which so many convicts fell victims on the march.

When, at the approach of darkness, the wretched band sought a night's rest in the midst of the wilderness, a terrible conflict of emotions was seething in Joshua's soul, and the scene around him fitly harmonized with his mood; for black clouds had again risen in the north from the sea and, before the thunder and lightning burst forth and the rain poured in torrents, howling, whistling winds swept masses of scorching sand upon the recumbent prisoners.

After these dense clouds had been their coverlet, pools and ponds were their beds. The guards had bound them together hand and foot and, dripping and shivering, held the ends of the ropes in their hands; for the night was as black as the embers of their fire which the rain had extinguished, and who could have pursued a fugitive through such darkness and tempest.

But Joshua had no thought of secret flight. While the Egyptians were trembling and moaning, when they fancied they heard the wrathful voice of Seth, and the blinding sheets of fire flamed from the clouds, he only felt the approach of the angry God, whose fury he shared, whose hatred was also his own. He felt himself a witness of His all-destroying omnipotence, and his breast swelled more proudly as he told himself that he was summoned to wield the sword in the service of this Mightiest of the Mighty.

CHAPTER XX

The storm which had risen as night closed in swept over the isthmus. The waves in its lakes dashed high, and the Red Sea, which thrust a bay shaped like the horn of a snail into it from the south, was lashed to the wildest fury.

Farther northward, where Pharaoh's army, protected by the Migdol of the South, the strongest fort of the Etham line, had encamped a short time before, the sand lashed by the storm whirled through the air and, in the quarter occupied by the king and his great officials, hammers were constantly busy driving the tent-pins deeper into the earth; for the brocades, cloths, and linen materials which formed the portable houses of Pharaoh and his court, struck by the gale, threatened to break from the poles by which they were supported.

Black clouds hung in the north, but the moon and stars were often visible, and flashes of distant lightning frequently brightened the horizon. Even now the moisture of heaven seemed to avoid this rainless region and in all directions fires were burning, which the soldiers surrounded in double rows, like a living shield, to keep the storm from scattering the fuel.

The sentries had a hard duty; for the atmosphere was sultry, in spite of the north wind, which still blew violently, driving fresh clouds of sand into their faces.

Only two sentinels were pacing watchfully to and fro at the most northern gate of the camp, but they were enough; for, on account of the storm, no one had appeared for a long time to demand entrance or egress. At last, three hours after sunset, a slender figure, scarcely beyond boyhood, approached the guards with a firm step and, showing a messenger's pass, asked the way to Prince Siptah's tent.

He seemed to have had a toilsome journey; for his thick black locks were tangled and his feet were covered with dust and dried clay. Yet he excited no suspicion; for his bearing was that of a self-reliant freeman, his messenger's pass was perfectly correct, and the letter he produced was really directed to Prince Siptah; a scribe of the corn storehouses, who was sitting at the nearest fire with other officials and subordinate officers, examined it.

As the youth's appearance pleased most of those present, and he came from Tanis and perhaps brought news, a seat at the fire and a share in the meal were offered; but he was in haste.

Declining the invitation with thanks, he answered the questions curtly and hurriedly and begged the resting soldiers for a guide. One was placed at his disposal without delay. But he was soon to learn that it would not be an easy matter to reach a member of the royal family; for the tents of Pharaoh, his relatives, and dignitaries stood in a special spot in the heart of the camp, hedged in by the shields of the heavily-armed troops.

When he entered he was challenged again and again, and his messenger's pass and the prince's letter were frequently inspected. The guide, too, was sent back, and his place was filled by an aristocratic lord, called I the 'eye and ear of the king,' who busied himself with the seal of the letter. But the messenger resolutely demanded it, and as soon as it was again in his hand, and two tents standing side by side rocking in the tempest had been pointed out to him, one as Prince Siptah's, the other as the shelter of Masana, the daughter of Hornecht, for whom he asked, he turned to the chamberlain who came out of the former one, showed him the letter, and asked to be taken to the prince; but the former offered to deliver the letter to his master—whose steward he was—and Ephraim—for he was the messenger—agreed, if he would obtain him immediate admission to the young widow.

The steward seemed to lay much stress upon getting possession of the letter and, after scanning Ephraim from top to toe, he asked if Kasana knew him, and when the other assented, adding that he brought her a verbal message, the Egyptian said smiling:

"Well then; but we must protect our carpets from such feet, and you seem weary and in need of refreshment. Follow me."

With these words he took him to a small tent, before which an old slave and one scarcely beyond childhood were sitting by the fire, finishing their late meal with a bunch of garlic.

They started up as they saw their master; but he ordered the old man to wash the messenger's feet, and bade the younger ask the prince's cook in his name for meat, bread, and wine. Then he led Ephraim to his tent, which was lighted by a lantern, and asked how he, who from his appearance was neither a slave nor a person of mean degree, had come into such a pitiable plight. The messenger replied that on his way he had bandaged the wounds of a severely injured man with the upper part of his apron, and the chamberlain instantly went to his baggage and gave him a piece of finely plaited linen.

Ephraim's reply, which was really very near the truth, had cost him so little thought and sounded so sincere, that it won credence, and the steward's kindness seemed to him so worthy of gratitude that he made no objection when the courtier, without injuring the seal, pressed the roll of papyrus with a skilful hand, separating the layers and peering into the openings to decipher the contents. While thus engaged, the corpulent courtier's round eyes sparkled brightly and it seemed to the youth as if the countenance of the man, whose comfortable plumpness and smooth rotundity at first appeared like a mirror of the utmost kindness of heart, now had the semblance of a cat's.

As soon as the steward had completed his task, he begged the youth to refresh himself in all comfort, and did not return until Ephraim had bathed, wrapped a fresh linen upper-garment around his hips, perfumed and anointed his hair, and, glancing into the mirror, was in the act of slipping a broad gold circlet upon his arm.

He had hesitated some time ere doing this; for he was aware that he would encounter great perils; but this circlet was his one costly possession and, during his captivity, it had been very difficult for him to hide it under his apron. It might be of much service to him but, if he put it on, it would attract attention and increase the danger of being recognized.

Yet the reflection he beheld in the mirror, vanity, and the desire to appear well in Kasana's eyes, conquered caution and prudent consideration, and the broad costly ornament soon glittered on his arm.

The steward stood in astonishment before the handsome, aristocratic youth, so haughty in his bearing, who had taken the place of the unassuming messenger. The question whether he was a relative of Kasana sprang to his lips, and receiving an answer in the negative, he asked to what family he belonged.

Ephraim bent his eyes on the ground for some time in embarrassment, and then requested the Egyptian to spare him an answer until he had talked with Hornecht's daughter.

The other, shaking his head, looked at him again, but pressed him no farther; for what he had read in the letter was a secret which might bring death to whoever was privy to it, and the aristocratic young messenger was doubtless the son of a dignitary who belonged to the circle of the fellow-conspirators of Prince Siptah, his master.

A chill ran through the courtier's strong, corpulent body, and he gazed with mingled sympathy and dread at the blooming human flower associated thus early in plans fraught with danger.

His master had hitherto only hinted at the secret, and it would still be possible for him to keep his own fate separate from his. Should he do so, an old age free from care lay before him; but, if he joined the prince and his plan succeeded, how high he might rise! Terribly momentous was the choice confronting him, the father of many children, and beads of perspiration stood on his brow as, incapable of any coherent thought, he led Ephraim to Kasana's tent, and then hastened to his master.

Silence reigned within the light structure, which was composed of poles and gay heavy stuffs, tenanted by the beautiful widow.

With a throbbing heart Ephraim approached the entrance, and when he at last summoned courage and drew aside the curtain fastened firmly to the earth, which the wind puffed out like a sail, he beheld a dark room, from which a similar one opened on the right and left. The one on the left was as dark as the central one; but a flickering light stole through numerous chinks of the one on the right. The tent was one of those with a flat roof, divided into three apartments, which he had often seen, and the woman who irresistibly attracted him was doubtless in the lighted one.

To avoid exposing himself to fresh suspicion, he must conquer his timid delay, and he had already stooped and loosed the loop which fastened the curtain to the hook in the floor, when the door of the lighted room opened and a woman's figure entered the dark central chamber.

Was it she?

Should he venture to speak to her? Yes, it must be done.

Panting for breath and clenching his hands, he summoned up his courage as if he were about to steal unbidden into the most sacred sanctuary of a temple. Then he pushed the curtain aside, and the woman whom he had just noticed greeted him with a low cry.

But he speedily regained his composure, for a ray of light had fallen on her face, revealing that the person who stood before him was not Kasana, but her nurse, who had accompanied her to the prisoners and then to the camp. She, too, recognized him and stared at him as though he had risen from the grave.

They were old acquaintances; for when he was first brought to the archer's house she had prepared his bath and moistened his wound with balsam, and during his second stay beneath the same roof, she had joined her mistress in nursing him. They had chatted away many an hour together, and he knew that she was kindly disposed toward him; for when midway between waking and sleeping, in his burning fever, her hand had stroked him with maternal tenderness, and afterwards she had never wearied of questioning him about his people and at last had acknowledged that she was descended from the Syrians, who were allied to the Hebrews. Nay, even his language was not wholly strange to her; for she had been a woman of twenty when dragged to Egypt with other prisoners of Rameses the Great. Ephraim, she was fond of saying, reminded her of her own son when he was still younger.

The youth had no ill to fear from her, so grasping her hand, he whispered that he had escaped from his guards and come to ask counsel from her mistress and herself.

The word "escaped" was sufficient to satisfy the old woman; for her idea of ghosts was that they put others to flight, but did not fly themselves. Relieved, she stroked the youth's curls and, ere his whispered explanation was ended, turned her back upon him and hurried into the lighted room to tell her mistress whom she had found outside.

A few minutes after Ephraim was standing before the woman who had become the guiding star of his life. With glowing cheeks he gazed into the beautiful face, still flushed by weeping, and though it gave his heart a pang when, before vouchsafing him a greeting, she enquired whether Hosea had accompanied him, he forgot the foolish pain when he saw her gaze warmly at him. Yet when the nurse asked whether she did not think he looked well and vigorous, and withal more manly in appearance, it seemed as though he had really grown taller, and his heart beat faster and faster.

Kasana desired to learn the minutest details of his uncle's experiences; but after he had done her bidding and finally yielded to the wish to speak of his own fate, she interrupted him to consult the nurse concerning the means of saving him from unbidden looks and fresh dangers—and the right expedient was soon found.

First, with Ephraim's help, the old woman closed the main entrance of the tent as firmly as possible, and then pointed to the dark room into which he must speedily and softly retire as soon as she beckoned to him.

Meanwhile Kasana had poured some wine into a goblet, and when he came back with the nurse she made him sit down on the giraffe skin at her feet and asked how he had succeeded in evading the guards, and what he expected from the future. She would tell him in advance that her father had remained in Tanis, so he need not fear recognition and betrayal.

Her pleasure in this meeting was evident to both eyes and ears; nay, when Ephraim commenced his story by saying that Prince Siptah's command to remove the prisoners' chains, for which they were indebted solely to her, had rendered his escape possible, she clapped her hands like a child. Then her face clouded and, with a deep sigh, she added that ere his arrival her heart had almost broken with grief and tears; but Hosea should learn what a woman would sacrifice for the most ardent desire of her heart.

She repaid with grateful words Ephraim's assurance that, before his flight, he had offered to release his uncle from his bonds and, when she learned that Joshua had refused to accept his nephew's aid, lest it might endanger the success of the plan he had cleverly devised for him, she cried out to her nurse, with tearful eyes, that Hosea alone would have been capable of such a deed.

To the remainder of the fugitive's tale she listened intently, often interrupting him with sympathizing questions.

The torturing days and nights of the past, which had reached such a happy termination, seemed now like a blissful dream, a bewildering fairy-tale, and the goblet she constantly replenished was not needed to lend fire to his narrative.

Never before had he been so eloquent as while describing how, in the ravine, he had stepped on some loose stones and rolled head foremost down into the chasm with them. On reaching the bottom he had believed that all was lost; for soon after extricating himself from the rubbish that had buried him, in order to hurry to the pool, he had heard the whistle of the guards.

Yet he had been a good runner from his childhood, had learned in his native pastures to guide himself by the light of the stars, so without glancing to the right or to the left, he had hastened southward as fast as his feet would carry him. Often in the darkness he had fallen over stones or tripped in the hollows of the desert sand, but only to rise again quickly and dash onward, onward toward the south, where he knew he should find her, Kasana, her for whose sake he recklessly flung to the winds what wiser-heads had counselled, her for whom he was ready to sacrifice liberty and life.

Whence he derived the courage to confess this, he knew not, and neither the blow from her fan, nor the warning exclamation of the nurse: "Just look at the boy!" sobered him. Nay, his sparkling eyes sought hers still mote frequently as he continued his story.

One of the hounds which attacked him he had flung against a rock, and the other he pelted with stones till it fled howling into a thicket. He had seen no other pursuers, either that night, or during the whole of the next day. At last he again reached a travelled road and found country people who told him which way Pharaoh's army had marched. At noon, overwhelmed by fatigue, he had fallen asleep under the shade of a sycamore, and when he awoke the sun was near its setting. He was very hungry, so he took a few turnips from a neighboring field. But their owner suddenly sprang from a ditch near by, and he barely escaped his pursuit.

He had wandered along during a part of the night, and then rested beside a well on the roadside, for he knew that wild beasts shun such frequented places.

After sunrise he continued his march, following the road taken by the army. Everywhere he found traces of it, and when, shortly before noon, exhausted and faint from hunger, he reached a village in the cornlands watered by the Seti-canal, he debated whether to sell his gold armlet, obtain more strengthening food, and receive some silver and copper in change. But he was afraid of being taken for a thief and again imprisoned, for his apron had been tattered by the thorns, and his sandals had long since dropped from his feet. He had believed that even the hardest hearts could not fail to pity his misery so, hard as it was for him, he had knocked at a peasant's door and begged. But the man gave him nothing save the jeering counsel that a strong young fellow like him ought to use his arms and leave begging to the old and weak. A second peasant had even threatened to beat him; but as he walked on with drooping bead, a young woman whom he had noticed in front of the barbarian's house followed him, thrust some bread and dates into his hand, and whispered hastily that heavy taxes had been levied on the village when Pharaoh marched through, or she would have given him something better.

This unexpected donation, which he had eaten at the next well, had not tasted exactly like a festal banquet, but he did not tell Kasana that it had been embittered by the doubt whether to fulfil Joshua's commission and return to his people or yield to the longing that drew him to her.

He moved forward irresolutely, but fate seemed to have undertaken to point out his way; for after walking a short half hour, the latter portion of the time through barren land, he had found by the wayside a youth of about his own age who, moaning with pain, held his foot clasped between both hands. Pity led him to go to him and, to his astonishment, he recognized the runner and messenger of Kasana's father, with whom he had often talked.

"Apu, our nimble Nubian runner?" cried the young widow, and Ephraim assented and then added that the messenger had been despatched to convey a letter to Prince Siptah as quickly as possible, and the swift-footed lad, who was wont to outstrip his master's noble steeds, had shot over the road like an arrow and would have reached his destination in two hours more, had he not stepped on the sharp edge of a bottle that had been shattered by a wagon-wheel—and made a deep and terrible wound.

"And you helped him?" asked Kasana.

"How could I do otherwise?" replied Ephraim. "He had already lost a great deal of blood and was pale as death. So I carried him to the nearest ditch, washed the gaping wound, and anointed it with his balsam."

"I put the little box in his pouch myself a year ago," said the nurse who was easily moved, wiping her eyes. Ephraim confirmed the statement, for Apu had gratefully told him of it. Then he went on.

"I tore my upper garment into strips and bandaged the wound as well as I could. Meanwhile he constantly urged haste, held out the pass and letter his master had given him and, knowing nothing of the misfortune which had befallen me, charged me to deliver the roll to the prince in his place. Oh, how willingly I undertook the task and, soon after the second hour had passed, I reached the camp. The letter is in the prince's hands, and here am I—and I can see that you are glad! But no one was ever so happy as I to sit here at your feet, and look up to you, so grateful as I am that you have listened to me so kindly, and if they load me with chains again I will bear it calmly, if you will but care for me. Ah, my misfortune has been so great! I have neither father nor mother, no one who loves me. You, you alone are dear, and you will not repulse me, will you?"

He had fairly shouted the last words, as if beside himself, and carried away by the might of passion and rendered incapable by the terrible experiences of the past few hours of controlling the emotions that assailed him, the youth, still scarcely beyond childhood, who saw himself torn away from and bereft of all that had usually sustained and supported him, sobbed aloud, and like a frightened birdling seeking protection under its mother's wings, hid his head, amid floods of tears, in Kasana's lap.

Warm compassion seized upon the tender-hearted young widow, and her own eyes grew dim. She laid her hands kindly upon his head, and feeling the tremor that shook the frame of the weeping lad, she raised his head with both hands, kissed his brow and cheeks, looked smilingly into his eyes with tears in her own, and exclaimed:

"You poor, foolish fellow! Why should I not care for you, why should I repel you? Your uncle is the most beloved of men to me, and you are like his son. For your sakes I have already accepted what I should otherwise have thrust far, far from me! But now I must go on, and must not care what others may think or say of me, if only I can accomplish the one thing for which I am risking person, life, all that I once prized! Wait, you poor, impulsive fellow!"—and here she again kissed him on the cheeks—"I shall succeed in smoothing the path for you also. That is enough now!"

This command sounded graver, and was intended to curb the increasing impetuosity of the ardent youth. But she suddenly started up, exclaiming with anxious haste: "Go, go, at once!"

The footsteps of men approaching the tent, and a warning word from the nurse had brought this stern order to the young widow's lips, and Ephraim's quick ear made him understand her anxiety and urged him to join the old nurse in the dark room. There he perceived that a few moments' delay would have betrayed him; for the curtain of the tent was drawn aside and a man passed through the central space straight to the lighted apartment, where Kasana—the youth heard it distinctly—welcomed the new guest only too cordially, as though his late arrival surprised her.

Meanwhile the nurse had seized her own cloak, flung it over the fugitive's bare shoulders, and whispered:

"Be near the tent just before sunrise, but do not enter it until I call you, if you value your life. You have neither mother nor father, and my child Kasana ah, what a dear, loving heart she has!—she is the best of all good women; but whether she is fit to be the guide of an inexperienced young blusterer, whose heart is blazing like dry straw with love for her, is another question. I considered many things, while listening to your story, and on account of my liking for you I will tell you this. You have an uncle who—my child is right there—is the best of men, and I know mankind. Whatever he advised, do; for it will surely benefit you. Obey him! If his bidding leads you far away from here and Kasana, so much the better for you. We are walking in dangerous paths, and had it not been done for Hosea's sake, I would have tried to hold her back with all my might. But for him—I am an old woman; but I would go through fire myself for that man. I am more grieved than I can tell, both for the pure, sweet child and for yourself, whom my own son was once so much like, so I repeat: Obey your uncle, boy! Do that, or you will go to ruin, and that would be a pity!"

With these words, without waiting for an answer, she drew the curtain of the tent aside, and waited until Ephraim had slipped through. Then, wiping her eyes, she entered, as if by chance, the lighted chamber; but Kasana and her late guest had matters to discuss that brooked no witnesses, and her "dear child" only permitted her to light her little lamp at the three-armed candelabra, and then sent her to rest.

She promptly obeyed and, in the dark room, where her couch stood beside that of her mistress, she sank down, hid her face in her hands, and wept.

She felt as though the world was upside down. She no longer understood her darling Kasana; for she was sacrificing purity and honor for the sake of a man whom—she knew it—her soul abhorred.

CHAPTER XXI

Ephriam cowered in the shadow of the tent, from which he had slipped, and pressed his ear close to the wall. He had cautiously ripped a small opening in a seam of the cloth, so he could see and hear what was passing in the lighted room of the woman he loved. The storm kept every one within the tents whom duty did not summon into the open air, and Ephraim had less reason to fear discovery on account of the deep shadow that rested on the spot where he lay. The nurse's cloak covered him and, though shiver after shiver shook his young limbs, it was due to the bitter anguish that pierced his soul.

The man on whose breast he saw Kasana lay her head was a prince, a person of high rank and great power, and the capricious beauty did not always repel the bold man, when his lips sought those for whose kiss Ephraim so ardently longed.

She owed him nothing, it is true, yet her heart belonged to his uncle, whom she had preferred to all others. She had declared herself ready to endure the most terrible things for his liberation; and now his own eyes told him that she was false and faithless, that she granted to another what belonged to one alone. She had bestowed caresses on him, too, but these were only the crumbs that fell from Hosea's table, a robbery—he confessed it with a blush—he had perpetrated on his uncle, yet he felt offended, insulted, deceived, and consumed to his inmost soul with fierce jealousy on behalf of his uncle, whom he honored, nay, loved, though he had opposed his wishes.

And Hosea? Why, he too, like himself, this princely suitor, and all other men, must love her, spite of his strange conduct at the well by the roadside—it was impossible for him to do otherwise—and now, safe from the poor prisoner's resentment, she was basely, treacherously enjoying another's tender caresses.

Siptah, he had heard at their last meeting, was his uncle's foe, and it was to him that she betrayed the man she loved!

The chink in the tent was ready to show him everything that occurred within, but he often closed his eyes that he might not behold it. Often, it is true, the hateful scene held him in thrall by a mysterious spell and he would fain have torn the walls of the tent asunder, struck the detested Egyptian to the ground, and shouted into the faithless woman's face the name of Hosea, coupled with the harshest reproaches.

The fervent passion which had taken possession of him was suddenly transformed to hate and scorn. He had believed himself to be the happiest of mortals, and he had suddenly become the most miserable; no one, he believed, had ever experienced such a fall from the loftiest heights to the lowest depths.

The nurse had been right. Naught save misery and despair could come to him from so faithless a woman.

Once he started up to fly, but he again heard the bewitching tones of her musical laugh, and mysterious powers detained him, forcing him to listen.

At first the seething blood had throbbed so violently in his ears that he felt unable to follow the dialogue in the lighted tent. But, by degrees, he grasped the purport of whole sentences, and now he understood all that they said, not a word of their further conversation escaped him, and it was absorbing enough, though it revealed a gulf from which he shrank shuddering.

Kasana refused the bold suitor many favors for which he pleaded, but this only impelled him to beseech her more fervently to give herself to him, and the prize he offered in return was the highest gift of earth, the place by his side as queen on the throne of Egypt, to which he aspired. He said this distinctly, but what followed was harder to understand; for the passionate suitor was in great haste and often interrupted his hasty sentences to assure Kasana, to whose hands in this hour he was committing his life and liberty, of his changeless love, or to soothe her when the boldness of his advances awakened fear and aversion. But he soon began to speak of the letter whose bearer Ephraim had been and, after reading it aloud and explaining it, the youth realized with a slight shudder that he had become an accomplice in the most criminal of all plots, and for a moment the longing stole over him to betray the traitors and deliver them into the hand of the mighty sovereign whose destruction they were plotting. But he repelled the thought and merely sunned himself in the pleasurable consciousness—the first during this cruel hour-of holding Kasana and her royal lover in his hand as one holds a beetle by a string. This had a favorable effect on him and restored the confidence and courage he had lost. The baser the things he continued to hear, the more clearly he learned to appreciate the value of the goodness and truth which he had lost. His uncle's words, too, came back to his memory.

"Give no man, from the loftiest to the lowliest, a right to regard you save with respect, and you can hold your head as high as the proudest warrior who ever wore purple robe and golden armor."

On the couch in Kasana's house, while shaking with fever, he had constantly repeated this sentence; but in the misery of captivity, and on his flight it had again vanished from his memory. In the courtier's tent when, after he had bathed and perfumed himself, the old slave held a mirror before him, he had given it a passing thought; but now it mastered his whole soul. And strange to say, the worthless traitor within wore a purple coat and golden mail, and looked like a military hero, but he could not hold his head erect, for the work he sought to accomplish could only succeed in the secrecy that shuns the light, and was like the labor of the hideous mole which undermines the ground in the darkness.

His tool was the repulsive cloven-footed trio, falsehood, fraud, and faithlessness, and she whom he had chosen for his help-mate was the woman—it shamed him to his inmost soul-for whom he had been in the act of sacrificing all that was honorable, precious, and dear to him.

The worst infamies which he had been taught to shun were the rounds of the ladder on which this evil man intended to mount.

The roll the youth had brought to the camp contained two letters. The first was from the conspirators in Tanis, the second from Siptah's mother.

The former desired his speedy return and told him that the Syrian Aarsu, the commander of the foreign mercenaries, who guarded the palace, as well as the women's house, was ready to do him homage. If the high-priest of Amon, who was at once chief-judge, viceroy and keeper of the seal, proclaimed him king, he was sovereign and could enter the palace which stood open to him and ascend the throne without resistance. If Pharaoh returned, the body-guards would take him prisoner and remove him as Siptah, who liked no halfway measures, had secretly directed, while the chief-priest insisted upon keeping him in mild imprisonment.

Nothing was to be feared save the premature return from Thebes of Seti, the second son of Menephtah; for the former, after his older brother's death, had become heir to the throne, and carrier doves had brought news yesterday that he was now on his way. Therefore Siptah and the powerful priest who was to proclaim him king were urged to the utmost haste.

The necessary measures had been adopted in case of possible resistance from the army; for as soon as the Hebrews had been destroyed, the larger portion of the troops, without any suspicion of the impending dethronement of their commander-in-chief, would be sent to their former stations. The body-guards were devoted to Siptah, and the others who entered the capital, should worst come to worst, could be easily overpowered by Aarsu and his mercenaries.

"There is nothing farther for me to do," said the prince, "stretching himself comfortably, like a man who has successfully accomplished a toilsome task," except to rush back to Tanis in a few hours with Bai, have myself crowned and proclaimed king in the temple of Amon, and finally received in the palace as Pharaoh. The rest will take care of itself. Seti, whom they call the heir to the throne, is just such another weakling as his father, and must submit to a fixed fact, or if necessary, be forced to do so. The captain of the body-guards will see that Menephtah does not again enter the palace in the city of Rameses."

The second letter which was addressed to the Pharaoh, had been written by the mother of the prince in order to recall her son and the chief-priest Bai to the capital as quickly as possible, without exposing the former to the reproach of cowardice for having quitted the army so shortly before the battle. Though she had never been better, she protested with hypocritical complaints and entreaties, that the hours of her life were numbered, and besought the king to send her son and the chief-priest Bai to her without delay, that she might be permitted to bless her only child before her death.

She was conscious of many a sin, and no one, save the high-priest, possessed the power of winning the favor of the gods for her, a dying woman. Without his intercession she would perish in despair.

This letter, too, the base robber of a crown read aloud, called it a clever bit of feminine strategy, and rubbed his hands gleefully.

Treason, murder, hypocrisy, fraud, shameful abuse of the most sacred feelings, nay all that was evil must serve Siptah to steal the throne, and though Kasana had wrung her hands and shed tears when she heard that he meant to remove Pharaoh from his path, she grew calmer after the prince had represented that her own father had approved of his arrangements for the deliverance of Egypt from the hand of the king, her destroyer.

The letter from the prince's mother to Pharaoh, the mother who urged her own son to the most atrocious crimes, was the last thing Ephraim heard; for it roused in the young Hebrew, who was wont to consider nothing purer and more sacred than the bonds which united parents and children, such fierce indignation, that he raised his fist threateningly and, springing up, opened his lips in muttered invective.

He did not hear that Kasana made the prince swear that, if he attained the sovereign power, he would grant her first request. It should cost him neither money nor lands, and only give her the right to exercise mercy where her heart demanded it; for things were in store which must challenge the wrath of the gods and he must leave her to soothe it.

Ephraim could not endure to see or hear more of these abominable things.

For the first time he felt how great a danger he ran of being dragged into this marsh and becoming a lost, evil man; but never, he thought, would he have been so corrupt, so worthless, as this prince. His uncle's words again returned to his mind, and he now raised his head proudly and arched his chest as if to assure himself of his own unbroken vigor, saying meanwhile, with a long breath, that he was of too much worth to ruin himself for the sake of a wicked woman, even though, like Kasana, she was the fairest and most bewitching under the sun.

Away, away from the neighborhood of this net, which threatened to entangle him in murder and every deed of infamy.

Resolved to seek his people, he turned toward the gate of the camp, but after a few hasty steps paused, and a glance at the sky showed him that it was the second hour past midnight. Every surrounding object was buried in silence save that from the neighboring Dens of the royal steeds, came the sound of the rattle of a chain, or of the stamp of a stallion's hoof.

If he risked escaping from the camp now, he could not fail to be seen and stopped. Prudence commanded him to curb his impatience and, as he glanced around, his eyes rested on the chamberlain's tent from which the old slave had just emerged to look for his master, who was still waiting in the prince's tent for his lord's return.

The old man had treated Ephraim kindly, and now asked him with good-natured urgency to come in and rest; for the youth needed sleep.

And Ephraim accepted the well-meant invitation. He felt for the first time how weary his feet were, and he had scarcely stretched himself upon the mat which the old slave—it was his own—spread on the floor of the tent for him, ere the feeling came over him that his limbs were relaxing; and yet he had expected to find here time and rest for calm deliberation.

He began, too, to think of the future and his uncle's commission.

That he must join his people without delay was decided. If they escaped Pharaoh's army, the others could do what they pleased, his duty was to summon his shepherds, servants, and the youths of his own age, and with them hurry to the mines to break Joshua's chains and bring him back to his old father and the people who needed him. He already saw himself with a sling in his girdle and a battle-axe in his hand, rushing on in advance of the others, when sleep overpowered him and bound the sorely wearied youth so firmly and sweetly that even dreams remained aloof from his couch and when morning came the old slave was obliged to shake him to rouse him.

The camp was already pervaded with bustling life. Tents were struck, asses and ox-carts laden, steeds curried and newly-shod, chariots washed, weapons and harnesses cleaned, breakfast was distributed and eaten.

At intervals the blare of trumpets was heard in one direction, loudly shouted commands in another, and from the eastern portion of the camp echoed the chanting of the priests, who devoutly greeted the new-born sun-god.

A gilded chariot, followed by a similar one, drove up to the costly purple tent beside Kasana's, which active servants were beginning to take down.

Prince Siptah and the chief-priest Bai had received Pharaoh's permission to set off for Tanis, to fulfil the wish of a "dying woman."

Soon after Ephraim took leave of the old slave and bade him give Kasana's nurse the cloak and tell her that the messenger had followed her advice and his uncle's.

Then he set off on his walk.

He escaped unchallenged from the Egyptian camp and, as he entered the wilderness, he heard the shout with which he called his shepherds in the pastures. The cry, resounding far over the plain, startled a sparrow-hawk which was gazing into the distance from a rock and, as the bird soared upward, the youth fancied that if he stretched out his arms, wings must unfold strong enough to bear him also through the air. Never had he felt so light and active, so strong and free, nay had the priest at this hour asked him the question whether he would accept the office of a captain of thousands in the Egyptian army, he would undoubtedly have answered, as he did before the ruined house of Nun, that his sole desire was to remain a shepherd and rule his flocks and servants.

He was an orphan, but he had a nation, and where his people were was his home.

Like a wanderer, who, after a long journey, sees his home in the distance, he quickened his pace.

He had reached Tanis on the night of the new moon and the round silver shield which was paling in the morning light was the same which had then risen before his eyes. Yet it seemed as though years lay between his farewell of Miriam and the present hour, and the experiences of a life had been compressed into these few days.

He had left his tribe a boy; he returned a man; yet, thanks to this one terrible night, he had remained unchanged, he could look those whom he loved and reverenced fearlessly in the face.

Nay, more!

He would show the man whom he most esteemed that he, too, Ephraim, could hold his head high. He would repay Joshua for what he had done, when he remained in chains and captivity that he, his nephew, might go forth as free as a bird.

After hurrying onward an hour, he reached a ruined watch-tower, climbed to its summit, and saw, at a short distance beyond the mount of Baal-zephon, which had long towered majestically on the horizon, the glittering northern point of the Red Sea.

The storm, it is true, had subsided, but he perceived by the surging of its emerald surface that the sea was by no means calm, and single black clouds in the sky, elsewhere perfectly clear, seemed to indicate an approaching tempest.

He gazed around him asking himself what the leader of the people probably intended, if—as the prince had told Kasana—they had encamped between Pihahiroth—whose huts and tents rose before him on the narrow gulf the northwestern arm of the Red Sea thrust into the land—and the mount of Baal-zephon.

Had Siptah lied in this too?

No. This time the malicious traitor had departed from his usual custom; for between the sea and the village, where the wind was blowing slender columns of smoke asunder, his falcon-eye discovered many light spots resembling a distant flock of sheep, and among and beside them a singular movement to and fro upon the sands.

It was the camp of his people.

How short seemed the distance that separated him from them!

Yet the nearer it was, the greater became his anxiety lest the great multitude, with the women and children, herds and tents, could not escape the vast army which must overtake them in a few hours.

His heart shrank as he gazed around him; for neither to the east, where a deeper estuary was surging, nor southward, where the Red Sea tossed its angry waves, nor even toward the north, whence Pharaoh's army was marching, was escape possible. To the west lay the wilderness of Aean, and if the wanderers escaped in that direction, and were pressed farther, they would again enter Egyptian soil and the exodus would be utterly defeated.

So there was nothing left save to risk a battle, and at the thought a chill ran through the youth's veins; for he knew how badly armed, untrained, savage, unmanageable, and cowardly were the men of his race, and had witnessed the march of the powerful, well-equipped Egyptian army, with its numerous foot-soldiers and superb war-chariots.

To him now, as to his uncle a short time before, his people seemed doomed to certain destruction, unless succored by the God of his fathers. In former years, and just before his departure, Miriam, with sparkling eyes and enthusiastic words, had praised the power and majesty of this omnipotent Lord, who preferred his people above all other nations; but the lofty words of the prophetess had filled his childish heart with a slight fear of the unapproachable greatness and terrible wrath of this God.

It had been easier for him to uplift his soul to the sun-god, when his teacher, a kind and merry-hearted Egyptian priest, led him to the temple of Pithom. In later years he had felt no necessity of appealing to any god; for he lacked nothing, and while other boys obeyed their parents' commands, the shepherds, who well knew that the flocks they tended belonged to him, called him their young master, and first in jest, then in earnest, paid him all the honor due a ruler, which prematurely increased his self-importance and made him an obstinate fellow.

He whom stalwart, strong men obeyed, was sufficient unto himself, and felt that others needed him and, as nothing was more difficult for him than to ask a favor, great or small, from any one, he rebelled against praying to a God so far off and high above him.

But now, when his heart was oppressed by the terrible destiny that threatened his people, he was overwhelmed by the feeling that only the

Greatest and Mightiest could deliver them from this terrible, unspeakable peril, as if no one could withstand this powerful army, save He whose might could destroy heaven and earth.

What were they that the Most High, whom Miriam and Hosea described as so pre-eminently great, should care for them? Yet his people numbered many thousands, and God had not disdained to make them His, and promise great things for them in the future. Now they were on the verge of destruction, and he, Ephraim, who came from the camp of the enemy, was perhaps the sole person who saw the full extent of the danger.

Suddenly he was filled with the conviction that it was incumbent upon him, above all others, to tell the God of his fathers,—who perhaps in caring for earth and heaven, sun and stars, had forgotten the fate of His people—of the terrible danger impending, and beseech Him to save them. He was still standing on the top of the ruined tower, and raised his arms and face toward heaven.

In the north he saw the black clouds which he had noticed in the blue sky swiftly massing and rolling hither and thither. The wind, which had subsided after sunrise, was increasing in strength and power, and rapidly becoming a storm. It swept across the isthmus in gusts, which followed one another more and more swiftly, driving before them dense clouds of yellow sand.

He must lift up his voice loudly, that the God to whom he prayed might hear him in His lofty heaven, so, with all the strength of his young lungs, he shouted into the storm:

"Adonai, Adonai! Thou, whom they call Jehovah, mighty God of my fathers, hear me, Ephraim, a young inexperienced lad, of whom, in his insignificance, Thou hast probably never thought. I ask nothing for myself. But the people, whom Thou dost call Thine, are in sore peril. They have left durable houses and good pastures because Thou didst promise them a better and more beautiful land, and they trusted in Thee and Thy promises. But now the army of Pharaoh is approaching, so great a host that our people will never be able to resist it. Thou must believe this, Eli, my Lord. I have seen it and been in its midst. So surely as I stand here, I know that it is too mighty for Thy people. Pharaoh's power will crush them as the hoofs of the cattle trample the grain on the threshing-floor. And my people, who are also Thine, are encamped in a spot where Pharaoh's warriors can cut them down from all directions, so that there is no way for them to fly, not one. I saw it distinctly from this very spot. Hear me now, Adonai. But canst Thou hear my words, oh Lord, in such a tempest? Surely Thou canst; for they call Thee omnipotent and, if Thou dost hear me and dost understand the meaning of my words, Thou wilt see with Thy mighty eyes, if such is Thy will, that I speak the truth. Then Thou wilt surely remember the vow Thou didst make to the people through Thy servant Moses.

"Among the Egyptians, I have witnessed treachery and murder and shameful wiles; their deeds have filled me, who am myself but a sinful, inexperienced youth, with horror and indignation. How couldst Thou, from whom all good is said to proceed, and whom Miriam calls truth itself, act like those abominable men and break faith with those who trusted in Thee? I know, Thou great and mighty One, that this is far from Thee, nay, perhaps it is a sin even to cherish such a thought. Hear me, Adonai! Look northward at the troops of the Egyptians, who will surely soon leave their camp and march forward, and southward to the peril of Thy people, for whom escape is no longer possible, and Thou wilt rescue them by Thy omnipotence and great wisdom; for Thou hast promised them a new country, and if they are destroyed, how can they reach it?"

With these words he finished his prayer, which, though boyish and incoherent, gushed from the inmost depths of his heart. Then he sprang with long leaps from the ruined tower to the barren plain at his feet, and ran southward as fleetly as if he were escaping from captivity a second time. He felt how the wind rushing from the north-east urged him forward, and told himself that it would also hasten the march of Pharaoh's soldiers. Perhaps the leaders of his people did not yet know how vast was the military power that threatened them, and undervalued the danger in which their position placed them. But he saw it, and could give them every information. Haste was necessary, and he felt as though he had gained wings in this race with the storm.

The village of Pihahiroth was soon gained, and while dashing by it without pausing, he noticed that its huts and tents were deserted by men and cattle. Perhaps its inhabitants had fled with their property to a place of safety before the advancing Egyptian troops or the hosts of his own people.

The farther he went, the more cloudy became the sky,—which here so rarely failed to show a sunny vault of blue at noonday,—the more fiercely howled the tempest. His thick locks fluttered wildly around his burning head, he panted for breath, yet flew on, on, while his sandals seemed to him to scarcely touch the ground.

The nearer he came to the sea, the louder grew the howling and whistling of the storm, the more furious the roar of the waves dashing against the rocks of Baal-zephon. Now—a short hour after he had left the tower—he reached the first tents of the camp, and the familiar cry: "Unclean!" as well as the mourning-robes of those whose scaly, disfigured faces looked forth from the ruins of the tents which the storm had overthrown, informed him that he had reached the lepers, whom Moses had commanded to remain outside the camp.

Yet so great was his haste that, instead of making a circuit around their quarter, he dashed straight through it at his utmost speed. Nor did he pause even when a lofty palm, uprooted by the tempest, fell to the ground so close beside him that the fan-shaped leaves in its crown brushed his face.

At last he gained the tents and pinfolds of his people, not a few of which had also been overthrown, and asked the first acquaintances he met for Nun, the father of his dead mother and of Joshua.

He had gone down to the shore with Moses and other elders of the people. Ephraim followed him there, and the damp, salt sea-air refreshed him and cooled his brow.

Yet he could not instantly get speech with him, so he collected his thoughts, and recovered his breath, while watching the men whom he sought talking eagerly with some gaily-clad Phoenician sailors. A youth like Ephraim might not venture to interrupt the grey-haired heads of the people in the discussion, which evidently referred to the sea; for the Hebrews constantly pointed to the end of the bay, and the Phoenicians sometimes thither, sometimes to the mountain and the sky, sometimes to the north, the center of the still increasing tempest.

A projecting wall sheltered the old men from the hurricane, yet they found it difficult to stand erect, even while supported by their staves and clinging to the stones of the masonry.

At last the conversation ended and while the youth saw the gigantic figure of Moses go with slow, yet firm steps among the leaders of the Hebrews down to the shore of the sea, Nun, supported by one of his shepherds, was working his way with difficulty, but as rapidly as possible toward the camp. He wore a mourning-robe, and while the others looked joyous and hopeful when they parted, his handsome face, framed by its snow-white beard and hair, had the expression of one whose mind and body were burdened by grief.

Not until Ephraim called him did he raise his drooping leonine head, and when he saw him he started back in surprise and terror, and clung more firmly to the strong arm of the shepherd who supported him.

Tidings of the cruel fate of his son and grandson had reached him through the freed slaves he had left in Tanis; and the old man had torn his garments, strewed ashes on his head, donned mourning robes, and grieved bitterly for his beloved, noble, only son and promising grandson.

Now Ephraim was standing before him; and after Nun had laid his hand on his shoulders, and kissed him again and again, he asked if his son was still alive and remembered him and his people.

As soon as the youth had joyfully assured him that such was the case, Nun threw his arms around the boy's shoulders, that henceforth his own blood, instead of a stranger, should protect him from the violence of the storm.

He had grave and urgent duties to fulfil, from which nothing might withhold him. Yet as the fiery youth shouted into his ear, through the roar of the hurricane, on their way through the camp, that he would summon his shepherds and the companions of his own age to release Hosea, who now called himself Joshua, old Nun's impetuous spirit awoke and, clasping Ephraim closer to his heart, he cried out that though an old man he was not yet too aged to swing an axe and go with Ephraim's youthful band to liberate his son. His eyes sparkled through his tears, and waving his free arm aloft, he cried:

"The God of my fathers, on whom I learned to rely, watches over His faithful people. Do you see the sand, sea-weed, and shells yonder at the end of the estuary? An hour ago the place was covered with water, and roaring waves were dashing their white spray upward. That is the way, boy, which promises escape; if the wind holds, the water—so the experienced Phoenicians assure us—will recede still farther toward the sea. Their god of the north wind, they say, is favorable to us, and their boys are already lighting a fire to him on the summit of Baal-zephon yonder, but we know that it is Another, Who is opening to us a path to the desert. We were in evil case, my boy!"

"Yes, grandfather!" cried the youth. "You were trapped like lions in the snare, and the Egyptian host—it passed me from the first man to the last—is mighty and unconquerable. I hurried as fast as my feet could carry me to tell you how many heavily-armed troops, bowmen, steeds, and chariots...."

"We know, we know," the old man interrupted, "but here we are."

He pointed to an overturned tent which his servants were trying to prop, and beside which an aged Hebrew, his father Elishama, wrapped in cloth, sat in the chair in which he was carried by bearers.

Nun hastily shouted a few words and led Ephraim toward him. But while the youth was embracing his great-grandfather, who hugged and caressed him, Nun, with youthful vivacity, was issuing orders to the shepherds and servants:

"Let the tent fall, men! The storm has begun the work for you! Wrap the covering round the poles, load the carts and beasts of burden. Move briskly, You, Gaddi, Shamma, and Jacob, join the others! The hour for departure has come! Everybody must hasten to harness the animals, put them in the wagons, and prepare all things as fast as possible. The Almighty shows us the way, and every one must hasten, in His name and by the command of Moses. Keep strictly to the old order. We head the procession, then come the other tribes, lastly the strangers and leprous men and women. Rejoice, oh, ye people; for our God is working a great miracle and making the sea dry land for us, His chosen people. Let everyone thank Him while working, and pray from the depths of the heart that He will continue to protect us. Let all who do not desire to be slain by the sword and crushed by the weight of Pharaoh's chariots put forth their best strength and forget rest! That will await us as soon as we have escaped the present peril. Down with the tent-cover yonder; I'll roll it up myself. Lay hold, boy! Look across at the children of Manasseh, they are already packing and loading. That's right, Ephraim, you know how to use your hands!

"What more have we to do! My head, my forgetful old head! So much has come upon me at once! You have nimble feet, Raphu;—I undertook to warn the strangers to prepare for a speedy departure. Run quickly and hurry them, that they may not linger too far behind the people. Time is precious! Lord, Lord, my God, extend Thy protecting hand over Thy people, and roll the waves still farther back with the tempest, Thy mighty breath! Let every one pray silently while working, the Omnipresent One, Who sees the heart, will hear it. That load is too heavy for you, Ephraim, you are lifting beyond your strength. No. The youth has mastered it. Follow his example, men, and ye of Succoth, rejoice in your master's strength."

The last words were addressed to Ephraim's shepherds, men and maid servants, most of whom shouted a greeting to him in the midst of their work, kissed his arm or hand, and rejoiced at his return. They were engaged in packing and wrapping their goods, and in gathering, harnessing, and loading the animals, which could only be kept together by blows and shouts.

The people from Succoth wished to vie with their young master, those from Tanis with their lord's grandson, and the other owners of flocks and lesser men of the tribe of Ephraim, whose tents surrounded that of their chief Nun, did the same, in order not to be surpassed by others; yet several hours elapsed ere all the tents, household utensils, and provisions for man and beast were again in their places on the animals and in the carts, and the aged, feeble and sick had been laid on litters or in wagons.

Sometimes the gale bore from the distance to the spot where the Ephraimites were busily working the sound of Moses' deep voice or the higher tones of Aaron. But neither they nor the men of the tribe of Judah heeded the monition; for the latter were ruled by Hur and Naashon, and beside the former stood his newly-wedded wife Miriam. It was different with the other tribes and the strangers, to the obstinacy and cowardice of whose chiefs was due the present critical position of the people.

CHAPTER XXII

To break through the center of the Etham line of fortifications and march toward the north-east along the nearest road leading to Palestine had proved impossible; but Moses' second plan of leading the people around the Migdol of the South had also been baffled; for spies had reported that the garrison of the latter had been greatly strengthened. Then the multitude had pressed around the man of God, declaring that they would rather return home with their families and appeal to Pharaoh's mercy than to let themselves, their wives, and their families be slaughtered.

Several days had been spent in detaining them; but when other messengers brought tidings that Pharaoh was approaching with a powerful army the time seemed to have come when the wanderers, in the utmost peril, might be forced to break through the forts, and Moses exerted the full might of his commanding personality, Aaron the whole power of his seductive eloquence, while old Nun and Hur essayed to kindle the others with their own bold spirit.

But the terrible news had robbed the majority of the last vestige of self reliance and trust in God, and they had already resolved to assure Pharaoh of their repentance when the messengers whom, without their leader's knowledge, they had sent forth, returned, announcing that the approaching army had been commanded to spare no Hebrew, and to show by the sharp edge of the sword, even to those who sued for mercy, how Pharaoh punished the men by whose shameful sorcery misery and woe had come upon so many Egyptians.

Then, too late, they became aware that to return would ensure more speedy destruction than to boldly press forward. But when the men capable of bearing arms followed Hur and Nun to the Migdol of the South, they turned to fly at the defiant blare of the Egyptian war trumpets. When they came back to the camp with weary limbs, depressed and disheartened, new and exaggerated reports of Pharaoh's military force had reached the people, and now terror and despair had taken possession of the bolder men. Every admonition was vain, every threat derided, and the rebellious people had forced their leaders to go with them till, after a short march, they reached the Red Sea, whose deep green waves had forced them to pause in their southward flight.

So they had encamped between Pihahiroth and Baal-zephon, and here the leaders again succeeded in turning the attention of the despairing people to the God of their fathers.

In the presence of sure destruction, from which no human power could save them, they had again learned to raise their eyes to Heaven; but Moses' soul had once more been thrilled with anxiety and compassion for the poor, sorely afflicted bands who had followed his summons. During the night preceding, he had climbed one of the lower peaks of Baal-zephon and, amid the raging of the tempest and the roar of the hissing surges, sought the Lord his God, and felt his presence near him. He, too, had not wearied of pleading the need of his people and adjuring him to save them.

At the same hour Miriam, the wife of Hur, had gone to the sea-shore where, under a solitary palmtree, she addressed the same petition to her God, whose trusted servant she still felt herself. Here she besought Him to remember the women and children who, trusting in Him, had wandered forth into distant lands. She had also knelt to pray for the friend of her youth, languishing in terrible captivity; but had only cried in low, timid accents: "Oh, Lord, do not forget the hapless Hosea, whom at Thy bidding I called Joshua, though he showed himself less obedient to Thy will than Moses, my brother, and Hur, my husband. Remember also the youthful Ephraim, the grandson of Nun, Thy faithful servant."

Then she returned to the tent of the chief, her husband, while many a lowly man and poor anxious woman, before their rude tents or on their thin, tear-drenched mats, uplifted their terrified souls to the God of their fathers and besought His care for those who were dearest to their hearts.

So, in this night of utmost need, the camp had become a temple in which high and low, the heads of families and the housewives, masters and slaves, nay, even the afflicted lepers sought and found their God.

At last the morning came on which Ephraim had shouted his childish prayer amid the roaring of the storm, and the waters of the sea had begun to recede.

When the Hebrews beheld with their own eyes the miracle that the Most High was working for His chosen people, even the discouraged and despairing became believing and hopeful.

Not only the Ephraimites, but the other tribes, the foreigners, and lepers felt the influence of the newly-awakened joyous confidence, which urged each individual to put forth all his powers to prepare for the journey and, for the first time, the multitude gathered and formed into ranks without strife, bickering, deeds of violence, curses, and tears.

After sunset Moses, holding his staff uplifted, and Aaron, singing and praying, entered at the head of the procession the end of the bay.

The storm, which continued to rage with the same violence, had swept the water out of it and blew the flame and smoke of the torches carried by the tribes toward the south-west.

The chief leaders, on whom all eyes rested with trusting eagerness, were followed by old Nun and the Ephraimites. The bottom of the sea on which they trod was firm, moist sand, on which even the herds could walk as if it were a smooth road, sloping gently toward the sea.

Ephraim, in whom the elders now saw the future chief, had been entrusted, at his grandfather's suggestion, with the duty of seeing that the procession did not stop and, for this purpose, had been given a leader's staff; for the fishermen whose huts stood at the foot of Baal-zephon, like the Phoenicians, believed that when the moon reached her zenith the sea would return to its old bed, and therefore all delay was to be avoided.

The youth enjoyed the storm, and when his locks fluttered and he battled victoriously against the gale in rushing hither and thither, as his office required, it seemed to him a foretaste of the venture he had in view.

So the procession moved on through the darkness which had speedily followed the dusk of evening. The acrid odor of the sea-weed and fishes which had been left stranded pleased the boy,—who felt that he had matured into manhood,—better than the sweet fragrance of spikenard in Kasana's tent. Once the memory of it flashed through his brain, but with that exception there was not a moment during these hours which gave him time to think of her.

He had his hands full of work; sometimes a heap of sea-weed flung on the path by a wave must be removed; sometimes a ram, the leader of a flock, refused to step on the wet sand and must be dragged forward by the horns, or cattle and beasts of burden must be driven through a pool of water from which they shrank.

Often, too, he was obliged to brace his shoulder against a heavily-laden cart, whose wheels had sunk too deeply into the soft sand; and when, even during this strange, momentous march, two bands of shepherds began to dispute about precedence close to the Egyptian shore, he quickly settled the dispute by making them draw lots to decide which party should go first.

Two little girls who, crying bitterly, refused to wade through a pool of water, while their mother was busy with the infant in her arms, he carried with prompt decision through the shallow puddle, and the cart with a broken wheel he had moved aside by the light of the torches and commanded some stalwart bondmen, who were carrying only small bundles, to load themselves with the sacks and bales, nay, even the fragments of the vehicle. He uttered a word of cheer to weeping women and children and, when the light of a torch fell upon the face of a companion of his own age, whose aid he hoped to obtain for the release of Joshua, he briefly told him that there was a bold adventure in prospect which he meant to dare in concert with him.

The torch-bearers who usually headed the procession this time were obliged to close its ranks, for the storm raging from the northeast would have blown the smoke into the people's faces. They stood on the Egyptian shore, and already the whole train had passed them except the lepers who, following the strangers, were the last of the whole multitude.

These "strangers" were a motley crew, comprising Asiatics of Semitic blood, who had escaped from the bondage or severe punishments which the Egyptian law imposed, traders who expected to find among the wanderers purchasers of their wares, or Shasu shepherds, whose return was prohibited by the officials on the frontier. Ephraim had much trouble with them, for they refused to leave the firm land until the lepers had been forced to keep farther away from them; yet the youth, with the aid of the elders of the tribe of Benjamin, who preceded them, brought them also to obedience by threatening them with the prediction of the Phoenicians and the fishermen that the moon, when it had passed its zenith, would draw the sea back to its old bed.

Finally he persuaded the leader of the lepers, who had once been an Egyptian priest, to keep at least half the distance demanded.

Meanwhile the tempest had continued to blow with increased violence, and its howling and whistling, blended with the roar of the dashing waves and the menacing thunder of the surf, drowned the elders' shouts of command, the terrified shrieks of the children, the lowing and bleating of the trembling herds, and the whining of the dogs. Ephraim's voice could be heard only by those nearest and, moreover, many of the torches were extinguished, while others were kept burning with the utmost difficulty. Seeking to recover his wind and get a little rest, he walked slowly for a time over the damp sand behind the last lepers, when he heard some one call his name and, turning, he saw one of his former playmates, who was returning from a reconnoitring expedition and who, with the sweat pouring from his brow and panting breath, shouted into the ear of the youth, in whose hand he saw the staff of a leader, that Pharaoh's chariots were approaching at the head of his army. He had left them at Pihahiroth and, if they did not stop there to give the other troops time to join them, they might overtake the fugitives at any moment. With these words he darted past the lepers to join the leaders; but Ephraim stopped in the middle of the road, pressing his hand upon his brow, while a new burden of care weighed heavily upon his soul.

He knew that the approaching army would crush the men, women, and children whose touching fear and helplessness he had just beheld, as a man's foot tramples on an ant-bill, and again every instinct of his being urged him to pray, while from his oppressed heart the imploring cry rose through the darkness:

"Eli, Eli, great God most high! Thou knowest—for I have told Thee, and Thine all-seeing eye must perceive it, spite of the darkness of this night—the strait of Thy people, whom Thou hast promised to lead into a new country. Remember Thy vow, Jehovah! Be merciful unto us, Thou great and mighty one! Our foe is approaching with resistless power! Stay him! Save us! Protect the poor women and children! Save us, be merciful to us!"

During this prayer he had raised his eyes heavenward and saw on the summit of Baal-zephon the red blaze of a fire. It had been lighted by the Phoenicians to make the Baal of the north-wind favorable to the men of kindred race and hostile to the hated Egyptians. This was a kindly deed; but he put his trust in another God and, as his eye glanced over the vault of heaven and noted the grey and black storm-clouds scurrying, gathering, parting, and then rushing in new directions, he perceived between two dispersing masses of clouds the silvery light of the full moon, which had now attained her zenith.

Fresh anxiety assailed him; for he remembered the prediction of men skilled in the changes of winds and waves. If the sea should now return to its ancient bed, his people would be lost; for there was no escape, even toward the north, where deep pools of water were standing amid the mire and cliffs. Should the waves flow back within the next hour, the seed of Abraham would be effaced from the earth, as writing inscribed on wax disappears from the tablet under the pressure of a warm hand.

Yet was not this people thus marked for destruction, the nation which the Lord had chosen for His own? Could He deliver it into the hand of those who were also His own foes?

No, no, a thousand times no!

And the moon, which was to cause this destruction, had but a short time before been the ally of his flight and favored him. Only let him keep up his hope and faith and not lose confidence.

Nothing, nothing was lost as yet.

Come what might, the whole nation need not perish, and his own tribe, which marched at the head of the procession, certainly would not; for many must have reached the opposite shore, nay, perhaps more than he supposed; for the bay was not wide, and even the lepers, the last of the train, had already advanced some distance across the wet sand.

Ephraim now remained alone behind them all to listen to the approach of the hostile chariots. He laid his ear to the ground on the shore of the bay, and he could trust to the sharpness of his hearing; how often, in this attitude, he had caught the distant tramp of stray cattle or, while hunting, the approach of a herd of antelopes or gazelles.

As the last, he was in the greatest danger; but what cared he for that?

How gladly he would have sacrificed his young life to save the others.

Since he had held in his hand the leader's staff, it seemed to him as if he had assumed the duty of watching over his people, so he listened and listened till he could hear a slight trembling of the ground and finally a low rumble. That was the foe, that must be Pharaoh's chariots, and how swiftly the proud steeds whirled them forward.

Springing up as if a lash had struck him, he dashed on to urge the others to hasten.

How oppressively sultry the air had grown, spite of the raging storm which extinguished so many torches! The moon was concealed by clouds, but the flickering fire on the summit of the lofty height of Baal-zephon blazed brighter and brighter. The sparks that rose from the midst of the flames glittered as they swept westward; for the wind now came more from the east.

Scarcely had he noticed this, when he hurried back to the boys bearing pans of pitch who closed the procession, to command them in the utmost haste to fill the copper vessels afresh and see that the smoke rose in dense, heavy clouds; for, he said to himself, the storm will drive the smoke into the faces of the stallions who draw the chariots and frighten or stop them.

No means seemed to him too insignificant, every moment that could be gained was precious; and as soon as he had convinced himself that the smoke-clouds were pouring densely from the vessels and making it difficult to breathe the air of the path over which the people had passed, he hurried forward, shouting to the elders whom he overtook that Pharaoh's chariots were close at hand and the march must be hastened. At once pedestrians, bearers, drivers, and shepherds exerted all their strength to advance faster; and though the wind, which blew more and more from the east, impeded their progress, all struggled stoutly against it, and dread of their approaching pursuers doubled their strength.

The youth seemed to the heads of the tribes, who nodded approval wherever he appeared, like a shepherd dog guarding and urging the flock; and when he had slipped through the moving bands and battled his way forward against the storm, the east wind bore to his ears as if in reward a strange shout; for the nearer he came to its source, the louder it rang, and the more surely he perceived that it was a cry of joy and exultation, the first that had burst from a Hebrew's breast for many a long day.

It refreshed Ephraim like a cool drink after long thirsting, and he could not refrain from shouting aloud and crying joyously to the others: "Saved, saved!" Two tribes had already reached the eastern shore of the bay and were raising the glad shouts which, with the fires blazing in huge pans on the shore, kindled the courage of the approaching fugitives and braced their failing strength. Ephraim saw by their light the majestic figure of Moses on a hill by the sea, extending his staff over the waters, and the spectacle impressed him, like all the other fugitives, from the highest to the lowest, more deeply than aught else and strongly increased the courage of his heart. This man was indeed the trusted servant of the Most High, and so long as he held his staff uplifted, the waves seemed spell-bound, and through him God forbade their return.

He, Ephraim, need no longer appeal to the Omnipotent One—that was the appointed task of this great and exalted personage; but he must continue to fulfil his little duty of watching the progress of individuals.

Back against the stream of fugitives to the lepers and torch-bearers he hastened, shouting to each division, "Saved! Saved! They have gained the goal. Moses' staff is staying the waves. Many have already reached the shore. Thank the Lord! Forward, that you, too, may join in the rejoicing! Fix your eyes on the two red beacons! The rescued ones lighted them! The servant of the Lord is standing between them with uplifted staff."

Then, kneeling on the wet sand, he again pressed his ear to the ground, and now heard distinctly, close at hand, the rattle of wheels and the swift beat of horses' hoofs.

But while still listening, the noise gradually ceased, and he heard nothing save the howling of the furious storm and the threatening dash of the surging waves, or a single cry borne by the east wind.

The chariots had reached the dry portion of the bay and lingered some time ere they continued their way along this dangerous path; but suddenly the Egyptian war-cry rang out, and the rattle of wheels was again heard. They advanced more slowly than before but faster than the people could walk.

For the Egyptians also the road remained dry; but if his people only kept a short distance in advance he need feel no anxiety; during the night the rescued tribes could disperse among the mountains and hide in places where no chariots nor horses could follow. Moses knew this region where he had lived so long as a fugitive; it was only necessary to inform him of the close vicinity of the foe. So he trusted one of his play-fellows of the tribe of Benjamin with the message, and the latter had not far to go to reach the shore. He himself remained behind to watch the approaching army; for already, without stooping or listening, spite of the storm raging around him, he heard the rattle of wheels and the neighing of the horses. But the lepers, whose ears also caught the sound, wailed and lamented, feeling themselves in imagination flung to the ground, crushed by the chariots, or crowded into a watery grave, for the pathway had grown narrower and the sea seemed to be trying in earnest to regain the land it had lost.

The men and cattle could no longer advance in ranks as wide as before, and while the files of the hurrying bodies narrowed they lengthened, and precious time was lost. Those on the right were already wading through the rising water in haste and terror; for already the commands of the Egyptian leaders were heard in the distance.

But the enemy was evidently delayed, and Ephraim easily perceived the cause of their diminished speed; for the road constantly grew softer and the narrow wheels of the chariots cut deeply into it and perhaps sank to the axles.

Protected by the darkness, he glided forward toward the pursuers, as far as he could, and heard here a curse, yonder a fierce command to ply the lash more vigorously; at last he distinctly heard one leader exclaim to the man next him:

"Accursed folly! If they had only let us start before noon, and not waited until the omen had been consulted and Anna had been installed with all due solemnity in Bai's place, it would have been easy work, and we should have caught them like a flock of quail! The chief-priest was wont to bear himself stoutly in the field, and now he gives up the command because a dying woman touches his heart."

"Siptah's mother!" said another soothingly. "Yet, after all, twenty princesses ought not to have turned him from his duty to us. Had he remained, there would have been no need of scourging our steeds to death, and that at an hour when every sensible leader lets his men gather round the camp-fires to eat their suppers and play draughts. Look to the horses, Heter! We are fast in the sand again!"

A loud out-cry rose behind the first chariot, and Ephraim heard another voice shout:

"Forward, if it costs the horses their lives!"

"If return were possible," said the commander of the chariot-soldiers, a relative of the king, "I would go back now. But as matters are, one would tumble over the other. So forward, whatever it may cost. We are close on their heels. Halt! Halt! That accursed stinging smoke! Wait, you dogs! As soon as the pathway widens, we'll run you down with scant ceremony, and may the gods deprive me of a day of life for each one I spare! Another torch out! One can't see one's hand before one's face! At a time like this a beggar's crutch would be better than a leader's staff."

"And an executioner's noose round the neck rather than a gold chain!" said another with a fierce oath.

"If the moon would only appear again! Because the astrologers predicted that it would shine in full splendor from evening till morning, I myself advised the late departure, turning night into day. If it were only lighter!..."

But this sentence remained unfinished, for a gust of wind, bursting like a wild beast from the south-eastern ravine of Mount Baal-zephon, rushed upon the fugitives, and a high wave drenched Ephraim from head to foot.

Gasping for breath, he flung back his hair and wiped his eyes; but loud cries of terror rang from the lips of the Egyptians behind him; for the same wave that struck the youth had hurled the foremost chariots into the sea.

Ephraim began to fear for his people and, while running forward to join them again, a brilliant flash of lightning illumined the bay, Mount Baal-zephon, and every surrounding object. The thunder was somewhat long in following, but the storm soon came nearer, and at last the lightning no longer flashed through the darkness in zigzag lines, but in shapeless sheets of flame, and ere they faded the deafening crash of the thunder pealed forth, reverberating in wild uproar amid the hard, rocky precipices of the rugged mountain, and dying away in deep, muttering echoes along the end of the bay and the shore.

Whenever the clouds, menacing destruction, discharged their lightnings, sea and land, human beings and animals, far and near, were illumined by the brilliant glare, while the waters and the sky above were tinged with a sulphurous yellow hue through which the vivid lightning shone and flamed as through a wall of yellow glass.

Ephraim now thought he perceived that the blackest thunder-clouds came from the south and not from the north, but the glare of the lightning showed behind him a span of frightened horses rushing into the sea, one chariot shattered against another, and farther on several jammed firmly together to the destruction of their occupants, while they barred the progress of others.

Yet the foe still advanced, and the space which separated pursued and pursuers did not increase. But the confusion among the latter had become so great that the warriors' cries of terror and their leaders' shouts of encouragement and menace were distinctly heard whenever the fierce crashing of the thunder died away.

Yet, black as were the clouds on the southern horizon, fiercely as the tempest raged, the gloomy sky still withheld its floods and the fugitives were wet, not with the water from the clouds but by the waves of the sea, whose surges constantly dashed higher and more and more frequently washed the dry bed of the bay.

Narrower and narrower grew the pathway, and with it the end of the procession.

Meanwhile the flames blazing in the pitch pans continued to show the terrified fugitives the goal of escape and remind them of Moses and the staff God had given him. Every step brought them nearer to it. Now a loud shout of joy announced that the tribe of Benjamin had also reached the shore; but they had at last been obliged to wade, and were drenched by the foaming surf. It had cost unspeakable effort to save the oxen from the surging waves, get the loaded carts forward, and keep the cattle together; but now man and beast stood safe on shore. Only the strangers and the lepers were still to be rescued. The latter possessed no herds of their own, but the former had many and both sheep and cattle were so terrified by the storm that they struggled against passing through the water, now a foot deep over the road. Ephraim hurried to the shore, called on the shepherds to follow him and, under his direction, they helped drive the herds forward.

The attempt was successful and, amid the thunder and lightning, greeted with loud cheers, the last man and the last head of cattle reached the land.

The lepers were obliged to wade through water rising to their knees and at last to their waists and, ere they had gained the shore, the sluices of heaven opened and the rain poured in torrents. Yet they, too, arrived at the goal and though many a mother who had carried her child a long time in her arms or on her shoulder, fell upon her knees exhausted on the land, and many a hapless sufferer who, aided by a stronger companion in misery, had dragged the carts through the yielding sand or wading in the water carried a litter, felt his disfigured head burn with fever, they, too, escaped destruction.

They were to wait beyond the palm-trees, whose green foliage appeared on the hilly ground at the edge of some springs near the shore; the others were to be led farther into the country to begin, at a given signal, the journey toward the southeast into the mountains, through whose inhospitable stony fastnesses a regular army and the war-chariots could advance only with the utmost difficulty.

Hur had assembled his shepherds and they stood armed with lances, slings, and short swords, ready to attack the enemy who ventured to step on shore. Horses and men were to be cut down and a high wall was to be made of the fragments of the chariots to bar the way of the pursuing Egyptians.

The pans of burning pitch on the shore were shielded and fed so industriously that neither the pouring rain nor the wind extinguished them. They were to light the shepherds who had undertaken to attack the chariot-soldiers, and were commanded by old Nun, Hur, and Ephraim.

But they waited in vain for the pursuers, and when the youth, first of all, perceived by the light of the torches that the way by which the rescued fugitives had come was now a wide sea, and the smoke was blown toward the north instead of toward the southwest—it was at the time of the first morning watch—his heart, surcharged with joy and gratitude, sent forth the jubilant shout: "Look at the pans. The wind has shifted! It is driving the sea northward. Pharaoh's army has been swallowed by the waves!"

The group of rescued Hebrews remained silent for a short time; but suddenly Nun's loud voice exclaimed:

"He has seen aright, children! What are we mortals! Lord, Lord! Stern and terrible art Thou in judgment upon Thy foes!"

Here loud cries interrupted him; for at the springs where Moses leaned exhausted against a palm-tree, and Aaron was resting with many others, the people had also perceived what Ephraim had noticed—and from lip to lip ran the glad, terrible, incredible, yet true tidings, which each passing moment more surely confirmed.

Many an eye was raised toward the sky, across which the black clouds were rushing farther and farther northward.

The rain was ceasing; instead of the lightning and thunder only a few pale flashes were seen over the isthmus and the distant sea at the north, while in the south the sky was brightening.

At last the setting moon emerged from the grey clouds, and her peaceful light silvered the heights of Baal-zephon and the shore of the bay, whose bottom was once more covered with tossing waves.

The raging, howling storm had passed into the low sighing of the morning breeze, and the sea, which had dashed against the rocks like a roaring wild-beast, now lay quivering with broken strength at the stone base of the mountain.

For a short time the sea still spread a dark pall over the many Egyptian corpses, but the paling moon, ere her setting, splendidly embellished the briny resting-place of a king and his nobles; for her rays illumined and bordered their coverlet, the sea, with a rich array of sparkling diamonds in a silver setting.

While the east was brightening and the sky had clothed itself in the glowing hues of dawn, the camp had been pitched; but little time remained for a hasty meal for, shortly after sunrise, the gong had summoned the people and, as soon as they gathered near the springs, Miriam swung her timbrel, shaking the bells and striking the calf-skin till it resounded again. As she moved lightly forward, the women and maidens followed her in the rhythmic step of the dance; but she sang:

"I will sing unto the Lord, for he hath triumphed gloriously: the horse and his rider hath he thrown into the sea.

"The Lord is my strength and song, and he is become my salvation: he is my God, and I will prepare him an habitation; my father's God, and I will exalt him.

"The Lord is a man of war: the Lord is his name. Pharaoh's chariots and his host hath he cast into the sea: his chosen captains also are drowned in the Red Sea.

"The depths have covered them: they sank into the bottom as a stone.

"Thy right hand, O Lord, is become glorious in power: thy right hand, O Lord, hath dashed in pieces the enemy.

"And in the greatness of thine excellency thou hast overthrown them that rose up against thee: thou sentest forth thy wrath, which consumed them as stubble.

"And with the blast of thy nostrils the waters were gathered together, the floods stood upright as an heap, and the depths were congealed in the heart of the sea.

"The enemy said, I will pursue, I will overtake, I will divide the spoil; my lust shall be satisfied upon them; I will draw my sword, my hand shall destroy them.

"Thou didst blow with thy wind, the sea covered them: they sank as lead in the mighty waters.

"Who is like unto thee, O Lord, among the gods? Who is like thee, glorious in holiness, fearful in praises, doing wonders?

"Thou stretchedst out thy right hand, the earth swallowed them.

"Thou, in thy mercy hast led forth the people which thou hast redeemed: thou hast guided them in thy strength unto thy holy habitation."

Men and women joined in the song, when she repeated the words:

"I will sing unto the Lord, for he hath triumphed gloriously: the horse and his rider hath he thrown into the sea."

This song and this hour of rejoicing were never forgotten by the Hebrews, and each heart was filled with the glory of God and the glad and grateful anticipation of better, happier days.

CHAPTER XXIII

The hymn of praise had died away, but though the storm had long since raged itself into calmness, the morning sky, which had been beautiful in the rosy flush of dawn, was again veiled by grey mists, and a strong wind still blew from the southwest, lashing the sea and shaking and swaying the tops of the palm-trees beside the springs.

The rescued people had paid due honor to the Most High, even the most indifferent and rebellious had joined in Miriam's song of praise; yet, when the ranks of the dancers approached the sea, many left the procession to hurry to the shore, which presented many attractions.

Hundreds had now gathered on the strand, where the waves, like generous robbers, washed ashore the booty they had seized during the night.

Even the women did not allow the wind to keep them back; for the two strongest impulses of the human heart, avarice and the longing for vengeance, drew them to the beach.

Some new object of desire appeared every moment; here lay the corpse of a warrior, yonder his shattered chariot. If the latter had belonged to a man of rank, its gold or silver ornaments were torn off, while the short sword or battle-axe was drawn from the girdle of the lifeless owner, and men and women of low degree, male and female slaves belonging to the Hebrews and foreigners, robbed the corpses of the clasps and circlets of the precious metal, or twisted the rings from the swollen fingers of the drowned.

The ravens which had followed the wandering tribes and vanished during the storm, again appeared and, croaking, struggled against the wind to maintain their places above the prey whose scent had attracted them.

But the dregs of the fugitive hordes were still more greedy than they, and wherever the sea washed a costly ornament ashore, there were fierce outcries and angry quarrelling. The leaders kept aloof; the people, they thought, had a right to this booty, and whenever one of them undertook to control their rude greed, he received no obedience.

The pass to which the Egyptians had brought them within the last few hours had been so terrible, that even the better natures among the Hebrews did not think of curbing the thirst for vengeance. Even grey-bearded men of dignified bearing, and wives and mothers whose looks augured gentle hearts thrust back the few hapless foes who had succeeded in reaching the land on the ruins of the war-chariots or baggage-wagons. With shepherds' crooks and travelling staves, knives and axes, stones and insults they forced their hands from the floating wood, and the few who nevertheless reached the land were flung by the furious mob into the sea which had taken pity on them in vain.

Their wrath was so great, and vengeance so sacred a duty, that no one thought of the respect, the pity, the consideration, which are misfortune's due, and not a word was uttered to appeal to generosity or compassion or even to remind the people of the profit which might be derived from holding the rescued soldiers as prisoners of war.

"Death to our mortal foes! Destruction to them! Down with them! Feed the fishes with them! You drove us into the sea with our children, now try the salt waves yourselves!"

Such were the shouts that rose everywhere, and which no one opposed, not even Miriam and Ephraim, who had also gone down to the shore to witness the scene it presented.

The maiden had become the wife of Hur, but her new condition had made little change in her nature and conduct. The fate of her people and the intercourse with God, whose prophetess she felt herself to be, were still her highest aims. Now that all for which she had hoped and prayed was fulfilled; now that at the first great triumph of her efforts she had expressed the feelings of the faithful in her song, she felt as if she were the leader of the grateful multitude at whose head she had marched singing and as if she had attained the goal of her life.

Ephraim had reminded her of Hosea and, while talking with him about the prisoner, she moved on as proudly as a queen, answering the greetings of the throng with majestic dignity. Her eyes sparkled with joy, and her features wore an expression of compassion only at brief intervals, when the youth spoke of the greatest sufferings which he had borne with his uncle. She doubtless still remembered the man she had loved, but he was no longer necessary to the lofty goal of her aspirations.

Ephraim had just spoken of the beautiful Egyptian, who had loved Hosea and at whose intercession the prisoner's chains had been removed, when loud outcries were heard at a part of the strand where many of the people had gathered. Shouts of joy mingled with yells of fury; and awakened the conjecture that the sea had washed some specially valuable prize ashore.

Curiosity drew both to the spot, and as Miriam's stately bearing made the throng move respectfully aside, they soon saw the mournful contents of a large travelling-chariot, which had lost its wheels. The linen canopy which had protected it was torn away, and on the floor lay two elderly Egyptian women; a third, who was much younger, leaned against the back of the vehicle thus strangely transformed into a boat. Her companions lay dead in the water which had covered its floor, and several Hebrew women were in the act of tearing the costly gold ornaments from the neck and arms of one of the corpses. Some chance had preserved this young woman's life, and she was now giving her rich jewels to the Israelites. Her pale lips and slender, half-frozen hands trembled as she did so, and in low, musical tones she promised the robbers to yield them all she possessed and pay a large ransom, if they would spare her. She was so young, and she had shown kindness to a Hebrew surely they might listen to her.

It was a touching entreaty, but so often interrupted by threats and curses that only a few could hear it. Just as Ephraim and Miriam reached the shore she shrieked aloud—a rude hand had torn the gold serpent from her ear.

The cry pierced the youth's heart like a dagger-thrust and his cheeks paled, for he recognized Kasana. The bodies beside her were those of her nurse and the wife of the chief priest Bai.

Scarcely able to control himself, Ephraim thrust aside the men who separated him from the object of the moment's assault, sprang on the sand-hill at whose foot the chariot had rested, and shouted with glowing cheeks in wild excitement:

"Back! Woe to any one who touches her!"

But a Hebrew woman, the wife of a brickmaker whose child had died in terrible convulsions during the passage through the sea, had already snatched the dagger from her girdle, and with the jeering cry "This for my little Ruth, you jade!" dealt her a blow in the back. Then she raised the tiny blood-stained weapon for a second stroke; but ere she could give her enemy another thrust, Ephraim flung himself between her and her victim and wrenched the dagger from her grasp. Then planting himself before the wounded girl, he swung the blade aloft exclaiming in loud, threatening tones:

"Whoever touches her, you robbers and murderers, shall mingle his blood with this woman's." Then he flung himself beside Kasana's bleeding form, and finding that she had lost consciousness, raised her in his arms and carried her to Miriam.

The astonished plunderers speechlessly made way for a few minutes, but ere he reached the prophetess shouts of: "Vengeance! Vengeance!" were heard in all directions. "We found the woman: the booty belongs to us alone!—How dares the insolent Ephraimite call us robbers and murderers?—Wherever Egyptian blood can be spilled, it must flow!—At him!—Snatch the girl from him!"

The youth paid no heed to these outbursts of wrath until he had laid Kasana's head in the lap of Miriam, who had seated herself on the nearest sand-hill, and as the angry throng, the women in front of the men, pressed upon him, he again waved his dagger, crying: "Back—I command you. Let all of the blood of Ephraim and Judah rally around me and Miriam, the wife of their chief! That's right, brothers, and woe betide any hand that touches her. Do you shriek for vengeance? Has it not been yours through yonder monster who murdered the poor defenceless one? Do you want your victim's jewels? Well, well; they belong to you, and I will give you mine to boot, if you will leave the wife of Hur to care for this dying girl!"

With these words he bent over Kasana, took off the clasps and rings she still wore, and gave them to the greedy hands outstretched to seize them. Lastly he stripped the broad gold circlet from his arm, and holding it aloft exclaimed:

"Here is the promised payment. If you will depart quietly and leave this woman to Miriam, I will give you the gold, and you can divide it among you. If you thirst for more blood, come on; but I will keep the armlet."

These words did not fail to produce their effect. The furious women looked at the heavy broad gold armlet, then at the handsome youth, and the men of Judah and Ephraim who had gathered around him, and finally glanced enquiringly into one another's faces. At last the wife of a foreign trader cried:

"Let him give us the gold, and we'll leave the handsome young chief his bleeding sweetheart."

To this decision the others agreed, and though the brickmaker's infuriated wife, who thought as the avenger of her child she had done an act pleasing in the sight of God, and was upbraided for it as a murderess, reviled the youth with frantic gestures, she was dragged away by the crowd to the shore where they hoped to find more booty.

During this threatening transaction, Miriam had fearlessly examined Kasana's wound and bound it up with skilful hands, The dagger which

Prince Siptah had jestingly given the beautiful lady of his love, that she might not go to war defenceless, had inflicted a deep wound under the shoulder, and the blood had flowed so abundantly that the feeble spark of life threatened to die out at any moment.

But she still lived, and in this condition was borne to the tent of Nun, which was the nearest within reach.

The old chief had just been supplying weapons to the shepherds and youths whom Ephraim had summoned to go to the relief of the imprisoned Hosea, and had promised to join them, when the mournful procession approached.

As Kasana loved the handsome old man, the latter had for many years kept a place in his heart for Captain Homecht's pretty daughter.

She had never met him without gladdening him by a greeting which he always returned with kind words, such as: "The Lord bless you, child!" or: "It is a delightful hour when an old man meets so fair a creature." Many years before—she had then worn the curls of childhood—he had even sent her a lamb, whose snowy fleece was specially silky, after having bartered the corn from her father's lands for cattle of his most famous breed—and what his son had told him of Kasana had been well fitted to increase his regard for her.

He beheld in the archer's daughter the most charming young girl in Tanis and, had she been the child of Hebrew parents, he would have rejoiced to wed her to his son.

To find his darling in such a state caused the old man grief so profound that bright tears ran down upon his snowy beard and his voice trembled as, while greeting her, he saw the blood-stained bandage on her shoulder.

After she had been laid on his couch, and Nun had placed his own chest of medicines at the disposal of the skilful prophetess, Miriam asked the men to leave her alone with the suffering Egyptian, and when she again called them into the tent she had revived the strength of the severely-wounded girl with cordials, and bandaged the hurt more carefully than had been possible before.

Kasana, cleansed from the blood-stains and with her hair neatly arranged, lay beneath the fresh linen coverings like a sleeping child just on the verge of maidenhood.

She was still breathing, but the color had not returned to cheeks or lips, and she did not open her eyes until she had drunk the cordial Miriam mixed for her a second time.

The old man and his grandson stood at the foot of her couch, and each would fain have asked the other why he could not restrain his tears whenever he looked at this stranger's face.

The certainty that Kasana was wicked and faithless, which had so unexpectedly forced itself upon Ephraim, had suddenly turned his heart from her and startled him back into the right path which he had abandoned. Yet what he had heard in her tent had remained a profound secret, and as he told his grandfather and Miriam that she had compassionately interceded for the prisoners, and both had desired to hear more of her, he had felt like a father who had witnessed the crime of a beloved son, and no word of the abominable things he had heard had escaped his lips.

Now he rejoiced that he had kept silence; for whatever he might have seen and heard, this fair creature certainly was capable of no base deed.

To the old man she had never ceased to be the lovely child whom he had known, the apple of his eye and the joy of his heart. So he gazed with tender anxiety at the features convulsed by pain and, when she at last opened her eyes, smiled at her with paternal affection. Her glance showed that she instantly recognized both him and Ephraim, but weakness baffled her attempt to nod to them. Yet her expressive face revealed surprise and joy, and when Miriam had given her the cordial a third time and bathed her brow with a powerful essence, her large eyes wandered from face to face and, noticing the troubled looks of the men, she managed to whisper:

"The wound aches—and death—must I die?" One looked enquiringly at another, and the men would gladly have concealed the terrible truth; but she went on:

"Oh, let me know. Ah, I pray you, tell me the truth!"

Miriam, who was kneeling beside her, found courage to answer:

"Yes, you poor young creature, the wound is deep, but whatever my skill can accomplish shall be done to preserve your life as long as possible."

The words sounded kind and full of compassion, yet the deep voice of the prophetess seemed to hurt Kasana; for her lips quivered painfully while Miriam was speaking, and when she ceased, her eyes closed and one large tear after another ran down her cheeks. Deep, anxious silence reigned around her until she again raised her lashes and, fixing her eyes wearily on Miriam, asked softly, as if perplexed by some strange spectacle:

"You are a woman, and yet practise the art of the leech."

"My God has commanded me to care for the suffering ones of our people," replied the other.

The dying girl's eyes began to glitter with a restless light, and she gasped in louder tones, nay with a firmness that surprised the others:

"You are Miriam, the woman who sent for Hosea." And when the other answered promptly and proudly: "It is as you say!" Kasana continued:

"And you possess striking, imperious beauty, and much influence. He obeyed your summons, and you—you consented to wed another?"

Again the prophetess answered, this time with gloomy earnestness: "It is as you say."

The dying girl closed her eyes once more, and a strange proud smile hovered around her lips. But it soon vanished and a great and painful restlessness seized upon her. The fingers of her little hands, her lips, nay, even her eyelids moved perpetually, and her smooth, narrow forehead contracted as if some great thought occupied her mind.

At last the ideas that troubled her found utterance and, as if roused from her repose, she exclaimed in terrified accents:

"You are Ephraim, who seemed like his son, and the old man is Nun, his dear father. There you stand and will live on.... But I—I... Oh, it is so hard to leave the light.... Anubis will lead me before the judgment seat of Osiris. My heart will be weighed, and then...."

Here she shuddered and opened and closed her trembling hands; but she soon regained her composure and began to speak again. Miriam, however, sternly forbade this, because it would hasten her death.

Then the sufferer, summoning all her strength, exclaimed hastily, as loudly as her voice would permit, after measuring the prophetess' tall figure with a long glance: "You wish to prevent me from doing my duty—you?"

There had been a slight touch of mockery in the question; but Kasana doubtless felt that it was necessary to spare her strength; for she continued far more quietly, as though talking to herself:

"I cannot die so, I cannot! How it happened; why I sacrificed all, all.... I must atone for it; I will not complain, if he only learns how it came to pass. Oh, Nun, dear old Nun, who gave me the lamb when I was a little thing—I loved it so dearly—and you, Ephraim, my dear boy, I will tell you everything."

Here a painful fit of coughing interrupted her; but as soon as she recovered her breath, she turned to Miriam, and called in a tone which so plainly expressed bitter dislike, that it would have surprised any one who knew her kindly nature:

"But you, yonder,—you tall woman with the deep voice who are a physician, you lured him from Tanis, from his soldiers and from me. He, he obeyed your summons. And you... you became another's wife; probably after his arrival... yes! For when Ephraim summoned him, he called you a maiden... I don't know whether this caused him, Hosea, pain.... But there is one thing I do know, and that is that I want to confess something and must do so, ere it is too late.... And no one must hear it save those who love him, and I—do you hear—I love him, love him better than aught else on earth! But you? You have a husband, and a God whose commands you eagerly obey—you say so yourself. What can Hosea be to you? So I beseech you to leave us. I have met few who repelled me, but you—your voice, your eyes— they pierce me to the heart—and if you were near I could not speak as I must.... and oh, talking hurts me so! But before you go—you are a leech—let me know this one thing—I have many messages to leave for him ere I die.... Will it kill me to talk?"

Again the prophetess found no other words in answer except the brief: "It is as you say," and this time they sounded harsh and ominous.

While wavering between the duty which, as a physician, she owed the sufferer and the impulse not to refuse the request of a dying woman, she read in old Nun's eyes an entreaty to obey Kasana's wish, and with drooping head left the tent. But the bitter words of the hapless girl pursued her and spoiled the day which had begun so gloriously and also many a later hour; nay, to her life's end she could not understand why, in the presence of this poor, dying woman, she had been overpowered by the feeling that she was her inferior and must take a secondary place.

As soon as Kasana was left alone with Nun and Ephraim, and the latter had flung himself on his knees beside her couch, while the old man kissed her brow, and bowed his white head to listen to her low words, she began:

"I feel better now. That tall woman... those gloomy brows that meet in the middle... those nightblack eyes... they glow with so fierce a fire, yet are so cold.... That woman... did Hosea love her, father? Tell me; I am not asking from idle curiosity!"

"He honored her," replied the old man in a troubled tone, "as did our whole nation; for she has a lofty spirit, and our God suffers her to hear His voice; but you, my darling, have been dear to him from childhood, I know."

A slight tremor shook the dying girl. She closed her eyes for a short time and a sunny smile hovered around her lips.

She lay in this attitude so long that Nun feared death had claimed her and, holding the medicine in his hand, listened to hear her breathing.

Kasana did not seem to notice it; but when she finally opened her eyes, she held out her hand for the cordial, drank it, and then began again:

"It seemed just as if I had seen him, Hosea. He wore the panoply of war just as he did the first time he took me into his arms. I was a little thing and felt afraid of him, he looked so grave, and my nurse had told me that he had slain a great many of our foes. Yet I was glad when he came and grieved when he went away. So the years passed, and love grew with my growth. My young heart was so full of him, so full.... Even when they forced me to wed another, and after I had become a widow."

The last words had been scarcely audible, and she rested some time ere she continued:

"Hosea knows all this, except how anxious I was when he was in the field, and how I longed for him ere he returned. At last, at last he came home, and how I rejoiced! But he, Hosea...? That woman—Ephraim told me so—that tall, arrogant woman summoned him to Pithom. But he returned, and then.... Oh, Nun, your son... that was the hardest thing! ... He refused my hand, which my father offered.... And how that hurt me!... I can say no more!... Give me the drink!"

Her cheeks had flushed crimson during these painful confessions, and when the experienced old man perceived how rapidly the excitement under which she was laboring hastened the approach of death, he begged her to keep silence; but she insisted upon profiting by the time still allowed her, and though the sharp pain with which a short cough tortured her forced her to press her hand upon her breast, she continued:

"Then hate came; but it did not last long—and never did I love him more ardently than when I drove after the poor convict—you remember, my boy. Then began the horrible, wicked, evil time... of which I must tell him that he may not despise me, if he hears about it. I never had a mother, and there was no one to warn me.... Where shall I begin? Prince Siptah—you know him, father—that wicked man will soon rule over my country. My father is in a conspiracy with him... merciful gods, I can say no more!"

Terror and despair convulsed her features as she uttered these words; but Ephraim interrupted her and, with tearful eyes and faltering voice, confessed that he knew all. Then he repeated what he had heard while listening outside of her tent, and her glance confirmed the tale.

When he finally spoke of the wife of the viceroy and chief-priest Bai, whose body had been borne to the shore with her, Kasana interrupted him with the low exclamation:

"She planned it all. Her husband was to be the greatest man in the country and rule even Pharaoh; for Siptah is not the son of a king."

"And," the old man interrupted, to quiet her and help her tell what she desired to say, "as Bai raised, he can overthrow him. He will become, even more certainly than the dethroned monarch, the tool of the man who made him king. But I know Aarsu the Syrian, and if I see aright, the time will come when he will himself strive, in distracted Egypt, rent by internal disturbances, for the power which, through his mercenaries, he aided others to grasp. But child, what induced you to follow the army and this shameful profligate?"

The dying girl's eyes sparkled, for the question brought her directly to what she desired to tell, and she answered as loudly and quickly as her weakness permitted:

"I did it for your son's sake, for love of him, to liberate Hosea. The evening before I had steadily and firmly refused the wife of Bai. But when I saw your son at the well and he, Hosea.... Oh, at last he was so affectionate and kissed me so kindly... and then—then.... My poor heart! I saw him, the best of men, perishing amid contumely and disease.

"And when he passed with chains one thought darted through my mind...."

"You determined, you dear, foolish, misguided child," cried the old man, "to win the heart of the future king in order, through him, to release my son, your friend?"

The dying girl again smiled assent and softly exclaimed:

"Yes, yes, I did it for that, for that alone. And the prince was so abhorrent to me. And the shame, the disgrace—oh, how terrible it was!"

"And you incurred it for my son's sake," the old man interrupted, raising her hand, wet with his tears, to his lips; but she fixed her eyes on Ephraim, sobbing softly:

"I thought of him too. He is so young, and it is so horrible in the mines."

She shuddered again as she spoke; but the youth covered her burning hand with kisses, while she gazed affectionately at him and the old man, adding in faltering accents:

"Oh, all is well now, and if the gods grant him freedom...."

Here Ephraim interrupted her to exclaim in fiery tones:

"We are going to the mines this very day. I and my comrades, and my grandfather with us, will put his guards to flight."

"And he shall hear from my lips," Nun added, "how faithfully Kasana loved him, and that his life will be too short to thank her for such a sacrifice."

His voice failed him—but every trace of suffering had vanished from the countenance of the dying girl, and for a long time she gazed heavenward silently with a happy look. By degrees, however, her smooth brow contracted in an anxious frown, and she gasped in low tones:

"Well, all is well... only one thing... my body... unembalmed ... without the sacred amulets...."

But the old man answered:

"As soon as you have closed your eyes, I will give it, carefully wrapped, to the Phoenician captain now tarrying here, that he may deliver it to your father."

Kasana tried to turn her head toward him to thank him with a loving glance, but she suddenly pressed both hands on her breast, crimson blood welled from her lips, her cheeks varied from livid white to fiery scarlet and, after a brief, painful convulsion, she sank back. Death laid his hand on the loving heart, and her features gained the expression of a child whose mother has forgiven its fault and clasped it to her heart ere it fell asleep.

The old man, weeping, closed the dead girl's eyes. Ephraim, deeply moved, kissed the closed lids, and after a short silence Nun said:

"I do not like to enquire about our fate beyond the grave, which Moses himself does not know; but whoever has lived so that his or her memory is tenderly cherished in the souls of loved ones, has, I think, done the utmost possible to secure a future existence. We will remember this dead girl in our most sacred hours. Let us do for her corpse what we promised, and then set forth to show the man for whom Kasana sacrificed what she most valued that we do not love him less than this Egyptian woman."

CHAPTER XXIV

The prisoners of state who were being transported to the mines made slow progress. Even the experienced captain of the guards had never had a more toilsome trip or one more full of annoyances, obstacles, and mishaps.

One of his moles, Ephraim, had escaped; he had lost his faithful hounds, and after his troop had been terrified and drenched by a storm such as scarcely occurred in these desert regions once in five years, a second had burst the next evening—the one which brought destruction on Pharaoh's army—and this had been still more violent and lasting.

The storm had delayed the march and, after the last cloud-burst, several convicts and guards had been attacked by fever owing to their wet night-quarters in the open air. The Egyptian asses, too, who were unused to rain, had suffered and some of the best had been left on the road.

Finally they had been obliged to bury two dead prisoners, and place three who were dangerously ill on the remaining asses; and the other prisoners were laden with the stores hitherto carried by the beasts of burden. This was the first time such a thing had happened during the leader's service of five and twenty years, and he expected severe reproofs.

All these things exerted a baneful influence on the disposition of the man, who was usually reputed one of the kindest-hearted of his companions in office; and Joshua, the accomplice of the bold lad whose flight was associated with the other vexations, suffered most sorely from his ill-humor.

Perhaps the irritated man would have dealt more gently with him, had he complained like the man behind him, or burst into fierce oaths like his yoke-mate, who made threatening allusions to the future when his sister-in-law would be in high favor with Pharaoh and know how to repay those who ill-treated her dear relative.

But Hosea had resolved to bear whatever the rude fellow and his mates chose to inflict with the same equanimity that he endured the scorching sun which, ever since he had served in the army, had tortured him during many a march through the desert, and his steadfast, manly character helped him keep this determination.

If the captain of the gang loaded him with extra heavy burdens, he summoned all the strength of his muscles and tottered forward without a word of complaint until his knees trembled under him; then the captain would rush to him, throw several packages from his shoulders, and exclaim that he understood his spite; he was only trying to be left on the road, to get him into fresh difficulties; but he would not allow himself to be robbed of the lives of the men who were needed in the mines.

Once the captain inflicted a wound that bled severely; but he instantly made every effort to cure it, gave him wine to restore his strength, and delayed the march half a day to permit him to rest.

He had not forgotten Prince Siptah's promise of a rich reward to any one who brought him tidings of Hosea's death, but this was the very reason that induced the honest-hearted man to watch carefully over his prisoner's life; for the consciousness of having violated his duty for the sake of reaping any advantage would have robbed him of all pleasure in food and drink, as well as of the sound sleep which were his greatest blessings.

So though the Hebrew prisoner was tortured, it was never beyond the limits of the endurable, and he had the pleasure of rendering, by his own great strength, many a service to his weaker companions.

He had commended his fate to the God who had summoned him to His service; but he was well aware that he must not rest content with mere pious confidence, and therefore thought by day and night of escape. But the chain that bound him to his companions in suffering was too firmly forged, and was so carefully examined and hammered every morning and evening, that the attempt to escape would only have plunged him into greater misery.

The prisoners had at first marched through a hilly region, then climbed upward, with a long mountain chain in view, and finally reached a desert country from which truncated sandstone cones rose singly from the rocky ground.

On the fifth evening they encamped near a large mountain which Nature seemed to have piled up from flat layers of stone and, as the sun of the sixth day rose, they turned into a side valley leading to the mines in the province of Bech.

During the first few days they had been overtaken by a messenger from the king's silver-house; but on the other hand they had met several little bands bearing to Egypt malachite, turquoise, and copper, as well as the green glass made at the mines.

Among those whom they met at the entrance of the cross-valley into which they turned on the last morning was a married couple on their way homeward, after having received a pardon from the king. The captain of the guards pointed them out to encourage his exhausted moles, but the spectacle produced the opposite effect; for the tangled locks of the man, who had scarcely passed his thirtieth year, were grey, his tall figure was bowed and emaciated, and his naked back was covered with scars and bleeding wales; the wife, who had shared his misery, was blind. She sat cowering on an ass, in the dull torpor of insanity, and though the passing of the convicts made a startling interruption to the silence of the wilderness, and her hearing had remained keen, she paid no heed, but continued to stare indifferently into vacancy.

The sight of the hapless pair placed Hosea's own terrible future before him as if in a mirror, and for the first time he groaned aloud and covered his face with his hands.

The captain of the guards perceived this and, touched by the horror of the man whose resolution had hitherto seemed peerless, called to him:

"They don't all come home like that, no indeed!"

"Because they are even worse off," he thought. "But the poor wights needn't know it beforehand. The next time I come this way I'll ask for Hosea; I shall want to know what has become of this bull of a man. The strongest and the most resolute succumb the most quickly."

Then, like a driver urging an unharnessed team forward, he swung the lash over the prisoners, but without touching them, and pointing to a column of smoke which rose behind a cliff at the right of the road, he exclaimed:

"There are the smelting furnaces! We shall reach our destination at noon. There will be no lack of fire to cook lentils, and doubtless you may have a bit of mutton, too; for we celebrate to-day the birth of the good god, the son of the sun; may life, health, and prosperity be his!"

For the next half-hour their road led between lofty cliffs through the dry bed of a river, down which, after the last rains, a deep mountain torrent had poured to the valley; but now only a few pools still remained.

After the melancholy procession had passed around a steep mountain whose summit was crowned with a small Egyptian temple of Hathor and a number of monuments, it approached a bend in the valley which led to the ravine where the mines were located.

Flags, hoisted in honor of Pharaoh's birth-day, were waving from tall masts before the gates of the little temple on the mountain; and when loud shouts, uproar, and clashing greeted the travellers in the valley of the mines, which was wont to be so silent, the captain of the guards thought that the prisoners' greatest festival was being celebrated in an unusually noisy way and communicated this conjecture to the other guards who had paused to listen.

Then the party pressed forward without delay, but no one raised his head; the noon-day sun blazed so fiercely, and the dazzling walls of the ravine sent forth a reflected glow as fierce as if they were striving to surpass the heat of the neighboring smelting furnaces.

Spite of the nearness of the goal the prisoners tottered forward as if asleep, only one held his breath in the intensity of suspense.

As the battle-charger in the plough arches his neck, and expands his nostrils, while his eyes flash fire, so Joshua's bowed figure, spite of the sack that burdened his shoulders, straightened itself, and his sparkling eyes were turned toward the spot whence came the sounds the captain of the guards had mistaken for the loud tumult of festal mirth.

He, Joshua, knew better. Never could he mistake the roar echoing there; it was the war-cry of Egyptian soldiers, the blast of the trumpet summoning the warriors, the clank of weapons, and the battle-shouts of hostile hordes.

Ready for prompt action, he bent toward his yokemate, and whispered imperiously:

"The hour of deliverance is at hand. Take heed, and obey me blindly."

Strong excitement overpowered his companion also, and Hosea had scarcely glanced into the side-valley ere he bade him hold himself in readiness.

The first look into the ravine had showed him, on the summit of a cliff, a venerable face framed in snowy locks—his father's. He would have recognized him among thousands and at a far greater distance! But from the beloved grey head he turned a swift glance at the guide, who had stopped in speechless horror, and supposing that a mutiny had broken out among the prisoners, with swift presence of mind shouted hoarsely to the other guards:

"Keep behind the convicts and cut down every one who attempts to escape!"

But scarcely had his subordinates hurried to the end of the train, ere Joshua whispered to his companion:

"At him!"

As he spoke the Hebrew, who, with his yoke-mate, headed the procession, attacked the astonished leader, and ere he was aware of it, Joshua seized his right arm, the other his left.

The strong man, whose powers were doubled by his rage, struggled furiously to escape, but Joshua and his companion held him in an iron grasp.

A single rapid glance had showed the chief the path he must take to join his people True, it led past a small band of Egyptian bow-men, who were discharging their arrows at the Hebrews on the opposite cliff, but the enemy would not venture to fire at him and his companion; for the powerful figure of the captain of the guards, clearly recognizable by his dress and weapons, shielded them both.

"Lift the chain with your right hand," whispered Joshua, "I will hold our living buckler. We must ascend the cliff crab-fashion."

His companion obeyed, and as they advanced within bow-shot of the enemy—moving sometimes backward, sometimes sideways—they held the Egyptian before them and with the ringing shout: "The son of Nun is returning to his father and to his people!" Joshua step by step drew nearer to the Hebrew combatants.

Not one of the Egyptians who knew the captain of the prisoners' guard had ventured to send an arrow at the escaping prisoners. While the fettered pair were ascending the cliff backward, Joshua heard his name shouted in joyous accents, and directly after Ephraim, with a band of youthful warriors, came rushing down the height toward him.

To his astonishment Joshua saw the huge shield, sword, or battle-axe of an Egyptian heavily-armed soldier in the hands of each of these sons of his people, but the shepherd's sling and the bag of round stones also hung from many girdles.

Ephraim led his companions and, before greeting his uncle, formed them into two ranks like a double wall between Joshua and the hostile bow-men.

Then he gave himself up to the delight of meeting, and a second glad greeting soon followed; for old Nun, protected by the tall Egyptian shields which the sea had washed ashore, had been guided to the projecting rock in whose shelter strong hands were filing the fetters from Joshua and his companion, while Ephraim, with several others, bound the captain.

The unfortunate man had given up all attempt at resistance and submitted to everything as if utterly crushed. He only asked permission to wipe his eyes ere his arms were bound behind his back; for tear after tear was falling on the grey beard of the warder who, outwitted and overpowered, no longer felt capable of discharging the duties of his office.

Nun clasped to his heart with passionate fervor the rescued son whom he had already mourned as lost. Then, releasing him, he stepped back and never wearied of feasting his eyes on him and hearing him repeat that, faithful to his God, he had consecrated himself to the service of his people.

But it was for a brief period only that they gave themselves up to the bliss of this happy meeting; the battle asserted its rights, and its direction fell, as a matter of course, to Joshua.

He had learned with grateful joy, yet not wholly untinged with melancholy, of the fate which had overtaken the brave army among whose leaders he had long proudly numbered himself, and also heard that another body of armed shepherds, under the command of Hur, Miriam's husband, had attacked the turquoise mines of Dophkah, which situated a little farther toward the south, could be reached in a few hours. If they conquered, they were to join the young followers of Ephraim before sunset.

The latter was burning with eagerness to rush upon the Egyptians, but the more prudent Joshua, who had scanned the foe, though he did not doubt that they must succumb to the fiery shepherds, who were far superior to them in numbers, was anxious to shed as little blood as possible in this conflict, which was waged on his account, so he bade Ephraim cut a palm from the nearest tree, ordered a shield to be handed to him and then, waving the branch as an omen of peace, yet cautiously protecting himself, advanced alone to meet the foe.

The main body were drawn up in front of the mines and, familiar with the signal which requested negotiations, asked their commander for an interview.

The latter was ready to grant it, but first desired to know the contents of a letter which had just been handed to him and must contain evil tidings. This was evident from the messenger's looks and the few words which, though broken, were pregnant with meaning, that he had whispered to his countryman.

While some of Pharaoh's warriors offered refreshments to the exhausted, dust-covered runner, and listened with every token of horror to the tidings he hoarsely gasped, the commander of the troops read the letter.

His features darkened and, when he had finished, he clenched the papyrus fiercely; for it had announced tidings no less momentous than the destruction of the army, the death of Pharaoh Menephtah, and the coronation of his oldest surviving son as Seti II., after the attempt of Prince

Siptah to seize the throne had been frustrated. The latter had fled to the marshy region of the Delta, and Aarsu, the Syrian, after abandoning him and supporting the new king, had been raised to the chief command of all the mercenaries. Bai, the high-priest and chief-judge, had been deprived of his rank and banished by Seti II. Siptah's confederates had been taken to the Ethiopian gold mines instead of to the copper mines. It was also stated that many women belonging to the House of the Separated had been strangled; and Siptah's mother had undoubtedly met the same fate. Every soldier who could be spared from the mines was to set off at once for Tanis, where veterans were needed for the new legions.

This news exerted a powerful influence; for after Joshua had told the commander that he was aware of the destruction of the Egyptian army and expected reinforcements which had been sent to capture Dophkah to arrive within a few hours, the Egyptian changed his imperious tone and endeavored merely to obtain favorable conditions for retreat. He was but too well aware of the weakness of the garrison of the turquoise mines and knew that he could expect no aid from home. Besides, the mediator inspired him with confidence; therefore, after many evasions and threats, he expressed himself satisfied with the assurance that the garrison, accompanied by the beasts of burden and necessary provisions, should be allowed to depart unharmed. This, however, was not to be done until after they had laid down their arms and showed the Hebrews all the galleries where the prisoners were at work.

The young Hebrews, who twice outnumbered the Egyptians, at once set about disarming them; and many an old warrior's eyes grew dim, many a man broke his lance or snapped his arrows amid execrations and curses, while some grey-beards who had formerly served under Joshua and recognized him, raised their clenched fists and upbraided him as a traitor.

The dregs of the army were sent for this duty in the wilderness and most of the men bore in their faces the impress of corruption and brutality. Those in authority on the Nile knew how to choose soldiers whose duty it was to exercise pitiless severity against the defenceless.

At last the mines were opened and Joshua himself seized a lamp and pressed forward into the hot galleries where the naked prisoners of state, loaded with fetters, were hewing the copper ore from the walls.

Already he could hear in the distance the picks, whose heads were shaped like a swallow's tail, bite the hard rock. Then he distinguished the piteous wails of tortured men and women; for cruel overseers had followed them into the mine and were urging the slow to greater haste.

To-day, Pharaoh's birthday, they had been driven to the temple of Hathor on the summit of the neighboring height, to pray for the king who had plunged them into the deepest misery, and they would have been released from labor until the next morning, had not the unexpected attack induced the commander to force them back into the mines. Therefore to-day the women, who were usually obliged merely to crush and sift the ores needed to make glass and dyes, were compelled to labor in the galleries.

When the convicts heard Joshua's shouts and footsteps, which echoed from the bare cliffs, they were afraid that some fresh misfortune was impending, and wailing and lamentations arose in all directions. But the deliverer soon reached the first convicts, and the glad tidings that he had come to save them from their misery speedily extended to the inmost depths of the mines.

Wild exultation filled the galleries which were wont to witness only sorrowful moans and burning tears; yet loud cries for help, piteous wailings, groans, and the death-rattle reached Joshua's ear; for a hot-blooded man had rushed upon the overseer most hated and felled him with his pick-axe. His example quickly inflamed the others' thirst for vengeance and, ere it could be prevented, the same fate overtook the other officials. But they had defended themselves and the corpse of many a prisoner strewed the ground beside their tormentors.

Obeying Joshua's call, the liberated multitude at last emerged into the light of day. Savage and fierce were the outcries which blended in sinister discord with the rattling of the chains they dragged after them. Even the most fearless among the Hebrews shrank in horror as they beheld the throng of hapless sufferers in the full radiance of the sunlight; for the dazzled, reddened eyes of the unfortunate sufferers,—many of whom had formerly enjoyed in their own homes or at the king's court every earthly blessing; who had been tender mothers and fathers, rejoiced in doing good, and shared all the blessings of the civilization of a richly gifted people,—these dazzled eyes which at first glittered through tears caused by the swift transition from the darkness of the mines to the glare of the noon-day sun, soon sparkled as fiercely and greedily as those of starving owls.

At first, overwhelmed by the singular change in their destiny, they struggled for composure and did not resist the Hebrews, who, at Joshua's signal, began to file the fetters from their ankles; but when they perceived the disarmed soldiers and overseers who, guarded by Ephraim and his companions, were ranged at the base of a cliff, a strange excitement overpowered them. Amid shrieks and yells which no name can designate, no words describe, they broke from those who were trying to remove their fetters and, though no glance or word had been exchanged between them, obeyed the same terrible impulse, and unheeding the chains that burdened them, rushed upon the defenceless Egyptians. Before the Hebrews could prevent it, each threw himself upon the one who had inflicted the worst suffering upon him; and here might be seen an emaciated man clutching the throat of his stronger foe, yonder a band of nude women horribly disfigured by want and neglect, rush upon the man who had most rudely insulted, beaten, and abused them, and with teeth and nails wreak upon him their long repressed fury.

It seemed as though the flood-tide of hate had burst its dam and, unfettered, was demanding its victims.

There was a horrible scene of attack and defence, a ferocious, bloody conflict on foot and amid the red sand of the desert, shrieks, yells, and howls pierced the ear; nay, it was difficult to distinguish individuals in this motley confusion of men and women, animated on the one side by the wildest passion, a yearning for vengeance amounting to blood-thirstiness, and on the other by the dread of death and the necessity for self-defence.

Only a few of the prisoners had succeeded in controlling themselves; but they, too, shouted irritating words to their fellows, reviled the Egyptians in violent excitement, and shook their clenched fists at the disarmed foe.

The fury with which the liberated serfs rushed upon their tormentors was as unprecedented as the cruelties they had suffered.

But Joshua had deprived the Egyptians of their weapons, and they were therefore under his protection.

So he commanded his men to separate the combatants, if possible without bloodshed; but the task was no easy one, and many new and horrible deeds were committed. At last, however, it was accomplished, and they now perceived how terribly rage had increased the strength of the exhausted and feeble sufferers; for though no weapons had been used in the conflict a number of corpses strewed the spot, and most of the guards were bleeding from terrible wounds.

After quiet had been restored, Joshua asked the wounded commander for the list of prisoners, but he pointed to the clerk of the mines, whom none of the convicts had assailed. He had been their physician and treated them kindly-an elderly man, he had himself undergone sore trials and, knowing the pain of suffering, was ready to alleviate the pangs of others.

He willingly read aloud the names of the prisoners, among which were several Hebrew ones, and after each individual had responded, many declared themselves ready to join the wandering tribes.

When the disarmed soldiers and guards at last set out on their way home, the captain of the band that had escorted Joshua and his companions left the other Egyptians, and with drooping head and embarrassed mien approached old Nun and his son, and begged permission to go with them; for he could expect no favor at home and there was no God in Egypt so mighty as theirs. It had not escaped his notice that Hosea, who had once been a chief in the Egyptian service, had raised his hands in the sorest straits to this God, and never had he witnessed the same degree of resolution that he possessed. Now he also knew that this same mighty God had buried Pharaoh's powerful army in the sea to save His people. Such a God was acceptable to his heart, and he desired nothing better than to remain henceforward with those who served Him.

Joshua willingly allowed him to join the Hebrews. Then it appeared that there were fifteen of the latter among the liberated prisoners and, to Ephraim's special delight, Reuben, the husband of poor melancholy Milcah, who clung so closely to Miriam. His reserved, laconic disposition had stood him in good stead, and the arduous forced labor seemed to have inflicted little injury on his robust frame.

The exultation of victory, the joy of success, had taken full possession of Ephraim and his youthful band; but when the sun set and there was still no sign of Hur and his band, Nun and his followers were seized with anxiety.

Ephraim had already proposed to go with some of his companions in quest of tidings, when a messenger announced that Hur's men had lost courage at the sight of the well-fortified Egyptian citadel. Their leader, it is true, had urged them to the assault, but his band had shrunk from the peril and, unless Nun and his men brought aid, they would return with their mission unfulfilled.

It was therefore resolved to go to the assistance of the timorous. With joyous confidence they marched forward and, during the journey through the cool night, Ephraim and Nun described to Joshua how they had found Kasana and how she had died. What she had desired to communicate to the man she loved was now made known to him, and the warrior listened with deep emotion and remained silent and thoughtful until they reached Dophkah, the valley of the turquoise mines, from whose center rose the fortress which contained the prisoners.

Hur and his men had remained concealed in a side-valley, and after Joshua had divided the Hebrew force into several bodies and assigned to each a certain task, he gave at dawn the signal for the assault.

After a brief struggle the little garrison was overpowered and the fortress taken. The disarmed Egyptians, like their companions at the copper mines, were sent home. The prisoners were released and the lepers, whose quarters were in a side-valley beyond the mines—among them were those who at Joshua's bidding had been brought here—were allowed to follow the conquerors at a certain distance.

What Hur, Miriam's husband, could not accomplish, Joshua had done, and ere the young soldiers departed with Ephraim, old Nun assembled them to offer thanks to the Lord. The men under Hur's command also joined in the prayer and wherever Joshua appeared Ephraim's companions greeted him with cheers.

"Hail to our chief!" often rang on the air, as they marched forward: "Hail to him whom the Most High Himself has chosen for His sword! We will gladly follow him; for through him God leads us to victory."

Hur's men also joined in these shouts, and he did not forbid them; nay, after the storming of the fortress, he had thanked Joshua and expressed his pleasure in his liberation.

At the departure, the younger man had stepped back to let the older one precede him; but Hur had entreated grey-haired Nun, who was greatly his senior, to take the head of the procession, though after the deliverance of the people on the shore of the Red Sea he had himself been appointed by Moses and the elders to the chief command of the Hebrew soldiers.

The road led first through a level mountain valley, then it crossed the pass known as the "Sword-point ", which was the only means of communication between the mines and the Red Sea.

The rocky landscape was wild and desolate, and the path to be climbed steep. Joshua's old father, who had grown up on the flat plains of Goshen and was unaccustomed to climbing mountains, was borne amid the joyous acclamations of the others, in the arms of his son and grandson, to the summit of the pass; but Miriam's husband who, at the head of his men, followed the division of Ephraim's companions, heard the shouts of the youths yet moved with drooping head and eyes bent on the ground.

At the summit they were to rest and wait for the people who were to be led through the wilderness of Sin to Dophkah.

The victors gazed from the top of the pass in search of the travellers; but as yet no sign of them appeared. But when they looked back along the mountain path whence they had come a different spectacle presented itself, a scene so grand, so marvellous, that it attracted every eye as though by a magic spell; for at their feet lay a circular valley, surrounded by lofty cliffs, mountain ridges, peaks, and summits, which here white as chalk, yonder raven-black, here grey and brown, yonder red and green, appeared to grow upward from the sand toward the azure sky of the wilderness, steeped in dazzling light, and unshadowed by the tiniest cloudlet.

All that the eye beheld was naked and bare, silent and lifeless. On the slopes of the many-colored rocks, which surrounded the sandy valley, grew no blade of grass nor smallest plant. Neither bird, worm, nor beetle stirred in these silent tracts, hostile to all life. Here the eye discerned no cultivation,—nothing that recalled human existence. God seemed to have created for Himself alone these vast tracts which were of service to no living creature. Whoever penetrated into this wilderness entered a spot which the Most High had perchance chosen for a place of rest and retreat, like the silent, inaccessible Holy of Holies of the temple.

The young men had gazed mutely at the wonderful scene at their feet. Now they prepared to encamp and showed themselves diligent in serving old Nun, whom they sincerely loved. Resting among them under a hastily erected canopy he related, with sparkling eyes, the deeds his son had performed.

Meanwhile Joshua and Hur were still standing at the top of the pass, the former gazing silently down into the dreary, rocky valley, which overarched by the blue dome of the sky, surrounded by the mountain pillars and columns from God's own workshop, opened before him as the mightiest of temples.

The old man had long gazed gloomily at the ground, but he suddenly interrupted the silence and said:

"In Succoth I erected a heap of stones and called upon the Lord to be a witness between us. But in this spot, amid this silence, it seems to me that without memorial or sign we are sure of His presence." Here he drew his figure to a greater height and continued: "And I now raise mine eyes to Thee, Adonai, and address my humble words to Thee, Jehovah, Thou God of Abraham and of our fathers, that Thou mayst a second time be a witness between me and this man whom Thou Thyself didst summon to Thy service, that he might be Thy sword."

He had uttered these words with eyes and hands uplifted, then turning to the other, he said with solemn earnestness:

"So I ask thee Hosea, son of Nun, dost thou remember the vow which thou and I made before the stones in Succoth?"

"I do," was the reply. "And in sore disaster and great peril I perceived what the Most High desired of me, and am resolved to devote to Him all the strength of body and soul with which He has endowed me, to Him alone, and to His people, who are also mine. Henceforward I will be called Joshua...

nor will I seek service with the Egyptians or any foreign king; for the Lord our God through the lips of thy wife bestowed this name upon me."

Then Hur, with solemn earnestness, broke in: "That is what I expected to hear and as, in this place also, the Most High is a witness between me and thee and hears this conversation, let the vow I made in His presence be here fulfilled. The heads of the tribes and Moses, the servant of the Lord, appointed me to the command of the fighting-men of our people. But now thou dost call thyself Joshua, and hast vowed to serve no other than the Lord our God. I am well aware thou canst accomplish far greater things as commander of an army than I, who have grown grey in driving herds, or than any other Hebrew, by whatever name he is known, so I will fulfil the vow sworn at Succoth. I will ask Moses, the servant of the Lord, and the elders to confide to thee the office of commander. In their hands will I place the decision and, because I feel that the Most High beholds my heart, let me confess that I have thought of thee with secret rancor. Yet, for the welfare of the people, I will forget what lies between us and offer thee my hand."

With these words he held out his hand to Joshua and the latter, grasping it, replied with generous candor:

"Thy words are manly and mine shall be also. For the sake of the people and the cause we both serve, I will accept thy offer. Yet since thou hast summoned the Most High as a witness and He hears me, I, too, will not withhold one iota of the truth. The Lord Himself has summoned me to the office of commander of the fighting-men which thou dost desire to commit to me. It was done through Miriam, thy wife, and is my due. Yet I recognize thy willingness to yield thy dignity to me as a praiseworthy deed, since I know how hard it is for a man to resign power, especially in favor of a younger one whom he does not love. Thou hast done this, and I am grateful. I, too, have thought of thee with secret rancor; for through thee I lost another possession harder for a man to renounce than office: the love of woman."

The hot blood mounted into Hur's cheeks, as he exclaimed:

"Miriam! I did not force her into marriage; nay I did not even purchase her, according to the custom of our fathers, with the bridal dowry—she became my wife of her own free will."

"I know it," replied Joshua quietly, "yet there was one man who had yearned to make her his longer and more ardently than thou, and the fire of jealousy burned fiercely in his heart. But have no anxiety; for wert thou now to give her a letter of divorce and lead her to me that I might open my arms and tent to receive her, I would exclaim:

"Why hast thou done this thing to thyself and to me? For a short time ago I learned what woman's love is, and that I was mistaken when I believed Miriam shared the ardor of my heart. Besides, during the march with fetters on my feet, in the heaviest misfortune, I vowed to devote all the strength and energy of soul and body to the welfare of our people. Nor shall the love of woman turn me from the great duty I have taken upon myself. As for thy wife, I shall treat her as a stranger unless, as a prophetess, she summons me to announce a new message from the Lord."

With these words he held out his hand to his companion and, as Hur grasped it, loud voices were heard from the fighting-men, for messengers were climbing the mountain, who, shouting and beckoning, pointed to the vast cloud of dust that preceded the march of the tribes.

CHAPTER XXV

The Hebrews came nearer and nearer, and many of the young combatants hastened to meet them. These were not the joyous bands, who had joined triumphantly in Miriam's song of praise, no, they tottered toward the mountain slowly, with drooping heads. They were obliged to scale the pass from the steeper side, and how the bearers sighed; how piteously the women and children wailed, how fiercely the drivers swore as they urged the beasts of burden up the narrow, rugged path; how hoarsely sounded the voices of the half fainting men as they braced their shoulders against the carts to aid the beasts of burden.

These thousands who, but a few short days before, had so gratefully felt the saving mercy of the Lord, seemed to Joshua, who stood watching their approach, like a defeated army.

But the path they had followed from their last encampment, the harbor by the Red Sea, was rugged, arid, and to them, who had grown up among the fruitful plains of Lower Egypt, toilsome and full of terror.

It had led through the midst of the bare rocky landscape, and their eyes, accustomed to distant horizons and luxuriant green foliage, met narrow boundaries and a barren wilderness.

Since passing through the Gate of Baba, they had beheld on their way through the valley of the same name and their subsequent pilgrimage through the wilderness of Sin, nothing save valleys with steep precipices on either side. A lofty mountain of the hue of death had towered, black and terrible, above the reddish-brown slopes, which seemed to the wanderers like the work of human hands, for the strata of stones rose at regular intervals. One might have supposed that the giant builders whose hands had toiled here in the service of the Sculptor of the world had been summoned away ere they had completed the task, which in this wilderness had no searching eye to fear and seemed destined for the service of no living creature. Grey and brown granite cliffs and ridges rose on both sides of the path, and in the sand which covered it lay heaps of small bits of red porphyry and coal-black stones that seemed as if they had been broken by the blows of a hammer and resembled the dross from which metal had been melted. Greenish masses of rock, most peculiar in form, surrounded the narrow, cliff circled mountain valleys, which opened into one another. The ascending path pierced them; and often the Hebrews, as they entered, feared that the lofty cliffs in the distance would compel them to return. Then murmurs and lamentations arose, but the mode of egress soon appeared and led to another rock-valley.

On departing from the harbor at the Red Sea they had often found thorny gum acacias and an aromatic desert plant, which the animals relished; but the farther they entered the rocky wilderness, the more scorching and arid the sand became, and at last the eye sought in vain for herbs and trees.

At Elim fresh springs and shade-giving palms were found, and at the Red Sea there were well-filled cisterns; but here at the camp in the wilderness of Sin nothing had been discovered to quench the thirst, and at noon it seemed as though an army of spiteful demons had banished every inch of shade cast by the cliffs; for every part of the valleys and ravines blazed and glowed, and nowhere was there the slightest protection from the scorching sun.

The last water brought with them had been distributed among the human beings and animals, and when the procession started in the morning not a drop could be found to quench their increasing thirst.

Then the old doubting rancor and rebelliousness took possession of the multitude. Curses directed against Moses and the elders, who had led them from the comfort of well-watered Egypt to this misery, never ceased; but when they climbed the pass of the "Swordpoint" their parched throats had become too dry for oaths and invectives.

Messengers from old Nun, Ephraim, and Hur had already informed the approaching throngs that the young men had gained a victory and liberated Joshua and the other captives; but their discouragement had become so great that even this good news made little change, and only a flitting smile on the bearded lips of the men, or a sudden flash of the old light in the dark eyes of the women appeared.

Miriam, accompanied by melancholy Milcah, had remained with her companions instead of, as usual, calling upon the women to thank the Most High.

Reuben, the husband of her sorrowful ward whom fear of disappointment still deterred from yielding to his newly-awakened hopes, was a quiet, reticent man, so the first messenger did not know whether he was among the liberated prisoners. But great excitement overpowered Milcah and, when Miriam bade her be patient, she hurried from one playmate to another assailing them with urgent questions. When even the last could give her no information concerning the husband she had loved and lost, she burst into loud sobs and fled back to the prophetess. But she received little consolation, for the woman who was expecting to greet her own husband as a conqueror and see the rescued friend of her childhood, was absent-minded and troubled, as if some heavy burden oppressed her soul.

Moses had left the tribes as soon as he learned that the attack upon the mines had succeeded and Joshua was rescued; for it had been reported that the warlike Amalekites, who dwelt in the oasis at the foot of Mt. Sinai, were preparing to resist the Hebrews' passage through their well-watered tract in the wilderness with its wealth of palms. Accompanied by a few picked men he set off across the mountains in quest of tidings, expecting to join his people between Alush and Rephidim in the valley before the oasis.

Abidan, the head of the tribe of Benjamin, with Hur and Nun, the princes of Judah and Ephraim after their return from the mines—were to represent him and his companions.

As the people approached the steep pass Hur, with more of the rescued prisoners, came to meet them, and hurrying in advance of all the rest was young Reuben, Milcah's lost husband. She had recognized him in the distance as he rushed down the mountain and, spite of Miriam's protest, darted into the midst of the tribe of Simeon which marched in front of hers.

The sight of their meeting cheered many a troubled spirit and when at last, clinging closely to each other, they hurried to Miriam and the latter beheld the face of her charge, it seemed as though a miracle had been wrought; for the pale lily had become in the hue of her cheeks a blooming rose. Her lips, too, which she had but rarely and timidly opened for a question or an answer, were in constant motion; for how much she desired to know, how many questions she had to ask the silent husband who had endured such terrible suffering.

They were a handsome, happy pair, and it seemed to them as if, instead of passing naked rocks over barren desert paths, they were journeying through a vernal landscape where springs were gushing and birds carolling their songs.

Miriam, who had done everything in her power to sustain the grieving wife, was also cheered by the sight of her happiness. But every trace of joyous sympathy soon vanished from her features; for while Reuben and Milcah, as if borne on wings, seemed scarcely to touch the soil of the wilderness, she moved forward with drooping head, oppressed by the thought that it was her own fault that no like happiness could bloom for her in this hour.

She told herself that she had made a sore sacrifice, worthy of the highest reward and pleasing in the sight of God, when she refused to obey the voice of her heart, yet she could not banish from her memory the dying Egyptian who had denied her right to be numbered among those who loved Hosea, the woman who for his sake had met so early a death.

She, Miriam, lived, yet she had killed the most fervent desire of her soul; duty forbade her thinking with ardent longing of him who lingered up yonder, devoted to the cause of his people and the God of his fathers, a free, noble man, perhaps the future leader of the warriors of her race, and if Moses so appointed, next to him the first and greatest of all the Hebrews, but lost, forever lost to her.

Had she on that fateful night obeyed the yearning of her woman's heart and not the demands of the vocation which placed her far above all other women, he would long since have clasped her in his arms, as quiet Reuben embraced his poor, feeble Milcah, now so joyous as she walked stoutly at his side.

What thoughts were these?

She must drive them back to the inmost recesses of her heart, seek to crush them; for it was a sin for her to long so ardently to meet another. She wished for her husband's presence, as a saviour from herself and the forbidden desires of this terrible hour.

Hur, the prince of the tribe of Judah, was her husband, not the former Egyptian, the liberated captive. What had she to ask from the Ephraimite, whom she had forever refused?

Why should it hurt her that the liberated prisoner did not seek her; why did she secretly cherish the foolish hope that momentous duties detained him?

She scarcely saw or heard what was passing around her, and Milcah's grateful greeting to her husband first informed her that Hur was approaching.

He had waved his hand to her while still afar, but he came alone, without Hosea or Joshua, she cared not what the rescued man called himself; and it angered her to feel that this hurt her, nay, pierced her to the heart. Yet she esteemed her elderly husband and it was not difficult for her to give him a cordial welcome.

He answered her greeting joyously and tenderly; but when she pointed to the re-united pair and extolled him as victor and deliverer of Reuben and so many hapless men, he frankly owned that he had no right to this praise, it was the due of "Joshua," whom she herself had summoned in the name of the Most High to command the warriors of the people.

Miriam turned pale and, in spite of the steepness of the road, pressed her husband with questions. When she heard that Joshua was resting on the heights with his father and the young men and refreshing themselves with wine, and that Hur had promised to resign voluntarily, if Moses desired to entrust the command to him, her heavy eye-brows contracted in a gloomy frown beneath her broad forehead and, with curt severity, she exclaimed:

"You are my lord, and it is not seemly for me to oppose you, not even if you forget your own wife so far that you give place to the man who once ventured to raise his eyes to her."

"He no longer cares for you," Hur eagerly interrupted; "nay, were I to give you a letter of divorce, he would no longer desire to possess you."

"Would he not?" asked Miriam with a forced smile. "Do you owe this information to him?"

"He has devoted himself, body and soul, to the welfare of the people and renounces the love of woman," replied Hur. But his wife exclaimed:

"Renunciation is easy, where desire would bring nothing save fresh rejection and shame. Not to him who, in the hour of the utmost peril, sought aid from the Egyptians is the honor of the chief command of the warriors due, but rather to you, who led the tribes to the first victory at the store-house in Succoth and to whom the Lord Himself, through Moses His servant, confided the command."

Hur looked anxiously at the woman for whom a late, fervent love had fired his heart, and seeing her glowing cheeks and hurried breathing, knew not whether to attribute these symptoms to the steep ascent or to the passionate ambition of her aspiring soul, which she now transferred to him, her husband.

That she held him in so much higher esteem than the younger hero, whose return he had dreaded, pleased him, but he had grown grey in the strict fulfilment of duty, and would not deviate from what he considered right. His mere hints had been commands to the wife of his youth whom he had borne to the grave a few years before, and as yet he had encountered no opposition from Miriam. That Joshua was best fitted to command the fighting-men of the people was unquestionable, so he answered, with panting breath, for the ascent taxed his strength also:

"Your good opinion is an honor and a pleasure to me; but even should Moses and the elders confer the chief command upon me, remember the heap of stones at Succoth and my vow. I have ever been mindful of and shall keep it."

Miriam looked angrily aside, and said nothing more till they had reached the summit of the pass.

The victorious youths were greeting their approaching kindred with loud shouts.

The joy of meeting, the provisions captured, and the drink which, though sparingly distributed, was divided among the greatest sufferers, raised the drooping courage of the exhausted wayfarers; and the thirsting Hebrews shortened the rest at the summit of the pass in order to reach Dophkah more quickly. They had heard from Joshua that they would find there not only ruined cisterns, but also a hidden spring whose existence had been revealed to him by the ex-captain of the prisoners' guards.

The way led down the mountain. "Haste" was the watchword of the fainting Hebrews on their way to a well; and thus, soon after sunset, they reached the valley of the turquoise mines, where they encamped around the hill crowned by the ruined fortress and burned store-houses of Dophkah.

The spring in an acacia grove dedicated to the goddess Hathor was speedily found, and fire after fire was quickly lighted. The wavering hearts which, in the desert of Sin, had been on the verge of despair were again filled with the anticipation of life, hope, and grateful faith. The beautiful acacias, it is true, had been felled to afford easier access to the spring whose refreshing waters had effected this wonderful change.

At the summit of the pass Joshua and Miriam had met again, but found time only for a hasty greeting. In the camp they were brought into closer relations.

Joshua had appeared among the people with his father. The heir of the princely old man who was held in such high esteem received joyous greetings from all sides, and his counsel to form a vanguard of the youthful warriors, a rear-guard of the older ones, and send out chosen bands of the former on reconnoitering expeditions was readily adopted.

He had a right to say that he was familiar with everything pertaining to the guidance and defence of a large army. God Himself had entrusted him with the chief command, and Moses, by sending him the monition to be strong and steadfast, had confirmed the office. Hur, too, who now possessed it, was willing to transfer it to him, and this man's promise was inviolable, though he had omitted to repeat it in the presence of the elders. Joshua was treated as if he held the chief command, and he himself felt his own authority supreme.

After the assembly dispersed, Hur had invited him, spite of the late hour, to go to his tent and the warrior accompanied him, for he desired to talk with Miriam. He would show her, in her husband's presence, that he had found the path which she had so zealously pointed out to him.

In the presence of another's wife the tender emotions of a Hebrew were silent. Hur's consort must be made aware that he, Joshua, no longer cherished any love for her. Even in his solitary hours, he had wholly ceased to think of her.

He confessed that she was a noble, a majestic woman, but the very memory of this grandeur now sent a chill through his veins.

Her actions, too, appeared in a new light. Nay, when at the summit of the pass she had greeted him with a cold smile, he felt convinced that they were utterly estranged from one another, and this feeling grew stronger and stronger beside the blazing fire in the stately tent of the chief, where they met a second time.

The rescued Reuben and his wife Milcah had deserted Miriam long before and, during her lonely waiting, many thoughts had passed through her mind which she meant to impress upon the man to whom she had granted so much that its memory now weighed on her heart like a crime.

We are most ready to be angry with those to whom we have been unjust, and this woman regarded the gift of her love as something so great, so precious, that it behooved even the man whom she had rejected never to cease to remember it with gratitude. But Joshua had boasted that he no longer desired, even were she offered to him, the woman whom he had once so fervently loved and clasped in his embrace. Nay, he had confirmed this assertion by leisurely waiting, without seeking her.

At last he came, and in company with her husband, who was ready to cede his place to him.

But she was present, ready to watch with open eyes for the welfare of the too generous Hur.

The elderly man, to whose fate she had linked her own, and whose faithful devotion touched her, should be defrauded by no rival of the position which was his due, and which he must retain, if only because she rebelled against being the wife of a man who could no longer claim next to her brothers the highest rank in the tribes.

Never before had the much-courted woman, who had full faith in her gift of prophesy, felt so bitter, sore, and irritated. She did not admit it even to herself, yet it seemed as if the hatred of the Egyptians with which Moses had inspired her, and which was now futile, had found a new purpose and was directed against the only man whom she had ever loved.

But a true woman can always show kindness to everyone whom she does not scorn, so though she blushed deeply at the sight of the man whose kiss she had returned, she received him cordially, and with sympathetic questions.

Meanwhile, however, she addressed him by his former name Hosea, and when he perceived it was intentional, he asked if she had forgotten that it was she herself who, as the confidante of the Most High, had commanded him henceforward to call himself "Joshua."

Her features grew sharper with anxiety as she replied that her memory was good but he reminded her of a time which she would prefer to forget. He had himself forfeited the name the Lord had given him by preferring the favor of the Egyptians to the help which God had promised. Faithful to the old custom, she would continue to call him "Hosea."

The honest-hearted soldier had not expected such hostility, but he maintained a tolerable degree of composure and answered quietly that he would rarely afford her an opportunity to address him by this or any other name. Those who were his friends readily adopted that of Joshua.

Miriam replied that she, too, would be ready to do so if her husband approved and he himself insisted upon it; for the name was only a garment. Of course offices and honors were another matter.

When Joshua then declared that he still believed God Himself had summoned him, through the lips of His prophetess, to command the Hebrew soldiers and that he would admit the right of no one save Moses to deprive him of his claim to this office, Hur assented and held out his hand to him.

Then Miriam dropped the restraint she had hitherto imposed on herself and, with defiant eagerness, continued:

"There I am of a different opinion. You did not obey the summons of the Most High. Can you deny this? And when the Omnipresent One found you at the feet of Pharaoh, instead of at the head of His people, He deprived you of the office with which He had entrusted you. He, the mightiest of generals, summoned the tempest and the waves, and they swallowed up the foe. So perished those who were your friends till their heavy fetters made you realize their true disposition toward you and your race. But I, meanwhile, was extolling the mercy of the Most High, and the people joined in my hymn of praise. On that very day the Lord summoned another to command the fighting-men in your stead, and that other, as you know, is my husband. If Hur has never learned the art of war, God will surely guide his arm, and it is He and none other who bestows victory.

"My husband—hear it again—is the sole commander of the hosts and if, in the abundance of his generosity, he has forgotten it, he will retain his office when he remembers whose hand chose him, and when I, his wife, raise my voice and recall it to his memory."

Joshua turned to go, in order to end the painful discussion, but Hur detained him, protesting that he was deeply incensed by his wife's unseemly interference in the affairs of men, and that he insisted on his promise. "A woman's disapproving words were blown away by the wind. It would be Moses' duty to declare whom Jehovah had chosen to be commander."

While making this reply Hur had gazed at his wife with stern dignity, as if admonishing discretion, and the look seemed to have effected its purpose; for Miriam had alternately flushed and paled as she listened; nay, she even detained the guest by beckoning him with a trembling hand to approach, as though she desired to soothe him.

"Let me say one thing more," she began, drawing a long breath, "that you may not misunderstand my meaning. I call everyone our friend who devotes himself to the cause of the people, and how self-sacrificingly you intend to do this, Hur has informed me. It was your confidence in Pharaoh's favor that parted us—therefore I know how to prize your firm and decisive breach with the Egyptians, but I did not correctly estimate the full grandeur of this deed until I learned that not only long custom, but other bonds, united you to the foe."

"What is the meaning of these words?" replied Joshua, convinced that she had just fitted to the bowstring another shaft intended to wound him. But Miriam, unheeding the question, calmly continued with a defiant keenness of glance that contradicted her measured speech:

"After the Lord's guidance had delivered us from the enemy, the Red Sea washed ashore the most beautiful woman we have seen for a long time. I bandaged the wound a Hebrew woman dealt her and she acknowledged that her heart was filled with love for you, and that on her dying bed she regarded you as the idol of her soul."

Joshua, thoroughly incensed, exclaimed: "If this is the whole truth, wife of Hur, my father has given me a false report; for according to what I heard from him, the hapless woman made her last confession only in the presence of those who love me; not in yours. And she was right to shun you—you would never have understood her."

Here he saw a smile of superiority hover around Miriam's lips; but he repelled it, as he went on:

"Ah, your intellect is tenfold keener than poor Kasana's ever was. But your heart, which was open to the Most High, had no room for love. It will grow old and cease to beat without having learned the feeling. And, spite of your flashing eyes, I will tell you you are more than a woman, you are a prophetess. I cannot boast of gifts so lofty. I am merely a plain man, who understands the art of fighting better than that of foretelling the future. Yet I can see what is to come. You will foster the hatred of me that glows in your breast, and will also implant it in your husband's heart and zealously strive to fan it there. And I know why. The fiery ambition which consumes you will not suffer you to be the wife of a man who is second to any other. You refuse to call me by the name I owe to you. But if hatred and arrogance do not stifle in your breast the one feeling that still unites us—love for our people, the day will come when you will voluntarily approach and, unasked, by the free impulse of your heart, call me 'Joshua.'"

With these words he took leave of Miriam and her husband by a short wave of the hand, and vanished in the darkness of the night.

Hur gazed gloomily after him in silence until the footsteps of the belated guest had died away in the sleeping camp; then the ill-repressed wrath of the grave man, who had hitherto regarded his young wife with tender admiration, knew no bounds.

With two long strides he stood directly before her as she gazed with a troubled look into the fire, her face even paler than his own. His voice had lost its metallic harmony, and sounded shrill and sharp as he exclaimed:

"I had the courage to woo a maiden who supposed herself to be nearer to God than other women, and now that she has become my wife she makes me atone for such presumption."

"Atone?" escaped Miriam's livid lips, and a defiant glance blazed at him from her black eyes. But, undismayed, he continued, grasping her hand with so firm a pressure that it hurt her:

"Aye, you make me atone for it!—Shame on me, if I permit this disgraceful hour to be followed by similar ones."

Miriam strove to wrest her hand from his clasp, but he would not release it, and went on:

"I sought you, that you might be the pride of my house. I expected to sow honor, and I reap disgrace; for what could be more humiliating to a man than to have a wife who rules him, who presumes to wound with hostile words the heart of the friend who is protected by the laws of hospitality? A woman of different mould, a simple-hearted, upright wife, who looked at her husband's past life, instead of planning how to increase his greatness, that she might share it with him, need not have had me shout into her ears that Hur has garnered honors and dignities enough, during his long existence, to be able to spare a portion of them without any loss of esteem. It is not the man who holds the chief command, but the one who shows the most self-sacrificing love for the people that is greatest in the eyes of Jehovah. You desire a high place, you seek to be honored by the multitude as one who is summoned by the Lord. I shall not forbid it, so long as you do not forget what the duty of a wife commands. You owe me love also; for you vowed to give it on your marriage day; but the human heart can bestow only what it possesses, and Hosea is right when he says that love, which is warm itself and warms others, is a feeling alien to your cold nature."

With these words he turned his back upon her and went to the dark portion of the tent, while Miriam remained standing by the fire, whose flickering light illumined her beautiful, pallid face.

With clenched teeth and hands pressed on her heaving bosom, she stood gazing at the spot where he had disappeared.

Her grey-haired husband had confronted her in the full consciousness of his dignity, a noble man worthy of reverence, a true, princely chief of his tribe, and infinitely her superior. His every word had pierced her bosom like the thrust of a lance. The power of truth had given each its full emphasis and held up to Miriam a mirror that showed her an image from which she shrank.

Now she longed to rush after him and beg him to restore the love with which he had hitherto surrounded her—and which the lonely woman had gratefully felt.

She knew that she could reciprocate his costly gift; for how ardently she longed to have one kind, forgiving word from his lips.

Her soul seemed withered, parched, torpid, like a corn-field on which a poisonous mildew has fallen; yet it had once been green and blooming.

She thought of the tilled fields in Goshen which, after having borne an abundant harvest, remained arid and bare till the moisture of the river came to soften the soil and quicken the seed which it had received. So it had been with her soul, only she had flung the ripening grain into the fire and, with blasphemous hand, erected a dam between the fructifying moisture and the dry earth.

But there was still time!

She knew that he erred in one respect; she knew she was like all other women, capable of yearning with ardent passion for the man she loved. It depended solely on herself to make him feel this in her arms.

Now, it is true, he was justified in thinking her harsh and unfeeling, for where love had once blossomed in her soul, a spring of bitterness now gushed forth poisoning all it touched.

Was this the vengeance of the heart whose ardent wishes she had heroically slain?

God had disdained her sorest sacrifice; this it was impossible to doubt; for His majesty was no longer revealed to her in visions that exalted the heart, and she was scarcely entitled to call herself His prophetess. This sacrifice had led her, the truth-loving woman, into falsehood and plunged her who, in the consciousness of seeking the right path lived at peace with herself, into torturing unrest. Since that great and difficult deed she, who had once been full of hope, had obtained nothing for which she longed. She, who recognized no woman as her superior, had been obliged to yield in shame her place to a poor dying Egyptian. She had been kindly disposed toward all who were of her blood, and were devoted to the sacred cause of her people, and now her hostile bitterness had wounded one of the best and noblest. The poorest bondman's wife rejoiced to bind more and more closely the husband who had once loved her—she had wickedly estranged hers.

Seeking protection she had approached his hearthstone shivering, but she had found it warmer than she had hoped, and his generosity and love fell upon her wounded soul like balm. True, he could not restore what she had lost, but he could give a welcome compensation.

Ah, he no longer believed her capable of a tender emotion, yet she needed love in order to live, and no sacrifice seemed to her too hard to regain his. But pride was also a condition of her very existence, and whenever she prepared to humbly open her heart to her husband, the fear of humiliating herself overpowered her, and she stood as though spell-bound till the blazing wood at her feet fell into smoking embers and darkness surrounded her.

Then a strange anxiety stole over her.

Two bats, which had come from the mines and circled round the fire darted past her like ghosts. Everything urged her back to the tent, to her husband, and with hasty resolution she entered the spacious room lighted by a lamp. But it was empty, and the female slave who received her said that Hur would spend the time until the departure of the people with his son and grandson.

A keen pang pierced her heart, and she lay down to rest with a sense of helplessness and shame which she had not felt since her childhood.

A few hours after the camp was astir and when her husband, in the grey dawn of morning, entered the tent with a curt greeting, pride again raised its head and her reply sounded cold and formal.

He did not come alone; his son Uri was with him.

But he looked graver than was his wont; for the men of Judah had assembled early and adjured him not to give up the chief command to any man who belonged to another tribe.

This had been unexpected. He had referred them to Moses' decision, and his desire that it might be adverse to him was intensified, as his young wife's self-reliant glance stirred fresh wrath in his soul.

CHAPTER XXVI

Early the following morning the people resumed their march with fresh vigor and renewed courage; but the little spring which, by digging, had at last been forced to flow was completely exhausted.

However, its refusal to bestow a supply of water to take with them was of no consequence; they expected to find another well at Alush.

The sun had risen in radiant majesty in a cloudless sky. The light showed its awakening power on the hearts of men, and the rocks and the yellow sand of the road sparkled like the blue vault above. The pure, light, spicy air of the desert, cooled by the freshness of the night, expanded the breasts of the wayfarers, and walking became a pleasure.

The men showed greater confidence, and the eyes of the women sparkled more brightly than they had done for a long time; for the Lord had again showed the people that He remembered them in their need; and fathers and mothers gazed proudly at the sons who had conquered the foe. Most of the tribes had greeted in the band of prisoners some one who had long been given up as lost, and it was a welcome duty to make amends for the injuries the terrible forced labor had inflicted. There was special rejoicing, not only among the Ephraimites, but everywhere, over the return of Joshua, as all, save the men of the tribe of Judah, now called him, remembering the cheering promise the name conveyed.

The youths who under his command had put the Egyptians to rout, told their relatives what manner of man the son of Nun was, how he thought of everything and assigned to each one the place for which he was best suited. His eye kindled the battle spirit in every one on whom it fell, and the foe retreated at his mere war-cry.

Those who spoke of old Nun and his grandson also did so with sparkling eyes. The tribe of Ephraim, whose lofty pretensions had been a source of much vexation, was willingly allowed precedence on this march, and only the men of Judah were heard to grumble. Doubtless there was reason for dissatisfaction; for Hur, the prince of their tribe, and his young wife walked as if oppressed by a heavy burden; whoever asked them anything would have been wiser to have chosen another hour.

So long as the sun's rays were oblique, there was still a little shade at the edge of the sandstone rocks which bordered the road on both sides or towered aloft in the center; and as the sons of Korah began a song of praise, young and old joined in, and most gladly and gratefully of all Milcah, now no longer pale, and Reuben, her happy, liberated husband.

The children picked up golden-yellow bitter apples, which having fallen from the withered vines, lay by the wayside as if they had dropped from the sky, and brought them to their parents. But they were bitter as gall and a morose old man of the tribe of Zebulun, who nevertheless kept their firm shells to hold ointment, said:

"These are a symbol of to-day. It looks pleasant now; but when the sun mounts higher and we find no water, we shall taste the bitterness."

His prediction was verified only too soon; for as the road which, after leaving the sandstone region, began to lead upward through a rocky landscape which resembled walls of red brick and grey stone, grew steeper, the sun rose higher and higher and the heat of the day hourly increased.

Never had the sun sent sharper arrows upon the travellers, and pitiless was their fall upon bare heads and shoulders.

Here an old man, yonder a younger one, sank prostrate under its scorching blaze or, supported by his friends, staggered on raving with his hand pressed to his brow like a drunken man. The blistered skin peeled from the hands and faces of men and women, and there was not one whose palate and tongue were not parched by the heat, or whose vigorous strength and newly-awakened courage it did not impair.

The cattle moved forward with drooping heads and dragging feet or rolled on the ground till the shepherds' lash compelled them to summon their failing powers.

At noon the people were permitted to rest, but there was not a hand's breadth of shade where they sought repose. Whoever lay down in the noonday heat found fresh tortures instead of relief. The sufferers themselves urged a fresh start for the spring at Alush.

Hitherto each day, after the sun had begun its course toward the west through the cloudless sky of the desert, the heat had diminished, and ere the approach of twilight a fresher breeze had fanned the brow; but to-day the rocks retained the glow of noonday for many hours, until a light cool breeze blew from sea at the west. At the same time the vanguard which, by Joshua's orders, preceded the travellers, halted, and the whole train stopped.

Men, women, and children fixed their eyes and waved hands, staves, and crutches toward the same spot, where the gaze was spell-bound by a wondrous spectacle never beheld before.

A cry of astonishment and admiration echoed from the parched weary lips, which had long since ceased to utter question or answer; and it soon rang from rank to rank, from tribe to tribe, to the very lepers at the end of the procession and the rear-guard which followed it. One touched another, and whispered a name familiar to every one, that of the sacred mountain where the Lord had promised Moses to "bring them unto a good land and a large, unto a land flowing with milk and honey."

No one had told the weary travellers, yet all knew that for the first time they beheld Horeb and the peak of Sinai, the most sacred summit of this granite range.

Though a mountain, it was also the throne of the omnipotent God of their fathers.

The holy mountain itself seemed at this hour to be on fire like the bush whence He had spoken to His chosen servant. Its summit, divided into seven peaks, towered majestically aloft in the distance, dominating the heights and valleys far and near, glowing before the people like a giant ruby, irradiated by the light of a conflagration which was consuming the world.

No eye had ever beheld a similar spectacle. Then the sun sank lower and lower, till it set in the sea concealed behind the mountains. The glowing ruby was transformed into a dark amethyst, and at last assumed the deep hue of a violet; but the eyes of the people continued to dwell on the sacred scenes as though spell-bound. Nay, when the day-star had completely disappeared, and its reflection gilded a long cloud with shining edges, their eyes dilated still more, for a man of the tribe of Benjamin, overwhelmed by the grandeur of the spectacle, beheld in it the floating gold-bordered mantle of Jehovah, and the neighbors to whom he showed it, believed him, and shared his pious excitement.

This inspiring sight had made the Hebrews for a short time forget thirst and weariness. But the highest exaltation was soon to be transformed into the deepest discouragement; for when night closed in and Alush was reached after a short march it appeared that the desert tribe which dwelt there, ere striking their tents the day before, had filled the brackish spring with pebbles and rubbish.

Everything fit to drink which had been brought with them had been consumed at Dophkah, and the exhausted spring at the mines had afforded no water to fill the skins. Thirst not only parched their palates but began to fever their bowels. Their dry throats refused to receive the solid food of which there was no lack. Scenes that could not fail to rouse both ruth and anger were seen and heard on all sides.

Here men and women raved and swore, wailed and moaned, yonder they gave themselves up to dull despair. Others, whose crying children shrieked for water, had gone to the choked spring and were quarrelling around a little spot on the ground, whence they hoped to collect a few drops of the precious fluid in a shallow dish. The cattle, too, lowed so mournfully and beseechingly that it pierced the shepherds' hearts like a reproach.

Few took the trouble to pitch a tent. The night was so warm, and the sooner they pressed forward the better, for Moses had promised to join them a few leagues hence. He alone could aid, it was his duty to protect man and beast from perishing.

If the God who had promised them such splendid gifts left them to die in the wilderness with their cattle, the man to whose guidance they had committed themselves was a cheat; and the God whose might and mercy he never ceased extolling was more false and powerless than the idols with heads of human beings and animals, to whom they had prayed in Egypt.

Threats, too, were loudly uttered amid curses and blasphemies. Wherever Aaron, who had returned to the people, appeared and addressed them, clenched fists were stretched toward him.

Miriam, too, by her husband's bidding, was compelled to desist from comforting the women with soothing words, after a mother whose infant was expiring at her dry breast, picked up a stone and others followed her example.

Old Nun and his son found more attentive hearers. Both agreed that Joshua must fight, no matter in what position Moses placed him; but Hur himself led him to the warriors, who joyously greeted him.

Both the old man and the younger one understood how to infuse confidence. They told them of the well-watered oasis of the Amalekites, which was not far distant, and pointed to the weapons in their hands, with which the Lord Himself had furnished them. Joshua assured them that they greatly outnumbered the warriors of the desert tribe. If the young men bore themselves as bravely as they had done at the copper mines and at Dophkah, with God's aid the victory would be theirs.

After midnight Joshua, having taken counsel with the elders, ordered the trumpets which summoned the fighting-men to be sounded. Under the bright starry sky he reviewed them, divided them into bands, gave to each a fitting leader, and impressed upon them the importance of the orders they were to obey.

They had assembled torpidly, half dead with thirst, but the new occupation to which their sturdy commander urged them, the hope of victory, and the great value of the prize: a piece of land at the foot of the sacred mountain, rich in springs and palm-trees, wonderfully strengthened their lost energy.

Ephraim was among them animating others by his tireless vigor. But when the ex-chief of the Egyptians—whom the Lord had already convinced that He considered him worthy of the aid his name promised—adjured them to rely on God's omnipotence, his words produced a very different effect from those uttered by Aaron whose monitions they had heard daily since their departure.

When Joshua had spoken, many youthful lips, though parched with thirst, shouted enthusiastically:

"Hail to the chief! You are our captain; we will obey no other."

But he now explained gravely and resolutely that the obedience he exacted from them he intended to practise rigidly himself. He would willingly take the last place in the ranks, if such was the command of Moses.

The stars were still shining brightly in a cloudless sky when the sound of the horns warned the people to set out on their march. Meanwhile the vanguard had been sent forward to inform Moses of the condition of the tribes, and after the review was over, Ephraim followed them.

During the march Joshua kept the warriors together as closely as though an attack might be expected; profiting meanwhile by every moment to give the men and their captains instructions for the coming battle, to inspect them, and range their ranks in closer order. Thus he kept them and their attention on the alert till the stars paled.

Opposition or complaint was rare among the warriors, but the murmurs, curses, and threats grew all the louder among those who bore no weapons. Even before the grey dawn of morning the thirsting men, whose knees trembled with weakness, and who beheld close before their eyes the suffering of their wives and children, shouted more and more frequently:

"On to Moses! We'll stone him when we find him!"

Many, with loud imprecations and flashing eyes, picked up bits of rock along the road, and the fury of the multitude at last expressed itself so fiercely and passionately that Hur took counsel with the well-disposed among the elders, and then hurried forward with the fighting-men of Judah to protect Moses, in case of extremity, from the rebels by force of arms.

Joshua was commissioned to detain the bands of rioters who, amid threats and curses, were striving to force their way past the warriors.

When the sun at last rose with dazzling splendor, the march had become a pitiful creeping and tottering onward. Even the soldiers moved as though they were paralysed. Only when the rebels tried to press onward, they did their duty and forced them back with swords and lances.

On both sides of the valley through which the Hebrews were passing towered lofty cliffs of grey granite, which glittered and flashed marvellously when the slanting sunbeams struck the bits of quartz thickly imbedded in the primeval rock.

At noon the heat could not fail to be scorching again between the bare precipices which in many places jutted very near one another; but the coolness of the morning still lingered. The cattle at least found some refreshment; for many a bush of the juicy, fragrant betharan—[Cantolina fragrantissima]—afforded them food, and the shepherd-lads lifted their short frocks, filled the aprons thus made with them and, spite of their own exhaustion, held them up to the hungry mouths of the animals.

They had passed an hour in this way, when a loud shout of joy suddenly rang out, passing from the vanguard through rank after rank till it reached the last roan in the rear.

No one had heard in words to what event it was due, yet every one knew that it meant nothing else than the discovery of fresh water.

Ephraim now returned to confirm the glad tidings, and what an effect it produced upon the discouraged hearts!

They straightened their bent figures and struggled onward with redoubled speed, as if they had already drained the water jar in long draughts. The bands of fighting-men put no farther obstacles in their way, and joyously greeted those who crowded past them.

But the swiftly flowing throng was soon dammed; for the spot which afforded refreshment detained the front ranks, which blocked the whole procession as thoroughly as a wall or moat.

The multitude became a mighty mob that filled the valley. At last men and women, with joyous faces, appeared bearing full jars and pails in their hands and on their heads, beckoning gaily to their friends, shouting words of cheer, and trying to force their way through the crowd to their relatives; but many had the precious liquid torn from them by force ere they reached their destination.

Joshua and his band had forced their way to the vicinity of the spring, to maintain order among the greedy drawers of water. But they were obliged to have patience for a time, for the strong men of the tribe of Judah, with whom Hur had led the way in advance of all the rest, were still swinging their axes and straining at the levers hastily prepared from the trunks of the thorny acacias to move huge blocks out of the way and widen the passage to the flow of water that was gushing from several clefts in the rock.

At first the spring had lost itself in a heap of moss-covered granite blocks and afterwards in the earth; but now the overflow and trickling away of the precious fluid had been stopped and a reservoir formed whence the cattle also could drink.

Whoever had already succeeded in filling a jar had obtained the water from the overflow which had escaped through the quickly-made dam. Now the men appointed to guard the camp were keeping every one back to give the water in the large new reservoir into which it flowed in surprising abundance, time to grow clear.

In the presence of the gift of God for which they had so passionately shouted, it was easy to be patient. They had discovered the treasure and only needed to preserve it. No word of discontent, murmuring, or reviling was heard; nay, many looked with shame and humiliation at the new gift of the Most High.

Loud, gladsome shouts and words echoed from the distance; but the man of God, who knew better than any one else, the valleys and rocks, pastures and springs of the Horeb region and had again obtained so great a blessing for the people, had retired into a neighboring ravine; he was seeking refuge from the thanks and greetings which rose with increasing enthusiasm from ever widening circles, and above all peace and calmness for his own deeply agitated soul.

Soon fervent hymns of praise to the Lord sounded from the midst of the refreshed, reinvigorated bands overflowing with ardent gratitude, who had never encamped richer in hope and joyous confidence.

Songs, merry laughter, jests, and glad shouts accompanied the pitching of every tent, and the camp sprung up as quickly as if it had been conjured from the earth by some magic spell.

The eyes of the young men sparkled with eagerness for the fray, and many a head of cattle was slaughtered to make the meal a festal banquet. Mothers who had done their duty in the camp, leading their children by the hand went to the spring and showed them the spot where Moses' staff had pointed out to his people the water gushing from the clefts in the granite. Many men also stood with hands and eyes uplifted around the place where Jehovah had shown Himself so merciful to His people; among them many a rebel who had stooped for the bit of rock with which he meant to stone the trusted servant of God. No one doubted that a new and great miracle had been performed.

Old people enjoined the young never to forget this day and this drink, and a grandmother sprinkled her grandchildren's brows at the edge of the spring with water to secure for them divine protection throughout their future lives.

Hope, gratitude, and warm confidence reigned wherever the gaze was turned, even fear of the warlike sons of Amalek had vanished; for what evil could befall those who trusted to the favor of such an Omnipotent Defender.

One tent alone, the stateliest of all, that of the prince of the tribe of Judah, did not share the joy of the others.

Miriam sat alone among her women, after having silently served the meal to the men who were overflowing with grateful enthusiasm; she had learned from Reuben, Milcah's husband, that Moses had given to Joshua in the presence of all the elders, the office of commander-in-chief. Hur, her husband, she had heard farther, had joyfully yielded the guidance of the warriors to the son of Nun.

This time the prophetess had held aloof from the people's hymns of praise. When Milcah and her women had urged her to accompany them to the spring, she had commanded the petitioners to go alone. She was expecting her husband and wished to greet him alone; she must show him that she desired his forgiveness. But he did not return home; for after the council of the elders had separated, he helped the new commander to marshal the soldiers and did so as an assistant, subordinate to Hosea, who owed to her his summons and the name of Joshua.

Her servants, who had returned, were now drawing threads from the distaff: but this humble toil was distasteful to her, and while she let her hands rest and gazed idly into vacancy, the hours dragged slowly along, while she felt her resolution of meekly approaching her husband become weaker and weaker. She longed to pray for strength to bow before the man who was her lord and master; but the prophetess, who was accustomed to fervent pleading, could not find inspiration. Whenever she succeeded in collecting her thoughts and uplifting her heart, she was disturbed. Each fresh report that reached her from the camp increased her displeasure.

When evening at last closed in, a messenger arrived and told her not to prepare the supper which, however, had long stood ready. Hur, his son, and grandson had accepted the invitation of Nun and Joshua.

It was a hard task for her to restrain her tears. But had she permitted them to flow uncontrolled, they would have been those of wrath and insulted womanly dignity, not of grief and longing.

During the hours of the evening watch soldiers marched past, and from troop after troop cheers for Joshua reached her.

Even when the words "strong and steadfast!" were heard, they recalled the man who had once been dear to her, and whom now—she freely admitted it—she hated. The men of his own tribe only had honored her husband with a cheer. Was this fitting gratitude for the generosity with which he had divested himself, for the sake of the younger man, of a dignity that belonged to him alone? To see her husband thus slighted pierced her to the heart and caused her more pain than Hur's leaving her, his newly-wedded wife, to solitude.

The supper before the tent of the Ephraimites lasted a long time. Miriam sent her women to rest before midnight, and lay down to await Hur's return and to confess to him all that had wounded and angered her, everything for which she longed.

She thought it would be an easy matter to keep awake while suffering such mental anguish. But the great fatigues and excitements of the last few days asserted their rights, and in the midst of a prayer for humility and her husband's love sleep overpowered her. At last, at the time of the first morning watch, just as day was dawning, the sound of trumpets announcing peril close at hand, startled her from sleep.

She rose hurriedly and glancing at her husband's couch found it empty. But it had been used, and on the sandy soil—for mats had been spread only in the living room of the tent—she saw close beside her own bed the prints of Hur's footsteps.

So he had stood close by it and perhaps, while she was sleeping, gazed yearningly into her face.

Ay, this had really happened; her old female slave told her so unasked. After she had roused Hur, she had seen him hold the light cautiously so that it illumined Miriam's face and then stoop over her a long time as if to kiss her.

This was good news, and so rejoiced the solitary woman that she forgot the formality which was peculiar to her and pressed her lips to the wrinkled brow of the crooked little crone who had served her parents. Then she had her hair arranged, donned the light-blue festal robe Hur had given her, and hurried out to bid him farewell.

Meanwhile the troops had formed in battle array.

The tents were being struck and for a long time Miriam vainly sought her husband. At last she found him; but he was engaged in earnest conversation with Joshua, and when she saw the latter a chill ran through the prophetess' blood, and she could not bring herself to approach the men.

CHAPTER XXVII

A severe struggle was impending; for as the spies reported, the Amalekites had been joined by other desert tribes. Nevertheless the Hebrew troops were twice their number. But how greatly inferior in warlike skill were Joshua's bands to the foes habituated to battle and attack.

The enemy was advancing from the south, from the oasis at the foot of the sacred mountain, which was the ancient home of their race, their supporter, the fair object of their love, their all, well worthy that they should shed their last drop of blood in her defence.

Joshua, now recognized by Moses and the whole Hebrew people as the commander of the fighting-men, led his new-formed troops to the widest portion of the valley, which permitted him to derive more advantage from the superior number of his force.

He ordered the camp to be broken up and again pitched in a narrower spot on the plain of Rephidim at the northern end of the battle-field, where it would be easier to defend the tents. The command of this camp and the soldiers left for its protection he confided to his cautious father.

He had wished to leave Moses and the older princes of the tribes within the precincts of the well-guarded camp, but the great leader of the people had anticipated him and, with Hur and Aaron, had climbed a granite cliff from whose lofty summit the battle could be witnessed. So the combatants saw Moses and his two companions on the peak dominating the valley, and knew that the trusted servant of the Most High would not cease to commend their cause to Him and pray for their success and deliverance.

But every private soldier in the army, every woman and old man in the camp knew how to find the God of their fathers in this hour of peril, and the war-cry Joshua had chosen: "Jehovah our standard!" bound the hearts of the warriors to the Ruler of Battles, and reminded the most despairing and untrained Hebrew that he could take no step and deal no blow which the Lord did not guide.

The trumpets and horns of the Hebrews sounded louder and louder; for the Amalekites were pressing into the plain which was to be the scene of the battle.

It was a strange place of conflict, which the experienced soldier would never have selected voluntarily; for it was enclosed on both sides by lofty, steep, grey granite cliffs. If the enemy conquered, the camp would be lost, and the aids the art of war afforded must be used within the smallest conceivable space.

To make a circuit round the foe or attack him unexpectedly in the flank seemed impossible; but the rocks themselves were made to serve Joshua; for he had commanded his skilful slingers and trained archers to climb the precipices to a moderate height and wait for the signal when they were to mingle in the battle.

At the first glance Joshua perceived that he had not overestimated the foe; for those who began the fray were bearded men with bronzed, keen, manly features, whose black eyes blazed with the zest of battle and fierce hatred of the enemy.

Like their grey-haired, scarred leader, all were slenderly formed and lithe of limb. They swung, like trained warriors, the brazen sickle-shaped sword, the curved shield of heavy wood, or the lance decked below its point with a bunch of camel's hair. The war-cry rang loud, fierce, and defiant, from the steadfast breasts of these sons of the desert, who must either conquer or lose their dearest possession.

The first assault was met by Joshua at the head of men, whom he had armed with the heavy shields and lances of the Egyptians; incited by their brave leader they resisted a long time—while the narrow entrance to the battle field prevented the savage foe from using his full strength.

But when the foe on foot retreated, and a band of warriors mounted on swift dromedaries dashed upon the Hebrews many were terrified by the strange aspect of the huge unwieldy beasts, known to them only by report.

With loud outcries they flung down their shields and fled. Wherever a gap appeared in the ranks the rider of a dromedary urged it in, striking downward with his long keen weapon at the foe. The shepherds, unused to such assaults, thought only of securing their own safety, and many turned to fly; for sudden terror seized them as they beheld the flaming eyes or heard the shrill, fierce shriek of one of the infuriated Amalekite women, who had entered the battle to fire the courage of their husbands and terrify the foe. Clinging with the left hand to leather thongs that hung from the saddles, they allowed themselves to be dragged along by the hump-backed beasts wherever they were guided. Hatred seemed to have steeled the weak women's hearts against the fear of death, pity, and feminine dread; and the furious yells of these Megaerae destroyed the courage of many of the braver Hebrews.

But scarcely did Joshua see his men yield than, profiting by the disaster, he commanded them to retreat still farther and give the foe admittance to the valley; for he told himself that he could turn the superior number of his forces to better account as soon as it was possible to press the enemy in front and on both sides at the same time, and allow the slingers and bowmen to take part in the fray.

Ephraim and his bravest comrades, who surrounded him as messengers, were now despatched to the northern end of the valley to inform the captains of the troops stationed there of Joshua's intention and command them to advance.

The swift-footed shepherd lads darted off as nimbly as gazelles, and it was soon evident that the commander had adopted the right course for, as soon as the Amalekites reached the center of the valley, they were attacked on all sides, and many who boldly rushed forward fell on the sand while still waving sword or lance, struck by the round stones or keen arrows discharged by the slingers and archers stationed on the cliffs.

Meanwhile Moses, with Aaron and Hur, remained on the cliff overlooking the battle-field.

Thence the former watched the conflict in which, grown grey in the arts of peace, he shared only with his heart and soul.

No movement, no uplifted or lowered sword of friend or foe escaped his watchful gaze; but when the attack began and the commander, with wise purpose, left the way to the heart of his army open to the enemy, Hur exclaimed to the grey-haired man of God:

"The lofty intellect of my wife and your sister perceived the right course. The son of Nun is unworthy of the summons of the Most High. What strategy! Our force is superior, yet the foe is pressing unimpeded into the midst of the army. Our troops are dividing as the waters of the Red Sea parted at God's command, and apparently by their leader's order."

"To swallow up the Amalekites as the waves of the sea engulfed the Egyptians," was Moses' answer. Then, stretching his arms toward heaven, he cried: "Look down, Jehovah, upon Thy people who are in fresh need. Steel the arm and sharpen the eyes of him whom Thou didst choose for Thy sword! Lend him the help Thou didst promise, when Thou didst name him Joshua! And if it is no longer Thy will that he who shows himself strong and steadfast, as beseems Thy captain, should lead our forces to the battle, place Thyself, with the hosts of Heaven, at the head of Thy people, that they may crush their foes."

Thus the man of God prayed with arms uplifted, never ceasing to beseech and appeal to God, whose lofty will guided his own, and soon Aaron whispered that their foes were sore beset and the Hebrews' courage was showing itself in magnificent guise.

Joshua was now here, now there, and the ranks of the enemy were already thinning, while the numbers of the Hebrews seemed increasing.

Hur confirmed these words, adding that the tireless zeal and heroic scorn of death displayed by the son of Nun could not be denied. He had just felled one of the fiercest Amalekites with his battle-axe.

Then Moses uttered a sigh of relief, let his arms fall, and eagerly watched the farther progress of the battle, which was surging, raging and roaring beneath him.

Meanwhile the sun had reached its zenith and shone with scorching fire upon the combatants. The grey granite walls of the valley exhaled fiercer and fiercer heat and drops of perspiration had long been pouring from the burning brows of the three men on the cliff. How the noon-tide heat must burden those who were fighting and struggling below; how the bleeding wounds of those who had fallen in the dust must burn!

Moses felt all this as if he were himself compelled to endure it; for his immovably steadfast soul was rich in compassion, and he had taken into his heart, as a father does his child, the people of his own blood for whom he lived and labored, prayed and planned.

The wounds of the Hebrews pained him, yet his heart throbbed with joyous pride, when he beheld how those whose cowardly submission had so powerfully stirred his wrath a short time before, had learned to act on the defensive and offensive; and saw one youthful band after another shouting: "Jehovah our standard!" rush upon the enemy.

In Joshua's proud, heroic figure he beheld the descendants of his people as he had imagined and desired them, and now he no longer doubted that the Lord Himself had summoned the son of Nun to the chief command. His eye had rarely beamed as brightly as in this hour.

But what was that?

A cry of alarm escaped the lips of Aaron, and Hur rose and gazed northward in anxious suspense for thence, where the tents of the people stood, fresh war-cries rose, blended with loud, piteous shrieks which seemed to be uttered, not only by men, but by women and children.

The camp had been attacked.

Long before the commencement of the battle a band of Amalekites had separated from the others and made their way to it through a path in the mountains with which they were familiar.

Hur thought of his young wife, while before Aaron's mind rose Elisheba, his faithful spouse, his children and grandchildren; and both, with imploring eyes, mutely entreated Moses to dismiss them to hasten to aid their dear ones; but the stern leader refused and detained them.

Then, drawing his figure to its full height, Moses again raised his hands and eyes to Heaven, appealing to the Most High with fervent warmth, and never ceasing in his prayers, which became more and more ardent as time passed on, for the vantage gained by the soldiers seemed lost. Each new glance at the battle-field, everything his companions told him, while his soul, dwelling with the Lord, had rendered him blind to the scene at his feet, increased the burden of his anxieties.

Joshua, at the head of a strong detachment, had retreated from the battle, accompanied by Bezaleel, Hur's grandson, Aholiab, his most beloved comrade, the youthful Ephraim, and Reuben, Milcah's husband.

Hur's eyes had followed them, while his heart was full of blessings; for they had evidently quitted the battle to save the camp. With straining ears he listened to the sounds from the north, as if suspecting how nearly he was affected by the broken cries and moans borne by the wind from the tents.

Old Nun had defended himself against the Amalekite troop that assailed the camp, and fought valiantly; but when he perceived that the men whom Joshua had placed under his command could no longer hold out against the attack of the enemy, he sent to ask for aid; Joshua instantly entrusted the farther guidance of the battle to the second head of the tribe of Judah, Naashon, and Uri the son of Hur, who had distinguished himself by courage and discretion and hastened, with other picked men, to his father's relief.

He had not lost a moment, yet the conflict was decided when he appeared on the scene of action; for when he approached the camp the Amalekites had already broken through his father's troops, cut it off from them, and rushed in.

Joshua first saved the brave old man from the foe; then the next thing was to drive the sons of the desert from the tents and, in so doing, there was a fierce hand to hand struggle of man against man, and as he himself could be in only one place he was forced to leave the young men to shift for themselves.

Here, too, he raised the war-cry: "Jehovah our standard!" and rushed upon the tent of Hur,—which the enemy had seized first and where the battle raged most fiercely.

Many, corpses already strewed the ground at its entrance, and furious Amalekites were still struggling with a band of Hebrews; but wild shrieks of terror rang from within its walls.

Joshua dashed across the threshold as if his feet were winged and beheld a scene which filled even the fearless man with horror; for at the left of the spacious floor Hebrews and Amalekites rolled fighting on the blood-stained mats, while at the right he saw Miriam and several of her women whose hands had been bound by the foe.

The men had desired to bear them away as a costly prize; but an Amalekite woman, frantic with rage and jealousy and thirsting for revenge, wished to devote the foreign women to a fiery death; fanning the embers upon the hearth she had brought them, with the help of the veil torn from Miriam's head, to a bright blaze.

A terrible uproar filled the spacious enclosure, when Joshua sprang into the tent.

Here furious men were fighting, yonder the female servants of the prophetess were shrieking loudly or, as they saw the approaching warrior, screaming for help and rescue.

Their mistress, deadly pale, knelt before the hostile chief whose wife had threatened her with death by fire. She gazed at her preserver as if she beheld a ghost that had just risen from the earth and what now happened remained imprinted on Miriam's memory as a series of bloody, horrible, disconnected, yet superb visions.

In the first place the Amalekite chieftain who had bound her was a strangely heroic figure.

The bronzed warrior, with his bold hooked nose, black beard, and fiery eyes, looked like an eagle of his own mountains. But another was soon to cope with him, and that other the man who had been dear to her heart.

She had often compared him to a lion, but never had he seemed more akin to the king of the wilderness.

Both were mighty and terrible men. No one could have predicted which would be the victor and which the vanquished; but she was permitted to watch their conflict, and already the hot-blooded son of the desert had raised his war-cry and rushed upon the more prudent Hebrew.

Every child knows that life cannot continue if the heart ceases to throb for a minute; yet Miriam felt that her own stood still as if benumbed and turned to stone, when the lion was in danger of succumbing to the eagle, and when the latter's glittering knife flashed, and she saw the blood gushing from the other's shoulder.

But the frozen heart had now begun to beat again, nay it pulsed faster than ever; for suddenly the leonine warrior, toward whom she had just felt such bitter hatred, had again become, as if by a miracle, the friend of her youth. With blast of trumpets and clash of cymbals love had again set forth to enter, with triumphant joy, the soul which had of late been so desolate, so impoverished. All that separated her from him was suddenly forgotten and buried, and never was a more fervent appeal addressed to the Most High than during the brief prayer for him which rose from her heart at that moment. And the swiftness with which the petition was granted equalled its ardor; for the eagle had fallen and lowered its pinions beneath the superior might of the lion.

Then darkness veiled Miriam's eyes and she felt as if in a dream Ephraim sever the ropes around her wrists.

Soon after she regained her full consciousness, and now beheld at her feet the bleeding form of the conquered chieftain; while on the other side of the tent the floor was strewed with dead and wounded men, Hebrews and Amalekites, among them many of her husband's slaves. But beside the fallen men stood erect, and exulting in victory, the stalwart warriors of her people, among them the venerable form of Nun, and Joshua, whose father was binding up his wounds.

To do this she felt was her duty and hers only, and a deep sense of shame, a burning grief took possession of her as she remembered how she had sinned against this man.

She knew not how she who had caused him such deep suffering could atone for it, how she could repay what she owed him.

Her whole heart was overflowing with longing for one kind word from his mouth, and she approached him on her knees across the blood-stained floor; but the lips of the prophetess, usually so eloquent, seemed paralyzed and could not find the right language till at last from her burdened breast the cry escaped in loud imploring accents:

"Joshua, oh, Joshua! I have sinned heavily against you and will atone for it all my life; but do not disdain my gratitude! Do not cast it from you and, if you can, forgive me."

She had been unable to say more; then—never would she forget it—burning tears had gushed from her eyes and he had raised her from the floor with irresistible strength, yet as gently as a mother touches her fallen child, and from his lips mild, gentle words, full of forgiveness, echoed in her ears. The very touch of his right hand had assured her that he was no longer angry.

She still felt the pressure of his hand, and heard his assurance that from no lips would he more gladly hear the name of Joshua than from hers.

With the war-cry "Jehovah our standard!" he at last turned his back upon her; for a long time its clear tones and the enthusiastic shouts of his soldiers echoed in her ears.

Finally everything around her had lapsed into silence and she only knew that never had she shed such bitter, burning tears as in this hour. And she made two solemn vows in the presence of the God who had summoned her to be His prophetess. Meanwhile both the men whom they concerned were surrounded by the tumult of battle.

One had again led his troops from the rescued camp against the foe; the other was watching with the leader of the people the surging to and fro of the ever-increasing fury of the conflict.

Joshua found his people in sore stress. Here they were yielding, yonder they were still feebly resisting the onslaught of the sons of the desert; but Hur gazed with increasing and redoubled anxiety at the progress of the battle; for in the camp he beheld wife and grandson, and below his son, in mortal peril.

His paternal heart ached as he saw Uri retreat, then as he pressed forward again and repelled the foe by a well-directed assault, it throbbed joyously, and he would gladly have shouted words of praise.

But whose ear would have been sharp enough to distinguish the voice of a single man amid the clash of arms and war-cries, the shrieks of women, the wails of the wounded, the discordant grunting of the camels, the blasts of horns and trumpets mingling below?

Now the foremost band of the Amalekites had forced itself like a wedge into the rear ranks of the Hebrews.

If the former succeeded in opening a way for those behind and joined the division which was attacking the camp, the battle was lost, and the destruction of the people sealed; for a body of Amalekites who had not mingled in the fray were still stationed at the southern entrance of the valley, apparently for the purpose of defending the oasis against the foe in case of need.

A fresh surprise followed.

The sons of the desert had fought their way forward so far that the missiles of the slingers and bowmen could scarcely reach them. If these men were not to be idle, it was needful that they should be summoned to the battle-field.

Hur had long since shouted to Uri to remember them and use their aid again; but now the figure of a youth suddenly appeared approaching from the direction of the camp as nimbly as a mountain goat, by climbing and leaping from one rock to another.

As soon as he reached the first ones he spoke to them, and made signs to the next, who passed the message on, and at last they all climbed down into the valley, scaled the western cliff to the height of several men, and suddenly vanished as though the rock had swallowed them.

The youth whom the slingers and archers had followed was Ephraim.

A black shadow on the cliff where he had disappeared with the others must be the opening of a ravine, through which they were doubtless to be guided to the men who had followed Joshua to the succor of the camp.

Such was the belief, not only of Hur but of Aaron, and the former again began to doubt Joshua's fitness for the Lord's call; for what benefited those in the tents weakened the army whose command devolved upon his son Uri and his associate in office Naashon. The battle around the camp had already lasted for hours and Moses had not ceased to pray with hands uplifted toward heaven, when the Amalekites succeeded in gaining a considerable vantage.

Then the leader of the Hebrews summoned his strength for a new and more earnest appeal to the Most High; but the exhausted man's knees tottered and his wearied arms fell. But his soul had retained its energy, his heart the desire not to cease pleading to the Ruler of Battles.

Moses was unwilling to remain inactive during this conflict and his weapon was prayer.

Like a child who will not cease urging its mother until she grants what it unselfishly beseeches for its brothers and sisters, he clung imploring to the Omnipotent One, who had hitherto proved Himself a father to him and to his people and wonderfully preserved them from the greatest perils.

But his physical strength was exhausted, so he summoned his companions who pushed forward a rock on which he seated himself, in order to assail the heart of the Most High with fresh prayers.

There he sat and though his wearied limbs refused their service, his soul was obedient and rose with all its fire to the Ruler of the destinies of men.

But his arms grew more and more paralysed, and at last fell as if weighted with lead; for years it had become a necessity to him to stretch them heavenward when he appealed with all his fervor to God on high.

This his companions knew, and they fancied they perceived that whenever the great leader's hands fell the sons of Amalek gained a fresh advantage.

Therefore they eagerly supported his arms, one at the right side, the other at the left, and though the mighty man could no longer lift his voice in intelligible words, though his giant frame reeled to and fro, and though more than once it seemed to him as if the stone which supported him, the valley and the whole earth rocked, still his hands and eyes remained uplifted. Not a moment did he cease to call upon the Most High till suddenly loud shouts of victory, which echoed clearly from the rocky sides of the valley, rose from the direction of the camp.

Joshua had again appeared on the battle-field and, at the head of his warriors, rushed with resistless energy upon the foe.

The battle now assumed a new aspect.

The result was still uncertain, and Moses could not cease uplifting his heart and arms to heaven, but at last, at last this long final struggle came to an end. The ranks of the Amalekites wavered and finally, scattered and disheartened, dashed toward the southern entrance of the valley whence they had come.

There also cries were heard and from a thousand lips rang the glad shout: "Jehovah our standard! Victory!" and again "Victory!"

Then the man of God removed his arms from the supporting shoulders of his companions, swung them aloft freely and with renewed and wonderfully invigorated strength shouted:

"I thank Thee, my God and my Lord! Jehovah our standard! The people are saved!"

Then darkness veiled the eyes of the exhausted man. But a little later he again opened them and saw Ephraim, with the slingers and bowmen, attack the body of Amalekites at the southern entrance of the valley, while Joshua drove the main army of the sons of the desert toward their retreating comrades.

Joshua had heard through some captives of a ravine which enabled good climbers to reach a defile which led to the southern end of the battle-field; and Ephraim, obedient to his command, had gone with the slingers and bowmen along this difficult path to assail in the rear the last band of foemen who were still capable of offering resistance.

Pressed, harassed from two sides, and disheartened, the sons of Amalek gave up the conflict and now the Hebrews beheld how these sons of the desert, who had grown up in this mountain region, understood how to use their feet; for at a sign from their leader they spurred the dromedaries and flew away like leaves blown by the wind. Rough mountain heights which seemed inaccessible to human beings they scaled on their hands and feet like nimble lizards; many others escaped through the ravine which the captured slaves had betrayed to Joshua.

CHAPTER XXVIII

The larger portion of the Amalekites had perished or lay wounded on the battle-field. Joshua knew that the other desert tribes, according to their custom, would abandon their defeated companions and return to their own homes.

Yet it seemed probable that despair would give the routed warriors courage not to let their oasis fall into the hands of the Hebrews without striking a blow.

But Joshua's warriors were too much exhausted for it to be possible to lead them onward at once.

He himself was bleeding from several slight wounds, and the exertions of the last few days were making themselves felt even on his hardened frame.

Besides the sun, which when the battle began had just risen, was already sinking to rest and should it prove necessary to force an entrance into the oasis it was not advisable to fight in darkness.

What he and still more his brave warriors needed was rest until the grey dawn of early morning.

He saw around him only glad faces, radiant with proud self-reliance, and as he commanded the troops to disband, in order to celebrate the victory in the camp with their relatives, each body that filed slowly and wearily past him burst into cheers as fresh and resonant as though they had forgotten the exhaustion which so short a time before had bowed every head and burdened every foot.

"Hail to Joshua! Hail to the victor!" still echoed from the cliffs after the last band had disappeared from his gaze. But far more distinctly the words with which Moses had thanked him rang in his soul. They were:

"Thou bast proved thyself a true sword of the Most High, strong and steadfast. So long as the Lord is thy help and Jehovah is our standard, we need fear no foes."

He fancied he still felt on his brow and hair the kiss of the mighty man of God who had clasped him to his breast in the presence of all the people, and it was no small thing to master the excitement which the close of this momentous day awakened in him.

A strong desire to regain perfect self-possession ere he again mingled in the jubilant throng and met his father, who shared every lofty emotion that stirred his own soul, detained him on the battle-field.

It was a scene where dread and horror reigned; for all save himself who lingered there were held by death or severe wounds.

The ravens which had followed the wanderers hovered above the corpses and already ventured to swoop nearer to the richly-spread banquet. The scent of blood had lured the beasts of prey from the mountains and dens in the rocks and their roaring and greedy growling were heard in all directions.

As darkness followed dusk lights began to flit over the blood-soaked ground. These were to aid the slaves and those who missed a relative to distinguish friend from foe, the wounded from the dead; and many a groan from the breast of some sorely-wounded man mingled with the croaking of the sable birds, and the howls of the hungry jackals and hyenas, foxes and panthers.

But Joshua was familiar with the horrors of the battle-field and did not heed them.

Leaning against a rock, he saw the same stars rise which had shone upon him before the tent in the camp at Tanis, when in the sorest conflict with himself he confronted the most difficult decision of his life.

A month had passed since then, yet that brief span of time had witnessed an unprecedented transformation of his whole inner and outward life.

What had seemed to him grand, lofty, and worthy of the exertion of all his strength on that night when he sat before the tent where lay the delirious Ephraim, to-day lay far behind him as idle and worthless.

He no longer cared for the honors, dignities and riches which the will of the whimsical, weak king of a foreign people could bestow upon him. What to him was the well-ordered and disciplined army, among whose leaders be had numbered himself with such joyous pride?

He could scarcely realize that there had been a time when he aspired to nothing higher than to command more and still more thousands of Egyptians, when his heart had swelled at the bestowal of a new title or glittering badge of honor by those whom he held most unworthy of his esteem.

From the Egyptians he had expected everything, from his own people nothing.

That very night before his tent the great mass of the men of his own blood had been repulsive to him as pitiful slaves languishing in dishonorable, servile toil. Even the better classes he had arrogantly patronized; for they were but shepherds and as such contemptible to the Egyptians, whose opinions he shared.

His own father was also the owner of herds and, though he held him in high esteem, it was in spite of his position and only because his whole character commanded reverence; because the superb old man's fiery vigor won love from every one, and above all from him, his grateful son.

He had never ceased to gladly acknowledge his kinship to him, but in other respects he had striven to so bear himself among his brothers-in-arms that they should forget his origin and regard him in everything as one of themselves. His ancestress Asenath, the wife of Joseph, had been an Egyptian and he had boasted of the fact.

And now,—to-day?

He would have made any one feel the weight of his wrath who reproached him with being an Egyptian; and what at the last new moon he would only too willingly have cast aside and concealed, as though it were a disgrace, made him on the night of the next new moon whose stars were just beginning to shine, raise his head with joyous pride.

What a lofty emotion it was to feel himself with just complacency the man he really was!

His life and deeds as an Egyptian chief now seemed like a perpetual lie, a constant desertion of his ideal.

His truthful nature exulted in the consciousness that the base denial and concealment of his birth was at an end.

With joyous gratitude he felt that he was one of the people whom the Most High preferred to all others, that he belonged to a community, whose humblest members, nay even the children, could raise their hands in prayer to the God whom the loftiest minds among the Egyptians surrounded with the barriers of secrecy, because they considered their people too feeble and dull of intellect to stand before His mighty grandeur and comprehend it.

And this one sole God, before whom all the whole motley world of Egyptian divinities sank into insignificance, had chosen him, the son of Nun, from among the thousands of his race to be the champion and defender of His chosen people and bestowed on him a name that assured him of His aid.

No man, he thought, had ever had a loftier aim than, obedient to his God and under His protection, to devote his blood and life to the service of his own people. His black eyes sparkled more brightly and joyously as he thought of it. His heart seemed too small to contain all the love with which he wished to make amends to his brothers for his sins against them in former years.

True, he had lost to another a grand and noble woman whom he had hoped to make his own; but this did not in the least sadden the joyous enthusiasm of his soul; for he had long ceased to desire her as his wife, high as her image still stood in his mind. He now thought of her with quiet gratitude only; for he willingly admitted that his new life had begun on the decisive night when Miriam set him the example of sacrificing everything, even the dearest object of love, to God and the people.

Miriam's sins against him were effaced from his memory; for he was wont to forget what he had forgiven. Now he felt only the grandeur of what he owed her. Like a magnificent tree, towering skyward on the frontier of two hostile countries, she stood between his past and his present life. Though love was buried, he and Miriam could never cease to walk hand in hand over the same road toward the same destination.

As he again surveyed the events of the past, he could truly say that under his leadership pitiful bondmen had speedily become brave warriors In the field they had been willing and obedient and, after the victory, behaved with manliness. And they could not fail to improve with each fresh success. To-day it seemed to him not only desirable, but quite possible, to win in battle at their head a land which they could love and where, in freedom and prosperity, they could become the able men he desired to make them.

Amid the horrors of the battle-field in the moonless night joy as bright as day entered his heart and with the low exclamation: "God and my people!" and a grateful glance upward to the starry firmament he left the corpse-strewn valley of death like a conqueror walking over palms and flowers scattered by a grateful people on the path of victory.

CONCLUSION

There was an active stir in the camp

Fires surrounded by groups of happy human beings were burning in front of the tents, and many a beast was slain, here as a thank-offering, yonder for the festal supper.

Wherever Joshua appeared glad cheers greeted him; but he did not find his father, for the latter had accepted an invitation from Hur, so it was before the prince of Judah's tent that the son embraced the old man, who was radiant with grateful joy.

Ere Joshua sat down Hur beckoned him aside, ordered a slave who had just killed a calf to divide it into two pieces and pointing to it, said:

"You have accomplished great deeds for the people and for me, son of Nun, and my life is too short for the gratitude which is your due from my wife and myself. If you can forget the bitter words which clouded our peace at Dophkah—and you say you have done so—let us in future keep together like brothers and stand by each other in joy and grief, in need and peril. The chief command henceforth belongs to you alone, Joshua, and to no other, and this is a source of joy to the whole people, above all to my wife and to me. So if you share my wish to form a brotherhood, walk with me, according to the custom of our fathers, between the halves of this slaughtered animal."

Joshua willingly accepted this invitation, and Miriam was the first to join in the loud acclamations of approval commenced by the grey-haired Nun. She did so with eager zeal; for it was she who had inspired her husband, before whom she had humbled herself, and whose love she now once more possessed, with the idea of inviting Joshua to the alliance both had now concluded.

This had not been difficult for her; for the two vows she had made after the son of Nun, whom she now gladly called "Joshua," had saved her from the hand of the foe were already approaching fulfilment, and she felt that she had resolved upon them in a happy hour.

The new and pleasant sensation of being a woman, like any other woman, lent her whole nature a gentleness hitherto foreign to it, and this retained the love of the husband whose full value she had learned to know during the sad time in which he had shut his heart against her.

In the self-same hour which made Hur and Joshua brothers, a pair of faithful lovers who had been sundered by sacred duties were once more united; for while the friends were still feasting before the tent of Hur, three of the people asked permission to speak to Nun, their master. These were the old freedwoman, who had remained in Tanis, her granddaughter Hogla and Assir, the latter's betrothed husband, from whom the girl had parted to nurse her grandparents.

Hoary Eliab had soon died, and the grandmother and Hogla—the former on the old man's ass—had followed the Hebrews amid unspeakable difficulties.

Nun welcomed the faithful couple with joy and gave Hogla to Assir for his wife.

So this blood-stained day had brought blessings to many, yet it was to end with a shrill discord.

While the fires in the camp were burning, loud voices were heard, and during the whole journey not an evening had passed without strife and sanguinary quarrels.

Wounds and fatal blows had often been given when an offended man revenged himself on his enemy, or a dishonest one seized the property of others or denied the obligations he had sworn to fulfil.

In such cases it had been difficult to restore peace and call the criminals to account; for the refractory refused to recognize any one as judge. Whoever felt himself injured banded with others, and strove to obtain justice by force.

On that festal evening Hur and his guests at first failed to notice the uproar to which every one was accustomed. But when close at hand, amid the fiercest yells, a bright glare of light arose, the chiefs began to fear for the safety of the camp, and rising to put an end to the disturbance, they became witnesses of a scene which filled some with wrath and horror, and the others with grief.

The rapture of victory had intoxicated the multitude.

They longed to express their gratitude to the deity, and in vivid remembrance of the cruel worship of their home, a band of Phoenicians among the strangers had kindled a huge fire to their Moloch and were in the act of hurling into the flames several Amalekite captives as the most welcome sacrifice to their god.

Close beside it the Israelites had erected on a tall wooden pillar a clay image of the Egyptian god Seth, which one of his Hebrew worshippers had brought with him to protect himself and his family.

Directly after their return to the camp Aaron had assembled the people to sing hymns of praise and offer prayers of thanksgiving; but to many the necessity of beholding, in the old-fashioned way, an image of the god to whom they were to uplift their souls, had been so strong that the mere sight of the clay idol had sufficed to bring them to their knees, and turn them from the true God.

At the sight of the servants of Moloch, who were already binding the human victims to hurl them into the flames, Joshua was seized with wrath and, when the deluded men resisted, he ordered the trumpets to be sounded and with his young men who blindly obeyed him and were by no means friendly to the strangers, drove them back, without bloodshed, to their quarters in the camp.

The impressive warnings of old Nun, Hur, and Naashon diverted the Hebrews from the crime which ingratitude made doubly culpable. Yet many of the latter found it hard to control themselves when the fiery old man shattered the idol which was dear to them, and had it not been for the love cherished for him, his son, and his grandson, and the respect due his snow-white hair, many a hand would doubtless have been raised against him.

Moses had retired to a solitary place, as was his wont after every great danger from which the mercy of the Most High brought deliverance, and tears filled Miriam's eyes as she thought of the grief which the tidings of such apostasy and ingratitude would cause her noble brother.

A gloomy shadow had also darkened Joshua's joyous confidence. He lay sleepless on the mat in his father's tent, reviewing the past.

His warrior-soul was elevated by the thought that a single, omnipotent, never-erring Power guided the universe and the lives of men and exacted implicit obedience from the whole creation. Every glance at nature and life showed him that everything depended upon One infinitely great and powerful Being, at whose sign all creatures rose, moved, or sank to rest.

To him, the chief of a little army, his God was the highest and most far-sighted of rulers, the only One, who was always certain of victory.

What a crime it was to offend such a Lord and repay His benefits with apostasy!

Yet the people had committed before his eyes this heinous sin and, as he recalled to mind the events which had compelled him to interpose, the question arose how they were to be protected from the wrath of the Most High, how the eyes of the dull multitude could be opened to His wonderful grandeur, which expanded the heart and the soul.

But he found no answer, saw no expedient, when he reflected upon the lawlessness and rebellion in the camp, which threatened to be fatal to his people.

He had succeeded in making his soldiers obedient. As soon as the trumpets summoned them, and he himself in full armor appeared at the head of his men, they yielded their own obstinate wills to his. Was there then nothing that could keep them, during peaceful daily life, within the bounds which in Egypt secured the existence of the meanest and weakest human beings and protected them from the attacks of those who were bolder and stronger?

Amid such reflections he remained awake until early morning; when the stars set, he started up, ordered the trumpets to be sounded, and as on the preceding days, the new-made troops assembled without opposition and in full force.

He was soon marching at their head through the narrow, rocky valley, and after moving silently an hour through the gloom the warriors enjoyed the refreshing coolness which precedes the young day.

Then the grey light of early dawn glimmered in the east, the sky began to brighten, and in the glowing splendor of the blushing morning rose solemnly in giant majesty the form of the sacred mountain.

Close at hand and distinctly visible it towered before the Hebrews with its brown masses of rock, cliffs, and chasms, while above the seven peaks of its summit hovered a pair of eagles on whose broad pinions the young day cast a shimmering golden glow.

A thrill of pious awe made the whole band halt as they had before Alush, and every man, from the first rank to the last, in mute devotion raised his hands to pray.

Then they moved on with hearts uplifted, and one shouted joyously to another as some pretty dark birds flew twittering toward them, a sign of the neighborhood of fresh water.

They had scarcely marched half an hour longer when they beheld the bluish-green foliage of tamarisk bushes and the towering palm-trees; at last, the most welcome of all sounds in the wilderness fell on their listening ears—the ripple of flowing water.

This cheered their hearts, and the majestic spectacle of Mount Sinai, whose heaven-touching summit was now concealed by a veil of blue mist, filled with devout amazement the souls of the men who had grown up on the flat plains of Goshen.

[The mountain known at the present day as Serbal, not the Sinai of the monks which in our opinion was first declared in the reign of Justinian to be the mount whence the laws were given. The detailed reasons for our opinion that Serbal is the Sinai of the Scriptures, which Lepsius expressed before its and others share with us may be found in our works: "Durch Gosen zum Sinai, aus dem Wanderbuch and

der Bibliothek." 2 Aufl. Leipzig. 1882. Wilh. Engelmann.]

They pressed cautiously forward; for the remainder of the defeated Amalekites might be lying in ambush. But no foe was seen or heard, and the Hebrews found some tokens of the thirst for vengeance of the sons of the wilderness in their ruined houses, the superb palm-trees felled, and little gardens destroyed. It was necessary now to remove from the road the slender trunks with their huge leafy crowns, that they might not impede the progress of the people; and, when this work was done, Joshua ascended through a ravine which led to the brook in the valley, up to the first terrace of the mountain, that he might gaze around him far and near for a view of the enemy.

The steep pathway led past masses of red granite, intersected by veins of greenish diorite, until he reached a level plateau high above the oasis, where, beside a clear spring, green bushes and delicate mountain flowers adorned the barren wilderness.

Here he intended to rest and, as he gazed around him, he perceived in the shadow of an overhanging cliff a man's tall figure.

It was Moses.

The flight of his thoughts had rapt him so far away from the present and his surroundings, that he did not perceive Joshua's approach, and the latter was restrained by respectful awe from approaching the man of God.

He waited patiently till the latter raised his bearded face and greeted him with friendly dignity.

Then they gazed together at the oasis and the desolate stony valleys of the mountain region at their feet. The emerald waters of a small portion of the Red Sea, which washed the western slope of the mountain, also glittered beneath them.

Meanwhile they talked of the people and the greatness and omnipotence of the God who had so wonderfully guided them, and as they looked northward, they beheld the endlessly long stream of Hebrews, which, following the curves of the rocky valley, was surging slowly toward the oasis.

Then Joshua opened his heart to the man of God and told him the questions he had asked himself during the past sleepless night, and to which he had found no answer. The latter listened quietly, and in deep, faltering tones answered in broken sentences:

"The lawlessness in the camp—ay, it is ruining the people! But the Lord placed the power to destroy it in our hands. Woe betide him who resists. They must feel this power, which is as sublime as yonder mountain, as immovable as its solid rock."

Then Moses' wrathful words ceased.

After both had gazed silently into vacancy a long time, Joshua broke the silence by asking:

"And what is the name of this power?"

Loudly and firmly from the bearded lips of the man of God rang the words; "THE LAW!"

He pointed with his staff to the summit of the mountain.

Then, waving his hand to his companion, he left him. Joshua completed his search for the foe and saw on the yellow sands of the valley dark figures moving to and fro.

They were the remnants of the defeated Amalekite bands seeking new abodes.

He watched them a short time and, after convincing himself that they were quitting the oasis, he thoughtfully returned to the valley.

"The law!" he repeated again and again.

Ay, that was what the wandering tribes lacked. It was doubtless reserved for its severity to transform the hordes which had escaped bondage into a people worthy of the God who preferred them above the other nations of the earth.

Here the chief's reflections were interrupted; for human voices, the lowing and bleating of herds, the barking of dogs, and the heavy blows of hammers rose to his ears from the oasis.

They were pitching the tents, a work of peace, for which no one needed him.

Lying down in the shadow of a thick tamarisk bush, above which a tall palm towered proudly, he stretched his limbs comfortably to rest in the assurance that the people were now provided for, in war by his good sword, in peace by the Law. This was much, it renewed his hopes; yet, no, no—it was not all, could not be the final goal. The longer he reflected, the more profoundly he felt that this was not enough to satisfy him concerning those below, whom he cherished in his heart as if they were brothers and sisters. His broad brow again clouded, and roused from his repose by fresh doubts, he gently shook his head.

No, again no! The Law could not afford to those who were so dear to him everything that he desired for them. Something else was needed to make their future as dignified and beautiful as he had beheld it before his mind's eye on his journey to the mines.

But what was it, what name did this other need bear?

He began to rack his brain to discover it, and while, with closed lids, he permitted his thoughts to rove to the other nations whom he had known in war and peace, in order to seek among them the one thing his own people lacked, sleep overpowered him and a dream showed him Miriam and a lovely girl, who looked like Kasana as she had so often rushed to meet him when a sweet, innocent child, followed by the white lamb which Nun had given to his favorite many years before.

Both figures offered him a gift and asked him to choose one or the other. Miriam's hand held a heavy gold tablet, at whose top was written in flaming letters: "The Law!" and which she offered with stern severity. The child extended one of the beautifully-curved palm-leaves which he had often waved as a messenger of peace.

The sight of the tablet filled him with pious awe, the palm-branch waved a friendly greeting and he quickly grasped it. But scarcely was it in his hand ere the figure of the prophetess melted into the air like mist, which the morning breeze blows away. In painful astonishment he now gazed at the spot where she had stood, and surprised and troubled by his strange choice, though he felt that he had made the right one, he asked the child what her gift imported to him and to the people.

She waved her hand to him, pointed into the distance, and uttered three words whose gentle musical sound sank deep into his heart. Yet hard as he strove to catch their purport, he did not succeed, and when he asked the child to explain them the sound of his own voice roused him and he returned to the camp, disappointed and thoughtful.

Afterwards he often tried to remember these words, but always in vain. All his great powers, both mental and physical, he continued to devote to the people; but his nephew Ephraim, as a powerful prince of his tribe, who well deserved the high honors he enjoyed in after years, founded a home of his own, where old Nun watched the growth of great-grand-children, who promised a long perpetuation of his noble race.

Everyone is familiar with Joshua's later life, so rich in action, and how he won in battle a new home for his people.

There in the Promised Land many centuries later was born, in Bethlehem, another Jehoshua who bestowed on all mankind what the son of Nun had vainly sought for the Hebrew nation.

The three words uttered by the child's lips which the chief had been unable to comprehend were:

"Love, Mercy, Redemption!"